Dymond Star Enterprise

Presents

Paid N Plea$ures

—Where fantasies get turned into reality

I0675497

This is a work of fiction. Names, characters, places, and

incidents either are the product of the author's imagination or are used fictitiously, and any resemblance to
actual persons, living or dead, business establishments,
events, or locales is entirely coincidental.

Paid N Plea$ures / July 2025
Copyright © 2025 by Dymond Star Enterprise
Dymond Star Enterprise is a registered LLC
Art and cover design by pk_art1
All rights reserved.
This book, or parts thereof, may not be reproduced in
any form without permission.
For information address: Dymond Star Enterprise, 5203
Juan Tabo Blvd. STE 2B, Albuquerque,New Mexico
87111
For more information on Dymond Star Enterprise, or
speedy contact, email at
Dymondstarpresident@yahoo.com
ISBN: 979-8-218-71352-2
Dymond Star Enterprise owns all rights to
Paid N Plea$ures

PRINTED IN THE UNITED STATES OF AMERICA

Acknowledgments

On behalf of Dymond Star Enterprise I would like to give special thanks to all those who were apart of my journey prior and during the process of me writing the Paid N Plea$ures series. Rather our bond shattered or blossomed, your presence or lack thereof was vital for the growth of me within and also the development of the Paid N Plea$ures world I created for my supportive readers. I want you all too know... A movie will surely be to come from this one of a kind urban, erotic tale.

I thank my incredibly strong co-partner and beautiful wife...
I thank my gorgeous intelligent mother...
And over all, I thank the most beneficent and most merciful one above. Without the Grace of Allah none of this would be possible.

Rest in Paradise to my brother from another mother Aaron James Hayes a.k.a (AJ). I'll forever keep your name alive in the flesh, through my success. Your presence will forever remain and live on.

Chapter:1
"Fare Exchange Ain't No Robbery"

Smack! Smack! Smack!

"Why da fuck you always playing with my money?! "

Smack! I whacked the older dope fiend again upside his head with my 1911 model, .45 caliber handgun. It was about two o'clock in the morning on a hot summer night in July in the gritty streets of Detroit. I was on Michigan avenue and Hard Body's night club was spilling out so many drunks that they were unknowingly blocking the hostile scene from the police seeing what was happening.

"Chedda please!" Johnny Boy begged. "I'll have your money, please just give me one more week!"

The fiend was ass first on the sidewalk, looking up at me with a mixture of blood, sweat and tears in his eyes. I could see that his pupils were dilated and it gave me even more of an urge to kill him; knowing he was probably high off the supply I fronted him. He cried begging for dear life as I stood over him, aiming my gun inches away from his forehead. I know I blanked out for a minute because I felt my dick getting hard as I thought about blowing three holes in his dome like a bowling ball. I been looking for this piece of shit three weeks straight and I finally caught up with his ass. He was the only foot runner I had left to help me move work but he fucked me over for the last time. I had enough, I'm killing this nigga. . .

"Nooo! Get away from him!" I snapped out of it as a chick with a high-pitched voice, screaming at the top of her lungs, interrupted my thoughts.

I turned to the right and noticed the bitch was running towards me from near the exit of the club. I pointed my gun at her out of reflex, but she paid it no mind and still ran over to block and shield the dirt bag's body with hers.

"Stop, don't shoot him. Please, please, please don't shoot him! Daddy are you ok?" she asked Johnny Boy.

I believed she was his daughter instantly when she addressed him as daddy, because the hoe nigga was screaming and begging for his life just like her a second ago. I guess like father, like daughter. After I seen that the bitch was no threat, I tried to get back in kill mode and finish the job but couldn't help noticing how mu'fuckin' sexy the hoe was. Her body was banging! She was a sunlight caramel complexion, with black long curly hair. She wore a white halter top with pink lettering that read SUPREME across her perfect cantaloupe shaped breast. She had a belly ring to compliment her fit stomach which forced my eyes to her small waist and perfectly shaped ass. Her cheeks were hanging out of the denim blue jean booty shorts that she was rocking, and she appeared to be high class from her pink Louis Vuitton belt and matching handbag. Thanks to her white open toe stilettos, you could see her flawless pink pedicure and she stood about 5 '6 with only inches between her and my pointed gun. She was so close I could smell the Chanel N0 5 perfume she was wearing.

"You just gonna shoot him right here in front of everybody?" she asked, breaking my train of thought again, but this time her money green eyes were staring directly into mines, through the two holes of the ski mask I was wearing.

"You do know my bullets will go through dat lil body of yours and still hit my target, right?" I said to her as her eyes began to water.

"Wat ever he did I'll fix it, just please let him live." she begged.

"This no-good piece of shit owes me twenty bands!" I said, as I aimed ready to shoot the pretty lil bitch if she tried anything slick.

"Wait! Here you go, take it all, just don't shoot."

Before I could squeeze the trigger, baby gurl was holding her Louis Vuitton bag upside down, dumping everything inside of it out on the pavement. I-phone, Louis Vuitton wallet, box of magnum condoms, eye liner, lip stick, a quarter of what looked to be some exotic ass weed, a chromed .38 special revolver with a pearl handle, a half ounce of coke and three rubber band stacks of money with Benjamin Franklin's face exposed on each of them. Jackpot! I looked from the stacks of the money on the ground, then back into her eyes.

"Take it!" she screamed in a loud aggressive manner, causing me to pull my gun out of Johnny Boy's mouth and push her to the ground on top of him.

I hurried and picked up the money, the gun, the coke, the weed and the wallet; then put it inside the pocket of my hoodie. I looked down at the beauty bunched up on top of her father, so that I could get a photographic memory of her face.

Then out of nowhere; I heard, "Lacey! Lacey! Get away from her you creep!"

I looked up and seen a bunch of drunk ass hoes hollering for the bitch on the ground. It was about seven of them and they were standing by Hard Body's exit; yelling and pointing in my direction, drawing way too much attention; one bitch even pulled out a can of pepper spray and threatened to

7

blind me if I didn't leave her manager alone. They must've been a group of singers or models or something; I don't know.

I looked in the direction of where my boy Dre was parked waiting on me, but I couldn't see through all the mufuckas' who just came out the club. I felt too many eyes on me, watching my every move but I didn't panic. I raised my gun and shot in the air twice. Bang! Bang! Niggas and bitches were ducking, screaming and running around everywhere just like I needed them to. The crowd began to scatter and the path to my getaway car started to clear.

I could see Dre's Infinity truck still parked in the same spot I left him in, with the hoes. I peeped his tail lights were on, so his engine must've been running. I had to get to him fast before he decided to pull off without me.

I tucked my gun in my pants and fled to the parking lot as fast as I could, as I approached the truck, I snatched off my mask and put it in my pants pocket and entered through the back passenger side. The lil freak who was waiting for me in the back seat seemed startled until she realized it was me. Dre started to complain immediately.

"Damn dawg, I was just calling yo phone, ready to leave yo ass. These niggas shooting out here, it's time to roll."

He was so nervous that he wasn't even looking back as he spoke to me. He was too busy switching his gear into drive and focusing on not hitting any of the ongoing traffic that was trying to get away from the gun shots as well.

"Yea, shit getting wild out there" I said, trying to sound convincing.

I still was looking out the back window making sure no one saw me run to his truck. The lil bitch Chyna, who was in the front passenger next to Dre; decided to turn all the way around in her seat and question me.

"Did you see what happen bro? It sounded close as hell'' She commented.

Damn this hoe nosey as hell, i thought to myself.
"Not really" I lied, then continued so I could kill her curiosity. "I went to take a piss on the side of that building then I heard gun shots rang out. I looked up and seen some nigga by the club with a black mask on but it looked like the police were already on him. I just ran back to the truck so I wouldn't be the next nigga shot on the news."

"Damn somebody must've got killed, hurry up and get us da fuck outta here bae!" she said to Dre.

Dre and I bumped into Chyna and her lil friend earlier tonight at the strip club. Dre plugged me in so we could tag team them for the night. Chyna been his lil jump off for a minute, so it was only right that I made her friend one of mine's. It just so happened as we were leaving the club, I spotted the ol'dirt bag Johnny Boy who owed me money and I wasn't missing my opportunity to get is punk ass; especially not for a piece of a pussy. I ended up grabbing my strap out of Dre's glove box, along with my mask and told them I was going to take a quick leak, and to wait on me in the truck. After all that, now I'm back in the truck hoping Dre get me the fuck away from the scene without me having to tell him bout what really just went down.

I was just starting to relax and get comfortable in my seat but when I glanced to my left, I caught the lil freak next to me staring at the ski mask that was slightly hanging out of my pants pocket. Fuck! She looked up at me and we locked eyes. I knew right then she probably knew I was the one shooting. I had to say something. . .

"Wassup baby, is it something inside my pants you looking for?" I pushed the mask deeper inside my pants pocket so it wouldn't be hanging out as much and waited for a response, but I never broke eye contact.

9

I was a little nervous she caught my slip up because she just stared at me for a good ten seconds, then to my surprise she reached to undo my pants but my gun was in her way. She pulled it out of my waistband, placed in on the floor, then without hesitation, wrapped her lips around my dick and began sucking.

"Yo Dre, turn da music up" I said, then I laid my head back and closed my eyes so I could enjoy the fiya ass head lil momma was putting on me. She was gripping the base of my dick with both hands, stroking it to the movement of her mouth. Her moist tongue and deep ass throat made my dick feel like it had its own personal water slide.

I drifted off in deep thoughts loving the fact that shorty was giving me neck to the beat of the music that was playing. Money bagg Yo feat. Megan Thee Stallion's song, was blasting thru the speakers and my freak's lip service was right on beat like the two artist's rap lyrics . . . *Wat you doing with all dat ass, imma touch it; She say it's mine's so I smack it while we fuckin; Freak in the bed, innocent when we in public..*

I placed my left hand on the back of her head to gain control of her rhythm, but to be honest, she didn't need any help. I just Love feeling like a boss in control of shit. As she sucked on my dick, I wondered had she realized I was the one to blame for the gunshots she heard? I'm pretty sure after she seen the ski mask and the gun, she was smart enough to put it all together. I gotta make sure she keeps her mouth shut.

 "Damn baby you doing it like a pro" I said loud enough for her to hear me, keeping her motivated in her performance.

My mind started to replay everything that happened. I thought about how bad that bitch was who saved Johnny Boy 's life. I still might kill him if I catch him again.

"Yea baby, right there" I grunted as she released her hands and began to deep throat me.

I thought about the name I heard the hoes screaming, Lacey.

"Oohh shit lil momma" I moaned while I felt her tongue ring playing with the head of my dick.

I thought about the stacks of money Lacey dumped out of her purse like it was nothing to her. I couldn't wait to count it!

"I'm about to buss baby gurl" I warned, but all that did was make her speed up her rhythm and encourage her to suck harder.

I thought to myself again. . . any bitch that fine with stacks of cash on her like that, gotta have some major connects in the streets.

"Fuck" I said a little too loud because I couldn't take it anymore.

The head hunter was going to work with the sloppy toppy. Her mouth was so wet that her spit was dripping down the inside of my legs. She was face fuckin my dick then taking it out her mouth to lick it up and down with her tongue all on the sides of it. She stuffed me back inside her warm mouth as she poked out her lips like a fish blowing bubbles under water, then took my whole ten-inch dick down her throat. My toes began to curl. She lifted her head, keeping her lips wrapped around only the tip of my dick, then she forced her mouth back down taking my whole dick in her throat again.

"Fuck!" I squealed out loud again forcing my eyes to stay shut, tryna hold back the urge my new supa freak was giving me. She worked her way back up to the tip with her lips and then pushed me right back down her throat.

"Ga'damn!" I shouted out loud as I began bussing a fat ass nut in her mouth and face.

The music turned down instantly and I felt the truck stop moving. I opened my eyes, saw Dre and Chyna turned in their seat looking back at me.

"Damn, is everything good back there bro?" Dre asked, with a concerned look on his face. I looked in my lap and seen baby gurl holding my dick, staring at me with nut on her cheek.
I felt Dre and Chyna still eyeing me, waiting for an answer.
I thought to myself one last time. . . Maybe I should lay low off the streets for a while until I do my homework on Johnny Boy's daughter.

Then I answered, "Yea everything good bro. Now turn the music back up."

All in all, Johnny Boy owed money and I could've easily taken his life for it. The way I see it, whoever his so-called daughter was felt like her father's life was more important to her than the money inside her purse. She traded it to me; I didn't rob her. It was her money for his life. She paid his fee, an even trade. Where I'm from fare exchange ain't no robbery.

Chapter: 2
"It's Mine's I Spend It"

"Twenty-seven thousand! One, two, three, four, five, six, seven, eight, nine; twenty-eight thousand! One, two, three, four, five, six, seven, eight, nine; twenty-nine thousand! One, two three, four, five, six, seven, eight, nine, thirty mutha fuckin thousand! hell, fuck yeah!"

After counting up all the money I got from Johnny Boy's daughter last night, I had Dre drop me off at this lil cheap motel on the eastside called the Suezz. I was feeling good with a pocket full of money, so I told the lil freak from the back seat that she could come with me. After all, baby do gotta mean head game on her, so I had to get an encore of that performance. I asked her to pay for the room just to see how far this relationship could go. She passed the test with no complaint... my kind of girl. I woke up this morning counting my money and just like before, it was all there. Thirty big bands for yo man to get on his feet, once and for all!

I heard the door knob turn and the motel door flew open. I jumped out of bed half naked in my boxers, reaching for my gun on the night stand. My heart was beating out of my fuckin chest, till I saw it was the little freak from last night walking in with some carry out bags of food in her hands. I was so worried about my money; I didn't even notice baby gurl wasn't lying next to me in the bed when I woke up and started counting this morning.

"Well good morning to you too!" she said, as she turned and closed the motel door behind her.

"I didn't mean to scare you. I just went out to get us some breakfast from Coney Island."

Soon as I glanced at dat ass and them juicy ass lips of hers, I quickly remembered why I chose to let her stay the night with me.

"You good." I replied as I sat my gun back on the night stand and took a seat on the bed next to my three neat stacks of money.

She walked towards the center table and started setting out the Styrofoam food containers as we continued in conversation.

"So do you smoke?" she asked as she pulled out a nice size bag of weed and held it in the air looking at me, waiting for a response.

"Only good shit" I answered.

She smirked then smacked her lips and rolled her eyes.

"Well why don't you come over here and eat yo breakfast while I roll us up a fat ass wood to blow, and for yo info; I only smoke the best shit poppin in these streets", she said arrogantly with attitude.

"Wats yo name cuteness?" I asked, hoping she didn't get mad because I didn't remember.

"I told you last night my name is Shakora, but you can just call me Stormy for short since you gotta short memory."

"Stormy huh?" I repeated out loud while walking up so close behind her she could feel my meat on half wood brushing up against her ass through my boxers.

She turned around with an answer.

"Yea Stormy, because I can make any man brainstorm out of his mind" she paused in mid-sentence, looked down at the print of my dick and back into my eyes, then finished her statement... "at any given-time".

My dick started rising instantly as I watched Stormy roll up the weed while I was eating my pancake, sausage, egg and bacon breakfast. She was licking all over the Backwood, wrapping her lips around it in a sexual manner, teasing me. She knew exactly what she was doing. She was brown skin complexion with slanted eyes that made her look like she was mixed with Chinese. She had mad sex appeal. Her frame was small and petite but she had titties and ass jumping out at you everywhere. I think her slimness made her body parts stand out more than average and the fact that she was only 5 '2, made a nigga wanna pick her up and drill her guts in all night long. She had jet black silk wavy hair, that was shoulder length. She wore it in a ponytail; but it was her lips that reminded me of Megan Good's was what I love most about her.

I grabbed the remote and clicked on the TV I turned it to ESPN so I could take my mind off wanting to put my dick down Stormy's throat again. I took a sip from my pink lemonade than broke the short moment of silence between us.

"So, tell me lil momma; how old are you?"

"Twenty-two. What about you?"

"Twenty-three" I said, as I watched her spark up the Backwood she just rolled. "Any kids?" I asked and waited for her to finish inhaling the cloud of smoke that erupted in front of her face.

Cough! Cough! Cough! Cough!
''Damn this shit strong" she struggled to say as she finished out her coughing. "But I love it, it's something about it that keeps me craving for it. Here."

Stormy walked over to pass me the blunt and sat next to me on the couch. I grabbed the blunt but kept my eyes focused on hers, waiting for a response to my question.

"So do you?" I asked again.

She scooted closer then sat on my lap cowgirl style facing me.

"Why? Do you want to put one in me?" she asked with a devilish grin. . .

"No, I don't have any kids" she answered before I could even respond to her brain teaser..

''How many do you have; mister I want some kids by Stormy?"

"Wat?" I said confused. She caught me off guard and I was tryna' figure out what gave this bitch the big head to think I wanted to make her my baby momma?

"You heard me." she popped back.

"Listen my baby" I started than continued.. ''first things first, I don't have no kids And yea, you cute and all but it's gonna take more than a pretty face and a fat booty for me to want to put a baby in you when I barely even know you.''

"Well, I damn sho can't tell you wasn't tryna get me pregnant, the way you was bussing nut after nut inside of me last night!"

I sat there with my mouth half way open, looking shocked. She stayed siting on my lap with her eyes piercing through me like AK bullets. I forgot about me fucking her raw all night long. That money I came up on had me feeling so good, plus her tight ass pussy didn't make it no easier for me to pull out like I meant to. Before the dumb look on my face could stay for another second, I grabbed the lighter, re-lit the blunt than took a big ass puff. Soon as I inhaled the smoke my lungs felt like somebody set them on fire. I couldn't take it. I thought I was goin to cough up a lung.

''Damn baby this shit is good" I said to Stormy, but all she did was get off of my lap and stare at the TV, as if she was interested in what was on ESPN.

I took another little puff just to make sure I wasn't trippin'.

"Cough! Cough." This shit was so strong I could feel it aggravating my asthma.

"Yea, this some fiya. Where you get this from baby gurl?" Stormy just looked at me and rolled her eyes ignoring my question.

I was hoping to get her mind off the topic of me bussing in her last night.I realized it wasn't no way around it. I decided to sweet talk her and put the lid back on the can of worms I just opened.

"Listen Stormy, I ain't saying you not good enough for me to plant my seed in you, I'm just saying I don't know enough bout you yet for me to be tryna start a family with you."

she finally looked at me and began to speak.

"Well say dat then nigga, but don't be tryna play me like I'm just some lame ass bitch begging' to have yo baby when I don't even know you like that myself. I met you thru Chyna and I admit; you turned me on with that Lil hot boy shit you pulled last night, but I was just confronting you on the fact that yo pullout game was weak as hell last night. So I'mma

17

need you to give me some of that money over there for a Plan B; unless you wanna take the chance of paying for an abortion later down the line? since you don't wanna be my baby daddy."

I burst out laughing and hit the blunt one mo time before I passed it back to her.

"Fa sho lil momma I got you, but you still ain't told me where you got this fiya ass shit from?"

She put the half smoked blunt in the ash tray, hopped back on my lap cowgirl style, kissed me on my cheek.

"wats in it fa me?" she asked.

My dick instantly jumped at the warmness I felt from between her legs, but before I started to think with my lower head, I remembered that I wanted to get my day started early, so I had no time to give her this morning dick. I licked my lips like LL Cool J and cut my eyes at her on the sexual tip just so I could soften her up. A little booty rub and a few kisses on her neck was all that she needed before opening right up to me, giving up all the info she had so I can get my hands on some more of this fiya ass smoke.

"They call it wedding cake and the nigga I get it from name is BB. He don't really meet up with people if he don't know them, so you'll have to go thru me if you want some."

"BB?" I said out-loud , not familiar with the name.

"Yea BB", she replied. "It stands for Benji Bands but its BB for short. They call him Benji Bands because all the rubber band stacks of money he keeps on him are full of nothing but Benjamin Franklin, hunnit dollar bills. He's some type of big-time money getta. I really don't even know what he does, other than sell weed. It's weird because he always gives it to me for free when I meet up with him, so I don't understand how he could make all that money off weed, when he's giving it out for free?"

The more Stormy talks about this nigga, the more interested I became in finding out who he is. Either he can be my next lick to hit or who knows, he could be my new plug!

"Maybe he just like you and that's maybe why he gives you weed for free?" I suggested to Stormy.

''Of course, he likes me Chedda, who wouldn't?" she asked arrogantly and then continued, "He always hits on me and tells me I can move in with him and make a lot more money than I'm making. I told him I'm not a drug dealer."

"Then wat does he say?" I asked.

"He says he's not talking about selling drugs, but I never take him serious because he always has a different girl with him in the passenger seat of his car every time we meet up."

"Oh yeah? Wat kind of car does he drive?"

"I only met up with him three times, but each time it was a different whip. One day it was a Benz , the second time a BMW and just yesterday he was in an all-black G-Wagon Benz truck." She answered without hesitating.

"Damn dude must really be paid."

Stormy placed her lips on top of mine, giving me a seductive kiss, then whispered in my ear softly, "Not as paid as we gonna be after you stick it to him and get him for everything he owns."

I ended up giving Stormy a hunnit dolla bill and paid an Uber for her to get to her spot. I locked her number in my phone and made her give up some of that supa head one last time to get my day started on the right foot. Something about shorty made me see a lot of potential for her future in Chedda's world. The lil bitch might be on to something.

It was about 10:15 in the morning and check out was scheduled for 11:00 AM. I had a lot on my mind, but even more on my to do list for the day. It was time for me to finally get my shit together and never look back. I been thinking bout that bad ass bitch who saved Johnny Boy's life since the moment I saw her. Lacey, who the fuck was this bitch? I gotta do a background check on her quick, because it's not every day I run into a chick that keeps thirty grand in cash on her just to give away to save their crackhead ass daddy's life.

The first thing I needed to do was buy me a set of wheels. There's no way I can move around and get to this money like I want without having my own transportation. My last car got a hunnit bullets sprayed through the windshield two months ago at a strip club called The Crazy Horse. Ever since then, I been calling my dawg Dre to drive me around.

I took a quick shower, googled the closest car lot and waited for my Uber to arrive so I could go buy me a car. I gathered up all my money, grabbed my pistol and opened up the night stand drawer to grab the room key for turn in. Soon as I glanced inside, I noticed the motel key, along with all the extra shit I got with the money from Lacey last night. I reached and grabbed the .38 special, the ounce of cocaine, the bag of weed and the Louis Vuitton wallet. I noticed the bag of weed had a logo on it that read Wedding Cake. Wedding cake? That's the name of the trees Stormy smoked with me earlier.

I examined the exotic looking weed then glanced over at the Louis Vuitton wallet. I picked it up and dumped out everything that was in it. There was an up-to-date Michigan State ID with a picture of Lacey smiling. Her full name was Lacey Renee Williams and her address was on Detroit's west side on a street called Lindsay. She was twenty-seven years old and her birthday was May 9th.

Everything I needed to know about her was in the palm of my hands. There was also what looked to be business cards. There were five of them along with seven small size pictures of different females that had their Instagram name and phone number on the back of each one. I picked up one of the business cards. It had a picture of a woman's lower body squatting down in the background with money coming out of her panties. It read: Diamond Star Entertainment, where fantasies get turned into reality. What the fuck? No phone number, no e-mail, no exact address to be reached. Wat type of business is this? I laid out all the business cards and looked at the pictures on them. The bitches all were sexy as hell. Then I recognized one of them. . . Stormy!

My phone lit up ringing, breaking my train of thought. I answered and it was the Uber driver, letting me know that he was outside. I quickly put everything in my pockets, tucked my gun in my pants, looked at the time 10:57, then headed out the door. I ran to the office, turned in the motel key and jumped inside the Uber. I was headed to the car lot.

We pulled up to the car lot about fifteen minutes later. I hopped out and as soon as I walked in the dealership A Chaldean man with slicked back hair approached me.

''What can I help you with today my man? "

''I need a car." I told him straight up.

"Buy, lease what?" he asked.

"Buy" I responded.

"Oh, ok, ok. So, what's your budget?"

"Ten bands' cash" I snapped back.

"Ok follow me." He said walking me out to the lot.

As I followed him outside, I eyed all the cars we were walking by, new Challengers, Durango's, Yukons, BMW's and Benzs. All out of my price range for the time being, but you betta believe one day I'm gonna be whipping something so foreign and so clean bitches gonna wanna lick the paint off that mufucka.

"So, are you looking for a truck or a car?" the salesman asked.

I would've answered him but we stopped in front a 2010 used Charger that caught my eye. It was dark grey, something lo-key to get around in and the price tag read $7,300. It was ten years old but fuck it, I just needed something to bust my joogs in until I could afford something better.

"I want this" I told the sales man referring to the 2010 Charger that I stood in front of.

"Well ok, I guess we're buying a car!" he shouted.

He walked me right over to the counter and retrieved all of the needed info from me. All together It came up to 9000 thousand dollars cash. That covered the car, the insurance, the new plates and taxes. As long as this mufucka get me from point A to point B, then it's all worth it.

We went back outside; he gave me the car keys and shook my hand. I thanked him, hopped in the car started the engine and sped out of the car lot as if the police were chasing me.

I looked at the time, it was 12:30 and I was cruising down eight-mile rd. heading to Action Impact to buy me some new fire arms. Driving my own car had me feeling kind of good, but I couldn't get my mind off of all the shit I seen in Lacey's wallet. I stopped at a red light and pulled the things out of my pocket to take another look. What the fuck is this bitch Lacey into? I wondered. How did she get this Wedding Cake weed if some nigga name BB is the only one with it? And why da fuck is this picture of Stormy inside her wallet?

The light turned green and I pulled into Action Impact's parking lot, but my head was still spinning. I put the ounce of coke, the weed and the belongings from Lacey's wallet inside the glove box and took the .38 special and my .45 along with me inside the gun shop to holla at my man Joey.

I spent about thirty minutes in there chopping it up with Joey about some new shipments of AR's he ordered.

I left out with two brand new gloc .22's all black handguns, two thirty round extended clips to go with them, three hundred blue steel bullets and a hundred .38 special bullets for the revolver Lacey gave me. I had special plans for that lil chrome baby. Out of all that, my boy Joey only charged me a smooth nine hunnit bucks. Who said all whites was races?

The clock on my i-phone read 1:35 p.m. I still had a few more moves to make before I turned it in to lay low for the rest of the weekend. I had to go to the mall and load up on some new trap gear, then call and book a room for tonight at the Marriot downtown. I still wanted to slide thru da hood to stash some shit and see if I could spot Johnny Boys crackhead ass running round the streets. I needed to find out the scoop on his daughter Lacey.

I made a quick stop at the gas station before I headed to Fairlane Mall. I bought a BOSS water, two strawberry nutrigran bars, a snicker and a pack of Russian Creme backwoods. The breakfast I ate with Stormy was wearing off and I knew I was going to need something to snack on after I smoked some more of this good ass weed. I pumped my gas until the tank was full, then I sat in my car and rolled up some of the wedding cake inside my Backwood and stashed the rest in my glove box.

"Cough! Cough! Cough!'' I starting choking immediately after I fired the mufucka up.

Damn this some good shit, I thought to myself. At that moment, I realized I'd be a fool not to make this new strand of exotic bud my next investment. I hit the blunt one mo time before I turned up the music and drove to the mall feeling high as a kite the whole trip there.

The weekends traffic was light but the mall's crowd was jammed packed. It was already 2:45 and I was just walking inside the doors of the mall. Fine bitches and bad ass kids and groups of young teenage thugs were walking and running around everywhere. I left all the guns in the car except for the .38 special I placed in my back pocket before exiting my car. The police were extra thick along with mall security and I had no need for an unnecessary gun case just because one of my glocs bulging too hard on my hip, so I chose to leave them inside. I maneuvered thru the wild crowd and found my way to the 4Men clothing store.

As soon as I walked in, I noticed there were all female staff members' working the floor, with one male behind the counter, working the register. The women were all cute and seemed to be between the ages twenty-one to twenty-five, but you could tell whoever was doing the hiring was making sure each of them had a nice ass and a nice set of tittles before he made them an official employee. 4Men always kept a lot of the latest fashion on display but I really wasn't looking to blow too much cash on clothes. I just needed a few nice outfits that I could grind in and pull a bitch in at the same damn time. I ain't got too much going on to be a flashy type of nigga yet, so Air max's and Nike track fits was more of my style for the moment. I searched around a while and picked up a few items that caught my eye, as I was checking out some of the gear. I reached to grab a set of jean shorts, but then this light skin cutie approached the rack of clothes and retrieved the pair of shorts for me.

"Let me help you with that" her soft voice said.

"Good lookin out " I replied back, then I held them up against my waist and asked her what she thought about them.

"They 're cool, but I like my man wearing something a little more fitted around the waist so I can see his dick print all day." The cutie responded flirtatiously.

She moved my hand that was holding the shorts in front of my waist and stared at my dick as if she had x-ray vision and could see thru my pants; then she looked back into my eyes and licked her lips.

I smirked and let out a little laugh at baby girl's gesture, then asked her name. She quickly pointed at her name tag.

"Tay Tay'', she said mouthing each syllable.

"Nawl, I mean yo real name?" I replied.
She continued to look at me with a little pink blush coming over her face.

''Its Taylor'' she admitted.

"Taylor, why don't you grab me a pair of these shorts one size smaller and take the rest of these items over there to the counter so you can ring em up and get me outta here."

She did everything I asked her to do with no complaint. I handed her the clothes I was carrying so she could take them to the counter.

''I like your cologne, maybe you could blow one with me one day?" She whispered in my ear before walking away.

I was puzzled for a minute, tryna catch on to what she was talking about. Then it finally struck me that I still reeked of the weed I smoked on the drive here, but it was too late, she was already headed to the counter.

I stood in the long ass line as patient as I could. The only thing got me outta having a fucked-up attitude was that Taylor appeared at the register the moment it was my turn for check out.

"Oh, it's you again?" she said with a smile.

''I thought you left already" she couldn't help but to let out a little giggle because we both knew that was a lie.

"Your total is $993.92."

I pulled out a dummy roll and peeled off ten, hunnit dollar bills than gave them to Taylor along with my i-phone.

"Wats this for?" she asked.

"That's for you to put yo number in" I said as if baby girl owed it to me.

She entered her number, gave me back my phone along with my shopping bags and receipt and change. I turned to walk out but before I could leave, Taylor called after me.

"Aye, you never told me your name."

"My name Chedda. . . and the name of my cologne is called Wedding Cake. One of these days I'll hit you up so we can wear it together."

She just stood there with the biggest kool-aid smile on her face, then I headed out.

Baggin' bitches was never nothing new to me, don't get it twisted I ain't the pretty boy type, but a light skin nigga with the waves knows how to have his way with the ladies.

I couldn't believe how packed the mall was today. I had only bought a few outfits, so I still had to go to Footlocker and pick up some shoes.

I was relieved when I walked in and seen that the store wasn't as crowded as the last one. I went straight to where the air max's were and picked out the five best pair I seen. I saw a few Nike shirts and one-track fit that matched my shoes, so I thought, fuck it and bought them as well. All together I spent a thousand dollars in Footlocker. As I was walking out the store, I felt my phone vibrate and seen that it was a text message from Stormy.

Stormy: WYD?

I started to put my phone back inside my pocket and continue towards an exit out of the mall but then the wheels started turning in my head. I remembered I had to draw up a plan to buy some of that wedding cake from BB and find out how close Stormy was with that girl Lacey? She had to know her, otherwise why would Stormy's picture be inside Lacey's wallet?

I sent Stormy a text back:

Me: I aint doin shit. u think u gonna be free 2nite so we can Link up?

Stormy: Time and location?

Me: Ten o'clock downtown Marriot

Stormy: Ooooohh the Marriot? See u there. Can' t wait

Me: Bet. Call me when u pull up

I put my phone back inside my pocket. I had to find a way to make wedding cake my new investment of stock since Johnny Boy was no longer a reliable foot runner to help me move my dope in these streets. And since Stormy was the only thing, I had to help me get closer to the source; I knew my plan had to start with her.

I walked in every direction searching for a jewelry store inside the mall until I found the perfect one.

"How much is this one?" I asked the older lady behind the counter. She put on her glasses as she tried to make out which necklace, I was pointing at thru the glass counter.

"Oh, you mean the Cartier one?" she asked unsure if that's the one I was pointing to.

"Yeah" I replied.

"That's a Little out dated for a youngster, but its on sale for $1,850."

"Would you be able to gift wrap it for me?"

"Sure, no problem" she answered with a smile.

I pulled out two thousand in cash and handed it to the sweet older lady. She counted it up then told me that I gave her a little too much and tried to hand me back the extra money.

"Maam I wanted to know if I gave that extra one-fifty, could you put this in a small gift box and gift wrap it for me as well?"

She looked at me confused.

"What are you talking about young man?" she asked.

I slipped the .38 special in one of my shopping bags and set it on the counter. I told her to look inside. She opened the bag, looked at the gun and then back at me.

"Young man, we usually don't gift wrap this type of jewelry. . . but since you were so generous and polite, let's see what I can do for you." She winked at me, took the whole shopping bag and necklace in the back.

When she returned and handed the bag back to me everything was gift wrapped. I told her thanks than strolled right out of the jewelry store with a white gold Cartier necklace for Stormy along with a giftwrapped gun as a gesture for her to be my new bitch.

I made my way out the mall, threw all of my shopping bags in the trunk, then jumped inside the driver seat of my car. I was already kind of exhausted and I still had a few more errands to run. I looked at the time; it was 5:30 PM I started the engine and turned on the a/c while I googled the Marriot on my phone. I called and booked a suite from tonight to next

Sunday. I ended the call, stored the information in my notes and I pulled out of Fairlane's parking lot.

Traffick was still light, so I ended up making it back to the east side around six o 'clock. I stopped at Captain J' s for some chicken, then went and got a clean cut from my neighborhood's barbershop. Everybody I asked in the shop about Johnny Boy's whereabouts hadn't seen him around da hood and nobody knew he had a daughter. After I left the barber shop, I headed to my spot so I could get ready for tonight with Stormy.

For the past year I been living in a vacant house that me and a crackhead name Jughead cleaned and fixed-up together. We had heat, water, electricity and even cable. It was our real home. Jughead claimed he didn't have any family. I didn't like mines, so me and him fit well together. He was like the uncle I never had. Together; me and him were all we wanted and needed for a family. I parked in the driveway and grabbed all of my things from the car. When I finally managed to make it thru the door. I found Jughead in the front room on the couch slumped over snoring with a needle on the table in front of him and a crack pipe in his lap. He gonna get enough of speed balling, I thought to myself. I closed the blinds so no one would see in and see him like this, then I headed up stairs to my room.

It felt good to finally be home where I could relax and get a clear mind. I unpacked all of my shopping bags and noticed the two-gold shiny gift-wrapped boxes. I laid them out on my bed, thinking how I couldn't wait to activate my plan by giving them to Stormy later. I stashed my guns inside my closet and loaded one thirty round clip for one of the new glocs I was going to keep on me.

I put twenty-nine-hunnit up inside the small safe I had under my bed and I kept thirteen-thousand out on the Dresser. Once I laid out what I was going to wear for the night, I packed my bags for the week since I knew I'd be staying at the hotel for a while. I hopped in the shower and let the steaming hot water run over my head and body while I thought about everything I had going on. The more I brainstormed, the more my plan started to come together.

Out of the $13,000 that I had sitting on the Dresser, I planned to spend $10,000 of it on the exotic weed from BB as long as Stormy could deliver the connect. $2 ,500 was going to be kept in my pocket as spending money and the other $500 would be a part of Stormy's gift package so she could have her own spending money. A part of the plan was to make her my ride or die bitch, so, it's only right I make sure my girl keeps some cash on hand, so she can get around.

Lacey crossed my mind as I stopped the water and dried off. It was so much more I wanted to learn about her and I was hoping that Stormy had some info for me. I got Dressed, putting on the red, white and black matching Jordan shorts, socks and shirt that I laid out. I topped it off with a fresh pair of red and black retro Jordan shoes. The number elevens and a spray of my YSL cologne, I looked at the clock on my night stand and saw that it was 8:37 p.m. I told Stormy to meet me by ten o'clock, I still had a little time before I headed to the hotel.

I took the few extra minutes to meditate and think out my plan a little more. My bag was already packed with everything I wanted to bring to the hotel, so there was no need to rush. I laid back on my bed, closed my eyes and calculated all of the money I spent from the thirty-thousand dollar come up. I spent nine thousand on a car, nine hunnit on two brand new glocs , a thousand on clothes , a thousand on shoes , two thousand on Stormy's necklace and another thousand for the room at the Marriot for the week. I had another five hunnit to give Stormy for own pocket change and I kept twenty-five hunnit for my pockets. I put twenty-nine hunnit up in the stash and got ten thousand on standby to shop with BB. Oh, and I most definitely can't forget about the hunnit I gave Stormy this morning for the Plan B pill and Uber fare.

All In all, I ran through the whole thirty thousand dollars in a split second. The money that's left over was already accounted for. I had big plans ahead of myself and while some may not agree about how quickly I move; at the end of the day... It's Mine I Spend It!

Chapter: 3
"Coach Chedda" (Play Maker)

I opened my eyes, looked at the clock and realized how far I got carried away with my thoughts. It was 9:05p.m. I finally got up, tucked my gloc inside my waistband and grabbed my duffle bag. Soon as I took the first step down the stairs, I smelled the aroma of food being cooked. When I entered the living room it was clear that Jughead was wide awake and capable of being active during his heroin and crack cocaine high.

"Wassup Nephew?" He said, as he rubbed his powdered hands together. It smelled like he was frying fish, and he had all the flour from the batter on his shirt and hands.

"Wassup unc? here check this out." I reached into one of the side pockets on the duffle bag, pulled out the ounce of cocaine I got from Lacey and handed it to him. He opened the zip lock bag and dug his long ass pinky nail inside and snorted a bump from it.

"Wheeeww shit!" he barked. "You gotta new connect, I see." Jughead said, while giving me the thumbs up.

"I got dat from Johnny Boy's daughter" I told him.

"Johnny Boy got a daughter? Well, she got some good shit here. You need to let me cook that shit up and sell it to all my smokin' buddies because I could make us some good money with dat . . . and get high at the same damn time!"

I burst out laughing at my funny ass uncle, I neva allowed him to run my product for me because I hate mixing family with bidness, but now I may be forced to give him a chance since imma kill Johnny Boy the next time I see him.

 "Yeah unc, dats for you. Just bag me up a quarter out of that soft so I can get going. You can keep the rest."

"Say no mo nephew, that's why I love ya like you my own. And remember when you out in dem streets, it's a game of chess not checkers."

Jughead gave me seven grams of the soft white powder inside a sandwich bag and tied it for me. I put it in my pocket and told him I'd be back home after the weekend then walked out the front door. One thing I loved about Jughead is that he didn't ask too many unnecessary questions about what I had going on.

I put my bag in the trunk and sat inside the driver's seat.

Before I pulled out the driveway, I sent Stormy a text. I stopped at the liquor store and bought a fifth of Don Julio 1942 and a case of red bull energy drink. I even kept Stormy in mind and grabbed a bottle of papaya juice just in case she wanted to chase her liquor with something. I made sure to grab two boxes of magnum condoms to avoid having to pay for another Plan B pill as well.

I arrived downtown at the Marriot Hotel at 9:50p.m. I checked in at the front desk picked up my room key and headed to my room.

After taking the elevator up to my floor, I walked into my suite and looked around. There was a refrigerator with freezer that also had a liquor bar attached at the bottom. There was a sixty-four-inch plasma television, a King size bed with a mirror above on the ceiling. There was a walk-in shower with a bath tub attached, but my favorite thing about the suite was the hot tub jacuzzi right next to the window.

I unpacked most of my belongings and placed my duffle bag inside the closet. I grabbed a glass cup, put a few ice cubes inside and then poured a little of the Don Julio inside of it. I took a nice gulp just to knock off the edge and I set the cup down. I placed my gun and a few more items inside the night stand next to the bed. I turned on the TV and changed it to the BET JAMZ channel where music videos played twenty-four-seven. I pushed the button to start up the jacuzzi and I took my shirt off as I felt the liquor heating up my body. My phone rang and I saw that it was Stormy.

"Wat up?"

"I'm downstairs in da lobby, wat room you in?" She asked, with her soft sweet voice coming thru the speaker.

"I'm on the seventeenth-floor room 1755B."

I ended the call and grabbed my gun out the Dresser. I cocked it back and put one in the head, just in case. I didn't think she was up to no shiesty shit, but you could never be too safe out here in these streets. I grabbed one of the golden wrapped gifts I bought her and put it in my pocket so I could surprise her.

Tap, tap, tap. I heard three knocks at the door and I opened it to let her in. My right hand was clutching my brand-new gloc. She stood there with one hand holding her phone and the other holding a party store bag filled with who knows what. She looked at my right hand holding the gun and smacked her lips at the sight of it.

She walked in and I closed the door behind her. I set my gun down, grabbed the bag out of her hand and placed it on the table. I walked up on her and without saying a word, I gave her a big ass hug, holding her tight. I lowered my hands to grip both her ass cheeks. She smelled good as hell, like peaches or something; and I swear the way she was looking tonight made me wanna eat her up from head to toe.

34

"Damn you smell good girl'' I said, as I let her go and took a step back to admire her sex appeal.

She had on a see thru purple lavender button up blouse with a matching purple bra with some purple booty shorts. Her hair was French braided to her scalp with long ass weave extensions that touched the bottom of her ass. It might've been the Julio in my system but I was ready to fuck instantly.

"Boy you hugging all on me like you really missed a bitch" She said, staring at me with a little blush rushing her cheeks.

 "I did miss you my baby; especially those lips of yours."

I leaned in and gave her a sensual kiss sucking on her bottom lip for a split second. I cringed inside cause kissin a bitch I barely knew wasn't my style but I knew it was all part of my plan. She chuckled and ran her hand across my six pack. I knew right now was the perfect time to press play on the first part of my plan to make Stormy my bitch. I reached in my pocket and pulled out the gift-wrapped Cartier necklace and handed it to her.

"Wats this?" She asked with one hand holding the gift and the other covering her mouth.

"It's just a lil sum-sum I thought you might like. Go head, open it" I told her.

As she ripped the wrapping off and opened the jewelry box, I grabbed the open bottle of Don and poured her a glass.

"OMG, Chedda! it's beautiful!" she yelled smiling ear to ear as she lifted the white gold Cartier necklace; examining it.

I dropped a few ice cubes in her cup and poured a little of the papaya juice as a chaser. I took the necklace from her and gave her the glass.

"Here drink this, and turn around so I can put your necklace on."

She took a sip from her cup and turned around with her ass rubbing up against my dick. I placed the chain around her neck and connected the clip together, making sure it was secure on her.

I placed my lips on the right side of her neck close to her collarbone. As I turned her around, I planted some kisses on her neck down to her upper chest. I began to unbutton her purple blouse. She set the glass down and hopped on top of the table, helping me take the blouse off of her body. I reached around to her back and unhooked her bra. I pulled it off and her perfect melons were exposed for me to feast on.

I grabbed one in my left hand, massaging and caressing it as I took the other one in my mouth, nipple first. She moaned with pleasure. I traced my tongue around her areola and sucked on one breast then did the same to the other. I ran my tongue all the way down her stomach to her belly button and she lifted up a little so I can pull her shorts all the way down to her ankles. She kicked off her sandals and I tossed her shorts on the floor. She wasn't wearing any panties. I began kissing her pelvis area gently, working my lips closer to her wet juicy pussy. She opened her legs wide, as she continued sitting on the table and I dropped to my knees in front of her. Her pussy was clean shaved. I spread the dark colored lips open and saw hot pink pussy staring me in my face. It was leaking wet and her clit was pulsating, begging me to put my dick inside her.

 I put my tongue right on top of her clit and went to work. She moaned even louder and threw her head back as her legs begin to cradle my neck. I licked and sucked on her clit and had her begging me for more. I stuck two fingers inside her pussy just to see how ready she was and I felt nothing but warm wetness. I stood to my feet, took off my shoes and came out of my clothes.

My dick was brick hard and standing at attention. I stepped in between her legs and held my dick with my right hand, staring at Stormy in her eyes.

"Chedda, give it to me baby; please, I want it bad!" Stormy begged for the dick like a bitch in heat.

I rubbed the tip of it against her clit to tease her even more. My dick got even harder at the feel of her Drenched pussy. I spread open her pussy lips and she grabbed hold of my dick and put me inside of her.

I grabbed her by the waist and pulled her into each stroke while she wrapped her legs around me, taking every inch of my dick.

"Damn daddy, give it to me." Stormy moaned, under her breath, as I deep stroked her on top of the table.

She laid back on the table, pulling me on top of her with her arms wrapped around my neck. I pounded her pussy even harder. I felt her pussy muscles contracting around my dick. As I pumped each stroke, her legs started trembling and shaking, and her pussy started to gush cum all over my dick. She screamed my name and climaxed in pure ecstasy. I pulled my still hard dick out of her leaving her sprawled out on the table and sat at the foot of the bed. She got up from the table breathing heavily. She walked over to me, kneeled in front of me and took my dick inside of her mouth. She sucked with both hands taking hold of it. I let the dick suckin' pro do her thang for a while and stopped her before she made me buss.

I walked her over to the jacuzzi. She started to climb the steps and get in, but when I saw dat ass bare naked from the back; I stopped her, bent her over the ledge of the hot tub so that I could hit It from the back. Every time I pounded away; it sounded like I was splashing in a wave pool. Splat! Splat! Splat! Splat!

"Yes Chedda, yes!"

"Who's pussy is this?" I asked as I started to feel my nut startin' to rise. I smacked her ass cheek, SMACK!

"It's your pussy daddy! all yours", Stormy screamed out of breath.

Stormy threw dat ass back on me and I started to put more back into it, making sure she had no choice but to run into nothing other than hard dick.

"Damn bitch" I moaned out loud. I put one leg up on the steps to get a better angle and I dug deeper inside of her from the back.

She cried out and moaned my name as I pulled her hair and fucked her harder, harder and harder. I felt my nut coming and I quickly pulled out and bussed all over her booty. Stormy looked back at me with the top of her forehead sweating. She reached back and ran her fingers through the nut that I let out on her ass. She made sure she had a nice amount on her index finger then stuck it in her mouth, sucking the nut off it, while she looked at me seductively. I stepped inside the hot tub and she followed me. She sat on my lap cowgirl style and I began to suck on her tittles. She felt my dick starting to rise again and she fit me back inside her warm pussy and rode me until we both came together at the same time. So much for the condoms, I thought to myself.

This bitch sex game was good, but I know, my dick is better. Even though it was a lot of pleasure in our sexapade; at the end of the day, it was still only business. To activate my game plan, I needed to make Stormy my bitch; and can't no bitch deny me as they nigga once I give them dick this good.

A couple more drinks and a few bussed nuts later; Me and Stormy was having our own little party. It was a sex fest. I ain't know this girl had all this freak in her, and to be all the way one hunnit with you. . . I loved it. She hit a few lines of the powder off my dick and then sucked the residue off until I bussed in her mouth. She was a sex demon in every type of way.

BET JAMZ was playing music for us nonstop and the Wedding Cake trees had us high, so we were both fully awake like the night just begun, and for us; it did.

I turned the music down a little and told Stormy to stop recording me on her social media so we could talk. It was time for me to get down to business.

"Stormy, I know that we just met, but I'mma come at you straight up like we've known each other foreva because dat just the type of nigga I am." I spoke every word with certainty in my tone and looked her dead in her eyes so she wouldn't second guess it. She stopped playing with her phone and locked eye contact to let me know I had her attention.

"I don't know everything about you, but I do know you got me interested in wanting to be with you so that I can learn more about you." I hit her with some basic game just to butter her up more.

"I want you to be mine" I told her. She walked up to me and gave me a kiss on the lips.

"Chedda you are the sweetest nigga I ever met. The way you just fucked me tonight, I'm already yours."

I smirked then let out a quiet laugh at her response.

"Good, now since you my girl, I'mma need you to always keep it a hunnit with me about any and everything from here on out. . .even shit you might think I'mma be mad about."

"Baby if you my nigga, it's neva shit I would keep from you. You can trust me with your life'' Stormy said as if she really believed I would believe her. I gotta admit, the bitch had a good poker face, I reached in the dresser and pulled out Lacey's state ID and handed it to her.

"Where you know her from?" She took the ID and looked at it with a puzzled expression, then read the name out loud.

"Lacey Renee Williams? I've seen her face somewhere but I can't remember where" She replied.

"You sure bout dat?" I asked.

"Yes, Chedda I'm sure; she looks familiar but I just can't remember where I ...—oh shit wait! Do you remember when I told you about the guy I get my weed from?" she asked me excited.

"Yeah, you talkin' bout that nigga you called BB right?"

"Yes Chedda, him. He pulled up and met me one day while she was in the car with him."

It took a minute to take in what Stormy just told me. At that moment I remembered the small bag of Wedding Cake marijuana that I got from Lacey. It was all coming together. I pulled out the other pictures that were in Lacey's wallet and gave them to Stormy.

"So, wat about them, do you know any of em?" She grabbed the pictures and looked through them.

"I don't know any of these girls; Chedda wat's this about?"

"I don't know wat it's about, why don't you tell me, why the first bitch I showed you had a picture of you in her wallet?" I asked while grabbing the picture of her and handing it to her.

Stormy stood there with her mouth opened, looking shocked that I pulled out a picture of her.

"Where did you say you got this from?"

"I told you the first chick I showed you, had this picture of you. So now, do you wanna tell me where you know her from?"

Stormy wrinkled her facial expression with attitude, "Chedda, the only time I saw dat girl was when she was with BB, I neva knew her name or nothing, she neva even said a word to me.

I sat on the bed and hit the blunt, hoping that it would help me put this shit together in my head. I knew Stormy wasn't lying because the bag of weed I got from Lacey clearly linked her to BB in some type of way. So Stormy saying she seen her in the car with him all makes sense.

"Why would she have a picture of me in her wallet?" Stormy asked with confusion written all over her face.

Lacey probably was just one of his hoes he happened to be fucking with the day Stormy seen them together. I don't know? I looked at the time and seen that it was 1:30 in the morning. A plan started to form in my head. I don't know if it was the cocaine that had me all hyped up, or if I was just eager to find out wat da fuck was going on with this Lacey chick and this Benji Bands ass nigga. I didn't know the relationship between Lacey and BB, but I did know from the sounds of it, BB was interested in Stormy and I could use that to my advantage. My main motive is to get a good price on dat strong ass weed he had his hands on. I could use Stormy to do that for me. The closer she gets with him, the more insight I 'll have on him. As far as Lacey's sexy ass; she wasn't going anywhere far because I had her government name and address. She's not hard to find at all.

"Aye baby girl go in that closet and grab that black duffle bag" I said to Stormy.

She brought the bag to me. Then I told her to take a seat and pay attention. I revealed to my new ride or die bitch my plan. I knew that it would look suspicious for me to have Stormy call BB at 1:30 in da morning tryna spend ten thousand with him on some weed; so, I lined things up to take place at a better time. Stormy was all in just like I needed her to be. It was time for things to go into motion, and I couldn't wait to press play.

Mean While

While Chedda and Stormy was at the Marriot plotting on Benji; Downtown Detroit was slapping harder than ever. Thanks to the operation that BB got his top bitch Lacey to push; the streets of Downtown became the epic playground for the biggest tricks and hottest women in the Motor City.

"Thanks Papi, Barbie will be out for you in a minute" Lacey said to the Mexican trick that just handed her a stack of bills. She turned her back towards the trick and counted the money while he sat in the car awaiting the time to enjoy his Dream girl. Lacey turned around, looked at the Mexican and smiled; alerting him that she was satisfied with his payment. She walked away from the car and worked the crowded sidewalk like a runway model. It didn't matter that she was wearing six-inch stilettos, she still moved swiftly and was flawless in every step she took. It was 1:45 in the morning, and even though the sky was pitch black; the headlights from all the cars lined up on Broadway St. lit up the city's block like the sun was still shining.

As Benji sat in the back seat of his black G-wagon, scrolling through Instagram searching for models on his I-pad; he heard a knock on his tinted window. The Italian blond hair beauty in the driver's seat turned around asked for his permission

"Daddy, Lacey's outside, do you want me to turn da music down?"

"Yeah," Benji responded. She turned the music down and Benji rolled down the back window to hear what Lacey had to say.

"Here Daddy, it's all there; he's waiting for her" Lacey said.

Benj grabbed the stack of bills from Lacey and snapped his fingers signaling to the Chocolate sexy chick called Barbie in the back seat with him to stop sucking his dick. She took her lips from around his pole and put it back inside his silk Gucci boxers.

"Get yo self together baby it's time for you to be a star and shine like a diamond."

She grabbed her purse and pulled out a small makeup kit. She opened the mirror and applied some lip gloss and exited the truck.

"Love you daddy", Barbie said before she shut the door and followed behind Lacey.

Benji continued looking on his I-pad, searching for Instagram models. It was a normal Saturday night for him; and business was booming as usual. He and Lacey were partners in their new found brand Diamond Star Entertainment.

Benji considered all of his girls that were a part of the business his Diamond Stars. He knew the night was still young and business was going to be booming around 2 a.m. when the clubs let out. Most of his girls were inside the club making money for him right now. He recruited his top girl Lacey to run things and be the face of things rather than his face. He knew everything about it wasn't legal and he didn't want people in the streets giving law enforcement any information attaching him to it.

His name was already hot in the streets of Detroit and in their local law enforcement database. Benji felt the business would stay afloat in Detroit long enough for him to line things up and move it to Nevada, as long as he didn't attach his face to it in the streets. His distant presence was good and bad for him; because even though it kept the heat away from the business, he still had to find a way to protect his girls and his money without being there. Just yesterday his girl Lacey got robbed and he didn't like that one bit. He had his weed connect in Vegas, his cocaine connects in Vegas and even had a mansion out there that no one knew about other than Lacey. The only thing holding back his big move was his older brother.

Benji had only one family member left living which was his older brother who was addicted to drugs. His brother was 46yrs old, but he looked like he was sixty. Benji was thirty-five. His brother saved his life and raised him since a child. Benji had a type of love for him that only God could explain. When Benji was only five yrs. old, his family was traveling from Las Vegas to Detroit and ended up in a deadly crash. His father had taken him, his older brother, and their mother and two sisters on a vacation to visit his father's best friend by the name of Dude. On the way back their father lost control of the wheel and hit a semi-truck that was carrying gasoline on the highway. Both vehicles went into scorching flames.

BB's older brother, who was sixteen yrs. old at the time, unbuckled BB's seatbelt and climbed out of the burning van's window with him in arms. Their father, mother and two sisters died. BB was the youngest and his brother Ka'Ron was the oldest.

When Benji was old enough to comprehend the heroic act of his brother. He made his self a vow to never leave Ka'Ron behind and to always look out for him.

Ka 'Ron and BB were placed in foster care, where Ka 'Ron found a way to keep in touch with their father's best friend

Dude. As Ka 'Ron got older, Dude started supplying Ka'Ron with cocaine so that he could make money and provide for him and his younger brother BB. Ka 'Ron then chose to run away with BB from foster care in fear that they would split them up through adoption.

   As life took its course, Ka 'Ron begun to buckle under pressure while trying to provide and care for BB. He drunk cheap liquor to deal with the pain of losing his parents and two sisters. He started snorting the cocaine he was selling and eventually he fell victim to smoking crack. He's been hooked on it ever since and BB grew to take over the role of protecting and providing for himself and his older brother.

Even though Ka'Ron fell victim to the drugs, BB still had mad love and respect for him. He taught BB everything he knew about the streets and survival. Hustling, Pimping, killing, and he even showed BB how to start up his own business.

Now a days BB can barely keep up with his night walking brother and only bumps into him every now and then. When their paths do cross BB gives him money and try to talk him into going to rehab, but Ka'Ron let it go in one ear and out the other. Even though Ka'Ron is rebellious against going to rehab, BB is finally fed up and determined to make his older brother take his advice and enroll in rehab once and for all.

BB had a million-dollar plans for Vegas and all he needed was his strung-out brother to clean up his act. His goal was to move them both into paradise and watch his newly found Business flourish.

 Benji had two small bags of weed in his hands; one said Wedding Cake and one wasn't labeled. Benji opened the one that wasn't labeled and rolled up a blunt. Benji set his I -pad on the side of him and then sparked up the freshly rolled blunt. He took a big puff, then instructed his blond hair driver to turn back up the music.

"Yes Daddy", she said. BB smoked and watched all the traffic around them through the windows of his G-Wagon, while he awaited for the clock to strike 2 a.m.

***Lacey stood outside of the Mexican trick's passenger door and closed it shut after Barbie got inside his car. Lacey than directed him to pull into the car lot down the street on the right. "Listen Papi, once you park your car in the lot, Barbie here, is going to walk you into the entrance of Diamond Star and show you the time of your life, ok?"

The horny Mexican nodded his head up and down in agreement to Lacey's directions with the biggest smile on his face. He hadn't taken his eyes off Barbie since she sat inside his car.

"Ok Barbie, you a big girl, you got this'' Lacey said, as she backed away from the car to let the Mexican drive away. Lacey pulled out a small bag of powder and dipped her finger nail inside to scoop up enough to hit a quick bump. Lacey always gets a little nervous when it was one of her girl's first night doing their thang. It was taking her some time to get used to this, so she started to use a little of the cocaine she was selling for Benji to knock off the edge. Her and Benji just bagged Barbie a week ago and tonight was Barbie's first night to shine like the star Benji saw her to be.

Lacey Looked at the time and realized the clubs would be closing soon. This was her usual time to go inside and gather up all of her girls so she could collect all of what they made from selling Benji's drugs and other services sold while in the club; such as turning fantasies into reality.

Benji had invested allot of money into the vacant building they were using for Diamond Star's festivities this weekend and Lacey was kind of worried that she would be short on reaching her set quota this week.

By the time it turned 1:00 a.m., she had seen how business was booming and she quickly lost her worries. Now her main concern was if she had enough girls on the payroll to keep up with the clientele. Lacey snorted a little powder and placed the coke back inside her Fendi handbag. She strutted across the street, switching her booty left to right. She placed her VIP rope around her neck and entered the club. It was time for her to gather the group of Diamond Stars and take them over to their set venue for the night. The place where fantasies get turned into reality.

***

Chapter: 4
"Sum'n Like A Pimp"

I felt myself about to buss a nut while I was sleeping, then opened my eyes and seen why. Stormy had her ass tooted in the air with her face between my legs, sucking on my dick like it was a firebomb popsicle. "Damn girl, it's like that?" I grunted out loud, just to let her know I was awake and enjoying the morning head.

She looked up at me while she was pleasing me, but never stopped sucking for one second. I felt the drool from her mouth all over my dick and balls and knew I was about to buss any minute now.

"Oh, shit baby; you gonna make a nigga fall in love", I said, as I couldn't hold off my nut any longer. She used her jaw muscles to suck even harder and swallowed every last drop of cum I shot down her throat.

"Ooh shit!" I shouted as my whole body shook. Stormy got from between my legs and laid next to me on the bed, stared at me and placed her right hand on top of my balls. "I knew that would wake you up." she said, as she cuffed my balls and massaged them. "Wat time, is it?" I asked.

"It's three o'clock baby, we been sleeping all day. I been trying to get you up for the past twenty minutes but you wouldn't move. I had to give you a little Stormy specialty to get your day started."

49

I looked around and grabbed my I-phone off the night stand to look at the time, Stormy wasn't lying at all; It was 3:05pm and I had to get out of bed asap. I stayed up so late last nite going over my plan with Stormy, that my body shut down on me. I saw that I had ten missed calls on my phone but I had bigger things to focus on, so I paid them no attention. I got out of bed and went to the bathroom to get myself together.

"Are you hungry?" Stormy yelled from the bed, "I'm about to order us a pizza baby".

"Do that" I hollered back from the bathroom and went back to brushing my teeth.

I turned the shower on and let the water run for a bit. I rinsed my face and tried to gather my thoughts of everything I wanted to put in motion today. Last night Me and Stormy did as much homework as we could to learn more about who this BB cat and Lacey chick was. I had Stormy follow those other girls from Lacey's wallet on Instagram, since their IG name was on the card. We also found an Instagram page for Lacey and hers was open to the public; but the one that we found for Benji Bands was private. Stormy followed and sent a request, but we still waiting for him to accept.

As I prepared to step in the shower, Stormy appeared in the doorway naked with a fresh lit blunt burning.

"You wanna' hit this?"

"Wat you talkin' bout, dat pussy or dat blunt?" I joked, as I reached out and smacked her on her ass.

"Oh my God, you so horny" she said and passed me the blunt.

I hit the blunt a couple times than gave it back. Stormy stood there and continued to smoke while I stepped in the shower. Stormy followed me and got into the shower with the lit blunt in hand and gave it to me. I stepped out the water a little and smoked. Stormy grabbed a wash cloth and covered both of our bodies with soap suds, washing all the dirty sex from last night off of our bodies.

After washing up with Stormy; I was ready to walk it like I talk it. We were chillin' and eating pizza but now that I had food in my stomach, I was ready to put food on the table. It was 5:15pm I grabbed the remote and turned the music off. I reached in my duffle bag and pulled out the ten thousand dollars that I had to spend on the weed with BB. I looked up and seen Stormy watching me.

"Call BB and tell him you want ten grand worth of that Wedding Cake".

 She grabbed her phone and began dialing. "Put it on speaker", I instructed.

I heard the phone ring five times and then went straight to voicemail. She ended the call. The moment I begun to get discouraged, Stormy's phone lit up with a text message from BB.

 "He's texting now" she said and brought the phone over for me to read.

"Text him back about buying the weed" I told her.

BB: who this?

Stormy: Da one and only Stormy

BB: My bad sweet thang. I don't answer unknown numbers and I keep forgetting to save you in my contacts. I'm gonna' do dat now. Wassup? you try'na meet up?

Stormy: Yeah, but I'm tryna talk bidness

BB: talk

Stormy: ten thousand dollars' worth of bidness

He didn't text her back and I was starting to think we may have scared him away, but then Stormy's phone rang, it was BB calling.

"Answer it and put it on speaker" I told her. Stormy answered the call.

"Hello" stormy answered.

"Hey how you doing Stormy?" a voice asked through the speaker, but it wasn't a nigga's voice, it was a female, Stormy looked confused.

"Hello, Stormy are you there?" the soft voice asked. I nodded my head at Stormy, giving her the green Light to continue talking.

"Yea I'm here, can I ask who I'm speaking with?" asked Stormy.

 "Oh yes, I'm sorry sweetie, my name is Lacey." My heart begin to speed up as I heard the voice say her name, she continued, ''I'm calling on behalf of Benji. He told me that you were interested in discussing business and I just wanted to know when you would be available for us to meet up with you?"

 "Lacey, huh?" Stormy repeated, then asked, "Have we met before?"

''No, we haven't cutie pie, but I 've been waiting for the day; so, when are you free?" Stormy looked at me as if she was a little shocked by Lacey's forwardness.

''Umm'' Stormy stuttered a little bit; but she finally spit it out. ''I can meet up in about an hour, is dat fine?" Stormy asked.

"Make it an hour and a half and meet me downtown" Lacey shot back.

''Downtown where?"

"Do you know where Woodward and Broadway Street is?"

"Yeah."

"Well when you arrive on Broadway and Woodward, call me and I'll text you the directions from there. I am also going to text you my number so you can call me instead of BB when you pull up."

"OK, I'll see you than, make sure you wear something sexy too" Lacey said, and ended the call.

As soon as she hung up, she text Stormy her number.

"Wat da fuck!?" Stormy said out loud. Was she hitting on me Chedda, or am I tripping?"

I sat there and stared at Stormy, a little confused myself. I wasn't sure if it was Benji who was interested in Stormy or if it was Lacey that wanted her?

"Why would he have her talk to her instead of him? He ain't never did that before.. and what does she have to do with any business that's supposed to be between me and him?"

Stormy was asking all the right questions but I had no answers for her.

"Calm down baby, we'll figure it out in due time. In the meantime, let's get you together so you can meet up with this Lacey bitch. How did you get here?" I asked Stormy.

"I drove; why?"

"Good, take this and go buy you something sexy to wear before everything close, you know it's Sunday" I said, handing her the five hundred dollars I had set aside for her. As Stormy got herself together and prepared to leave, I turned back on the music and sparked up the half of blunt I left in the ashtray. I had to get my plan together ASAP because this nigga BB just hit me with a curve ball. I don't know if he's going to be there with Lacey to meet with

Stormy or not? Stormy shut the hotel room door behind her as I inhaled a cloud of smoke while listened to Lil Durk play through the speakers. I had an hour and half to get my plan together. I didn't know everything yet but I did know there was two things I wanted for sure; that's a plug on this Wedding Cake I 'm smoking on.. and Lacey as my bitch.

Mean While

''Oh, daddy yes! right there! Yes, keep going, yes! ugh ooh, yes! I love this dick! "

Benji Bands was enjoying a Sunday threesome with Lacey straddling him, and Kharisma sitting on his face. He gripped onto Lacey's waist and pulled her into every stroke as she bounced up and down on his dick like a wild cowgirl. Kharisma rocked her body front to back as Benji worked his tongue like a snake, licking away on her clit. Both the sexy vixens screamed in unison at the top of their lungs as Benji Bands made them climax at the same damn time, making sure he held his nut back from bussing inside of Lacey. They both got off him and laid beside him on the king size bed. One on the Left and one on the right.

Benji wiped Kharisma's cum off of his face and sat up. He smacked the tattoo on Lacey's ass, which read "Daddy's", and started to put on his boxers.

"C'mon get up baby, we got a long night ahead of us" BB said to Lacey as he was getting Dressed.

His tatted body was covered with sweat from the hot sex that just took place and his Dread locked hair hung to his belly button, covering his tattooed face. Even though Benji was thirty-five years old, he still was in shape like a twenty-five-year-old and he stayed active on the grind. He already cornered the market with high quality cocaine that he was flooding the streets of Detroit with and now he was working on locking down the city with his latest marijuana brand "Wedding Cake".

Benji was on to something exclusive with his hot new Diamond Star Entertainment girls, making him a whole different kind of money.

Benji learned at a young age from his older brother that the fastest way to create new opportunities for money came through women. Benji wasn't only making money off his women but he was also using them to handle all of his dirty work without lifting a finger. The majority of his money came from strip clubs. He used his Diamond Star girls to traffic weed and cocaine through the clubs and offering their bodies for fulfilling a trick's fantasy by turning it into reality. Benji was using vacant buildings downtown for the past three months for the Diamond star girls to host their sexual business of pleasure.

It's been the most rapid growing operation that Benji was a part of and he's been working Lacey overtime trying to keep up with the pace. Money was flying in his direction from every trick that stepped foot in Detroit; but more money meant more clientele to please and more clients meant the need for more girls.

Benji searched Instagram and recruited more and more women for his Diamond Star Empire, using his top girl Lacey and highly addictive drugs. The more money DSE made, the more Benji would smother his girls with the latest fashion and top designer out fits and accessories. He supplied them with a lavish lifestyle that any girl would Dream of. Benji and Lacey only set Venue' Events for Friday, Saturday and Sundays until he could move to Vegas; he knew the DSE operations was illegal and he didn't want the events in the same place every weekend just in case twelve caught wind. Monday thru Thursday, Lacey spent her time going after and courting Benji's recruits, while the other Diamond Star girls part timed in the strip club, selling Benji's drugs. BB never sat still for long. If he wasn't getting the next vacant building setup for the upcoming weekend, then he was out of town in

Vegas picking up more drugs from his father's old friend Dude.

As Lacey got up out of the bed to pull her yellow thong above her ass cheeks, she thought about her phone conversation with Stormy.

"So, what you think our girl is up to? I mean, ten thousand dollars' worth of that strong ass weed is a lot for a girl like her?"

"I ont' know, I was thinkin bout that myself. I hope she ain't get that addicted to it; I wasn't tryna' turn her out that bad'' Benji said, shaking his head because only him and Lacey knew the truth about the weed, they were selling.

"Maybe she tryna sell it?" Lacey shot back.

"Yeah, but where da fuck did, she get ten thousand dollas from, just to invest in weed all of a sudden?"

Lacey zipped up her skirt, stood in front of Benji and rubbed on his Dreads while they searched for an answer about the cutie they were after to recruit.

"Don't stress daddy, the ball is in my hands now; I'll handle err thing" Lacey tried to assure Benji that she had it under control, but there was something about Stormy popping up with ten thousand dollars to spend, that just didn't sit right with him.

"I want you to speak with her personally to find out wat she got going on, understood?"

"I got you daddy trust me, after tonight she'll be blowing our phones up, dying to be a Diamond Star. So, how much do you want to give her for the ten thousand she's bringing?" Lacey asked.

"We gonna give her three pounds."

"Three pounds? Don't you mean two?"

Benji stared at Lacey through his Dreads, biting his lip. She knew she was outta line. Benji hated repeating himself and most definitely hated for his orders to be questioned.

"Give her three, only because I need some security that she's gonna come back. As long as she keeps coming back, we will always have another opportunity to lock her in on our team. Business been picking up, so we need every bitch in Detroit that got a pussy to be one of our stars."

Lacey should 've already knew that anything BB said was already well thought out.

"Ok daddy, I'll go pick up the three and make it back before she calls."

Lacey finished gettin' dressed, grabbed her handbag, and keys then started walking towards the exit.

"make sure you add the special ingredients to them" Benji ordered.

"No problem daddy" She said while struttin her curves through the door of their pleasurable venue.

Benji sat on the edge of the king size mattress and finished putting on his clothes. He looked over his shoulder and seen that Kharisma was into a deep sleep. He didn't mind because he knew that once the sunset; her and the rest of the girls would be working hard for him until sunrise. He looked on the Dresser at the monitors connected to the portable video surveillance camera and watched as Lacey climbed into his Benz truck and pulled out of the parking lot.

Benji got on his phone and logged into his Instagram account. He knew that he was expecting Stormy to show up in about an hour, and he wanted to gather his thoughts on how he wanted to play the whole situation with her. Benji had been baiting her in since day one so she could be one of his girls but he never expected her to approach him with ten grand of her own money. Benji typed in Stormy's Instagram and noticed that she sent him a follow request. He ignored it. He found her page and seen that it was open to the public. He browsed through her story and most recent video post. As Benji was looking at her story he noticed videos of Stormy dancing to music in a hotel room with a light skinned nigga, with a short fade haircut. He eyed the video for several minutes and then logged off of Stormy's page. BB sat there in deep thought for a minute, wondering if the guy in the video with Stormy was her boyfriend.

He thought, maybe that's where Stormy's getting ten thousand dollars from.

He logged back onto her Instagram to look at the video again and took a mental photographic memory of the nigga who was in the video with Stormy. He noticed the nigga in the video setting a black handgun down on a Dresser.

Benji stood up and put his platinum VS diamond chain around his neck and placed his 41 millimeter sky dweller Rolex around his left wrist, He reached under the king size mattress and pulled out his FN 5-7 handgun and tucked it inside his waistband. He walked out of the room he was in and went over to the section where he kept the money that was made from last night. He stared at the stacks of money in front of him. He couldn't believe how much money he was making just by recruiting Instagram models and motivating them to fulfill fantasies with pleasure.

He and Lacey were a dynamic duo. Benji spoiled the girls with a lavish lifestyle and Lacey influenced them to sell sex and drugs for her. BB looked at the time on his Rolex and couldn't wait to see how much more money the night would bring him.

***

** "Cmon' Stormy its time to get moving, you been in there for over 30 minutes" I yelled through the bathroom door.

It was 5:25pm and Stormy been in the bathroom taking her sweet ass time like she didn't have somewhere to be. We had about twenty minutes before we had to meet up with Lacey. The only good thing about that was that we were already downtown, so it wouldn't take us long to get to her.

"How do I look?" Stormy asked, as she opened the bathroom door and stepped out, twirling around, showing off her outfit.

She had on a sleeveless spaghetti string white halter top, with some skin tight, red mesh checkered leggings. You could see a camel toe pussy print from the front. She also had on some white designer sandals to coordinate with her top.

"Chedda are you just gonna just sit there and stare, or you gonna tell me dat ya girl got taste?"

"You look good my baby" I said with a smirk. "Now before we leave, I want you to open this." I reached out and gave her a gift-wrapped box.

"Chedda another gift?" Stormy asked with excitement.

"Just open it" I said.

Stormy unwrapped the gift and opened the box. She stared at it surprised.

"You know how to use one of them?" I asked her.

She took the .38 special and aimed it at me as if she was about to shoot me.

"Whoa, careful that thang loaded!" I said jumping from in front of the barrel. Stormy burst out laughing.

"I 'm just playing and yeah, I know how to use one of these, my ex taught me. I always wanted my own, but he never bought me one."

"Well good, put it inside your purse with the money and make sure you don't pull it out unless you about to use it. Aight?"

"Ok baby, I got it, you're such a sweetheart" Stormy said, then gave me a kiss while rubbing on my dick.

"Listen; you're going to drive your car and I'm going to trail behind you in mines." I said to Stormy.

" Wat? Why won't we just ride together?"

"Because we can't chance being seen together."

" Why not?" Stormy asked.

"Because we can't! BB will let you get closer if he doesn't know that you have a man. Where ever you meet up with Lacey, I will be parked out front to make sure you good. I gave you a lil something to protect yourself just in case any thing happens; plus, imma be out front with this" I lifted up my gloc with the thirty-clip hanging from it.

"Just text me if you need me and I'll slide thru. The goal is just to pay who ever got the weed and come back with it. I also want you to be nicer to Lacey."

"Wat you mean by that?"

"I mean you had a little attitude with her on the phone and I don't want you to be that way in person with her. Just feel her out and see wat she's about. From the sound of it, she might got a crush on you."

"Sorry Chedda, but I don't swing dat way and how could she have a crush on me when she doesn't even know me!?" Stormy asked, sounding pist.

" You said she saw you one day when she was in the car with BB right?"

"Yea."

"Well maybe she liked wat she saw? I mean, she did have a picture of you in her wallet with yo Instagram on it, like she was a fan or sumn. Listen baby, I know you probably not into girls and prolly never did this before, but just hear her out and see what type of shit she on. Do it for me sweetie."

I tried to butter her up with my words and I think it was working.

"So, wat if BB's the one with the weed?" Stormy asked asked.

"That 'll be even better. Just deal with him the same way you dealt with him in the past. But I want you to do wat you gotta do so we can lock him in on plugging you with dat weed of his."

"So, this is all for weed?"

"Baby, this is all for money. We can be one of the first ones with this Wedding Cake strand in Detroit and it ain't no telling wat else BB or Lacey can offer us. So just play yo role and see where it goes." I gave Stormy the money, smacked her on her ass and told her come on.

Stormy got inside her white Honda and I followed behind her in my Charger. We had everything set. She was going to call to meet up with BB just as she normally would; but this time she was going to play whatever role she needed in order to get even closer to him so he would start supplying her with more weight of his exclusive Wedding Cake marijuana.

I followed Stormy as she turned off Jefferson and onto Broadway Street. She slowed down her speed and clicked on her blinker, signaling that she was making a right. Stormy turned into a parking lot that only had a few cars in it along with an all-black Benz truck.

It stuck out like a sore thumb because of the Forgiato rims that were on it. I figured that must be the one Stormy seen Benji in before. I kept straight and found a parking spot on the street. It had a nice view for me to keep an eye on Stormy.

I turned off the car and watched closely as I noticed the same lite caramel complexion dime piece, who said Johnny Boy was her daddy; step out of a building that looked abandoned. It was Lacey. Stormy exited her Honda and Lacey approached her in the parking lot. Lacey walked up to her and gave her a long hug and a peck on the cheek as if she had already known her. She said a few words to her then took herby the hand then walked her over to the black Benz truck. Lacey opened the passenger door and helped Stormy get in the passenger seat before she shut it behind her as if she was a gentleman taking a lady on a date.

Lacey got in the driver's seat and pulled out of the lot. I started my engine and followed them. Lacey droved about ten minutes before she parked and took Stormy inside a Spots called Starters.

I found a spot where I could keep an eye on them and parked. I didn't know what Lacey was up to but I was kind of relieved that they were in a public place. I knew that Stormy was safer in public. I sat in my car and listened to the music as I waited. I thought about how everything was playing out and I realized that I still haven't seen Benji Bands show his face for the transaction with Stormy. I wondered if he was inside that abandoned building where Lacey came from and if so; why was he having Lacey deal with Stormy instead of him? As I sat there in deep thought; I looked at the time and noticed that hours had gone by. It was 8:07pm and I was starting to worry wat da fuck was taking so long? I know damn well that it didn't take that long for either one of them to finish a dinner plate. They been in there three hours. I looked at my phone for a text from Stormy but I never got one, so I continued to wait.

Mean While

"All right girls, it's time to blow this popsicle stand and go get to this money!" Lacey said to the three Diamond Star girls that she had meet her and Stormy inside the sports bar.

It was a little past eight o'clock and Lacey's plan was all starting to come together. Lacey had ordered twenty-five shots of Platinum Patron and she made sure that Stormy and the girls ran through all of them, and just to get Stormy to loosen up for her she emptied the two capsules of molly in one of the last 2 shot glass as Stormy and the girls were busy gathering all their belongings.

"Stormy, sweetie," Lacey called out.

"Yeah girl?" Stormy answered slurring her speech.

"Let's you and me make a toast and take a shot together."

Lacey handed Stormy the spiked shot and then she held her own shot glass in the air...

"Too our new friendship!" Stormy shouted, and then tossed the Molly Juice right down her throat.

Lacey and the girls left out the bar and went to their cars.

"Damn girl, watch yo step," one of the girls said to Stormy, as she stumbled coming out of the exit.

Chedda was relieved to finally see Stormy and Lacey come outside the bar. He noticed that they were with three other girls. He watched as all of them switched their amazing asses and trimmed hips side to side, walking to their vehicles. He peeped that one of the three girls got inside the Benz truck with Lacey and Stormy, while the other two got inside the

S550 Benz car that was parked behind it. Both cars drove away, while Chedda trailed behind them.

They arrived back at the same parking lot where Stormy parked her car; only this time, Chedda noticed that the parking lot was jammed packed and it was hard for him to spot Stormy's Honda. He watched the girls park their vehicles in front of the building and went inside. He searched for a parking space and texted Stormy immediately.

"Wow!" Stormy said excitedly! as she walked side by side with Lacey and the other Diamond Stars into their venue for the night.

The event was in full effect with the Diamond Star women serving and catering to every trick in the building. There was even a little "girl on girl" action going on in front for everybody to see and the clients were loving It. The music was blasting through six-foot-tall speakers and the place was dim, but was lit up with all type of colorful flashing lights, flickering like a disco show. It smelt like nothing but good sex and Wedding Cake marijuana in the atmosphere. There was all type of personal cabanas setup like tents so you couldn't see what was going on inside them. There were naked women in body paint with heels on walking and mingling with the men. There was a bar area in the corner surrounded by more men and naked women. There was a center stage set up for the "girl on girl" entertainment and the final thing that Stormy notice was a VIP sign with flashing red lights that hung on the wall over the entrance of the walkway which led to another section of the building. The whole thing reminded Stormy of a big strip club without the poles for the women to dance on.

"Do you like it?!" Lacey asked Stormy, screaming over the music into her ear.

"Oh my God! Wat is this place?"

"This is Diamond Star Entertainment!" Lacey answered.

65

"Well, I love it!" Stormy told Lacey with her eyes as big as moon pies, looking at all the sexual entertainment going on around them.

A girl they called Blondie walked up to Lacey and begin speaking..

"it's pretty busy, I've been holding it down while you were gone, but daddy is waiting on you in the back." She then looked At the Diamond Stars standing with Lacey, "Girls, I need you to go get changed out over there at booth number thirty-three and get to work."

The three girls walked off. Blondie then looked at Stormy up and down then licked her lips.

"Mhm, you must be who Daddy was talking about, he's waiting in the back. Welcome to Diamond Star Entertainment baby." Blondie kissed Stormy in the mouth and slid in a little tongue without an apology, then walked away towards the bar section.

"C'mon keep up", Lacey told Stormy and then grabbed held of her hand as she led the way through the crowd towards the VIP section.

Stormy still shocked from the kiss Blondie laid on her, walked closely behind Lacey and tried to speak into her ear.

"I'm just, here to get some weed" Stormy said as she walked pass all the naked women and a lot of thirsty men, who were undressing her with their eyeballs.

"You will, I promise" Lacey said as she continued to lead Stormy down the VIP hallway and into the back room where Benji awaited.

They walked pass several closed doors where Stormy could hear sexual moans and screams over the music that blasted out front. Lacey stopped at the door towards the end of the hall and opened it.

When the door opened Stormy saw BB standing in a Black and gold trimmed Versace robe with his back turned towards them and his focus on the monitors that displayed live video of what was going on inside the building and outside around it as well. Lacey closed the door behind them, after her and Stormy stepped inside, Benji turned around, moved his dreads from in front of his face and walked towards Stormy.

"Where you been at cutie? I been waiting for you" Benji said as he looked Stormy up and down admiring her frame.

"I was with your girl having a bite to eat and a lil sum, sum to drink."

" Oh, is dat so?" Benji replied as he walked over towards a black garbage bag in the corner. He started to untie it while he continued talking to Stormy.

"So, Lacey told me that you got ten thousand dollars for some of this weed. Why you want so much? You throwing a party or sum'n?"

"Wat; a girl can't get her hustle on too?" Stormy asked sarcastically quick on her toes.

"Oh, so you tryna sell it huh?" Benji asked.

"Yeah, I couldn't think of no faster way for me to double my money and since you got the best shit I ever smoked; I thought why not turn people on to some strong and make a profit at da same damn time?" Benji laughed at how sexy Stormy's response was.

There is nothing more BB loved than a bad bitch that was a hustler and Stormy was definitely playing her role to fit the part.

Benji finally untied the bag, reached inside and tossed three zip locks full of the Wedding Cake marijuana in the middle of the floor. Stormy unzipped her purse and pulled out the ten thousand dollars.

"I don't want your money sweetheart" Benji said with a full grin on his face.

Stormy then felt Lacey's hand caressing her breast from behind. She turned around and notice that Lacey was fully naked. Lacey smiled at the fact that Stormy's eyes were stuck on her naked body.

Lacey stepped towards Stormy and begun tongue kissing her like she never been kissed before. Stormy's pussy started to tingle and she didn't understand how another female was able to get her pussy moist just from a kiss. Stormy felt her pussy getting even more wet from Lacey's kiss and she dropped the money and her purse on the floor from her grip and started unconsciously kissing Lacey back. Lacey ran her hands up Stormy's body and started to undress her while they were kissing. Benji stood there watching them with his robe undone stroking his dick. Lacey finally got Stormy fully naked then dropped to her knees in front of Stormy and begun to eat her pussy. Stormy felt an uncontrollable sensation that ran through her whole body when Lacey's tongue touched her.

She never felt like this before. Her pussy was now leaking like a faucet. Benji took off his robe and stepped in front of Stormy for her to see him stroking his dick to Lacey eating her pussy. Stormy moaned and got even more wetter at the sight of Benji's body and how big his dick was. Lacey stood to her feet and BB took control by moving her to the side, he lifted Stormy's little body in the air and placed her right on top of his dick. Her pussy was so fuckin' wet that he slid right in. He held her in his arms and pressed her back up against the wall for balance and started fucking her while Stormy had her legs wrapped around his waist and her arms around his neck. Benji pounded and pounded Stormy's back in while she took BB's big dick like a champ.

Benji walked Stormy over to the king size bed and threw her onto the mattress with Lacey. Lacey put her face in between

Stormy's legs again and started to drive her insane by licking and sucking on her pussy. Benji got on the bed with them and stuck his dick inside Lacey's warm wet pussy. Benji began to stroke Lacey from the back, her pussy was tight and wet.

"Oh Benji!" Lacey moaned under her breath while eating Stormy's pussy.

"Oh my god Lacey!" Stormy moaned out loud as if she knew Lacey's name for years.

Stormy grabbed hold of Lacey's head and pushed her face inside of her pussy begging for more pleasure. Lacey started to suck on Stormy's clit and stuck two fingers inside of her pussy at the same time.

"Oh god Lacey, yes! " Stormy screamed.

Benji deep stroked Lacey even harder and stuck his thumb inside her butt.

" OOOOh, Daddy!" moaned Lacey.

''Oh yes, I' m cumming!" Stormy shouted.

Benji sped up his strokes at the sounds from Stormy and Lacey.

"Yes Daddy! Harder!'' Lacey moaned, taking her tongue away from Stormy's clit just for a second to scream out too Benji.

"I'm cum-ming!" Stormy cried.

"Daddy yes, give me dat Daddy dick." Lacey shouted as she came all over Benji's dick at the same time Stormy was cumming all over her face.

Benji crawled to the head of the bed where Stormy's face was and put his dick inside of her mouth. Stormy began sucking him like a pro.

"Oh shit!" Benji grunted.

"Oh, damn baby, I ain't know it was like that'' Benji moaned in pleasure, expressing how good Stormy's deep throating skills were

Stormy than focused her tongue on the head of his dick, then used one hand to jack him off and the other one to play with his balls.

"Oh fuck, I love dat!" Benji shouted as he bussed a fat ass nut in Stormy's mouth. It was nut running down her chin and Stormy just began licking every drop of nut she could.

Benji, Stormy and Lacey all laid on the king size mattresses trying to regain some of their energy from the wild sex.

"BB I'm thirsty is there any water around?" Stormy asked as she began to feel the dehydration side effects of the molly.

BB turned his head towards Lacey. Lacey got out of the bed and walked across the room to get her clothes on so she could go fetch some water for Stormy but she stepped on something hard.

"Ouch!" Lacey said as she felt her foot step on hard metal.

"wat da fuck?" She looked down and seen her chrome .38 Special handgun with the pearl handle hanging halfway out of Stormy's purse next to the ten thousand dollars in the middle of the floor. Lacey bent down to take a closer look at the gun and saw her initials LRW engraved in the pearl handle of the gun.

"Wats wrong?" Benji asked from the bed.

Lacey grabbed the gun and held it in the air, showing Benji.

"This my gun that got took from me on Friday, during the robbery I told you about, She had it in her purse." Benji lifted up from the mattress and stared at Stormy as his killer instincts begun to take effect ...

70

Meanwhile continued...

-Chedda

"Man wat da fuck is taking this girl so long?" Chedda said aloud to himself while waiting for Stormy to come out the building.

Chedda was parked on the curb, going on two hours now and he was starting to get worried. He was paying close attention to the heavy traffic going in and out of the abandoned building and he was getting curious as to what was happening inside. Every time the entrance door swung open; he could hear the sounds of music being played inside as if there was some type of party going on.

He looked at his phone and got even more impatient because he still hadn't received a text back from Stormy. Chedda sat in his car a little while longer in hopes that Stormy Would come out or send him a text or call or something. He started thinking more on how Benji was playing his hand, with this whole transaction. The more he thought, the more Chedda understood wat was going on. BB's main focus wasn't the ten thousand dollars just like Chedda's main focus wasn't the Wedding Cake weed. Don't get it wrong; Chedda wanted the plug on the weed so he could hustle but he wanted Lacey much more.

Chedda was mimicking Benji's moves without even knowing until now. BB was using Lacey and his weed to get closer to Stormy just like Chedda was using Stormy along with ten thousand dollars to get closer to Lacey. Chedda wondered who BB was, and now he realized Benji Bands wasn't only sumtin like a hustla; who had the most exclusive weed in the city, but he was also a mu'fuckin pimp!

Chedda grabbed his phone and sent Stormy another text message instantly as he now felt vulnerable of Losing his money and his new bitch to Lacey and Benji Bands.

Meanwhile continued...

-Stormy

"Who did you get this from?" Lacey asked Stormy.

Stormy was speechless. The room was quiet, but the silence was broken by the sound of a text message alert going off from Stormy's phone inside of her purse. Lacey reached into Stormy's purse and grabbed the phone. Lacey opened up the text and read it easily because Stormy didn't have a lock on her phone.

Chedda: Damn wat da fuck is taking so long? It's getting crowded out here and I'm tired of waiting for you. Did u get da weed or not?

"I think you need to see this daddy" Lacey said as she handed Benji, Stormy's phone so he could read the same text she just read.

Benji took Stormy's phone out of Lacey's hand and read the text Chedda sent her, he looked back at Stormy and saw that she still had not said a word since Lacey asked her where she got the gun from. Benji thought about Lacey getting robbed on Friday night then looked at the 10 thousand dollars on the floor. He was sure that was the same money taken from the robbery. Benji reached under his mattress and pulled out his FN 5-7 handgun and cocked it back; putting one in the head. Stormy's body tensed up as Benji aimed and pointed the gun at her. Stormy jumped out of the bed naked and made a run for the door but Lacey was quick, like a cat pouncing on it's prey. She tackled Stomy to the ground and placed all of her body weight on top of her while Stormy screamed and cried for help.

"Please, please don't shoot me! Please!" Stormy begged.

Benji walked and stood over them, adjusting his robe back onto his body.

"Shut da fuck up!" Benji yelled, "I'm not gon' shoot you; as long as you calm the fuck down and tell me wat I wanna know... You got it?"

Stormy's eyes watered with tears.

"Y-y-yes, I got it," she managed to get out in between her cries.

"Good, now Lacey get the girl some water; and Stormy, you take a seat on the bed."

Lacey got off Stormy then got dress to go get the water.

"Make sho things runnin' smooth out there too" Benji said, before Lacey shut the door behind her.

Stormy, took a seat on the foot of the bed. Benji tucked his gun inside the belt of his robe. He held Stormy's phone in one hand and grabbed his phone with the other hand. BB logged into his Instagram account and went onto Stormy's page. He played the video that showed Stormy dancing on a guy in a hotel room and held it in front of Stormy's face.

"Is this the nigga named Chedda who just texted you?" Benji asked Stormy. Stormy lifted her head up to watch the video and nodded her head, up and down assuring BB that he was correct about his assumption.

"So, wat is this, some type of setup or sumthin?"

"No BB, I swear I was just buying some weed for him".

"So, you called me to buy my weed with the same money y'all took from me, when y'all robbed Lacey?"

''I didn't rob Lacey" Stormy said, with a confused look on her face.

Benji stared at Stormy with a stern grill.

"Well, how the fuck did you get her gun?" Stormy put her face in her palms and cried harder. Her nerves was still shaking up from Lacey jumping on her and her head was spinning from the molly he didn't even know was in her system.

"C'mon baby, save them water works for the wave pool, that shit don't float my boat, now where the fuck did you get the gun and money?"

"Chedda gave me the gun as a gift to protect myself and he gave me the money to give you, so I could buy the weed for him."

Who da fuck is this Chedda nigga?"

''My boyfriend,...but I just met him" answered Stormy.

Benji started pacing the floor back and forth as he though hard about what to do next. He was pissed at what Stormy told him and he knew he needed to make an example out of her so call boyfriend Chedda. Lacey came back with a cup of water and gave it to Stormy. Benji played the video of Stormy and Chedda again for Lacey to see.

"Do dat nigga look familiar to you?" Lacey grabbed the phone to examine the video closely.

"No, who's dat?", Lacey asked, handing the phone back to Benji.

"Dats the nigga who robbed you," Benji said.

"Daddy, I have something to tell you," Lacey said, as she put her head down with a sad look on her face.

"Wats dat baby gurl", Benji asked. "Well, I never really got robbed."

"Wat?" Benji said looking confused.

"I caught a guy with a mask on holding Johnny Boy at gun point for some money that he owed him. I was scared he was going to kill him, so I pored everything out of my purse and told him to take it."

BB cut his eyes at Lacey and grilled her.

"Make dat da last fuckin' time you lie to me about anything" Benji said through gritted teeth.

Benji looked at the time and saw that it was ten thirty.

"Where he at right now?" Benji asked Stormy.

Stormy felt threatened by his question. She just met Chedda but she was into him a lot and was not the type of bitch to turn on someone if they hadn't turned on her first. Lacey sensed the hesitation in Stormy to give BB an answer; she raised the.38 special that she took from Stormy's purse and pointed it at Storm's dome.

"Answer the fuckin' question!" Lacey demanded. Stormy was scared shitless.

"He's parked outside. Please just don't kill us!" Stormy begged.

Benji handed Stormy her phone and told her to call him.

"Ok... but wat am I supposed to say to him?" she asked.

"Tell him I said to come Inside, I want to meet him."

As Stormy called and talked to Chedda, Benji begun to get dressed and prepare for the unexpected. He couldn't believe the nerve of this young punk taking his money and then attempting to send a bitch in his direction to get drugs from him. Even though Lacey cleared things up about it not being a robbery, it still didn't sit well with him. Johnny Boy was a whole nother story and the fact that his drug habits were starting to mess with him and Lacey's business was a clear sign to Benji that it was bout time he finally set him straight.

"He said alright, he's gonna' come in" said Stormy.

Benji threw Stormy her clothes "Good gurl, now get dressed; oh and Stormy, you can text him and tell him dat I said he should leave dat gun he's showing off in y'all video inside his car before he comes in.''

***

Chapter: 5
"Get Down or Lay Down"

Man, wat da fuck?! I don't know wat the hell going on right about now. Stormy just called me with some bullshit, talkin' bout BB wants to meet me and talk to me. The nigga want me to come inside that fucking building. Then she just texted me, telling me to leave my gun inside the car. I was starting to think this Bitch Stormy was tryna' set me up, but then that didn't make sense because she already had the ten thousand dollars. If she wanted the money, she could've just kept it and left; she wouldn't need me to come inside. Something ain't right! Why da fuck is she telling BB about me anyway? He shouldn't know anything about me. I was pist and thinkin wat to do next? But one thing fa-sho, I ain't going inside without my gun.

I waited in the car for ten minutes before I finally seen a dark skin chick about to walk across the street towards the packed parking lot. It looked like she was going to attend whatever party that was going on in that building so I had to shoot my shot. I opened my car door and hollered at her.

"Aye wassup baby, can I ask you a favor?"

I approached her with respect so she wouldn't just keep walking on me.

"Well it depends on wat it is handsome", the slim chick said as she waited to hear wat I was requesting.

''If I'm right, you bout to go inside the same place I'm headed."

"And where are you headed?"she snapped back.

"In that building across the street."

"Wat's the favor?"

"Well, I was out here two nights ago and I saw someone get robbed not too far away. I don't want to end up no victim tonight, and they always search me when I go inside that place."

"Ok; so, wat you gettin' at?" she asked tryna get me to quit beating round the bush with her.

"I was wondering if I gave you a hunnit dollars, could you put my gun inside your purse and give it to me after they searched me on the inside?"

The bitch just stood there with her arms folded, tapping her foot as if she was considering telling me no.

"A'ight, I'll give you two hunnit" I said; because this bitch was acting as if this was a million-dollar jeopardy question.

She rolled her eyes, smacked her lips and held out her hand. I happily reached in my waistband to hand her my gun

"No, no, no, money first fool" she snapped.

"Oh, my bad, here" I reached in my pocket and pealed her off two one-hundred dollar bills.

"You, betta be lucky you cute, cause if BB knew I was doing this I could get in trouble for it. Now give me the gun" She demanded.

I gave her the gun and she put it inside her designer handbag.

"Let me go in before you, so they don't think you with me. I'll keep an eye on wherever they seat you and I'll get your gun to you" She said, then walked across the street, clicking her heels, not even giving me a chance to respond.

I sat back inside the car to give her a few minutes to enter the building, I thought about how things could turn for the worst inside, but I wasn't afraid of shit, so I was definitely going in. At times like this I wished I had a solid mufucka I could depend on so that I could at least call or text for back up. The only true homeboy I had was Dre and I knew my lifestyle and his existed in two different worlds. I would never drag him into none of my hot boy shit I had going on in the streets.

I got out the car, and closed the door. I walked across the street into the busy parking lot and up to the building entrance. As soon as I got closer, I could hear loud hip hop music banging and even smell the aroma of marijuana creeping out of the building. I opened the door and walked in. As I stepped in the packed place, I was approached by two huge mufuckas one tall white guy and a short black one who appeared to be working security. They both had on shirts that was too tight with letters that read DSE across the chest.

"Hey, hold ya' arms out and spread ya legs so we can wand and pat ya down" The black stocky one ordered me.

As soon as I did so, the white guy held out a metal detector hand wand and ran it across my whole body. It went off beeping loud as hell. He reached inside my pocket and pulled out my cell phone and waved the wand across my body one more time. They cleared me to enter and gave me back my phone.

"You go to booth forty-eight, she'll show you" The white bouncer said out loud above the music and pointed in the direction of a fine ass white girl with blond hair. She smiled and took hold of my hand, leading me through the crowded event. As we were walking to the booth, I couldn't help but notice how mind blowing this shit was. It was naked bitches everywhere, walking around, dancing and catering to the niggas that filled the building.

 All of the women bodies were covered with glitter and body paint and they all wore tall stilettos that jacked their beautiful bodies inches higher off the ground to give you an even better view of their voluptuous booties. I saw big logos lit up, all over the walls with Diamonds and stars inside them, that read Diamond Star Entertainment. There were about a hundred booths. The booths were separated and covered with dark cloth like material that surrounded it like a big tent or something so no one could see what was going on inside. The white girl in front of me approached a tent with the number forty-eight at the top of it. She pulled one end of the cloth to the side and walked me in. The lights were dim inside and I took a seat in the booth and noticed the three-seat leather cushion couch that was right next to it.

"Welcome to Diamond Star Entertainment; here is our menu for tonight" the blond hair white chick said while handing me two menus like I was at a restaurant.

"One is for your choice of alcohol beverages and the other is for your choice of pleasure. We serve food at the bar up front but there is absolutely no eating of any food inside the tent. You will have to eat at one of the tables, located in front of the stage. I understand this is your first time at a DSE event, so just take your time looking through our menu and if you see something you desire, just press the red button located on the right of the table, it will light up and someone will come take your order. As a compliment from Benji Bands himself, there is a fifth of Patron and a bottle of Moet Rose on ice for you. Is there anything else I can get for you?"

I looked at this white bitch, stuck for a minute. I was tryna' to take everything in before I answered her. Shit was moving way too fast and she was talking even faster.

"Nawl, I'm not going to order I ju-"

"Good! then just sit tight, have a drink and someone will come get you and let you know when Benji's ready for you. She turned around and switched her small booty right up out of the tent before I could even finish my sentence or say anything else.

I grabbed the bottle of Patron and poured me a nice amount in one of the glass cups that was sitten' on the table in front of me. I took a big swallow, hoping that it would help relax me and clear my mind. I took a peek outside the curtain of the tent to see if I could spot the dark skin chick who I paid to sneak my gun in for me, but she was nowhere in sight. I sat back down and sent Stormy a text to let her know I was inside, and tried to keep my mind from racing while I waited for her to text back.

I glanced at the front of the menu that ol' girl gave me and saw the Diamond Star Entertainment logo again on the cover. I decided to open it up and take a look to see what the hell that bitch was talking about?

When I opened it, I saw a row of pictures with naked women. There were so many bitches, I even thought I seen one that looked really familiar but I couldn't recall where I knew her from, they had hourly rates with prices for as short as thirty minutes all the way up to twenty-four hours. They even had some type of special for a threesome with your choice of any two girls you wanted on the menu as if it was a sex buffet restaurant. I couldn't believe what I was looking at. It was now clear to me that this was an event especially for women to sell sexual favors and for niggas to trick off money on whatever bitch they wanted to fuck; and however, they wanted to; as well.

Mean While

BB stood directly behind Lacey inside the money room with his arms wrapped around her waist and his dick pressed up against her ass while they both stood watching the video monitors. They were focusing on the one that was specifically connected to the hidden camera installed in tent number forty-eight; where Chedda was specifically assigned.

"So, wat do you want me to do with it daddy?" Hershey asked BB while standing on the side of him and Lacey, extending the black handgun in her hand towards BB's direction. BB turned, grabbed it out of her hand and popped the clip out of it. He pushed each bullet out of the loaded magazine into his hand and placed them on top of the table with the monitors.

He cocked the gloc back, spilling out the remaining bullet left in the chamber of the .40 caliber handgun. He wiped the clip down with the material of his robe before placing it back inside the gun. He wiped the unloaded handgun down quickly as well, then handed it back to Hershey.

"Get out of them clothes, give it to him just like he paid you to; then get to work."

Hershey placed the piece inside a small hand-held pouch and turned around. Benji smacked the chocolate Instagram model on her ass before she walked out.

Lacey stood there in a daze the whole time, stalking Chedda's every move on the video screen. She remembered how strong the demeanor was from the person who held Johnny Boy at gun point, and ever since BB showed her the video of him on Stormy's IG; she couldn't stop imagining how a nigga as sexy and innocent looking like Chedda, could be so ruthless and aggressive at the same time. Even though he held her and Johnny Boy at gunpoint, she couldn't deny she was getting turned on. Her pussy was dripping wet just watching him on a security monitor.

"Wats on your mind?'' Benji Interrupted.

"You", Lacey lied as she turned and gave Benji a peck on the lips.

"Where's our girl?" Benji asked referring to Stormy.

"She's gettin' dressed and ready for the night. I gave her something simple to put on, but we'll have to take her shopping before next week. She has a unique frame and not too many of the other stars have anything that fits her body right", Lacey expressed.

"That's not a problem. I want you to make sure you take it easy on her, it's only her first night."

"I will Daddy. Now wats the plan for this one here?" Lacey pointed at Chedda on the monitor and waited for an answer from BB.

He stood there eyeing Chedda on the screen as the vision of his plan played out inside his mind like a visionary. He had already got Stormy on his team thanks to the help of his top girl Lacey; and even though Benji was bothered by the antics that Chedda attempted to pull, he admired the young nigga's cleverness. He reminded Benji a little of himself when he was younger and being that BB was planning to take his D-S-E operations to Vegas, he needed someone just like Chedda, so he could school and teach to run his drug operation through D-S-E, while he aimed to move his new found Empire to Vegas.

"He is not going to have too many options; he owes us, so either he is going to get on board like his girl Stormy or they are both going to leave out in body bags" BB said meaning every word.

''I want you to go talk to him and give him the heads up that you're aware of who he is and wat he did, but don't scare him too much. Then, I want you to send Stormy in there so she can let him know the deal. After that, I'll send for him to talk to me in here where it's quiet and we'll go from there.''

As she started to walk away, he came over the top of her right ass cheek with his right hand. SMACK!

"Ooohh Daddy, I like it when you play rough!" Lacey joked, and jiggled her booty as she walked out the room.

Benji stood in silence looking at the monitor that showed Chedda sitting down, looking at a DSE menu. BB thought about how perfect things would go for him if he could get a young nigga like Chedda on his team to run the Detroit location for him and then he could get his brother into a rehab and all cleaned up before taking him to Vegas for them to prosper. Benji saw Lacey entered tent number forty-eight on the video monitor and he began to focus in. He reached in his pocket and retrieved an already rolled blunt. He sparked it up, inhaled and watched how the events of the night played out on the screens in front of him.

***

** "Hey stranger," a soft voice said interrupting my thoughts.

I looked from the menu and seen the fine mufucka who they called Lacey,standing inside my tent in front of me with absolutely nothing on except for a pink thong and matching heels, her hair was down to her shoulders, and she wore pink and silver glitter that covered her nipples in the design of a star.

"Wats up li'l momma are you for looking for someone?" I played dumb as if I never seen her face before in my life.

"Actually, I'm looking for you" She walked over to me and sat on my lap. My dick instantly began to come to life as I took in the scent of this bad ass bitch sitting on top of my dick. She leaned forward and put her lips close to my ear then whispered... "I know a little secret about you Chedda" Lacey stuck her tongue in my ear and my dick became as hard as a brick.

"I'll be right back," she said as she jumped off my lap and walked out of the tent.

My mind was wandering and I ain't know what to do next; so, I just poured another glass of Patron and took it straight to the head. I saw the curtain in the tent move and then Stormy entered looking like she was going to a beach body photo shoot. The necklace I bought her hung from her neck. She had on a white bikini top with small circles cut out just perfect enough for her nipples to poke out and was also wearing a matching thong. Her pussy lips made the biggest camel toe.

"Stormy, wassup; wat da fuck goin' on?'' I questioned with no hesitation.

Stormy walked over to me and I stood up to give her a hug. She looked like she'd been crying.

"Wats da deal baby girl, are you good?"

"Yeah I'm good, but we have to talk" She said as she sat down on the leather couch inside the tent next to me.

"Chedda they know you the one who robbed Lacey. Why didn't you tell me before I met up with them? You could've gotten me killed!"

"Wat you talking bout? I ain't rob Lacey, who told you that shit?"

''Chedda, you gave me her gun and her money to buy weed from BB and he already knows."

Fuck! I knew it was a reason why she asked me to come inside. Before I could give Stormy an explanation; the dark skin chocolate bitch who I gave my gun to, slid inside the tent like a swift cat burglar. She was topless with diamond designs painted over her nipples. She wore a black mini skirt so short and tight that you could tell she didn't have any panties on.

"Here you are boy, I was looking all over for you." I stood up immediately and

"Looking for me? I been looking for yo ass. You told me that you were gonna' find me as soon as I walked in. Wat happened?" I said straight up.

"I know, I'm sorry, I had to change and get ready for work. Who is she?" The dark beauty asked, referring to Stormy.

"I'm Stormy. I'm Lacey's; I mean... BB's and Lacey's girl. This is my boyfriend Chedda. I just started."

"So you a diamond star or what?" the girl asked Stormy with attitude.

"Y-yes. . . I guess so?"

The chocolate bitch rolled her eyes at Stormy than turned her attention back to me. "Well anyway, here you go handsome."

She reached inside the small hand pouch she was carrying and gave me my gloc.

"Thanks sweetie" I said, feeling better that I finally reunited with my blic.

"Mm-huh anytime, you can find me at every DSE event, if you ever looking to take a dip inside some real chocolate cream. They call me Hershey."

As soon as she said her name, I realized she was the one I seen inside the sex menu that I said looked familiar to me. She looked Stormy up and down, then rolled her eyes at her again before walking out.

I looked back at Stormy and seen a look of frustration.

"Wat was all dat about?" I asked, while placing my gloc inside my pants.

"I don't know, you tell me? She the one act like ya'll fuckin or something?"Stormy replied.

"Nawl fuck all that, I'm talking bout you sayin' all dat shit about you being BB's and Lacey's girl and sum'n bout you being a diamond star or some shit? Wat da fuck is you on? I told you to play a part; not be a part in it!"

"Wat did you expect me to do? you put me in a fucked-up situation. Now I owe BB and this is how he wants me to repay my debt to him... besides, it might not be such a bad idea anyway."

I stared at Stormy tryna' determine if this bitch knew what she was saying.

"How the fuck did they get the gun I gave you in the first place and how does Lacey know who I am?"

''Well; The gun fell out of my purse when me and Lacey were...'' she paused.

"When you and Lacey were wat Stormy?" I asked tryna get to the bottom of it.

"When we were having sex with Benji!"

Steam boiled inside of me. I grabbed the bottle of Patron and took a gulp of it from the neck. First this nigga lured me into this fake ass playboy party and then I gotta find out he fucked my bitch exactly a day after I made her my bitch? I didn't like this nigga already and we haven't even met yet. Long as I leave with what I came for, I ain't tripin'. Stormy was just a piece on the board for me to use to execute my plan.

"Chedda it wasn't even like that at first and then I don't know wat came over me, one thing just led to another. I' m still yours, I promise. I was doing it all for you."

I ain't gona' front I was a little upset bout it cause I thought I might've had a rider, but I was more concerned about the seriousness of the situation. This nigga BB may have home court advantage but I got my strap; and that's all I needed.

"So how does Lacey know who I am?" I asked her.

"They looked on my Instagram and saw the video of us at the hotel room."

"Stormy!"

''I know, you told me not to record you and I'm sorry but can we please not get into it at this place baby? I'll make it up to you later."

She begged me like she been my bitch for years and I'd be lying to you if I told you this situation didn't make me feel like she was.

I had to figure out my next move quick. All type of shit was running through my mind. Who knew what this nigga BB had planned now that he knew I robbed Lacey. It must 've been his money I got from her. But in reality, I didn't rob her, she gave it to me in exchange for Johnny Boy's life. That's her fault. She should've just let me kill the piece of shit if the money was that important. I don't know what the fuck was going on with Stormy and her little Diamond Star Dreams, but I wasn't taking any chance meeting up with no nigga who felt like I robbed him for thirty grand.

The only thing I could think to do was to try and get us the fuck up out of this bitch. I grabbed Stormy by the arm and started to head out the tent along with the bottle of Rose gripped in the other hand; but I was stopped by the two bouncers blocking my way and barging their way inside.

"Hey little fella, where ya going? The boss is ready to see you, come on with us.''

 I looked at both of them and read their facial expressions, it was clear they meant bidness. I swung the Rose bottle over the top of the white bouncer's head, splitting his shit wide open. The bottle came out of my hand as blood erupted out of his wig like lava out of a volcano. I attempted to push through him out of the tent but was rushed by the short black bouncer. We threw blows left to right inside the tent, wrestling all over the little furniture there was. He hit me right in my shit, turning my nose into a blood faucet and dazed me a little. I was on the ground when I saw Stormy hop on the back of the bouncer like a baby monkey, tryna take down a silver back gorilla. I reached in my waistband and grabbed my gloc. I aimed it right at the center of the stocky bouncer's stomach; but soon as I pulled the trigger, my gloc clicked and de-cocked, signaling that there were no bullets inside the chamber or clip. Click! Wat da Fuck!

I threw my gun on the floor and tried to get on my feet and shake off my dizziness. I heard a lot of screaming and hollering, then I seen the white bouncer walk up on Stormy while she was hanging on to the other one's back. He was holding his head with one hand and holding a taser in the other one. He had it up against Stormy's body and shocked the living shit out of her. ZAP! she dropped to the ground like a rag doll.

I saw him look to me while I was using the couch to hold my balance. Him and the black bouncer started towards me and I attempted to walk through the cloth material on the tent, The whole tent collapsed and I stumbled to the ground. I couldn't see shit with the tent covering my eyes but I heard loud screams as the music stopped and I felt a bunch of feet trampling my body. ZAP! Zap! The next thing I felt was my whole body lock up and go into shock from electricity and everything went dark.

** "Chedda get up, are you ok?" I heard Stormy ask while I felt her take the cloth filled with ice off of my face.

I opened my eyes and saw that I was laying on a blow-up mattress with Stormy on the side of me, holding a homemade icepack. I heard a faint sound of loud music playing in the background as if I was still at that event. I looked around and seen tables with stacks of money piled up everywhere. The dark skin bitch who told me her name was Hershey was standing up placing neat handfuls of money through a money counter machine. It kept making loud irritating beeping noises; after each stack of money that it separated and all she did was keep adding more to it. Hershey was standing next to Lacey. She passed each stack of money that came out of the money counter to Lacey then Lacey placed rubber bands around each stack. I look to the other site of the half-lit room and spotted a nigga that had long ass Dreadlocks and tattoos everywhere with a red five-point star under his left eye. He was just standing there with a robe on, staring at a bunch of video monitors that were lined up on another table. I looked at one of the screens to see what he was watching, but it was way too far away from me to make out what was on the monitor. On top of that, my vision in my left eye was still kind of blurry from one of the punches that caught me during the fight.

"Chedda baby it's ok, I'm here" Stormy said as if she saved the day.

"Wat da fuck is this?" I said, feeling frustrated and confused.

"Oh! your finally awake after your little scuffle, I see" Lacey blurted out after noticing I was speaking to Stormy.

"Hey Benji look, our little friend is finally up after the ass whooping, he just got" Hershey said sounding like she was excited to see what I had coming next.

She looked at me from the table she was standing at, then winked her eye and blew me a kiss; then smiled. It hit me right then and there, that this bitch had unloaded my gun and was a part of their plan the whole fuckin time.

"Snake ass bitch!" I shouted.

"I can only be loyal to one honey" she said, and continued counting money as if I was a non-factor.

I noticed the nigga with the Dreads turn towards me and stare, in response to Lacey and Hershey alerting him about me being awake. I tried to get up but didn't realize my left wrist was handcuffed to Stormy's right.

"Wat the fuck is this all about?" I said loud enough for everybody in the room to hear.

The tatted nigga who must've been Benji Bands, started walking towards me and I sat up in the bed as much as I could.

"Chedda, Chedda, Chedda... I hope they call you that for a reason, because you gonna' need allot of it to pay me back for all the chedda I been losing due to yo bullshit. By the way, I'm Benji Bands but you can call me BB. Our girl Stormy here told me a lot bout you. Nice to finally meet you" He laughed out loud and smirked a little bit just to let me know he was being an ass hole.

I cut my eyes at Stormy and she stared at the ground like a sad puppy. Beep! The money counter sounded off again and I could hear Hershey prepare another stack of cash for it to shuffle through. I sat there and continued to let the nigga run his dick suckers before I gave him a piece of my mind.

"Let's see... thirty-thousand Friday night..the ounce of coke and not to mention the embarrassment you took my girl Lacey through from having her at gun point.. and about another twenty-thousand dollars' worth of damage you caused to one of my booths and the furniture you destroyed. And let's just say about another twenty-thousand dollars' worth of business that I missed out on because we had to shut down for an hour just to clean up the mess you created in my place of business. But the you know wats gonna' cost you the most?" He paused as if I was really gonna' try to answer his sarcastic ass question, then he continued..

"the fact that yo premature wanna be a playa ass had the courage to take my money and then attempt to send a pretty young thang in my direction, thinkin' you was gonna be able to catch a good price on the most exclusive weed in da city and buy it from me with my own money...Now that's classic."

CLAP! CLAP! CLAP! CLAP! BB clapped his hands together as if he was giving me an a round of applause, then Lacey and Hershey joined in, laughing and snickering at his sarcasm.

"I give you an E for effort lil nigga; that means you failed, you gotta come with more than that before you step to the plate with a heavy weight."

Even though, I didn't like the fact that I was on the ass-end of the stick, I was listening to how he viewed my moves. The nigga didn't miss a beat; and I despised him for it. BB reached inside his robe and pulled out a freshly rolled backwood, then sparked a liter and fired it up. He inhaled a huge cloud of smoke and then blew it out.

"Cough! Cough! You smoke lil nigga?"

He reached his hand out holding the blunt in my direction, offering me a hit. I looked at it with my grill twisted in silence.

" I guess not, good, it's bad for ya health."

He inhaled another cloud and then continued to talk to me like he was some sort of big shot in control of my life.

That's the type of energy I was getting' from this nigga; like he thought he was God or some shit.

"Now listen closely because the next decision you make in this room is going to determine how you and Stormy leave this building. Now Lacey already explained to me the situation about the so-called robbery that took place on Friday."

"How the fuck I rob a nigga who owe me money?!" I said with aggression finally breaking my silence.

"Hold on lil nigga, let me finish."

I just continued to bite my tongue so this nigga could hurry up and get to the point.

"Now, like I was saying. Lacey explained to me that Johnny Boy as you know him, had owed you some money; So, she ended up taking the initiative to give you the money that she had on her in exchange for you not to kill him. Is that right?"

I just looked at him in his eyes without blinking or saying a word keeping my mug ripped.

"Normally when a nigga takes some shit that belongs to me, I don't let him live to see tomorrow once I catch up with him; but I can't blame you for rightfully wanting what another man owes you. I salute a man who's about his business and doesn't hold a nigga up when it comes to his money. However lil nigga, Johnny Boy as you know him, may have owed you but now you two owe me."

He took another puff from the lit blunt and then put it out inside of an ashtray that set on one the tables covered in money.

"Hershey."

"Yes, Daddy?"

"Go get Road Kill and Hitman for me."

The dark skin diva set the pile of money that she had in her hand down on the table and swiftly walked out the money room closing the door behind her to fulfill Benji's order.

Lacey walked up to Benji and stood by his Side, placing her hands on the back of his shoulders, giving him a gentle massage. BB reached inside his robe pocket and pulled out two state ID cards and a small silver key. He read the first ID aloud. "Shakora Janae Evans, born February 27, 1998 He switched and read the other ID. Seven Aaron Thomas, born June 28, 1997. I guess the nigga thought he was scaring me just because he took my ID out my pocket while I was knocked out, and now knew my government name. He tossed the silver key onto the blow-up mattress.

"Stormy uncuff yo self-sweetheart and come stand by daddy so this nigga could get the picture."

Stormy grabbed the key and unlocked her wrist from the cuffs, then Benji started back talking to me.

"See; Me, Stormy and Lacey here already had a discussion and came to an agreement. You just happened to be late to the party."

Stormy got up from the blow-up mattress leaving my hand inside the cuffs and prepared herself to leave my side as well.

"You and ya gurl tried to pull the wool over my eyes in order for you to come up and I ain't mad at that, because I respect the grind but during yall little scheme of things, I lost out on some of my profit... now in some form of way you two gotta find a way to repay my loses".

Stormy looked at me with tears in her eyes before she approached BB and stood next to him on the opposite side of Lacey while he continued speaking.

"Stormy's gonna handle her half of the debt by fulfilling a position with Diamond Star Entertainment. Don't get it twisted, she's still your girl, she's just our star now" Benji said with a serious facial expression.

I gritted my teeth in disbelief to the shit I was hearing, then out of nowhere, Hershey entered back into the room with the two bouncers I got into a fight with. The stocky black one had duct tape and rope in his hands and the tall white chunky one had a white bandage wrapped around his wounded head with a mossberg shotgun clutched in his palms.

"Being that you wanted to make you some money anyway; I'm giving you an opportunity for you to pay yo debt to me by taking on the responsibility, distributing my products throughout the Diamond Star Entertainment's events, or, you can deal with the ultimatum, because I'm sure Road Kill here has a lot of aggression he wants to let out, concerning that Rose bottle you took across his skull."

He turned and nodded his head at the big white bouncer who then cocked the shotgun back and aimed it in my direction. I looked at everybody standing in front of me and suddenly understood clearly what 2Pac meant when he said, Me against the world. I tore my mug up even more as the spirit of defeat attempted to take over my heart and soul; but I didn't let it. One thing my crackhead Uncle JugHead always told me is that life is a game of chess, not checkers. So even though this nigga BB felt that he had me conquered you can best believe this shit was far from over.

"It's four in the morning lil nigga, I ain't got all day. Either you gone get down or lay down!"

Chapter: 6
"Game Time"

Six months later. . .

It was the day after Christmas and I was finally about to bring in the New Year. I couldn't wait to celebrate! It's been going on six months since I been working under the OG Benji and I couldn't fix my lips to lie to you if I wanted to; life's been treating a nigga like a king! Even though BB pulled some disrespectful ass shit on me to make me get down for the cause; my decision to let go of my pride for the moment end up paying off good. I was out here living my best life like Lil Duval. Smile Bitch! Smile Bitch! I moved into my new loft and was rolling in a brand-new gold Track hawk Jeep for the winter. I still had my lil out of date Charger but I only drove that when I was tryna be low—key or up to no good. BB plugged me with the strongest trees that was gettin' smoked in the city, along with the purest of cocaine and MDMA molly that existed on this side of the border from Canada. I was grinding 24/7. I can't remember the last time I had a good night's sleep.

The money kept calling and I was picking up, running to it every time. I gave Stormy the silent treatment for a whole month after that bull-shit she pulled with BB and Lacey, but once I let her put that fiya ass head on me again; we was back going stronger than ever. She felt so bad after letting me down, that she's been doing any and everything under the sun, just to stay number one on my roster. The bitch bossed her game all the way up. She been working side by side with Lacey and even became one of the most wanted females at every Diamond Star event.

Don't think I 'm slippin' tho, because I will never overlook the fact that she folded on me during her first mission, and neither would the press-play that Benji laid on me be forgotten either.

BB and Lacey were a whole nother story. Benji was traveling in and out of town, left and right as if he owned the airlines. Lacey was flying in Instagram models from different states for them to work for Diamond Star Entertainment. Business was doing so good that BB and Lacey invested a portion of their funds into buying out a small apartment complex to start their girls off with a place to stay. It was located on the east side of Detroit on east 7-mile rd. and Outer Drive. It was named Anthos Garden, but it was known throughout the east side as the Sun Rise Apartments. It was nothing luxurious but after thirty to sixty days working for DSE; the girls would have saved up enough money to move anywhere in the city they wanted, so it was worth the stay.

Lacey had her own place on the west side but she mainly lived with Benji in his seven-bedroom mini-mansion that was in West Bloomfield. It was about forty-five minutes outside of Detroit and was a small city in Oakland County, one of the richest county's in the state of Michigan. Only Diamond Stars' top models stayed in the house with him and you can bet that Stormy also had a room there with her name written all over it. Most of the times she stayed the night with me at my new loft inside the Plasma Building, Downtown Detroit. She wasn't too fond of sharing me and watching me fuck my other girl.

Whenever I had my other girl Taylor or one of the other Diamond Star's occupying my time she would run and cry her ass to sleep in the room she had at BB's house.

I was banking about forty to fifty grand a month. As Long as BB wasn't out of town, he'd hit me off with however many bows of trees that I needed and it he did the same with the coke and molly. I was responsible for supplying all the Diamond Star ladies with the product so they could sell at the night clubs and strip clubs they attended on the side, as well as the DSE events they catered to every weekend. They brought the drug money back to me and I gave it to Benji.

I would've been pulling in way more dough if I could've supplied all the hustlers in the city with the product I was handling, but OG BB had this one rule that limited my grind and I hated it. Only supply the Diamond Star Models for distribution of the product. He felt that if we supplied hustling niggas in the streets that it would bring too much heat from the law and open up the door for other bull shit to come our way as well, such as robberies, or beef with competition over drug territory. "It's not about the sprint, it's about the marathon" is what he loved to tell me anytime I asked him about serving more weight in the streets. BB believed as long as he only used his Diamond Stars to distribute the best product in the city, then he could conceal his identity as the man behind the product and secure an everlasting position in the drug game. He also felt that if we supplied all the drug dealers, then our clientele wouldn't have the need to come back and shop with us because everybody else would have it for them to buy.

We were the only mufuka's in Detroit with the Wedding Cake strand of marijuana; the I-can't-feel-my-face powder; and the up-for-three-days-straight molly. If you wanted the best in da city then you had to shop with a Diamond Star model and guess wat? Nine times out of ten you were going to trick with her for some pleasure as well.

Benji cornered the market for his self with his wittiness in the drug and sex entertainment game. Everything that he was breathing on me, made a lot of sense and no matter how ill I felt towards the nigga, I would 've been a fool not to take notes and soak up game. To be one hunnid, i ain't neva had nobody worth looking up to in my life until I got held at gunpoint by this nigga BB. I would never let him know that tho. The nigga's ego was already big enough and I ain't neva been no dick suckin' ass nigga to stroke another man's ego. Honestly, I'd probably still be out here robbin' or tryna' sell ten-dollar rocks, or twenty-dollar blow packs if it wasn't for him. Who would've ever thought all this good fortune would've come just from me aiming to blow Johnny Boy's head off for a debt his sexy ass daughter was willing to pay for him?

So far, I stacked one-hundred twenty-seven thousand in my stash and I had access to the best weed, coke and molly floating around the city; not to mention Lacey been on ya manz dick lately. She been sending shots, eyeing me every time she get a chance to. So I'ma just get this money, continue enjoying the ride and soak up as much game as I can until it's my time to shine. It's Game Time!

   It was Thursday morning, the day after Christmas and I was waking up to my girl Tay Tay ass naked on one side of me and Stormy butt booty naked on the other side. I finally talked both of them into giving me the perfect threesome for my Christmas gift and it was all what I hoped it to be. Tay Tay' is the lil chick Taylor, I met at the mall a while back. I ended up hitting hér up to keep my dick occupied the moment I had put Stormy on punishment for failing the mission I sent her on. Conversation and Fuck session after fuck session; I decided that Tay Tay was worth keeping.

Good pussy, good head and good housekeeping was hard to find these days; so why not make her girlfriend number two? Not only could the bitch ride a mean dick, but lil momma knew how to throw down in the kitchen like a chef! Stormy always felt as if I treated Tay Tay like she was number one and Taylor felt the same as if I treated Stormy like she was the main; but if they knew the truth, they would both hit the roof, that number one spot beneath my money was remaining open and soon to be filled; and the one I had my eye on to fill it was neither Taylor or Stormy. I reached over the sleeping beauties and grabbed my phone, I had a bunch of missed calls as usual but I see that there was one from BB, so I got up and called him.

"Ho-ho-ho Merry Christmas li'l nigga" I heard BB's voice say thru the speaker of my phone.

"Man Christmas was yesterday, wat da fuck you talkin' bout?"

''Aaah you right; well fuck Christmas because every day's a holiday when you fuckin with Benji B! Did you get the gift I sent you?"

"Wat gift?" I asked confused to what he was talking bout.

"I gave it to Stormy to bring with her when she left the DSE Christmas special event last night, she said she was on her way to you so I told her to give it to you."

"Oh, well she sleep right na; I'll get on her head about it when she wake up."

"Yeah make sho you do dat, but listen. . . We got bidness on da floor. I'm about to fly out to Vegas in about an hour. I won't be back in time for this weekend's DSE events, so I'm counting on you and Lacey to make sure shit run the way it's supposed to. You think you can handle that?"

I was surprised at what I was hearing. This nigga ain't neva missed a DSE event; and what threw me for another loop even more, was that he trusted me enough to run shit for him while he was gone. I knew I was growing on him but to be real, I thought he was just using me. I ain't know he would fuck with me on that level.

"Hello, Hello? You there?" BB thought the call dropped or sumn because I took a slight pause to think about wat he just said to me.

"Yeah, I'm here, heard everything OG. I got you, I'ma hold it down."

''A'ight good. I left Lacey with all the product that you need for the stars. I even left double the amount because it can get busy round the holidays. I'mma be back on New Year's Eve, just in time for our New Year's Eve celebration. You hold it down till then, and I promise you when I get back, we gon' have the time of our lives at the Party''.

"No problem OG, fly safe, I'll holla at you when you get back."

I ended the call and looked at the time. It was nine in the morning and I already could see I had a busy day on my hands. It was Thursday, so I had to pick up the product from Lacey and then meet up with all the Diamond Stars who hustled, in order to get them their weekly supply before Friday night. Now that BB's going to be out of town, I'll have to help Lacey with preparing the Venue for the events this weekend as well. I wasn't mad about it either, because I been waiting on BB to give Lacey some breathing room. It's time to see wats really good with shorty and dem cheeks dat she got on her. I slid out the bed and snatched the sheets off of Stormy.

"Wat You doing? Cover me back up, it's cold'' Stormy whined as I woke her up.

''Where the gift at that BB gave you to give me?" I asked while rubbing on her naked booty.

"Oh, I forgot it in my car. It's in the glove box. Go get it Chedda, leave me alone I'm tired."

I threw the sheet back on top of Stormy's naked body then put on some sweat pants with a shirt, so I could go to her car and retrieve this mysterious gift that BB sent. I took the elevator down to the lobby and walked past the front desk and went out of the building into the parking lot. I searched for Stormy's car. I was freezing my balls off, then I looked at the electronic key in my hand and remembered that the bitch just bought her a new 2024 Durango. I pressed the panic button on the key and heard the car horn repeatedly going off. I followed the sound and spotted the white Durango sitting on red colored Ashanti rims. I can't lie, Stormy had style and taste when it came to luxury. The Diamond Star lifestyle and fame was getting to her head and I knew how fast things were moving; it was only going to get worst. I got inside the driver's seat and shut the door so that I could get away from the cold wind that was blowing. I popped open the glove box and saw a jewelry box with a green bow on top. I grabbed it and opened it, to see what was inside. It was a gold 41-millimeter Daytona Rolex watch. The face on the inside of it was white and the bezel had flawless Rolex diamonds going around it. I pulled it out the box and placed it on my left wrist immediately. It fit perfectly. I twisted my wrist; then I sent BB the picture with a text attached that said, "Good looking out big homie".

This trophy had to hit his pockets for a nice piece of change, but shit it was the least he could do after all the money I been helping him make over these past months. I was responsible for collecting all of the drug money that the girls brought back for him, so I get to see exactly how much he's clocking in just off the drugs alone. The small forty to fifty grand I was making didn't compare not even a little bit. Lacey was responsible for collecting all the money made off pleasures from the Diamond Stars, it was a smooth two-way operation. Some models sold drugs and pleasure; some just sold pleasure. But make no mistake about it, all of them was bout they paper and down for Benji. Just as I was bracing myself to exit the truck and step back out into the cold air, I notice an open card with a small jewelry box next to it on the passenger side seat. The Chanel logo was stamped on the jewelry box. I opened the card and read what it said...

To the cutie pie that rewards my eye. I've been watching you from the day I saw you and haven't stopped yet. I always knew you had in you, what all of your past overlooked. I could spot a diamond from a mile away. Wear this bracelet and remember I'm the one who helped you shine like a star today. Merry Christmas Lil momma, continue shining like the star you are. BB

I sat back in the driver seat a little while longer to collect my thoughts. I felt my adrenaline began to rush a little bit from what I just read but I kept my cool. I kind of figured that BB was probably fucking Stormy once he gave her a room in his house. Stormy told me that it only happened that one time when she had a threesome with him and Lacey, but I neva trusted a bitch's word for shit anyway. So I ain't surprised. Even though this ain't stone cold proof that they still fucking, it damn sure makes it look like it. I knew Stormy was sick about me keeping Taylor around and even more hurt that I was slaying dick like a porn star to any Diamond Star model that wanted to spread her legs. This was expected out of her. I just didn't respect the fact that BB had the nerve to continue fucking my bitch when I'm supposed to be his so called lil homie. On top of that he already had the coldest bitch as his main squeeze in Lacey; and she even allowed him to fuck every Diamond Star diva that walked through the doors, without trippin, so the million-dollar question was; Why continue fucking my bitch?

This shit right here proves to me again that it ain't no love in this game and you can't let your guards down for the slightest second; not even with the bitch you sleeping with.

"Chess, not Checkers" I mumbled to myself as I scrolled through my phone contacts, found Lacey's name and sent her a text.

Me: Wassup, wyd?

It ain't take her no time to text back.

Lacey: Nothing, just got out the shower bout to get my day started. Did BB talk to you yet?

Me: Yeah, he called me. Told me he was headed out of town and he wanted me to handle things. That's why I'm hittin' you up wondering wat's a good time for us to meetup?

Lacey: "Oh, so you only reaching out to take care of business?

Me: Yeah. I mean wat else was I supposed to be reaching out for?"

Lacey: Oh, ok. Well, I was gonna' say you can pull up on me now before I put some clothes on. . . but since it's only business then u can meet me later.

Me: Fuck bidness WYA?

Lacey: 18580 Lindsay Street

Me: On my way

I got out of Stormy's truck and hurried back into my loft.

I took a quick shower to wash the pussy off me from last night. I brushed my grill, got dressed and headed out the door leaving Stormy and Tay Tay asleep in bed.

Mean While

Lacey set her phone down on the bathroom sink and finished drying off her voluptuous body. She lotioned up with some of her most exclusive Victoria's secret product. She was so excited to finally have a chance for some one-on-one time with Chedda that her pussy began to pulsate just thinking about him. Benji had only been gone a good thirty minutes and if you asked her; Chedda couldn't have picked a better time to text her. She had been sending indicators with her actions every time she was around him, but to her; Chedda seemed to never catch on that she was craving him on a level that was hard for her to conceal any longer.

Lacey rubbed her body down one last time with the scented body oils and then slipped into her yellow see-through lingerie.

She dolled herself up with a little eye liner and a small amount of lipstick from the Kylie Jenner cosmetic make up line, then walked in her bedroom and lit the aphrodisiac candles that set on her Dresser, she adjusted the hidden video camera in her bedroom mirror, then exited her room, shutting the door so the scent from the sexual candles could build up and remain within. Lacey danced her way down the stairs into the living room and turned on her favorite R and B singer's album so it played through her top-of-the-line Sony surround sound system. She had speakers everywhere, so it could be heard throughout the entire house.

Lacey walked in the kitchen looked through her cabinets and refrigerator trying to determine what to cook for breakfast for her new boo.

She started the fire on the stove and sat at the table in her dining room, day dreaming about Chedda while she waited for the butter in the pan to melt. She wandered why it took so long for this day to finally come and she couldn't wait to ask him when he arrived.

Chedda was an Alpha straight forward type of nigga just like Benji, so Lacey couldn't figure why ne never took the initiative to pursue her after she was showing him all the necessary signs. She knew that he was in a relationship with Stormy but she also knew Chedda wanted more. He needed more. He deserved a woman that could put it down and also hold it down; like herself, not Stormy.

Bing! Lacey glanced at her phone as the sound of a text message coming though alerted her. She hoped it was Chedda, but it was Benji letting her know that his flight was about to take Off to Vegas. She texted back an I love you than continued thinking about Chedda, Lacey Loved Benji and wouldn't dare think to put no other nigga before him but it was something about Chedda that kept her sweet parts tingling. She was tired of BB promising her a family without actually giving it to her. Lacey ran the Diamond Star ENT. company just like Benji wanted and the only thing she wanted in return was a baby from BB; but she noticed every time they had sex he would pull out and buss instead of planting his seeds inside her. Whenever she confronted him about it, he'd always say it wasn't the right time yet; but now dat Chedda was around she had hopes for a family with another baby daddy.

The fact that the other Diamond Stars were bragging about how big his dick was and how good he broke their backs, didn't make it any easier for her to contain herself either. She just had to get a piece of Chedda. Her pussy began leaking. Lacey stood up immediately taking herself out of the daze and entered the kitchen to prepare breakfast for Chedda as she waited for him to arrive.

She grabbed the sandwich bag full of Molly from out of the cereal box, on top of her refrigerator. Lacey took one capsule out of the bag and tucked it under her left tittie inside her bra. There was no way she was missing out on her opportunity to fuck Chedda.

* * *

** I pulled up at Lacey's crib and parked my Track hawk on right behind the black S550 Mercedes Benz, sitting in her driveway, then I sent her a text letting her know I was outside. I peeped the blinds move a little in the center window frame; then I received a text from Lacey saying the door was unlocked and to come in. I walked in and locked the door behind me. Immediately the smell of turkey bacon and pancakes filled my nostrils and my stomach started begging for it immediately. There was a stair case leading to the top floor located right at the doorway, but I heard sounds of dishes being handled like she was cooking and there was music coming from the same direction; so, I walked past the steps, deeper into the house searching for her; I walked into the living room that was decorated with lavish furniture and electronics. She had summer Walker featuring, Usher playing on her sound system. They were blowing on the vocals, setting the mood right with a song called Come thru. I looked around at all the expensive furniture and all of the Christmas decorations, not knowing where to go next inside her house.

"Come in, I'm back here cooking" she called out from the kitchen and I followed the sound of her voice.

"Damn check you out!" I said as I took in the scene in front of me.

Lacey was standing in front of the stove, wearing a yellow see thru robe that was trimmed with fur on the end part of her sleeves. You could see the trace of her thong she had on through her robe and her ass was sitting up like a donkey. She couldn't hide it if she wanted too. Her hair was in a ponytail that sat like a big curly fluffy ball on top of her head and it made me envision grabbing ahold of it while I fucked her from the back.

110

''Well, you could give a bitch a hug or something, instead of just standing there." Lacey snapped me out of my imagination with her sassiness.

I never been touchy feely with her before, but I ain't drive all the way over here this early just to tuck my tail, so if this what she wanted, then this what I was gonna give her. I walked up behind her while she was cooking and wrapped my arms around her body, pressing my dick up against her ass so she could feel the print.

She smelled like honey and I couldn't wait to get a taste. I gave her a small peck on her cheek and then backed away to let her finish cooking.

"Was dat a good enough hug for you?"

"I guess that'll have to do for now" she said. All I saw was a big smile on Lacey's face and at that moment, I knew I should've been shooting my shot at this bad ass bitch a long time ago.

"I see you got the gift I picked out for you" she said referring to my Rolex watch. "

You picked it out? BB told me he got it for me."

"Yeah, he paid for it, but I picked it for you. I knew you would look cute in it."

She looked at me than back in the direction of the stove where she was cooking.

"Look like you bout to eat good, why you ain't make me none?"

"How you know I didn't?" She shifted to one side of the kitchen counter and started loading a plate.

I might 've been tripping but it looked like she was swinging her hips side to Side just to tease me with her candy.

"Follow me" She demanded while carrying the plate of food.

I followed behind her and admired watching her ass bounce from left to right through the see-through robe she was wearing. She set the plate of food down on the table in her dining room and pulled out a chair for me. She took my Montclair jacket off of me and placed it on the back of the chair.

"Now take a seat king" she said, in a seductive tone and scooted the chair up under me as I sat down.

I looked at the fully loaded breakfast plate that Lacey was serving me; turkey bacon, sausage patties, eggs with cheese and three stacks of pancakes with whip cream and cut up strawberries on top. It looked like a plate off one of them I-HOP commercials.

"Mmmhhh, this look good as hell. I ain't know you was gonna get a nigga together like this!"

"I ain't did nothing yet, just wait and see. Now wat do you want to drink; OJ, cranberry juice or apple juice?" she asked me.

"OJ", I said.

"I knew you were an OJ man" She replied then left and came back with a tall glass of orange juice that had crushed ice floating at the top.

Lacey brought me some Aunt Jemima maple syrup and placed the silverware on a cloth in front of me. She walked over towards the windows, closed the curtains and turned the music up a little louder for us to hear it clearer. Lacey dimmed the lights, lit a candle in the center of the table and then took a seat across from me so that we were staring face to face.

"Now eat up'' She directed, focusing her attention on nothing but My every move. I was on my way to take a bite until I realized she'd didn't have anything in front of her.

"Where's yo plate?" I asked as I started to cut my pancakes into fours.

"Oh, my food is right in front of me, I'mma eat sumthin else for breakfast" Lacey said with an angelic grin.

I took a bite of the pancakes and tried to focus on how good it tasted but couldn't get my mind off wat Lacey just said to me. She had my dick hard as arithmetic and the way she was eyeing me from across the table made me wanna stick my dick so deep inside her that she feel me in her stomach.

"So Chedda, tell me... why did it take so long for you to stop by and visit me at my place?"

"Wat you mean? You never invited me."

"Well, you neva asked either. I mean, you already had my address from when you took my ID when I gave you that money for Johnny Boy. I'm just wondering why you didn't ever stop by and pay me a visit? I didn't ask for my ID back for a reason."

"And wat reason was that?"

"So I wouldn't be hard for you to find. I was hoping you would've caught on by now; or maybe you just don't like wat you see?" Lacey said while standing up and holding her robe wide open for me to see her goodies than sitting back down.

I took a big gulp of my orange juice and continued cleaning my plate; then I entertained this little game that Lacey wanted to play.

"Listen sexy, you damn right I liked what I seen from the moment I saw you. but let's be real. . . You know me for holding yo daddy at gunpoint; so how I know you ain't still mad bout dat? And on the other hand, you stay attached to that nigga BB making it clear you belong to him. So you tell me wats good?"

"You afraid of BB or something?" She surprisingly asked me.

"My baby, I ain't afraid of shit."

"So, why does it matter if I belong to him or not? I mean, yeah I'm his, but sometimes I can be yours. And far as the shit you pulled in the past; that's exactly where it's at. . .in the past. I ain't mad about that lil stick up, I forgive you boo."

I finished drinking the last of my orange juice and was finishing up the rest of the eggs and sausage left on my plate. I don t know if I was just that turned on by Lacey, but for some reason, my dick was getting hard as fuck!

"Soooo , did you like my cooking?"

"I ain't gonna lie; you did yo thang. I wasn't expecting that. Now you got a nigga tryna' figure it out."

"Figure wat out?"

"You sexy; you about yo money; and you can cook... I'm tryna' figure out why it ain't a ring on yo finger yet?"

She put her head down a little and smiled as I made her blush. I knew exactly what I was doing too. BB wanted to have one up on me with Stormy, so now it was time to set the grounds for dividing and conquering. Nine out of ten women Dream for love and happiness. Since BB never wifed Lacey up to show her he was committed to her like she was committed to him; it was time for me to point that out to her and gravitate her my way.

"That was cute. Where you get dat from, Benji?" Lacey questioned sarcastically.

"My name Chedda baby, ain't nothing about me Benji; except for my pockets."

"Ooh well Mr. Chedda, now that you finally came over, I wanna know do you like my house?"

"It makes a nigga feel comfortable with all this fancy furniture and hospitality you showering me with; so yeah I like it, but I wanna see more of it."

Lacey scooted her chair back and stood up. She opened up her robe and took it off, letting it drop to the floor. She started undoing her bra.

"You wanna see more of my house or do you wanna see more of this?"

She turned side to side showing off her ass and then pulled off her bra and threw it on the table. she stood there biting her lips with her perfect breast exposed to me while her gumdrop size nipples stared me in my eyes.

"Damn baby" I said as I licked my lips, wanting to suck on one of the juicy fruits in front of me. I'm loving all that.. Shiiiitt gon head and show me some mo."

Lacey grabbed the remote control and turned the volume up on the music before tossing it on her living room couch. Summer Walker's song, Body played throughout the whole house. She bent down, got on all fours and crawled under the table I was eating on. I didn't know what she was doing until I felt her hands unbuckling my Versace belt and pulling down my Amiri jeans.

I let go of the fork I was holding in my hand and tilted my head back as my dick rose to the occasion and filled Lacey's mouth and throat. I couldn't believe how good Lacey's mouth felt around my meat. It was so wet and warm it felt

115

like she had a pussy for a mouth. I reached under the table to make sure it was real and felt the top of her ponytail. I took hold of it and guided her head back and forth while she enjoyed her morning breakfast. I don't know if I was just geeked off the fact that I finally had Lacey in rare form, or, was it just her head game to blame? It seemed like the slightest touch from her mouth made my dick harder than usual making me want more and more. I couldn't take it. I gripped the top of her ponytail and pulled her up from under the table by her hair. I slid the plate and the lit candle that was on the table, to the floor; with no regards. I helped her out of her thong, sat her on top of the table and began eating her pussy. She used her thumbs to spread her pretty pink pussy lips open while I licked on her clit and massaged both her breast with the palms of my hand at the same time. She laid back on the table and moaned in pleasure.

"Oh my god Chedda Yes! yes baby! right there!" I took my tongue off her clit and stuck it deep in her pussy a few times then back to butterflying on her clit again with my tongue. I gently squeezed her titties with my palm; and caressed her nipples between my fingers, while my face was deep inside her honeypot.

 "Oh my god Chedda yes!" Lacey screamed above the music. I tasted her sweet juice as it began to leak more and more.

"Give me that dick now!" She demanded.

I stood up and came out the rest of my clothes, I rubbed the tip of my anaconda up and down against her pussy lips just to tease her and play with her even more.

"Oh my God, please Chedda, give it to me!" she begged.

I smacked her pussy gently with the tip of my dick.

"Ooohhh shit! please Chedda please, I want you to take this pussy now!"

I slowly entered the tip of my dick and Lacey started grinding her hips and grabbing my waist and pulling me in deeper. I resisted, standing firm; making sure I drive this car at the speed of my race not hers. I pulled back a little then entered in deeper and she moaned even more. I slow stroked her entering deeper and deeper each time careful not to give her the whole thing at once.

"Ooh yes; keep going!" Lacey couldn't control her cries!

I sped up my pace sticking dick to her more, opening her walls to what I'ma about to break her in with.

 "Oh God Yes!" I gripped her hips and started to pull her into every stroke, pounding my dick deep inside her. SMACK! SMACK! SMACK! SMACK! SMACK! SMACK! SMACK' SMACK! SMACK! SMACK!

"Ooh daddy!'' Ooo Ahh oooohhhh Chedda! Yes daddy, right there, please don't stop!"

 I pounded her pussy out nonstop, making her juices splash all over me and her dining table. I felt her nails dig into my back as her legs started to shake while she climaxed, screaming my name.

"Chedda! Oh my God Chedda, I love this dick!" Her legs started shaking and she squirted all over my dick. I pulled out and picked her up as she held on to me with a vice grip while I carried her over to the couch in the living room.

"Don't tell me you done already Daddy? I just wanted to make her squirt for you one time. I'm ready for some more of daddy dick."

"You the one breathing hard out of breath and shit. I ain't even got started yet'' I told her.

Lacey sat up on the couch while I stood in front of her with my dick in my hand.

"Come here so I can taste myself" she said.

I stepped closer while Lacey freaky ass took my whole dick in her mouth and began sucking and licking on it like a lollipop. She grabbed hold of my balls and played with them in her palm while she kept on sucking. I felt my nut start to rise and had to pull out of her mouth cause I was bout ready to buss and I wasn't ready yet.

"Wats the matter, you can't handle it?"

''Oh, I can handle it a'ight.''

"Well sit down right here and let mama put this wap on you" She teased, then pulled me on to the couch and sat on my dick, face to face.

She straddled me like she was riding a bull and my dick slipped right inside her wet ass pussy. She leaned all the way towards me with her titties pressed against me while she bounced up and down on my dick. She stuck her tongue in my mouth and began kissing me while she continued going to work on my dick.

Splash! Splash! Splash! Splash! Splash! Splash! It sounded like I was playing in a puddle of water. I pulled from our lip lock than I sucked on her neck and kissed all over her chest while she continued to ride me.

"You like dat daddy?"

"Yea, keep going." I groaned.

"This my dick daddy! Oh, Chedda, I love this dick!", she screamed.

"Dammn baby. . oh shit, this pussy wet as fuck!" I shouted back.

Lacey was putting it down on me and I had to get her off of me before I let a set of twins off inside of her. Her pussy felt so good, tight, wet and warm. It was hard for me to pull out but I had to. I grabbed held of her body and lifted her up just enough to slide my dick out.

"Damn baby girl, you gona make a nigga give you a baby, sittin' on my dick like dat. Turn dat ass around and bend over so I can beat it up from the back.

She got off my lap, and stood naked in front of me.

"Let's take this upstairs baby boy.''

Lacey grabbed my hand and walked me up the steps into a bedroom full of lit candles. The room was extra warm and the scent from the candles made my dick even harder. I started to think of doing some real freaky things to Lacey even more. Lacey got into the bed and got on all fours. She wiggled her booty left to right, moving her torso like a snake or some shit.

It made me think her pussy was calling my name; like she was hypnotizing me or something. She looked back at me with a devilish grin and put one hand on her ass cheeks and spread it to the sides so that I could get a good look at her pussy. I seen a tattoo on her ass that read Daddy's

"Come and get it" she purred. I climbed onto the bed with Lacey and stuck my dick right into her pussy.

"Oh, shit," she said under her breath. I began to stroke her soul to another planet.

"Oh, God!" she cried! I thrust my whole dick in her pussy.

Her pussy started to cream for me and that just made me pound even harder. I put my thumb deep in her ass, while I kept stroking harder and harder.

"Goh-whom-haaaaa! I couldn't even understand what Lacey was saying any more.

I took my thumb out her butt and grabbed hold of her ponytail so tight that the band she had holding it together came out. All of her hair was in my hands and I was pulling it and dawg fucking her like a mad man.

"Who yo daddy now?" I growled.

"You daddy-oh yes! I been a bad girl!" Lacey screamed.

"Shut up and take this dick!" I shouted out of breath.

"Oh my God, I'm sorry daddy. Oh my. . . Chedda, oh God!" Lacey screamed at the top of her lungs and I pushed her face into her pillow to shut her up.

I pounded and pounded away, deep stroke after deep stroke, chasing my nut. Her pussy felt so good it was hard for me to pull out like I was off a pill or something, I finished beating her shit down, smacking out so hard that it sounded like a round of applause. Clap! Clap! clap! clap! clap! clap! clap!

As I felt me bussin, I pulled out and shot it all over the top of her ass cheek. It was nut all over the Daddy tattoo she had engraved on her. I did that on purpose because I knew it had to be referring to Benji. She laid there stuck in that position, breathing hard like she just ran in a track meet. Her face was down and her ass was up. she was stuck. I looked on her dresser and grabbed a strawberry flavored lubricant oil and squirted some of it on her ass hole since she still had it tooted in the air. I spread her ass cheeks open and began tongue fucking her butt while I jammed two fingers in and out of her pussy from the back.

"Oh Lord, Chedda you fuckin my head up!" she admitted through her whine.

I thought to myself. If Benji want to play these games... then let the games begin!

Chapter: 7
"Money, Pu$$y... Power!"

I stopped at the red light on the corner of Gratiot and 7 mile and checked the rearview mirror while I waited for the green signal. It was bout four o'clock in the evening and I had left Lacey's house bout twenty minutes ago. She hit me off with all the work that BB left for me and I couldn't wait to get off the road with this shit before the narcs catch a nigga riding dirty.

The light turned green and I cruised around the neighborhood for a while until I found myself in the driveway of me and Jughead's spot. I made driving up different blocks in the hood a regular habit lately after that night with Johnny Boy. I haven't seen him since but that shit with him was still a thought in my head, so I stayed alert and on point. I don't think the nigga dead cause I been around Lacey enough for me to catch wind of some serious news like her father dying. I never asked her about him because the fact I held him at gun point and even aimed my gun at her wouldn't a comfortable topic of convo for me to bring up. I didn't give a fuck about him and damn sure ain't worried about no retaliation from the dope fiend but his disappearance was kinda weird to me; that's all.

I hopped out with the duffle bag and stomped through the snow with my new all-black Nike boots. I'mma have to get on Jughead's ass about not having our walkway shoveled. I unlocked the door and to my surprise; I walked in on Jughead getting his dick sucked by Mrs. Johnson who lived next door.

"Oh, shit, my bad'' I said, as Mrs. Johnson Jumped up scrambling to cover her bare titties. Jughead took the crack-pipe out his mouth and begun pulling his pants up, trying to conceal his saggy ass balls. It was the most fucked up scene I've seen this year.

"My bad Unc" I repeated.

"My God I'm so embarrassed, I'm so sorry young man" Mrs. Johnson said, as she was putting on her clothes.

"Jughead sweetie, I have to go" Mrs Johnson said as she hurriedly grabbed her purse and headed toward the door.

"No, it's just my nephew, he's about to leave. Don't go, he'll only be here a minute."

My uncle begged and tried to convince Mrs. Johnson to stay but she was already outta there. She brushed pass me and was through the front door in a flash.

 "Dawg-gon-it nephew, you dun ran the cat away! I been working on that one there for about a year and when I finally bout to get me some ass, here you come fucking shit up!" My uncle said.

I couldn't do shit but laugh and that wasn't making it no better.

"Hold up unc. . . Ain't Mrs. Johnson married?"

"So freakin' wat! Yeah, she married! That li'l cheap ass wedding band ain't gon' stop a real playa from gettin' his mack on. You been missing all week and you pick today to pop-up. I don't pop up at your li'l fancy spot downtown when you dippin' the dawg!"

Unc was pist. He took the lighter to his crack-pipe than sat down on the leather couch. He had the place looking like a five-star residence on the inside but a trap spot on the outside.

Ever since I been hitting Jughead with a little of the powder I was getting from Benji, he been making a lot of extra money selling to his crack head friends. I never give him a lot, but I could tell by all the furniture and electronics he bought that he was making good money from it. I guess he was also getting some old worn out pussy too! I shook my head and went upstairs to my room.

I opened the duffle bag as soon as I got in my room. This shit was heavier than usual and the smell of the weed was strong as fuck. My whole room was reeking. I dumped everything out on my bed. I separated the pounds of weed; the molly and the powder. All together I counted twenty pounds of the Wedding Cake marijuana, then weighed up two bricks worth of Molly and two bricks worth of soft white cocaine. It was most definitely double the amount of product he usually gives me every week and I was geeked. I ain't neva had this much work in my possession and this time I wanted to take advantage of it instead of holding myself back. I was tired of bringing in loafs of bread for Benji, only for me to get the crumbs from it. I understand that he had to pay all the Diamond Star bitches who was selling it for him, and yeah, I knew he also had to fund the DSE operations, but fuck that; when was I going to get paid? He was getting money off bitches selling pleasures and drugs for him. I even tried to use my own money to shop with BB in order for me to buy my own work and serve my own clientele, but he wouldn't even supply me. He kept saying wait until he moves DSE to Vegas before I flooded the city; but I was tired of waiting. He claimed that he didn't want me to supply other niggas because that would bring heat, but now I'm starting to think he's just try'na hold me back and keep me under his thumb so he can be the only one making the real money. Well guess what? It's time for all that shit to STOP!

After about thirty minutes worth of me plotting and scheming my next move, I came up with a plan and starting looking through my contacts and decided to text a nigga who I knew kept a hustle going in the streets. His name was Dirty. He was a Little older than me and from a neighborhood called Beirut. The niggas over there were known for selling drugs to majority white clientele by eight-mile road, but they also was known for being some sketchy grimy ass mufuckas towards niggas who wasn't from their hood. Dirty took me under his wing for a while and taught me how to sell crack when I was younger, so he had a different type of relationship with me than he did with other niggas outside of his hood.

Me: Wats good my dawg? I got some shit on da floor I want you to check out. I ain't got much so hit me up asap.

I sent the text, then I divided up the drugs that I was going to give to the Diamond Stars and set aside the other half for me to move on my own. I calculated the math so I could pay Benji all the money that he was expecting and still leave room for myself to make extra profit. His prices weren't hard for me to work with. He expected the Diamond Star models to bring back thirty-six-thousand off each key of coke, meaning each ounce of coke was worth a thousand dollars.

I'mma take one brick of coke for myself and sell each ounce for twelve hundred a piece, which would leave me bout eight thousand dollars' worth of profit after I minus the thirty six thousand paid back to Benji for it. He expected fifty-four thousand off each brick of molly; meaning each ounce of molly was worth about fourteen hundred dollars apiece. I'mma take a brick of that for myself and hustle each ounce for eighteen hundred a piece, which would Leave me ten thousand-eight hundred dollars' worth of profit from that after paying Benji back the fifty-four thousand for it. BB wanted four thousand dollars for each pound of Wedding Cake Kush and if I sold each pound for five thousand dollars, I would make ten thousand dollars' worth of profit from ten pounds of the twenty, he supplied me with.

All together that would be twenty—eight thousand dollars' worth of profit from side hustling; not to mention the twelve thousand-five hundred that BB pays me weekly just for distributing to the models. That's bout forty thousand, five hundred dollars total that I could make from the product in front of me and still pay BB his usual expected tab without him knowing I served on the side.

My adrenaline started to rush just thinking about the money. Bing!Bing! My phone went off interrupting my thoughts from a text message alert. It was Dirty.

Dirty: Wats da deal? I' m still in da same hood, same block, just slide thru anytime between noon and midnight and we can talk bidness my nigga. I'm out here.

I read the text and my palms of my hands starting to itch as I thought about how the streets was gonna love the exclusive product I had on deck. I knew BB had some strong shit and I knew nobody had it in da city. It was so strong that I contemplated adding some cut on the molly and coke just to stretch it so I could make more money, but the plan was to first get the streets hooked and then once my clientele was official; I could add some cut to stretch it out and make more extras. That's when I will be able to make the real money. Jughead was a scientist when it came to stretching drugs and one day I'mma use him to do just that.

I Laid a big plastic garbage bag over my bed, then I began to break down the product on top of it, so none of the residue would get on my sheets. I separated each brick of molly and coke into ounces and kept the weed divided in pounds.

125

I placed my thirty-six ounces of coke to the side along with my ten pounds of weed and thirty-six ounces of molly as well. I bagged up each package that I had for the Diamond Stars individually so I could deliver each one of them their weekly supply. Once I got done, I put everything back into my duffle bag and zipped it up. I reached under bed and pulled out my small safe. I entered the combination, opened it and stared at the money that I had saved up inside of it. I had sixty thousand stored here and another sixty thousand in my loft for back-up. I thought about how far away I was from reaching my set goal and felt more motivated to make my next dollar. Benji wasn't the only one with plans and it was time for me to stop letting him hold me back. I locked the safe, grabbed my duffle bag and headed back down stairs.

Soon as I reached the bottom of the stairs I seen Jughead. I could see that he was high. He sat on the couch with his mug tore up, letting me know that he was still mad. I reached in my duffle bag and threw three ounces of soft white cocaine on the table in front of him.

"Here you go, you old fart . . .I want twelve hunnit for each ounce.

He jumped off the couch like an acrobat.

"Thanks nephew! Shit, I knew you was about to come through with something. You always come through!"

"Yeah, yeah, shut up. You was just throwing a fit over that old piece of dried up pussy. Just make sho you have my money by New Years Eve. You think you can handle that?"

"Yeah, I can handle that; my name Jughead nephew. I been wheeling and dealing since before C-Murda was killing. I got you and that's on the love!"

I was about to walk out the door but Jughead stopped me.

"Aye nephew".

"Wassup now Jughead?"

"Aye, you wouldn't happen to have none of dat pinkish clear shit you had last time, would you?"

"Wat?"

"You know, the crystal shard looking shit that look like meth, you called it Mary or Jolly or something?"

"You mean Molly? "

"Yep! dats it. You got some?"

"Don't tell me you strung out off of molly now?" I said with a serious look on my face.

"Naw, well... I be mixing it with the powder when I cook up the rock and my friends be loving it! Shit they'd spend every dime they got for the shit I be cooking with that. They can't get enough of it. I can make a lot more money with the both of them" He said.

I shook my head at the experimenting ass dope fiend in front of me, then reached in my bag and tossed him three ounces of Molly.

"That's gonna cost you eighteen hunnit a piece" I told him.

"Yeah, that's my nephew! I got you. I can really get busy now!" Jughead shouted.

"Just make sho you have all my money by New Year's Eve. . . And make sho you get yo ass out there and shovel the snow from our walkway before you call over that cheating ass old lady of yours."

"A'ight nephew, Merry Christmas."

I slammed the door, walked out the house than got in my track hawk. I looked at the time and seen that it was 5:45pm. I told Lacey that I was going to meet up with her and help her prepare the Venue tonight at eight o'clock. That meant I only had a couple hours to shoot these other moves before I headed her way. I pulled off to handle my bidness. I was on my way to the Anthos Garden Apartments to drop off a few packages for the Diamond Stars who stayed in the complex. The others who didn't live there planned to meet me at the Venue tonight or tomorrow evening to get their weekly supply.

I pulled into the parking lot of the complex and hopped out of the truck with the duffle hanging off of my shoulder. As I was walking up the stairs to the apartment, I couldn't seem to get Lacey out of my mind. I always imagined how the pussy might 've been, but actually feeling that mu'fucka was something on a level I didn't expect.

 I was definitely slippin' hard right now. I was in such a rush to get to Lacey' s house this morning that I ended up leaving my pistol at the loft. If a nigga wanted to rob me, this would be the perfect opportunity too. I wasn't too worried though because BB made sure it was only his females that worked for DSE who were allowed to live in his Anthos Garden apartments.

Knock! Knock! Knock! I stood outside of Apt. B5 waiting for Daisy to open the door. Daisy was a twenty-one yr. old sexy Mexican chick who BB flew out from Arizona. She been out here for three months and still hadn't moved out these ghetto ass apartments. It wasn't that she didn't have enough money; she just would rather send her money back to Mexico and help take care of her family instead of splurging on the lavish things. That's what made me like her more than all of the other Diamond Stars. She had morals, principals and stuck to her priorities. She had her mother and ten brothers and sisters to take care of. They were all poor and struggling until she was able to start sending them money.

She thought BB was going to make her his wife so she could have a permanent green card when she joined DSE. She was disappointed when she noticed the only time, she saw Benji was at work during the DSE events. It crushed her that he didn't even allow her to move in the mansion with him, so she loved the little attention I showed her because she felt neglected from BB.

Knock! Knock! Knock! Kno-, the door swung open.

"Hola Papi!"

Daisy spoke with a heavy sexy Spanish accent that made a nigga want to fuck her just from how she sounded. She stood in front of me with grey sweat pants and a tank top on.

"Why da fuck it took you so long to answer the door?" I asked her.

"Sorry Papi, I was in the back running my water for a bubble bath."

I stepped in her small apartment and shut the door. I sat down in her Lazy boy chair and set the bag of drugs in front of me on the floor. I pulled out my phone and sent a text to all the Diamond Stars who lived in the complex and told them I was there with the supply.

"Come here Mami and sit on Papi lap" I told her.

Daisy came and sat her petite body on top of my stiff dick and I went straight to pulling out one of her titties and began sucking on it like a baby.

"Oooh Papi, you a little frisky today huh?" She said with her heavy Spanish accent.

I continued to suck on her small breast and slid one of my hands into her sweat pants and felt straight up pussy. Daisy wasn't wearing any panties, but as soon as I slid two fingers inside her. Knock! Knock! Knock!

I got interrupted by knocks at her apartment door

"Fuck!" I blurted out.

"Sorry Papi, maybe later huh?" She said as she got off my lap and went to answer the door.

"It's La La" Daisy said, after peeping through the window. She opened the door and let big booty La La in as I prepared to give her the product.

" Sup big booty?" I said, pist cause she just interrupted my freak session with the sexy latina.

"Hey big dick Chedda" La La said popping her gum.

 "Oooooo wee, how you know what his pito look like chica?" Damn cut into La La instantly before I could get a word out.

"Gurl please you think you the only one getting some of that? Guess again, Said La La.

Daisy stood there with her mouth dropped open to the floor looking at me while I acted like I was busy retrieving the drugs out of my duffle bag.

"Is that true?" Daisy asked. La La just stood there laughing.

Knock! Knock! Knock!

Somebody else was outside of Daisy's apartment and I was glad. Daisy answered the door and the two twins, Tee Tee and Nee Nee walked in. Before I knew it Daisy's apartment was looking like a Diamond Star family reunion. I was trying my best to hurry up and give the girls their work so they could leave but all of them was flirting and tryna to get me to come to their apartment. One of em even offered to suck my dick in Daisy's bedroom while she was taking a bubble bath and for a minute, I actually thought about letting her do it. They were all on my dick asking me was I gonna be the one to take over the DSE events from now on? I told them that this was only a one-time thing because Benji was out of town. By the time I was leaving Daisy's place; it was already 7:00pm and I only had an hour to pull down on Dirty in Beirut.

I licked my lips from eating Daisy's pussy after the diamonds were gone drom her apartment then I headed out the door to take care of bidness. She wouldn't let me get my dick wet but there was no way I could resist eating that latina pussy fresh out of the tub. Plus, I had to make up for La La big booty ass putting me on blast to her.

I drove down the one-way street, then turned on Dirty's block and seen a bunch of niggas crowded on the porch of the corner house. I tried to look at the faces of the niggas but I couldn't see if one of them was Dirty or not. I continued riding slow up his block then I called his phone.

"Yo", Dirty answered.

"Wass da deal Dirtball, I'm riding down yo block right now, you out here?"

 "Oh, that you in that jeep that just went by?"

"Yeah" I confirmed to him.

I heard him talking to some niggas in the background, then he got back on the phone with me.

"Oh ok. Nigga you can't be riding up this street all slow like that without alerting me that it's you. These niggas was bout to light yo shit up and put you on Fox 2 News. It's all good doe, just turn around I'mma bout to walk off the porch and meet you on the curb. I'm, at the corner house."

I pulled up and parked across the street from the corner house. Dirty got in the passenger seat of my ride.

"Wats good my nigga? I see you out here in new wheels and shit, look at you" Dirty said, greeting me with a hand shake.

"Yea my nigga, I been trying to find my way. I see you still out here holding it down on the same block huh?" I replied.

"C'mon now, you know what it is my guy; if Dirty don't serve the hood than who will? I ain't seen you around lately, what, you been going O.T. or something, like everybody else?"

Dirty was curious if I been taking out of town trips to sell drugs.

"Nawl, nawl bro, I really been on some lo-key shit, just tryna stack my paypa, but all that lo-key shit bout to stop because I got work to put on the block" I told him.

"Word? ok then, dats wat I like to hear, cause for a minute I thought you Let them niggas run you off the streets."

"Wat niggas run me off the streets?" I asked.

"You know; them niggas who sprayed yo li'l car up at the strip club."

I burst out in laughter at what this nigga Dirty was talking bout. Some bitch ass niggas I was into it with, caught me slippin' this past spring and gunned my shit down but them niggas was bull shittin' they let off a hunnit shots and ain't hit me not one time. They ain't ready for Chedda.

"Man if you don't knock it off," I said laughing, then continued,

''Real shit, them niggas is dog food if I catch them, so if you ever run into them niggas, hit me up and let me know. On another note, I got some shit I want you to check out. You one of the realest hustlers I know in these streets, so I wanted you to be the first nigga I fucks with."

I reached in the back and grabbed my duffle bag; I took one pound of weed, one ounce of molly and one ounce of soft; then tossed it all in his lap.

"Oh shit, you bought some goodies for me huh?" Dirty said surprised at what I just tossed him.

"Yea, you can call it that. Check that out and give me a call back to let me know wat you think."

"This shit smelling real good bro", Dirty replied while he placed the Ziplock bag of weed up to his nose.

"Yeah, they call that shit there, Wedding Cake."

"Wedding Cake huh? Wat, you want for all this?"

"Look, just check it out first and see how yo peoples like it, then Just give me a call and we'll talk numbers later. I got somewhere to be before eight, so I gotta go."

I had to dismiss Dirty quick because one, I ain't feel right sitting on this hot ass block with all this work for twelve to catch me with, and two; I didn't have my strap to protect myself. I knew Dirty was a getting money ass nigga & so this lil shit prolly was nothing major to him, but it was still rules to the game and me being over here with this bag and no pistol was breaking one of them.

"A'ight fasho my nigga. I'mma check this shit out to see wat you working with and get back with you. Look at my dawg Chedda shooting moves out here in these streets! Boy O boy. . .dats wassup my dawg. Much love my nigga" Dirty said, opening my truck door to get out.

"Aye Dirty?" I said before he exited.

"Wass Good?"

"You happen to see Johnny Boy round here?" I asked him still on my toes.

133

"Nawl..now that I think about it, I ain't seen him in a while. Wassup with his crackhead ass?"

"Nothing. If you see him, just give me a call" I told him.

" I got you" Dirty said as he exited my vehicle with the drugs tucked in his pants.

I pulled off and headed towards the address that Lacey texted me for where the DSE event was going to be held. I sent a text of the location to Road Kill and Hitman. Me and them haven't been on the best of terms since our fight from a while back but BB wanted me to have a clear understanding with them to make sure everything ran smoothly at the events while he was gone. These were his two heads of security, so I had no choice.

It was Thursday night and I almost had all my duties done for the day. I gave majority of the Diamond Stars their supply to sell for Benji but I still had an handful to meet up with. I knew I probably wouldn't see the rest of them until tomorrow.

I'm hoping that Dirty can help me sell the lil work I took for myself before Benji came back on New Year's Eve, but I'm thinking bout making a few more calls to some other hustlers I know just to secure my options.

Bing! My phone lit up with a text message from Stormy. I didn't even read it. She called me and text me a few times earlier, but I missed them and paid them no mind. The only thing on my mind other than this Chedda. . . was Lacey.

I pulled up to the tall building that was located in Downtown Detroit where DSE was holding this week's events. They made it their signature to always find an available space that was downtown in the city for their regular clientele to always know what area for them to look to find a DSE event. This week it was taking place at a night club that was shut down, due to new ownership and remodeling. It used to be called the Zoo bar and it was right next door to a club called St. Andrew's. Benji ended up brushing shoulders with the new owner of it and talked him into letting DSE rent it out for the weekend even though it was supposed to be under construction. There were a lot of U-Haul trucks parked out front with movers unloading furniture and equipment for the venue setting. I walked pass them and entered inside.

"Move these other three over there and setup the booths to the left." I heard Lacey directing and instructing the moving team as soon as I walked into the building.

I noticed a few of the main Diamond Stars were there as well and that was good because I could give them their weekly supply tonight instead of waiting until tomorrow.

"Wassup gorgeous?" I said as I approached Lacey.

"About time, now maybe you could help these niggas carry in some of the furniture; dats wassup." Lacey said.

I laughed out loud at Lacey's comment.

"I see you got jokes. You know damn well I ain't lifting a damn thing but a bag of money.

" Oh, is dat right? cause I was hoping you lift all this ass up and fuck me in the shower tonight" She shot back.

"Damn, It's like dat huh?" I said and grabbed on my dick, gripping the hardness through my pants.

"Yeah, so are you gonna come through or wat?"

"You know dat!" I replied.

"Good. Now let's get this shit done so we can hurry up and head to my place, because I been thinking bout dat dick all day" She replied.

"Wassup, what you need me to do here?" I asked, ready to get shit wrapped up so we can head to her house.

"First I need you to pick a place in here where you want them to set up the money room and your own private room.

"Wat?" I asked, clueless to wat she was talking bout.

"You know; like the rooms you mainly see Benji in when we're running the events. The room where all the money and the video monitors are, is the money room and the room where the kings size bed is the sex... I mean personal room" She replied.

"Oh, well shit why you don't just pick a spot and tell them where to set it up?" I asked, not understanding what the hold up was.

"Well because normally Benji picks the spot and since he's not here; you are the one calling the shots, so I figured I'd wait till you got here so you can choose where you want it. So where do you want it, Daddy?" she asked.

I stood there feeling like a boss and looked at the sexiness in Lacey' s eyes as if her sex appeal already wasn't enough. She made my dick crave for her even more just by letting me take charge and giving me all the power to do so. My dick was busting through my Amiri jeans.

"So, I can pick anywhere in this building for our... I mean my private room and a place where I want to keep all the money we make?" I asked.

"Yeah, it's all on you. She said waiting for my response.

"Wat gives me all this power to do things how I want them to be done instead of how Benji's been doing them?" I asked her.

"The same thing that gives Benji his power to run the show " she responded.

"And wats that?tha lil momma?" I asked.

She walked and stood in front of me and took hold of my right hand. She slid it inside the front of her tight black leggings and placed it right in between her legs. My fingers were moistened from the wetness of her pussy.

"This pussy, that's what. My pussy gives you power" She replied.

Lacey clearly answered my question. I let my fingers fondle her cat a little until I was snapped out of my daze by someone clearing their throat purposely, loud enough to interrupt what was happening. I looked up and seen Hitman standing about five feet behind Lacey, watching everything that just went on between us. I pulled my hands out of her pants as if nothing happened; but it was too late, he peeped it all.

By eleven thirty I was following behind Lacey, walking up her stairs for the second time today. We had spent three hours back at the venue setting up and it was all ready for tomorrow. I even smashed most of the remaining work on the Diamond Stars' that was at the venue meeting with Lacey. I had three more to catch up with tomorrow but that was going to be a cakewalk. Road Kill ended up showing his face and he joined Hitman in company. I had a talk with both of them about how we were going to run things for the weekend and then left. You could tell that they were still holding ill feelings from our little fight and was pist that I was in charge over them this weekend.

I 'm sure Hitman more than likely, ran his dick suckas to Road Kill about what he saw happened between me and Lacey. They probably couldn't wait to break the news to Benji and I wasn't tryna even stress myself worrying about it right now. Stormy continued calling my phone and texting, asking me was I coming home tonight; but that shit was dead.

The only thing I was worried about was this fine good pussy having ass beauty that was about to spread her legs so I could enter paradise again. Soon as we reached the top stair, Lacey made a right, stepping into her bathroom and I followed her every move. She turned on the shower water and began to undressing. She took off all of her clothes and stood in front of me. She slid her hand between her legs and began playing with her pussy. She stuck two fingers inside her slit and finger fucked herself until she was leaking like a faucet.

"Ooohhh yeah", she moaned and put on a show for me while she squirted all over herself.

"Damn baby girl" I said, grabbing hold of my dick.

"I had a long day and I been a dirty girl. . .I need daddy to help clean up my mess" Lacey cooed, then pushed up on me and started to undress me.

I kicked off my shoes and unbuckled my belt to help her out. Before you knew it, we were both ass naked, covered in soap suds having steamy hot sex under the sprinkling water from her shower head.

I lifted her up and pressed her back up against the wall for balance, while she wrapped her legs around my waist and her arms around my neck. I pounded away giving her every inch of my manhood while she bounced up and down on top of it. Her pussy gripped around my girth so tight that no matter how wild she bounced on my dick; it wasn't sliding out of her until the show was over.

"Gotdamn" I let out as I felt her pussy muscles gripping my dick.

"Yes God! Chedda give it to me. Buss in me! Daddy Please! "

"Damn baby, I love this pussy!" I couldn't help but to let her know. We both rocked each other's world until I couldn't hold it anymore.

"Oh shit!" I hollered as I bussed the fattest nut inside of Lacey.

Her pussy had power.

"Chedda, Chedda, wake up."

All I felt was somebody shaking my body, waking me up out of my sleep. I was mad as fuck about it too because for some reason no matter how much I fucked Lacey last night, my body would just not let me go to sleep. It felt like I had drunk ten cans of red bull and as soon as I was finally able to doze off; here goes Lacey waking a nigga right back up at eight-thirty in the fuckin morning.

"Damn girl, wassup? I know you fell in love with the dick but you gonna have to let a nigga get a few hours of sleep before I can fuck the shit out you again" I said to her as I rolled over, still keeping my eyes shut.

"C'mon Chedda get up, I'm not playing, I gotta be somewhere."

Whoosh! Lacey pulled the pillow from under my head, waking me up immediately.

"Wat da fuck?!" I said, lifting my head up off the flat mattress.

"Get up, I said I got somewhere to be!" Lacey screamed as she scrambled around her bedroom picking my clothes up and throwing them on the bed at me.

"Alright damn, I'm gettin' up. Where da fuck you gotta be so damn early anyway; court or something?" I asked.

"Ha Ha, very funny nigga, I'mma have to be going to court for fucking you up in a minute if you don't hurry and get yo shit on, so I can leave" She shot back.

I sat up in the bed and started putting my clothes on so this bitch could shut da fuck up complaining.

"Damn; you wake a nigga up just to kick me out? No breakfast or nothing?"

"No Chedda I'm already late; so, can you just hurry up, so I can leave?"

"You could've left me sleep and went to wherever you had to go. I would 've found my way out when I got up."

"Leave you in my home by yo self? Nigga don't even think about it! now come on!"

Lacey rushed me like she was about to miss out a on a billion dollars or something. I finished pulling my pants up, grabbed my phone and car keys then started towards the front door. She brought my shoes down behind me and handed them to me.

"Damn; I can't believe you kicking me out yo house You owe me for this shit" I told her.

"I ain't telling you where to go . . . but you gotta get da hell outta here!" Lacey said jokingly as she locked the front door to the house and got inside her all-Black Benz.

"It was fun, call me later sugar muahhh!" She said blowing me a kiss, as she started her engine and drove off.

I don't know what da fuck dat bitch had going on but she had me fucked up.

I got inside my Track Hawk and started up the motor. I turned the heat on and chilled for a second, while it warmed up. I looked at my phone and saw one missed call. It was from Taylor and she just called thirty minutes ago. I know I had it coming from her because I didn't go home last night. Stormy probably headed back to her room at BB's house with the rest of the Diamond Stars after she seen I wasn't accepting her calls; but I knew Taylor wasn't going anywhere. She was going to be waiting for me to show up so she could let me have it. I put my Hawk in drive and headed back to the Loft.

I walked through the lobby and got onto the elevator. The usual African dude was working at the front desk and he gave me the thumbs up when I walked by, signaling to me that everything was normal. I drop him a few dollars every week just to alert me and keep me on notice if he sees anything funny or strange associated with my loft.

I put it in Taylor name and she's been one hunnit with me so far, but I didn't trust anybody. She could've had niggas up in here while I was gone or anything. I once heard a story about a chick running out with a million-dollars' worth of her man's money while he was out running the streets and when he came home there was nothing but a Dear John letter waiting for him.

I don't have a million dollars but I'm gonna' make sure this bitch don't get away with the lil shit I do have. I made a deal with the African to call me ASAP and hold her off from leaving the building if he ever seen anything suspicious like that happening.

The elevator door opened and I stepped onto my floor. I was bracing myself for the backlash I was about to receive. I saw Stormy's Durango still parked in the parking lot when I was walking into the building, so that meant I had double the trouble coming my way from her and Tay Tay. Stormy usually would 've thrown a temper tantrum then drove herself out to BB's for the night but I guess she was fed up and wanted to give me a piece of her mind, or maybe the bitch just didn't drive there because BB was out of town and wouldn't be there to keep her company? I don't know, but her actions sho was strange.

I unlocked the door and walked in. I shut the door softly, being careful not to make too much noise and wake them if they were sleeping. I looked around and seen that everything seemed to be in place. It was quiet, so Stormy and Taylor must still be sleep. That wasn't odd because it still was early in the morning and Tay Tay didn't have to be at work till noon. I went into the kitchen looking for something to eat since Lacey rushed me out of her crib without fixing a nigga some breakfast.

I ate a nutrigran bar and fixed me a bowl of Honey Bunches of Oats then sat on my couch in front of the TV to eat. I turned on the television and turned to the news so I could see what's been poppin' in the streets. It been a lot of weird shit going on since Trump been back in office and I only expected it to get weirder. As I was watching the news and eating my bowl of cereal, I thought I heard something. I turned down the volume to make sure I wasn't trippin'.

(Faint sounds)

"Uhhh, huh yea" a girl moaned.

"Ooohh yes, right there.

I jumped up off the couch set my bowl down on the table and tiptoed to my bedroom following the sounds of somebody moaning in pleasure. When I got to my bedroom door, it was cracked halfway open and I couldn't see in but I heard everything clear as day.

"Oh yes right there... Stormy you gonna make me cum!" I heard Taylor squirm in bliss.

I tiptoed closer to the door and gently pushed it open wider so I could see in. I couldn't believe the sight in front of me.

Taylor was handcuffed to my bed post, laying on her back, while Stormy had a bowl of ice next to her on the bed with her face deep off in between Taylor's legs.

"Oh shit, I'mma bout to cum! Oh, shit dat feels so so gooood!" I stood in the doorway and started to stroke my dick to the surprise freak show going on in front of me.

Bing! The sound of my iphone alerting me of an incoming text echoed throughout the room and Stormy's kinky deeds were interrupted.

Shocked by the sound of my phone, Stormy took her head out of Tay's pussy and turned around with an ice cube in her mouth. I had my dick in my hand with my pants half way to my ankles, and the girls were staring surprised to see me, just as I was surprised to see them.

Stormy swallowed the whole ice cube as if it was a small peanut.

"Where da fuck you been?!" They both yelled at the same damn time, as if they had practiced the moment. I still was stroking my dick, ecstatic from the live show I walked in on. On top of that, I didn't have an honest answer for neither one of them about my where abouts, so; I'd rather just join the festivities with my actions instead of my words.

"Ya'll missed me?" is all I could come up with.

Stormy got her naked body out the bed and approached me while I entered inside the room, closer to the bed. I kicked off my shoes and pants. I wanted Stormy to continue so I could he behind her and tear DAT ass up while she finished eating out Tay Tay but she just started running her mouth.

"Chedda, I been doing a lot of thinking while you were gone. Remember how you always tell me that I should try to get along with Taylor because you felt that Me and her together would make the perfect bitch?"

145

"Yea baby girl, I remember that," I said in a smooth Smokey Robinson type voice.

"Well, after the way we all put it down on each other Christmas night, it made me consider that you might be right? Maybe if Me, you and Tay Tay tried this out, then maybe it wouldn't be no need for you to stay out all night with other women, or, fuck any of the Diamond Stars because you'll have all that you need right here at home. So, I decided to put my big girl panties on and show Tay here how happy my mouth could make her feel, just so she'll understand that she's not losing her man, but rather gaining a bad bitch" Stormy said while crawling back into the bed and grabbing some ice before smashing her face back in between Taylor's legs.

"Oh yes Stormy, yes!" Taylor screamed as the touch of Stormy's tongue drove her crazy.

Stormy turned around, looked at me and tooted her ass in my direction, signaling for me to get behind her and beat it up.

"So, you gonna join us or what?" she asked and then turned back around to eat Taylor's pussy cat.

I finally got a few hours of rest than woke up to the sound of my phone going off on the floor. Stormy's head was resting on my shoulder and she was slumped, exhausted from the beating I just put on her monkey. I looked over and seen Taylor still handcuffed, knocked out and drained from the tongue-lashing Stormy laid on her as well. I was fucked up by the initiative that Stormy took and it made me confused with my feelings; to be all the way one hunnit with you, just when I thought I finally bagged Lacey and was cornering her to soon be my bitch instead of Benji's, Stormy went and pulled some mind-blowing shit like this. How could I pass up the opportunity to have two pretty bitches on the same accord under the same roof? This is what I been tryna' get Stormy on the whole time because it's just something about her that just makes anybody fall for her; man or woman. I sparked up a blunt and shook Stormy, tryna' wake her, offering her a hit of the wedding cake, but she refused. She ain't neva passed on a wake and bake session. I looked at Stormy's arm resting on my stomach and noticed the Chanel bracelet on her wrist, that must've been the one Benji bought her. I can't lie; it was icey as fuck! The thought of her and Benji still fuckin' instantly crossed my mind. I wanted to wake her up and question her about it but then again, fuck it. I'mma play dumb like I don't know shit and continue fuckin' Lacey behind both their backs.

I got out of bed and picked my phone up to see whose call I had missed. I had one missed call from Benji and two missed calls from Dirty. I scrolled down and seen a text message from him as well.

Dirty: Dawg get at me ASAP! dat shit was a thumbs up. Got some mo?

He sent that text around nine this morning. So, I guess it was him who blew my cover when I crept up on Stormy eating out Taylor. I looked at the time, feeling good bout the text I read. It was eleven thirty. I grabbed the handcuff key off the dresser and uncuffed Taylor from the bed post.

"Get up lil' momma, it's time for you to go to work." She tossed and turned for a minute, then finally spoke.

"Chedda, I'm tired of dat place, I don't wanna go to work" she whined.

"Wat?" I asked.

"I don't like it there, I'm tired of dealing with all the people at the mall; especially on the weekend. Why can't I just sleep with Stormy all day?" she whined.

"Look baby, Stormy sleeps all day because she grinds at night. I'll figure out somewhere else for you to make some money but till then, get up and get ready for work" I told her.

Taylor finally decided to get out of the bed. Sometimes it was like I had two grown ass daughters living with me. I knew once the bitch seen I could handle all of the bills and afford the lifestyle we were living that she was gonna try to get lazy on me. Fuck that, ain't nothing worse than a lazy ass bitch; so if Tay Tay was tired of working at the mall, that just meant I'll have to find something that she's good at in order to bring us in more money.

 I stepped out the room and called Benji, he answered after the fourth ring.

"Yo wats good lil homie?"

'Dat lil' homie always bothered me but I stomached it when it was coming from a nigga who was putting food on the table for me..but in due time even he gona learn who Chedda really is...''

"Wass good OG?"

"You tell me?"

I got quiet for a minute because I wasn't sure if Hitman told him about me having my hands inside Lacey pants at the venue

 '' You still there lil homie?"

"Yea errthang good, I'm here" I replied so he wouldn't think the call signal was bad.

"OK then, lemme know something. Today supposed to be yo big day to run the show while I'm gone. Lemme know if you shook and can't hold it down" BB said thru the phone tryna test me.

"Shook? You should know betta than that O.G. Da last thing da streets gonna say bout Chedda when I'm dead and gone is that I was shook. This shit ain't nothing to a Boss. I got errthang setup and ready to roll for tonight."

"Dat's wat I like to hear, now that I know everything good out there, I can lay my ass down and get some rest. We three hours behind ya'll. If anything, go sideways tonight just hit me up. I'll get at you."

"A'ight fa sho'."

I ended the call. Now that he was out the way, it was time for me to hit up Dirty and see what he was talking 'bout because from what I read in his text, he was talking my language. I heard Taylor singing in the shower while I waited for Dirty to answer.

"Waddup Doe!" Dirty voice shot through the speaker of my phone so loud that it was static in my ear. I turned the volume down so I could hear him better.

"Wats good my guy, I got yo text earlier but I was sleep. Talk to me and tell me sumn' good.

"Awww man ain't no sleep when it come to gettin' this money. You gotta change dat, yo name Chedda, you suppose to know dat... but listen, that shit you smashed on me was all the way around the board Like a piece on the monopoly board. I'm all out and need some more today. Nawl my bad, not today, I need it right now!"

"Damn, straight up? Tha streets like it huh?"

"Straight up! Slide down on me as soon as you get a chance" he reassured.

"How much you need?"

149

"How much I need? Nigga did you hear wat I just said? If how much I need is yo question; than the answer is how much you got!?"

I got off the phone with Dirty in a hurry and started getting myself together so I could hit the streets. I eased inside the bathroom and got inside the shower with Taylor so I wouldn't have to wait.

"I knew you was missing me" Taylor said as I started to soap up my body.

"I'm always missing you baby" I said to satisfy her.

"Good, because I been missing you too."

She squatted down in the shower and started blowing me. I continued soaping up my body thinking about how much money I was about to make today. I couldn't believe how good my day was starting.

"Damn baby, I ain't neva told a bitch I love them, but if you keep this shit up; you gon make a nigga like me fall in love."

When I finally bussed, Taylor swallowed every drop of it.

By 12:15PM Taylor was out the door on her way to work and I was placing my feet inside my size eleven butter scotch wheat Timberlands. They say the mu'fucka who made Timberland was a white racist but I ain't give a fuck; shit, I hated niggas my damn self, so how could I blame him?

I zipped up my Polo hoodie, put on my Rolex and started to prepare to leave. I let Stormy get her rest because I knew she had a long night ahead of her. She was one of the top stars so she only sold pleasures to the top spenders in the building, but it was stunning to me how a bitch could please all these different niggas and a douche with apple vinegar bath could still keep her pussy fresh and tight like she's a Nunn.

Stormy soaked her pussy in apple vinegar every night when she left the venue from selling pleasures and every time I hit that mu'fucka, it still felt amazing with the same tight grip and stern walls for me to knock down. I texted the three Diamond Stars, that I still had to meet up with in order to get them their supply before the weekend began; Barbie, Kharisma and Hershey. They wanted me to drive out to BB's house to deliver it to them before 5:00 pm. Their usual routine was to start their nights either strippin' at the club or partying at a club before they showed up to the venue. They'd normally pop up at the event by one or two o'clock and all their drugs would already be sold. They could've easily met me at the venue yesterday when I was with Lacey, but Benji be having his so-called Top diamonds feeling like they really some five-star Divas. They wore expensive shit and dressed like it too. I grabbed my gloc., brushed my 360 waves and locked the door behind me as I left the loft. I walked past the African at the front desk and headed out into the cool winter breeze to start my day.

I smoked a fat ass blunt while I was driving to Dirty's hood. I had to be careful smokin' this strong shit alone because last time I almost had an asthma attack. I usually don't smoke while Im riding dirty because that would give the police probable cause to search; but weed legal in Michigan now, so fuck twelve! I texted Dirty beforehand, to let him know I was on my way and as soon as I pulled up, he came running off the porch to hop in my whip. I made sure it was one in the head of my .40 cal just in case somebody tried some bullshit.

"My dawg Chedda, wat's good?" Dirty greeted and gave me dap as soon as he entered the passenger seat.

"You, sometimes me" I replied.

"Damn I smell you boy, I see you definitely still a weed head" Dirty joked, referring to the strong smell of the Wedding Cake I just blew in the ride.

"Know dat!" I replied, high as hell with my eyes bloodshot red.

"Man listen, dat shit you gave me was some fiya! I need the plug on dat, just tell me wat da ticket is?" Dirty was pleased with the quality of the work I hit him with.

"Depend on what you want" I replied.

"I want it all my nigga; the weed, the molly and the soft!"

I looked Dirty in his eyes and you could tell he wasn't bull-shitten. I glanced at the rare view mirror above me and seen my duffle bag sitting on the back seat.

"A'ight look, I need five thousand a pound for the tree; twelve hunnit an ounce for the soft and eighteen hunnit an ounce for the molly."

Dirty just sat there staring in space like he was searching for some words to come to his mind.

"You good my nigga?" I asked him with a serious look on my face.

"Yeah, hold up nigga I'm doing the math!" he snapped, then continued looking into space whispering and mouthing math problems; under his breath.

"Bet!" Dirty shouted, then reached in his pocket and counted out eight thousand dollars.

"Here, dats for the shit you gave me last night I counted it twice making sho it was all there and feeling to see if the bills had any signs of counterfeit. Dirty was my dawg, but this was Detroit. Fuck the double cross, you gotta' watch for the triple. On top of that, his name Dirty for a reason.

I took sixteen hunnit from the eight thousand and placed it in my right pocket, careful not to mix up the extra money I was making with the money that belonged to Benji.

"Now give me four mo pounds of dat green, ten ounces of dat soft and ten ounces of dat Molly. All dat come up to fifty thousand. I got dat in the crib for you right now. You got the work on you?"

He asked sounding a little thirsty.

"You got the money nigga?" I shot back.

"Yeah, I just told you it's in the crib. I can go grab it right now."

"Well go grab the chedda and I 'll give you wat you need."

He opened the door with a little attitude.

"I'll be right back nigga" He jumped out and shut my door and went inside the corner house.

I did the math in my head to make sure his calculation was right, then I reached in the back and grabbed everything Dirty asked for. I opened my glove compartment and grabbed an empty party store bag out of it. I put all the drugs dirty wanted inside of the party store bag and stuffed it under the passenger seat, then I placed the sixty-four hunnit inside my Louie duffle bag, zipped it up and placed it in the back; but on the floor this time so that it was out of sight. I put my right hand back inside the pocket of my hoodie and clutched on my pistol. My head was on the swivel, watching for anybody to try some bull shit. I looked at all the niggas on the crowded porch and started to feel uncomfortable parked on the curb, because Dirty had me waiting longer than I expected. I turned on the music to ease my nerves and listend to Future's "Honest" song. I don't know if it was because of the weed I smoked or because the lack of sleep I ain't been getting but I was paranoid than a mu'fucka. I saw Dirty walking out the door of the house. He said something to one of the niggas on the porch than headed down the stairs. He carried a small back pack on his shoulders as he crossed the street and opened my passenger door. I clutched on my pistol tight, ready to fire. He got inside and closed the door.

"Here man, let's make this quick because the block been hot all week," he said as he unzipped his bag.

I began to get ready to pull the trigger while I looked to see what was inside his bag. He reached in taking all day to show what he was digging for.. Finally his hand came out holding rubber banded stacks of money. I relaxed my trigger finger and eased my hand off my gloc, then started counting the money up as he passed it to me. It took us about three to five minutes but my ass was paranoid and it felt like an hour.

"This only forty-nine my nigga" I said, as I counted the last rubber band stack.

"Wat?" Dirty said with a puzzled look on his face.

He opened his back pack, looked inside, then flipped it upside down, dumping out the last thousand-dollar stack that was in there.

"Fifty. Now c'mon with the work so we can get off da block with this shit," he said sounding more paranoid than me.

"Reach under yo seat and grab it" I told him.

Dirty reached under the passenger seat then pulled out the party store bag that I filled with the drugs he wanted. He opened it up and peeked inside.

"My manz" he said, satisfied with the content. He placed the sack inside his back pack and zipped it up.

"I'mma go in here and weigh this shit. If anything short,or this ain't the same product, I'mma be on your head like cheese on a Packer's fan.''

I had to laugh at his friendly threat.

''You ain't got to worry bout nun dat nigga. This me you dealing with. I stood on bidness'' I told him than extended my hand for some play and we shook up.

''You came through with this, good looking out my nigga, I'm bout to make a fortune off the block today! Now hurry up and get yo ass out this hot ass hood, riden' round dirty like that. You got some nuts, pulling up on my block like you bullet proof. I'mma get at you my nigga, just make sho' you keep me locked in" Dirty said while exiting my Hawk and closing the door.

I counted out the ten thousand I just profited from the middle man tax I placed on the transaction and put it in my pocket. I reached in the back and placed the other forty thousand I made for Benji inside my duffle bag then peeled off...SKRRT!!!

I looked at the time and seen that it was a little pass one o'clock, so I decided to jump on the freeway and head towards BB's house so I could drop these packages off to the Stars. I was feeling geeked like a mu'fucka from the flip I just made with Dirty and I couldn't wait to get the rest of this shit gone. So far, shit was going smooth and everything I visioned was starting to formulate. I still had five pounds of weed; twenty-two ounces of coke and twenty-two ounces of molly left with four days to sell the shit before Benji came back.

If worst came to worst, I could always hit my stash and pay Benji for the work with my own money if it wasn't sold before he got back in town. But I was tryna hustle forwards not backwards; so my goal is to have it gone before he stepped foot back into the city.

The DSE event didn't really start until about ten or eleven at night but Lacey wanted me to meet her at the venue along with some Diamond stars way before then. She was in such a rush to go wherever she went this morning that she forgot to tell me what time to meet her. I guess I'll just wait till she calls me.

I cruised in the fast lane itching to open up the motor in my track hawk but kept my composure because I knew I was riding with drugs and a gun on me. I had no time to be in a high-speed chase because I wasn't pulling over. I was listening to young Dolph on the sounds. That country nigga talk so much about shipping pounds of weed and getting rich off drugs that he had me feeling like I was the next up and coming King Pin of Detroit. I knew I was no where near King Pin status; but Dolph sho motivated a nigga and made me feel like I could get there.

About forty minutes later, I was arriving at the gated complex. I pressed the numbers on the dial pad to contact somebody in the house so they could open up the security fence for me to pass through.

"Who is it?" A voice said through the speaker box, sounding like Blondie.

"It's Chedda" I shouted thru the mic.

"Oh, ok Chedda, I' m buzzing you in" Blondie replied.

The security bar raised allowing me to drive into the complex, I pulled up to BB's house but had to park down the street in front of one of his neighbors' places because there were so many cars parked outside of his house. He had six girls living with him and they each owned a car. There was Lacey, Stormy, Kharisma, Barbie, Hershey, and Blondie. There were seven Bedrooms in his house all together. He and Lacey shared a room, so that left one vacant. BB claimed to be leaving it open for some chick he planned on flying in from overseas but I haven't seen her yet.

I carried the duffle bag full of drugs to the front porch and rang the doorbell. I caught a little chill waiting for someone to let me in. The stupid bitch Blondie knew she just buzzed

156

me into the damn complex, I don't know why the fuck she wouldn't be waiting by the door for me? I pressed the doorbell again. Ding, dong!

"Who is it?" a soft voice said on the other side of the door.

"It's yo Daddy!" I shouted, pist at how cold I was gettin' from standing out in the freezing winter weather.

The locks clicked and then the door swung open. Hershey was in front of me with a bra and some boy shorts on.

"Boy you wish you was my daddy, hurry up and come in, you letting all that cold air in the house."

"I've been standing out there foreva waiting on one of ya'll to let me in."

I stepped inside they luxurious house. Hershey closed the door and locked it, then switched her small little booty in front of me.

"How come you ain't call nobody and let us know you was outside?"

" Shit I did. Blondie opened the gate and let me in, or at least I think it was Blondie's ass."

I walked deeper in the house checking out how fancy it was. It seems like every time I come over something new was added to the place.

"Uh-huh, no sweetie, you gotta' take them boots off before you get to walking all over our carpet" Hershey said poppin' her neck and snapping her fingers.

"Hershey who you down there talking to?" A voice shouted from upstairs.

I looked up and saw Barbie leaning over the banister looking down on us. She had nothing on but a white towel covering her body and a white towel wrapped around her hair like she had just gotten out of the shower. I peeked under the towel from below and got a good look at her kitty cat. It was shaved.

"Oh, hey Chedda" Barbie said with a blush on her face.

"Wassup Barbie Doll, I responded to the thick vixen above.

She walked away from the rail and went back to doing whatever it was she was doing.

"So wat you got for me cutie?" Hershey asked while taking a sip of wine from a glass made of crystal.

"The same as usual. BB wanted me to give ya'll a lil weed, Molly and powder.

"Oh yea?" Wat about dat dick I been hearing about?" She asked.

I started to unzip my duffle bag ignoring her question.

"You aint gotta be shy Chedda, I already heard wassup. Why don't you pull it out and lemme see it since Stormy ain't around" Hershey said, while sitting on the couch with her legs crossed licking her lips seductively. If it was any other Diamond Star, I would've upped my beef stick so quick that you would 've thought I was headed to a cook out; but it was Hershey and I still couldn't let go of the fact that she played me in unloading the gun the first time I met her.

"C'mon ain't shit up, you know that."

"Awww da lil baby still mad at mommy for playing with his toy?" she whined sarcastically.

I didn't respond. Kharisma walked in the room talking on her phone but ended the call as soon as she seen me.

"Oh, wasn't nobody gonna' tell me dat the party favors were here?"

Kharisma asked Hershey, eyeing her while she sipped her wine on the white couch. She walked up on Hershey and gently took the half-filled glass from her hand.

"And wat we keep telling you bout drinking this red wine in our white room!? Girl we gonna evict yo ass!" She told her.

"Shut up girl, I be catching you in here too!" Hershey popped back.

Kharisma took a sip from Hershey's glass than smacked her lips loud as fuck like it was the best drink on earth.

"Mmm-hmm girl, you a'int neva lied this one right here is good," Kharisma turned her attention back to me.

"Chedda, why you standing over there all suited and booted? You might as well take yo shoes off and get comfortable, we aint gonna be ready to leave for another two hours."

I looked at Kharisma fine ass puzzled.

"Two hours?"

"Yeah, since you running shit this weekend me and Blondie riding with you to the venue so we can meet up with Lacey. So, like I said; you might as well get comfortable and give us our product so I can fiya dat shit up. A bitch ain't smoked all day."

I took off my limbs, found a seat on the couch in front of the seventy-two-inch plasma and got comfortable like they Just told me to. I ain't have shit else to do before I went to the event, so I might as well chill with the stars of the show before it started. Besides; they did belong to me for the weekend since BB left me in charge. I opened the bag and started pulling out the three packages I came to deliver.

"Ooowwee you brought me some money too?" Kharisma said sarcastically, catching a glimpse of the money that was inside my Louie duffle with the drugs.

I closed it back up fast.

"Mind ya bidness, gold digger" I whispered to her and winked.

I threw her the package she had coming and handed Hershey's hers. The other one belonged to Barbie and I was still waiting on her fat pussy having ass to come down stairs. Kharisma opened up the Ziplock pound of weed and smelled it.

"Ummm yeah, dats the good shit girl" She said to Hershey.

Kharisma reached for the backwoods that was laying out on the oyster table and took a squat next to me on the couch, preparing to roll up a blunt.

"Naw, uh-huh hell to the no!" Hershey shouted then continued going... "You not about to roll dat up, you know we ain't supposed to be smoking dat. Don't you got any more of the clean shit upstairs?" she asked Kharisma with a serious look on her face.

"No, I don't got no more, I smoked it all up. I told you that."

"Well, I don't care girl, you betta call Lacey and tell her to bring you some more clean shit because you know dat once you get a room in this house, it ain't no more of smoking dat shit. Save that for them low ranking hoes in Anthos Garden that don't know any better" Hershey said referring to the stars who were staying in BB's low class apartments on the eastside because they weren't requested for as much as them.

Kharisma pouted, looking disappointed that Hershey just rained on her parade.

"Fine I'll just pop Molly and drink myself into a coma for the party to begin," Kharisma whined; then started to open the molly bag.

I sat there deep in thought for a minute as I watched Kharisma snort a line of Molly.

"Mmm-hmm damn dat shit strong, here it's on you bitch" she said, passing Hershey the rolled up hunnit dollar bill that she used to catch the line on the table.

I wasn't surprised at how they were dirtying up their noses in front of me; I was more so tryna' figure out why they couldn't smoke the Wedding Cake weed that I brought over for them from Benji? Wat da fuck did she mean by, the clean shit? I kept it as a mental note and ain't say shit because I was gonna do my homework quietly.

Hershey turned on some music and brought out two bottles of liquor. They had fifth of Belvedere and a fifth of Don Julio. I guess it was gonna be a hyped white night for me and the Diamond Stars.

''Woooohh this my shit!" Kharisma said, as she took a shot of Don and started bouncing her ass to Sada Baby's song playing through the speakers.

Hershey poured me a glass of Julio, sat on my lap, and felt on my dick. I started to push the bitch off of me, but fuck it; why not let her touch on what she'll never get? When I looked back up, Blondie and Barbie joined the party. we were all drinking, turning up, getting ready for the night.

Barbie and Kharisma started coming in and out wearing different lingerie's, asking my opinion on what they should wear at the event tonight. I was enjoying their company. If this is what Benji goes through every weekend; I want in! I poured me another glass of Don and dropped a little Molly inside of it.

"You know Molly make you horny right?" Blondie asked, shouting over the music.

I looked at her; guzzled the cup of Molly filled liquor to the head and then blew her a kiss. The liquor was in my system, full effect. This was my day to run DSE and it felt like the position of power I deserved in life. Without Benji, these were my bitches, my drugs and my money! It was time to turn up!

Mean While

"Bye Daddy, I love you!!" Lacey shouted back to Johnny Boy as she exited the drug rehabilitation center; waving goodbye to him. It was 3:30pm and Johnny Boy's visiting hours had just come to an end. Lacey rushed to her car but quickly slowed down her walk when she almost slipped on a patch of ice. She made it inside her Benz without falling and started up the engine hoping that the heat would defrost the ice on her windshield. She scrolled through her missed call log while waiting for the car to warm up a little. Cardi B crept through her car speakers. She felt relieved she finally had a chance to visit Johnny Boy. She talked him into enrolling in the institute a month ago and he'd finally controlled his behavior enough for him to be allowed visitors every Friday. He was still having trouble coping without the drugs and alcohol he was addicted too, but the doctor said it was a day-to-day process, Johnny Boy's assigned social worker told Lacey to look for him to have his treatment completed anywhere from six months to a year. Lacey hated to see Johnny Boy in there down and depressed like he was; but she knew it was for his own good. No one knew about Johnny Boy's where abouts but her. Johnny Boy didn't have much family or friends anyway and Lacey vowed to keep his secret only between them, not even Benji could know.

Lacey dialed BB's number on the face time, returning his missed call. She turned the music down as she saw his face appear on the screen.

"Wassup supastar, where you been?"

"Hey bae, I was just finishing a few touches for the event tonight, that's why I missed your call" she lied, then continued.. "I'm headed to the house to grab a few things before tonight. Is everything good with you?"

"Yeah, everything is looking beautiful. Dude put something nice and heavy together for us for the New Years. He said it might be the last shipment we get for a few months because of some political shit that he got wind of, so be easy on what we got put up. President Trump been having disagreements with China and North Korea and I guess one of them threatened to release something deadly into the United States that could shut down the U.S. Mail and the Airlines. You know Dude got all kind of sources that put him up on game about that type of shit; so, all we can do is take heed. I'mma send the shipment to yo crib from Fed-Ex on the day I board the plane."

"Wow.. well how is it going with finding a place for the Diamond Star headquarters out there?" Lacey asked.

"Damn; you know how to spoil my New Year's surprise don't you?" Benji said laughing out loud. "We found one and I just laid the first half of the payment down, today."

"Oh my God Benji? dats great!"

"Yeah, yeah everything is coming together. I'm just working this deal out to receive our escort license for the company then we're set to go."

"That's good baby, I'm so happy for you."

"Not me baby; us. None of this would've been possible without you."

Lacey blushed a rush of red from hearing those words come out of BB's mouth. He always knew how to touch her soft spot; even from thousands of miles away.

"Thanks Daddy."

"I'mma let you go head and get ready for later. I know you gotta big night on your hands without me."

"Yea I do and it's my first time doing this without you. I'm kind of nervous Daddy."

"You a big girl, you got it; this where all them building sessions we had come in at. How's Chedda doing? Is he ready?"

"He acts like he is, but I guess we'll find out tonight. I'm about to call him and tell him to meet up with me now."

"Fasho. remember, you make the money, don't let it make you."

"I know Daddy."

"Oh, and one mo thing I need you to do before I get back", Benji requested.

"Wats dat?"

"I want you to find my brother before the New Years, I ain't seen him in a while and I'm starting to get worried. I need him to get his act together so we can move to Vegas together once I close this deal."

"Ok, I'll get on it. I love you" Lacey said as she blew him a kiss goodbye on camera.

"Always" Benji said.

They disconnected the face time call.

Lacey turned her music back up feeling re-energized after speaking with Benji. Out of all the men she been with in her life, no man has ever had as strong effect on her like Benji did except her first love. Benji knew how to make Lacey's heart and pussy melt just from words out of his mouth and Lacey knew that she would never find that with anybody else. A guilty conscious set inside of Lacey as she thought about her

165

infidelity, motives and betrayal that transpired with Chedda recently. She was thrilled that she succeeded at forcing Chedda to nut inside her last night but she more so wished that it could be BB's sperm cells fertilizing her eggs. She wasn't sure if she was going to end up pregnant or not from their last sex session, but just the thought that there was a possibility excited her and gave her hope that she held on to with a firm grip.

Lacey looked at the time and seen that it was creeping up on four o'clock. She texted all of her Diamond Stars and notified them of the venue's location and what time to arrive. Un aware that Chedda was there with her top diamonds she texted him and told him to meet her at the venue by five o clock. She was anticipating being side by side with Chedda so she could watch him take control for the first time. His presence made her pussy drip every time she was around him and she couldn't get enough of being aroused. She viewed tonight as his graduation from a prince to a king and she couldn't wait to cater to him like one. Lacey switched her gear into drive than headed home so she could change into her attire for the special occasion she had planned for later.

***

Chapter: 9
"Turn Down for Wat!"

"Ayyee, turn dat shit up Chedda!" Kharisma yelled from back seat of my Track Hawk.

I turned the volume up a little more so she could vibe to the beat of Lil Baby's new song. Blondie was in the passenger seat smelling good and looking even better. We were all high off Molly and she kept licking her lips at me. I put my Jeep in drive and pulled out of the sub division with Barbie and Hershey trailing behind us preparing to go their separate ways. They were headed to a night club to distribute product and sexual pleasures on the side until it was time for them to arrive at the venue for the DSE event. Lacey sent me a text and told me to meet her at the venue by six O'clock. It was already 5:05 and it was going to take us about forty minutes to get to the city. Luckily, I convinced the stars to leave early, in order for us to make it there on time.

I stopped at the light, waiting to merge onto the freeway. Blondie leaned over and went inside my pants, pulling my dick out. She started jacking me off, grippen' my pole and stroking it; she even kissed the tip of it while batting her eye lashes at me. My pole came to life from the touch of her lips.

"Why you teasing me sexy?" I asked her with a stiff dick.

She didn't even speak, she just reached in her purse an pulled out some flavorful lubricant gel. She squirted it on my dick and rubbed it in like it was lotion. Next thing I know, Blondie had her head in my lap bobbin' up and down, giving me that good o'l Becky.

"Oh, shit girl, do yo thang then" I said encouraging her skills.

The light turned green and I placed my right hand on the back of her head then pressed on the gas, burning up the road heading back to da city.

Blondie, Barbie and me stepped in the building looking like we were there to start the party early. Lacey was surprised to see all three of us show up at the same time, you could tell she was a little curious but chose not to ask. The DJ booth was all setup along with the tables and alcohol section. I smelled the scent of good fried chicken and French fries so I knew the catering service was on point and ready to do they thang. There was no need for the usual body paint crew for the girls because DSE's theme was Angels and Demons this whole weekend. They were only going to wear halos around their heads and angel wings attached to the back of their bras. The demons were going to wear devil horns and remain topless with a pitchfork as a miniature stripper pole.

 We divided half and half. On Saturday we were switching their roles; making the angels from Friday into the Saturday night demons; and turning the Friday night demons into the Saturday's Angels. Sunday we were making all the Diamond Star's demons; so bare titties and nipples was gonna be all over the place for our clients.

"Chedda, come here lemme show you sumthin" Lacey said, taking me away from Blondie and Barbie.

She walked me upstairs to where I chose for the money room to setup.

"This is the money room right where you wanted it. Wat, you think?"

I looked the place up and down then focused my attention on the security camera monitors and the money counting machines that sat across from them. There were 12 different HD screens. There were cameras outside of the building and cameras that pointed in all directions of the booths inside the venue.

"I like it I'm impressed" I told her.

"Good, now if you like this, just wait until you see what I'm bout to show you next."

Lacey grabbed my hand and led me down the hall to where my personal room was set up. She walked me through the curtain that draped over the doorway. We entered the room which was dimly lit inside with purple black lights. There was a portable stripper pole that was set up in the center of the room. A king side bed was position right behind the pole about 6 feet away. A Dresser sat to the right that had a full-length mirror with purple light bulbs lit up all around it. The room had four space heaters, one in each corner that made the room feel warm and cozy. There was a table next to the bed that had a bucket of ice with 4 bottles of Moet inside.

"Well, do you like it?" Lacey asked with a big smile on her face.

I don't know why she asked cause no nigga in his right mind wouldn't like how this room was set up. It was a playground for the pussy to come play; but I hesitated a bit just to make her sweat.

"Chedda, do you?" she asked again in a whiney voice.

"This room makes me want to bend you over and fuck the shit outta you right now" I said to her, biting my lip and grippin my dick to let her know I was serious.

"MMMMM that exactly what I wanted to hear.. but save that same energy for later because right now we have work to do" She said as if her pussy wasn't fiending for my dick right now.

Lacey walked over to the bed, crouched down and pulled two gift boxes from under it the handed them to me.

"Wats this"I asked.

"It's what you're wearing tonight, so get out of them close and put dat on."

I opened the box and pulled out a silk Fendi robe, with three pairs of boxers. I opened the other box and it was a pair of Fendi slippers.

I was strutting my stuff around the place like I was king Tut. I saw Lacey in the back with a group of Diamond Stars by their changing booths. It seemed like more had arrived while I was upstairs. I walked up to the DJ booth and told him to play some music to liven up the mood. He put on that new Future and mixed it up with some Drake. I don't know what it is about Drake but when the hoes hear that nigga's music, they can't contain themselves. I headed over to the changing booth with Lacey and the other Diamond Stars. I walked over with two Moet bottles in each hand.

"Y'all ladies doing alright over here?" I asked, while looking inside catching a view of some naked ass titties.

"Hey Chedda, I ain't know you was here," one of the Stars named Wet Wet said to me as I walked inside the crowded tent.

"Yeah, you know I was upstairs hiding in the VIP room but I had to come down and bring y'all some champagne. I made sure that each one of the Diamond Stars that were present had a glass. I came out the tent to motion for the DJ to cut the music then stepped back inside to make a toast.

"Lemme get y'all attention for a minute" I said over the small chatter.

"Awe shit! Chedda bout to propose to one of us," one of the Diamond Stars joked amongst the crew and we all couldn't help but laugh.

"Good one, good one, but, y'all know ain't none of y'all got enough Chedda for me to propose...none of y'all" I shot back.

All I heard was a bunch of "ah no he didn't" coming from the divas in front of me.

"Nawl, but on a serious note, I wanted to just holla at y'all before we get our last weekend of the year started. I know everybody aint here but fuck it, the ones I see in front of me is plenty."

As soon as I finish the statement, I was interrupted by Stormy walking into the tent, looking bad than a mu'fucka. She had a sparkly gold halo around her head and a shiny gold bra with big white angel feather wings attached to the back. She looked like a bronze Goddess or sum shit. All eyes were on her.

"I went upstairs looking for you so I figured I would just change into this while I was up there. Wats going on in here?" Stormy asked wondering why everybody had champagne glasses in their hand.

"You just in time I said and rapped my arm around he while giving her her my champagne glass. I then grabbed the half-filled Moet bottle from the table with my free hand and continued with my speech. I saw Lacey side eye Stormy but I paid it no attention.

171

"As I was saying, the stars who are in front of me are the ones that I want to connect with most. We all know that the first time I met most of y'all it wasn't a pretty sight. I was getting stumped out and electrocuted with tasers in the middle of the floor."

They all bussed out laughing remembering the day that I reminisced about.

"I've come a long way from that day. My girl Stormy did too. We came a long way with BB and Lacey and all y'all and we've come a long way with Diamond Star Entertainment. This is my first weekend overseeing the DSE event and who knows; this may be my only time of having the opportunity to turn up and make money with y'all like this. So, I just wanted to say that I recognized all y'all grind, I recognized all y'all struggles and I recognized all y'all beauty."

"Awwweeee," The group of models all said in unison cutting me off.

They played tough but at the end of the day they still were women who fell victim to kind words. I continued my speech.

"I couldn't be more honored than to have this opportunity with y'all and I wouldn't pick any other group of stars in the world if I could. Now let's turn this bitch up to the max on the last weekend before the New Year!"

All the Diamonds shouted out with excitement, toasting their glass in the air and I signaled for the DJ to turn the music back on. The sounds blasted thru-out the venue and we all celebrated my first night in charge, waiting for the money to come rolling in.

By one o'clock the Diamond Star event was slappin' harder than a Jeezy concert at the Fox theater. I could barely keep up with all the money that Lacey and Blondie were bringing into the money room, from the clients. I was still waiting on Hershey to show up so she could help me run all these bills through the money counters but I guess they were still out club hopping distributing the drugs I gave them. I stood there watching the whole show on the video monitors in front of me. It was like a movie. Niggas was coming in paying top dollar for the chick they wanted to fuck and the pussy was delivered to them right there inside their own private booth. For the big spenders; there was a VIP section that provided them a closed off space along with a bed for them to enjoy their pick of pleasure. Traffic was coming left to right like a two-way intersection and the money was piling up right in front of me.

I stared at one of the monitors watching Blondie and Lacey work the floor. Lacey grasped every man's attention just from her looking fine. She was dressed as a demon tonight and her titties were out looking like erotic eye candy. I saw one trick on camera give her a stack of money just to suck on one of her nipples. Stormy was bouncing booth to booth, meaning a lot of niggas was requesting her as usual. Not one Diamond Star was un—occupied and that was good, because that meant everybody was making money. I saw Hitman guarding the door while Road Kill kept an eye on the entertainment taking place. Hershey finally entered the building with Barbie right next to her. They managed to find their way through the horny crowd and I noticed Hershey on the video monitor making her way up the stairs while Barbie headed towards the changing booth.

Knock! Knock! Knock!

I opened the door and undressed Hershey with my eyes as she stepped in.

"You miss me?" She said arrogantly, walking up to the table which held piles of money and the money counter machines.

"You damn right I miss you. Money been coming in like crazy and I don't even know how to work these damn machines in here to count it."

173

"Lacey ain't show you?"

"Nawl, Lacey been out there working her ass off. It's been busy."

"I see" Hershey said, pointing at all the money that was sitting on the table.

"Well, come here, lemme show you."

I walked up beside Hershey then she started explaining and showing me how to run the bills through the machine correctly. Once I was sure I knew how to do it, I quickly turned my attention to the chocolate bunny that I was fighting to stay away from. The MDMA was in my system so I had an excuse for my actions. I stepped behind her and rubbed my dick head against her small frame just to show her how ready the Molly be making me.

"Ooooooh, well somebody's excited to see me. I guess you a'int mad at me no more" Hershey said, reaching back tugging on my dick through my boxers. I opened my robe so she could get a better feel.

"Nawl I ain't mad at you, but I guess he is. Can't you tell he wanna beat you up till you scream?" I whispered in her ear; referring to my dick who I knew couldn't wait to break her back.

She turned around to look me in my eyes.

"Chedda, I been wanted to apologize and explain myself to you about that situation for the last couple of months. I put my finger over her lips cutting her off.

"Shhh, don't apologize to me; apologize to him" I told her pointing down at my dick.

Hershey licked her lips and prepared to drop to her knees in front of me until Stormy stormed in breaking up our vibe.

174

"Chedda! " I heard her voice come from behind me and I reached for a stack of money like I was placing it inside the money counter.

"Wassup baby, everything good?" I asked her hoping she hadn't seen anything.

"Yeah, I Just need you for a minute Daddy."

Hershey smacked her lips than rolled her eyes at me and Stormy as I began walking towards the door where she stood. She kissed me and sucked on my lip for a split second. I knew that was just to piss Hershey off even more, but I liked it.

"Daddy my pussy dripping wet and I need to ride yo dick right now," Stormy said with a look in her eyes I neva seen before.

"Hershey I'mma be right back. I want you out of those club clothes and into yo attire for the event before I get back. Hershey stuck her middle finger up at me than I left out with Stormy, headed to my private room.

"Damn baby, ride this dick.''

I was talking shit while Stormy was bouncing up and down on my dick with her Angel wings spread behind her. She wasn't flying, her pussy was soaking wet and when we made it to my king size bed, she hopped right on top and my manhood

slid right in.

"Uh-yeah, Daddy yes! Oh, I love this dick, keep it hard for me daddy!" Stormy cooed and shouted in pleasure as I gripped her waist, lifting her up and pulling her down into every stroke of my dick. Her pussy was extra slippery like she was off a sex pill or something.

"Oh Chedda!" Stormy screamed.

I looked at her while she was taking control. The wings that were still attached to the back of her bra made her look like the most devilish angel I ever seen and she was blessing me with the wettest pussy that came from heaven. I wasn't sure whose pussy was better between her's and Lacey's; but new pussy is always better.

"Oh shit, bitch you bout to make a nigga buss!" I hollered out as the feeling got more intense. Her pussy muscles were grippin' and tuggin' on my dick while her wetness was splashing all over it. She started riding me harder and faster until that was all she wrote.

"Ugghh! Fuck!" I hollered than pushed her off of me onto the bed then raised too buss my nut all over her face. She laid there looking at me squeezing my dick with her hand, making sure all the nut was out, then she got up to go clean herself with some wet wipes and headed back to work.

After about twenty minutes of me laying there, re-cooperating from the wap Stormy just put on me; I got my ass up and tossed my robe back on. I heard the music from down stairs setting the tone in the building and I couldn't take it anymore. I was done playing the background; it was time for me to join the party. Maybe Benji played the background when he was running things, but my name Chedda; im running the show this week and it's time to run shit my way. I went in the dresser and pulled out my duffle bag. I went inside it and grabbed an ounce of Molly. I was charging this one to my profit. I placed it in the pocket on my robe and grabbed another bottle of Moet out of the bucket, then headed towards the money room. Hershey was dressed as a demon with a black thong on, devil horns and no bra. She was running the money through the money counter and rubber banding another stack but I cut her short before she could finish.

"Hershey, c'mon, we going downstairs to turn this bitch up even mo!"

I handed her the bottle of Rose and started walking down the steps.

"Slow down, damn Chedda" Hershey complained behind me, but I ain't give a fuck wat she was talkin' bout. I came down the stairs with my Fendi slippers and Fendi robe, holding the bag of Molly in my hand. I was seeing so much pussy and titties circulating around me that I was feeling like a black Hugh Hefner.

I walked up to a table where two niggas were sitting down eating chicken and I sprinkled a chunk of Molly on their table.

"Turn up!" I hollerd over the music to them and gave em some dap before i carried on.

I worked my way throughout the crowd sprinkling the Molly into everybody's hands who were accepting it. I even gave some to the DJ.
Hitman and Road Kill acted like they didn't wanna accept anything from me, so I handed some to Hershey then made her give it to them. They popped it right there on the spot with a splash of the Moet I had her carrying around. I went inside the changing booth where some of the girls were taking a break, I re-energized they ass with a sprinkle of Molly and a splash of Moet. I found my way back to the DJ booth, grabbed the microphone and ordered him to turn it on.

"This da last weekend of the year, err body in this bitch turn up one last time for Diamond Star Entertainment!" I shouted into the mic.

The tricks all started yelling and whistling while the DJ and the Stars were right on cue with the music and dancing.

Niggas was throwing money everywhere; it was starting to look like a scene from Magic City. I guzzled some more Rose and went Molly crazy with them.

Everybody in the building was lit and wired. Clients wasn't even worried about being in closed off booths and neither were the bitches, they were fuckin right there on the spot, giving Diamond Stars back shots. I even caught Hitman getting his dick sucked by big booty LaLa in the Men's bathroom, shit was epic.

Hours into partying, Lacey walked up on me while I was finishing up a plate of chicken and fries. It was 5:00AM. The event was still rocking and I was still geeked up from all the Molly I popped.

"Let's go upstairs," Lacey said directly in my ear, so that I heard her above the DJ's tunes.

I looked her up and down, noticing the fish net stockings she had on. Her breast were out and her nipples were hard and perky. Right then I knew what time it was. I got up from the table and we went upstairs into my private room. She sat me on the edge of the bed making sure I didn't move. We could hear the Chris Brown song playing from down stairs called No bull shit. Lacey begun dancing to the beat on the pole giving me my own personal strip show. she spun around the dance pole like an acrobat than dropped down in front of it and bounced her ass like Meghan Thee Stallion. She walked over to the dresser and pulled out a dill doe from the bottom drawer. She came back in front of the pole, twirled around it, then did the splits on the floor, staying into the position with her legs wide open. She lifted her ass and pussy off the ground just enough to stick the sex toy inside her pussy. Hershey appeared in the doorway and then entered inside to watch the show. Lacey started bouncing up and down on top of the dill doe like she was making love to it. She took it from out of her pussy and lifted it into the air, showing me how wet her pussy was.

Her juices dripped all over it, from the top down to the bottom, even soaking her hand.

"Damn baby, it's like dat?" I asked, amazed at how drenched the toy appeared. She looked behind her and seen Hershey. Hershey approached her and joined in. Lacey held the wet dill doe in front of Hershey's mouth and she wrapped her lips around the tip of the fake dick, tasting Lacey's sweetness.

"Mmmm taste good, don't I?" Lacey asked her, while Hershey continued showing off her dick sucking skills to me on the sex toy Lacey just fucked. Lacey pushed and pulled the Dildoe in and out of Hershey's mouth. She damn near pushed it down her throat and Hershey didn't even gag. My dick turned into a rock and stood tall like the Eifel Tower. I took off my robe and got up trying to join in but Lacey shook her finger at me and stopped me.

"Didn't I tell you not to move? Now sit back down" Lacey demanded and I couldn't believe her, but I followed her orders like a kid tryna behave for a piece of candy. They continued the freak show. Lacey took the toy out of Hershey's mouth.

 "Now take dem panties off and assume the position bitch!" Lacey ordered.

Hershey came out of her panties and bent over on all fours then placed her head forward on the ground with her ass tooted in the air like she was preparing for a whooping.

All I saw was Hershey's fat moist monkey with hot pink lips peeking at me. Lacey slid the dildoe inside of Hershey's wet monkey from the back and Hershey moaned out loud.

"Mmmm—yes!"

Lacey went in deep, drilling her from the back with the toy, Jamming it in and out of her.

"Oh shit! ooh shit! Oh, shit yes!" cried Hershey.

Lacey continued fucking her harder and faster while Hershey was throwing her slim booty back like she had a real dick behind her.

"Oh, shit Lacey! Lacey, yes, yes, yesss! I'm cumming mommy, I'm cumming!" Hershey screamed, and white cream began oozing out of her chocolate candy. It was hard for me to contain myself. I was naked playing with my dick as I watched the water works. The tip of my dick began leaking with pre-cum, craving to dive inside one of the swimming pools in front of me. Lacey began sticking her tongue inside of Hershey, eating her pussy from the back.

"Oh, fuck yes! Mmm fuuucckk-yesss!" Hershey screamed. Lacey took her tongue away from Hershey's pussy, then spit directly in her brown eye. Lacey begin entering the dildoe inside Hershey's Asshole.

"Fuck! Oh, my goodness yes!" Hershey shouted in pain and pleasure at the same time. Lacey butt fucked her with the dildoe and fingered Hershey's pussy all at once. The shit was wild.

"Oh my gooooodness! Lacey, I love it, I love it Mommy, fuck me Harder!" The chocolate diva begged like I never seen before. I couldn't believe my eyes or ears. Hershey started gushing more white cream all over Lacey's fingers. Her legs were shaking uncontrollably.

Lacey stood up in front of her while Hershey was trying to gain her composure back from the breath taking experience she just endured.

"You know wat time it is" Lacey said to Hershey as if she was her hoe.

Hershey sat up, put her back against the dance pole— with her ass cheeks sitting on the floor. Lacey stood above her, grabbed hold of the pole and put each Leg over Hershey's shoulder. She squatted down in front of her, sitting her pussy right on her face. Hershey ate away while Lacey smothered her with wet pussy on her dinner plate.

"Mmm yea," Lacey moaned. "Eat yo dessert" she instructed her sex slave while bouncing up and down on Hershey's shoulders.

"Oooohh yea, you hitting the spot", Lacey said as she crossed her legs around Hershey's head, gripping her neck with her thighs until she came all over Hershey's face. Lacey took her legs from around Hershey's neck.

"Now you dismissed" she said to Hershey, then smacked her on her ass while she made her way towards the door way. I know she got that from BB because I seen him do the same shit several times to Diamond Star's that was leaving his presence. Lacey walked over to me and sat her booty on my hard dick.

"Is dat dick ready for me yet?" she asked, giving me the green light to enter inside paradise again.

**I opened my eyes to a banging ass headache. I looked to the left and to the right of me inside the king size mattress I was laying in and didn't see a soul insight. I heard a lot of noise coming from downstairs so I put my robe on to check it out and see what was going on. I was just waking up from the night before. After I had fucked the shit out of Laccy, I ended up shutting down the event at about seven—thirty in the morning. If I didn't, mu'fuckas would still be here tricking and fucking off of molly. They damned near turned the event into a rave party. I got up and stepped outside of my private room. I looked over the banister and seen what appeared to be a cleaning crew or something? They were sweeping and cleaning up the trash from the event.

"Hey sleepy head" Lacey said from behind me, standing in the door way of the money room.

She was dressed in a new outfit with a new hairstyle and everything; holding a Starbucks cup in her hand, looking like she been up for hours.

"Wat time, is it? And who all dem people downstairs?" I asked.

"Well, it's three o'clock in the afternoon and those people are actually DSE's sanitary team. You didn't think us ladies shared our goodies without keeping ourselves and our area clean, did you? They don't call us Diamonds for no reason Chedda; we gotta stay shined up and clean."

She walked up to me and handed me the Starbucks cup that was full of French Vanilla cappuccino.

"I'm glad you awake, now they can come up here spray the room down and change the sheets."

"Damn, how long you been up? I see you Dressed all fresh with cups of coffee and shit." I said to her.

"First off, I don't sleep on the weekends honey; once you get use to this DSE night life, you won't t be sleeping either. I been up inside the money room, counting up all the profit from last night. And yeah, I ran a few errands and went to my house to take a shower. I bought that coffee for me, but since you obviously need the caffeine boost more than I do, I 'd rather you drink it. You did good last night, plus I need you energized to do it all over again tonight" Lacey said, while rubbing her hand up and down my stomach.

"Hey guys I need this room cleaned; up here, with a set of new sheets as well." Lacey yelled over the banister to the so called DSE sanitary team.

"Aye Chedda, you should check your phone too it's been ringing nonstop" Lacey said, then walked back inside the money room. I could hear the money counting machines start back up, Beep!

Chapter: 10
"Diamond Star Addicts"

After the cleaning crew was done sterilizing my private room. I grabbed my phone and looked at all the missed calls. Benji called; Dirty, Taylor, Stormy and even my dawg Dre called me a few times. I knew I had to talk to Benji but money comes first; so, I decided to call Dirty first to see if he had any money on the floor for me.

"Hello." Dirty answered first ring.

"Dirtball, wass good my man?"

"Chedda?! Man, I been blowing yo shit up all day. I need some more of that shit ASAP my nigga. Mu'fuckas goin' crazy for that shit can you' come through?"

I turned my volume down a little because Dirty's voice was echoing in my ear when he spoke. He probably had one of those cheap ass trac phones that everybody be hustling off of.

"Naw. I really can't pull up on you right now but you can pull up on me. Is that cool?"

"Damn dawg, I ain't gonna be able to leave the block until after midnight, you know this bitch a nonstop operation. I'm close to selling out and I wanted to grab some mo before I go dry. Is midnight too late for me to pull up on you?" He asked.

"Naw, Naw, that's straight. Do you know where the old Zoo Bar was ?"

"You talkin' bout the club downtown?"

"Yeah, that club"I responded

"Yeah, I know where it's at. Wat da fuck you got going on up there? I thought dat bitch was shut down?"

Dirty had no idea about the type of shit I was surrounded by, since the last time we use to hustled together and I knew he was going to be in for a big surprise.

"It is, but. . . just text me when you on yo way and then slide through; I can show you better than I can tell you.

"Alright bet" Dirty replied as he prepared to end the call, but I stopped him.

"Aye Dirty.."

"Yeah wassup?"

"About how much you had in mind to spend?

"A hunnit." Dirty said. I was caught off guard from the amount he just said and I froze for a minute. "Hello. You hear me nigga?" Dirty asked, making sure I was still on the phone.

"Yea, Yea, I heard you."

"Is dat straight or what? Because you sounding like you unsure my nigga," Dirty questioned.

"Naw, its good. I got you. Like I said just text me when you on you yo way".

I ended the call with Dirty and thought to myself how the fuck was I going to get a hunnit grand worth of work for him to buy from me tonight? Benji was out of town, plus I didn't want him getting suspicious of me selling to out siders, so calling him was my last option.

I calculated in my head how much I had left to sell. Five pounds of trees; twenty-two ounces of soft; and twenty-one ounces of Molly left. I would've had twenty-two ounces of

Molly but I had to remember I passed out a whole ounce for free during the event I last night.

Altogether the shit I had left to sell came up to eighty-nine thousand worth of cash for the prices I was pitching. Therefore, I was short the hunnit but not that far from it. I still had set to the side for the Diamond Stars to sell at the event for tonight and tomorrow but I can't dip into that because than the girls would be short on drugs to sell and BB would know I'm doing something on the side. I took another sip from my French Vanilla cappuccino and tried to figure out how I was going to get my hands on more pounds of green before midnight? If I sold Dirty the rest of the pounds I had left, I wouldn't have any for back up, in case the Diamonds ran out. They still had to make it through tonight and tomorrow. If they ran out of Coke or Molly, we still can manage... but everybody and they momma smokes weed. I remembered when I was at BB' s house chilling with Kharisma yesterday, I heard Hershey tell her to call Lacey for some of the clean shit, referring to the weed. I still didn't know wat she meant by clean shit, but obviously Lacey was the one to get the weed from and that's the only thing that mattered for my dilemma right now. I got up and headed to the money room where Lacey was still rubber banding knots of cash.

"Wassup sexy?" I said as I entered through the door.

Beep! the money counter went off as she loaded another stack.

"Just counting up.. oh, My God Chedda! you won't believe how much we made last night and I ain't even done counting yet. I don't know if it's because of the holidays or how turned up you had us last night, but we ain't neva made this much money in just one night."

I looked at all the neat piles of money stacked on top of the tables. My mind was so focused on the other shit I had going

187

on with Dirty, that I didn't pay attention to how much money was in front of me just from the DSE event.

"Well damn, how much did we make?" I asked, aiming to know how much money this nigga Benji was really pulling in off of this DSE tricking service he was running. Lacey waved me closer to the tables so she could explain.

"First lemme break down to you how I have the table setup, so you can understand it better. Usually the girls bring all their drug money to you but since your here with me this week, I just had Blondie and Hershey collect it and bring it to the money room along with the rest of our money, So this table to the left is filled with all the money that the Diamonds made from drugs throughout the night; this table to the right is for all the.... well, you know, it's for all the money that the Diamond Stars made from turning fantasies into reality."

"You mean from selling pussy?" I interrupted, clarifying things for her.

"We don't sell pussy Chedda, we turn fantasies into reality" Lacey snapped back, then continued... "But like I was saying...this table is the drug money and this table over here is the money from the Diamond Stars desirable pleasure."

"Ok, so you still didn't tell me how much we made'?"

"Well, if you just listen instead of interrupting me daddy, than I could. So, ever since you came along, I haven't been collecting the money made from the drugs because that's been your job, but I do know every last one of the girls told me they were sold completely out and that's never happened in one night alone. We made a hundred and twenty-six thousand and four hundred dollars just from drugs yesterday."

"Ain't dat some shit" I said out loud looking at the stacks of money on the table.

188

"Yeah, it is we never sold out that fast and it's a good thing that Benji left you double the amount of drugs, because if he didn't then we wouldn't have any to sell at the clubs or during the event tonight. That means we would've been losing out on a lot of money if he wasn't such a thinker."

As soon as the words left her mouth, my heart dropped. Here I was about to try to get more drugs from her and she was looking forward to me having more drugs to supply the Diamond Star models in order for them to sell tonight. I let her continue while I thought of wat to do next.

"Now over here on this tables we 're use to bringing in about a hunnit thousand a night."

"A hunnit thousand?" I murmured.

"Yeah; but Sundays numbers are usually a little lower because our clients would have been then burnt themselves out from Friday and Saturday. But, so far I counted up a hundred and forty thousand; and I still have this pile of money to finish counting" Lacey said, while pointing at a separate stack of money.

My mind was speed racing, I couldn't believe these girls was bringing Benji in all this money just from selling pussy. I mean, I already knew he was making a grip off the dope he had his girls selling, because I was the one pushing it on them and collecting the pros. But a hunnit thousand plus in one night just from selling pussy had me stuck. I clearly been in the wrong business my whole Twenty-three years of living.

"Chedda can you believe it?" Lacey asked, breaking me out of my thoughts.

"You mean to tell me, y'all hoes. . . Lacey squinted her eyes at me with terror and I stopped to reword my question. "I mean, you telling me y'all Diamond Stars made a hunnit and forty bands last night just from selling pu-. . .I mean from turning fantasies into reality?"

189

"Yep!" Lacey said with a smile on her face, then ran another stack of money thru the machine... Beep! That's over two hundred and fifty thousand that BB made in just one night between drugs and pussy together. Not to mention we still had tonight and tomorrow.

"Them some expensive ass fantasies y'all selling" I said in disbelief.

"He's going to be happy to hear these numbers Chedda. We neva made this much in one night and it's all thanks to you. I owe you big time for this" Lacey said, then turned her head and eyed me while she finished rubber banding a wad of money.

"I'mma suck the skin off yo dick tonight" She said smirking and licking her lips looking like she meant every word she said.

"Oh, and Chedda before I forget, he wanted me to tell you to call him when you woke up" She said flat out.

I knew she was talking bout Benji. I was gonna call him, but first I had to figure out how to get some more drugs because the ones Lacey thought the girls had coming tonight was already spoken for and sold to the bigger bidder.

"You said the girls sold out of all the product I supplied them with yesterday?" I asked, hoping she miss spoke the first time. I heard here I know she did but it was just my way of easing back onto the topic of drugs.

"Sure did. I told them to show up here first so they could pick up some more from you before they went out to the clubs and came back for the event; that way they could talk these horny niggas into buying it from them" She said, as if this was a part their million-dollar game plan.

"Wat if I told you I needed something that only you could give me?"

190

She set the money that she was counting, down on the table, turned around and stared at me.

"Like wat Chedda?" She said in a seductive tone. I knew she probably thought I was talking bout fuckin, but it was nothing but dollar signs on my mind at this time.

"Well. I may need some more of dat wedding cake before Benji gets back."

"Wedding cake? Chedda, he told me to put twenty pounds of that stuff in the bag, you couldn't have given it all to the girls; so wat did you do with it?" Lacey had a disturbed look on her face and I had to turn the tables quick.

"Wat happened to it? " She asked again, folding her arms waiting for a response.

"Baby just relax, everything is fine. The money for everything you gave me is safe and secure. You just would make daddy's day better if you gave me ten more pound."

I walked up close to her, set my coffee cup on the table and began kissing her on the sides of her neck.

"MUUUUUUUM," Lacey moaned, but you could tell she was tryna to fight it.

"Chedda, I need to know wat you did with dat stuff because it's dangerous... she stopped herself in midsentence then started back talking... "you just shouldn't be smoking it like dat It's very strong she finished saying.

"Naw baby, I promise it ain't for me to smoke. It's for the girls to supply at the event for tonight and tomorrow."

"Wat happened to the extra ten pounds your supposed to have on standby?" she asked, tryna to keep tabs on the work she dropped on me the other day."

"If I give them the ten pounds tonight and they sell out; then tell me wat will I give them to sell at tomorrows event?"

191

Why don't you just give them five pounds tonight and five tomorrow?" she asked, not going for the Oki-dokiee I was tryna pull on her. It was no way around it. I had to keep it all the way real with her so I could get what I wanted. I kissed on her neck a little more before I spoke.

"Listen, I just need you to come thru with the ten extra pounds for me. I'll give Benji the money for them along with all the other money; but I need you to get them for me before tonight." I went back to kissing on her neck.

"MuuuuuuuuuuuuuuuM, dat feels so good. I'mma have to talk to Benji first.

"Well talk. . . to.... him then" I said in between kisses then kept shooting my shot.

"Just tell him that the girls sold out during the event and we need more to proceed. I told you; I'll have the money before the night ends. My word," I told her one last time than started back sucking on her neck while she threw her head back.

"Oh my God, you know how to find my spot. OOOOh yes!" Lacey sounded like I was making her pussy wet. I ran my tongue across her neck, down to her chest, I popped one of her tittles out of her bra and started sucking on it while I massaged her other one.

"Oooohh shit . . .Ok I'll do it!" Lacey finally committed,

"But I need you to do something for me," she said with a devilish look in her eyes. I stopped sucking on her titty to face her and asked, "wat you got in mind sweetheart?"

She reached her hand down and grabbed my hard dick and said,

"I want this now!" She turned around, bent over in front of me and lifted up her skirt. She wasn't wearing any panties so all I seen was her moist pussy staring at me.

"Fuck me and nut all inside of me right now!" she tooted and waved her ass in my direction even more, enticing me with her dripping wet pussy.

I followed my lower head and dove right in. I let my robe drop to the floor as I back stroked Lacey over the table with nothing on, but the pair of Fendi slippers she gave me yesterday. I power stroked her with all my might, pulling her hair and smacking on her ass while she threw it back at me.

SMACK!
''OOOh Daddy!'' she screamed.
I dug my dick deep in her pussy and let my kids off in her willingly as her pussy clenched on to my dick, swallowing every last drop of cum. This may have been BB's bitch, but this weekend she was mine.

**After I gave Lacey some good dick, I got Dressed in a hurry and headed to my spot so I could put my uncle Jughead to work. I thought of a way where I could serve Dirty wat he wanted and supply the girls with enough party favors for the events. I had everything figured out. When I was selling soft and crack before I met Benji; Jughead use to cut my dope to stretch it and he was a master chemist at it. My plan was to have him stretch the twenty-two ounces of coke I had left and the twenty-one ounces Molly into enough for me to supply Dirty and the Diamond Stars for the weekend. Lacey was on her way to get ten more pounds of that fiya ass Wedding Cake strand for me from her house, while I was taking care of my business with Jughead.

Those ten pounds were going to be for the girls to serve at the event tonight and tomorrow, while I sold the five, I had left to Dirty. I pulled up in front of my spot but had nowhere to park. There were cars in my driveway blocking my old Charger that sat in the drive way and cars parked on the sides of the street in front of the place. I didn't know what the hell Jughead had going on. I started to beep the horn on my jeep nonstop until somebody came out and moved their car to free up a parking space for me but I remembered that I was pressed for time. I found somewhere to park a few houses down, grabbed my duffle bag and made my way into the spot. Jughead had people shoveling the walk way and sprinkling salt down in front of the house and how fast they were moving, I could tell they were high off the product I left him. I stepped foot on the porch and heard old school music playing and a lot of chattering like there was some type of party going on. As soon as I opened the door a strong smell of crack cocaine entered inside my nostrils. There were people everywhere bunched up inside our small house smoking and passing crack pipes left to right. One of the old mu'fuckas tried to pass me one as I looked for Jughead amongst them.

"Anybody seen Jughead?" I asked the smoked-out crowd but nobody answered. They all continued lighting up their pipes and blowing smoke in the air, bobbing to the sounds of Sade blasting through the new sound system Jughead bought.I walked over to the stereo and pressed pause on the music to get their attention.

"Aye wat you think ya doing over there, dats my jam!" An old dope fiend shouted.

"Listen, have any of y'all seen jughead?" I asked, over the voices of the annoyed crowd.

"Chedda?" I heard Jughead call out from the kitchen.

"Aye Jughead you betta get this cock sucka, he just turned off my jam!" the old fiend yelled.

194

"Y'all take it easy, this my nephew. Just take it easy, the party is still going, chill out" Jughead said, while clearing his way through the crowd.

"Wat da fuck is all this?" I said to him as soon as he approached me.

"Chedda my boy, good to see you. Come talk to me in the kitchen man, away from these people" Jughead said, while pressing play on the stereo before leading me back into the kitchen.

Once we got inside the kitchen, I set my duffle bag down and took a seat. Jughead had pots and jars all over the place with a little bit of the drugs I left him, just sitting out on the table.

"Wat da fuck is all this unc? Wat you got going on?"

"Chedda, they love it, look!" Jughead said excitingly as he reached under the sink and pulled out two small grocery bags full of money. "They really love it nephew, we're going to be rich." Jughead couldn't keep his self together.

"Calm down unc, calm down and put that money back up before somebody walks in and sees it" I warned him.

"First lemme give this to you." Jughead counted out ninety-six hunnit dollars and gave it to me.

"That's wat I owe you from the stuff you gave me, every last penny of it too!" He assured me, while tying up the bag that held the rest of his money.

I placed eighteen hunnit of it in my pocket and Benji's seventy-two hunnit inside my duffle bag. I even threw in another fourteen hunnit in the bag for Benji cause of the free ounce of molly I passed around last nite, then I got straight to bidness.

"Unc good looking on my cheese, but I need you to take care of something for me asap, nine-one-one."

"Wat is It nephew? If I could help do, Jughead gonna come through!" my uncle joked. I reached in my duffle bag and pulled out the twenty ounces of coke and set it on the table.

"I need you to put a two on dat for me" I said to him then continued digging in my bag. I pulled out the twenty-one ounces of Molly and tossed it on the table next to the powder. "I also need you to put a two on dat for me as well; and I need it within the next two hours" I told him.

Jughead's eyes was as big as moon pies. He stared at me then looked at all the drugs on the table then looked back at me again.

"now that's allot of drugs nephew. I can help you get it done, but you say I only got two hours?" He asked.

"Two hours unc; that's it" I repeated, hoping he could work his magic. He picked up one of the bags of Molly and examined it.

"Now I ain't neva had my hands on this until you came around so I don't know wat to use to cut it with. But I do know this shit here is powerful enough for you to stretch it to Alaska" he said, glorifying the strength of the Molly, BB supplied me with.

Wait a minute, I'll be right back, don't move" Jughead said, as he walked out the kitchen into the party he was hosting. Before I knew it, he was back with some old bald head mu'fucka who he called Dee.

"Now take a look at this Dee" Jughead told D, while handing him the Molly.

"They call that Molly on the streets. Its an upper," unc explained to him. "Now tell me wat you use to add a little bit of cut on it, without fuckin up the quality? Because, that there wat my nephew got is some good shit."

Dee held the bag of Molly up to the light as if he really was searching for the answer. "This looks just like that crystal meth shit that my white girl like in the hills."

"Fuck wat it looks like, wat do we need to cut it with Dee? C'mon now stop playing around" Jughead barked to his homeboy.

"Easy now, Easy now Jugg, I know exactly wat to use for this."

"Wat? Said jughead.

"You gotta go get some bath salt."

"Bath salt?" I asked.

"Dats right, Trust me, bath salt will do the trick and won't even take away from the quality" Dee said.

I looked at Jughead, wondering should I trust the info that this bald head nigga Dee was offering to us.

"Wat u think Jughead, you think bath salt is our answer?" I asked him.

"Well nephew, bath salt do look just like it, so it won't change the appearance of it. . . and I ain't gonna lie to you, my partner Dee here been cutting dope and stretching drugs for years, so I'mma have to trust him on this."

At this point I didn't have a choice but to put my trust into the two dope fiends that stood in front of me. I reached in my pockets and pulled out three hunnit dollars than gave it to Dee.

"Run to the store and buy however much bath salt you need, so you can put a two of cut on the twenty-one ounces."

I looked at Jughead. "Unc, I need you to start adding the cut to the Coke while I go up-stairs and take a shower. I need this shit done quick, I got somewhere to be. I'mma throw you something nice for taking care of this" I told him.

"Don't worry nephew, Jughead got you. But it's only one problem."

"Wat" I asked.

"I need the cut for the Coke. Do you have it?"

I took a deep sigh, reached in my pocket and gave him three hunnit dollars.

"Go to the corner store and buy some dorms. Use them to cut the soft and don't put more than a two on it" I instructed.

I walked through the crowd and went upstairs to my room with my duffle bag and then started to unload all the cash that was inside it from the previous sales I made. Jughead had given me the money for the product I gave him and that was right on time, now I needed him to come through for me with this so the show could continue.

I told him to add a two worth of cut to the drugs; which meant add two times the amount of cut to the amount of drugs I had. For example; If I only had three ounces of coke; putting a two on that would be me adding six ounces worth of cut to the cocaine; which would give me nine ounces of cocaine total once it all mixed together. If Jughead and Dee did everything right, I would end up with sixty—six ounces of cocaine and sixty— three ounces of Molly. That would be perfect. I could take thirty-six ounces of Coke and thirty-six ounces of Molly to give to the Diamond Stars in order to supply the events for tonight and tomorrow. Then, I would still have enough to sell Dirty in order to fulfill the hunnit thousand dollar order he placed with me.

I opened my duffle bag; I took a look at all the money I was making from the drugs since I started selling on the side. I thought about dividing it up as usual, placing half of it in my safe here and placing the other half at my loft, but I changed my mind when the sound of all those people down stairs disturbed my thoughts. It seemed like Jughead was turning this spot into a one stop shop drug house and I ain't feel safe keeping too much money here anymore. I placed my money back into my duffle bag and grabbed my twin gloc .23 so that I can take it to the loft with its sibling. I reached under my bed and opened the small safe that held the sixty thousand, then put it all inside my duffle bag along with the other money. Since I had my loft, I didn't keep much here at the spot with Jughead anymore. The only things here were my gun arsenal, a few out fits and a few pairs of shoes. I kept my old charger parked in the driveway so Jughead could use it to get around while I was gone but that was about it.

My money was coming with me, I hopped in the shower and got Dressed, hoping that Jughead and Dee took care of everything. I looked at the time and seen that it was six o'clock. I knew I was running late and had to hurry, so I could meet Lacey at her house to pick up the pounds she had for me. She didn't wanna ride with any drugs in the car with her and I had to respect that. She was waiting for me to show up at her place, and grab the weed so that she could head back to the venue.

I was expecting the stars to show up at the venue for the product by eight o'clock, which meant I only had two hours left to handle my business. I picked up my Louie duffle bag and grabbed an extra backpack for the drugs, then walked down stairs to the kitchen. The smoke session was still going on in our living and dining room and I thought I was catching a contact from all the crack smoke that was lingering in the air.

"Hey, there he is. We been waiting on you" Jughead said, while passing his friend Dee the crack pipe across the kitchen counter. I looked on the table and seen two big piles of the product. One pile was the cocaine and one pile was the Molly.

"We were just about to bag it up in some zip locks for you."

"Naw, you good unc, I 'm glad you didn't. I need y'all to help me separate it, weigh it and bag it up into all ounces."

"All ounces? That's gonna take forever nephew" Jughead complained.

"Not if we work together. Now c'mon I told you I got something nice for you when we done."

I grabbed both of my scales out the cabinet and set them on the counter. Jughead pulled out the zip locks and we all got to work.

It took about 45 minutes to complete the mission.

"All done nephew, you need anything else?" Jughead asked me.

I separated the thirty-six ounces of cocaine and the thirty-six ounces of molly that I planned to give the Diamond Stars. I counted another twenty-seven ounces of soft and twenty—four ounces of Molly, then set them aside for Dirty. There was three ounces of Molly and three ounces of cocaine left. I picked them up off the table and handed them to Jughead.

"This for you unc, make sho you give yo boy Dee something too."

"I'll be damned! Have I ever told you, I love you nephew?" Jughead said while Dee held out his fist in front of me, tryna give me some dap. I dapped him up, then tossed all the drugs into my backpack and left out.

"I'mma get at you next week unc," I told him as I was walking out the door.

"Take it easy out there nephew, and remember, this a game of chess not checkers!" he hollered over the old school music that was playing.

I walked down the street, jumped in my Track Hawk and tossed my bags into the backseat. I started my engine and texted Lacey to let her know, I was on my way to her house. I had just enough time to get to her and make it back to the venue before the girls showed up to pick up their supply for the night.

I arrived at Lacey's house and seen her car parked in the driveway. I looked at my phone and seen that I still hadn't received a call nor a text back from her since I sent her a message. I knocked on her door and rang the doorbell.

Knock! Knock! Knock! Ring! Ring! Boom! Boom! Boom! I banged on her door waiting for an answer but she didn't respond. I pulled out my phone and called her number. It just rang, and rang, then went to voicemail. I don't know wat da fuck she was doing. I knew she was inside because her car was here. I twisted the door knob to see if it was unlocked and come to find out it was. I opened the door and walked inside her house. The lights were off but the music was playing. I shut the door behind me and entered her living room.

"Lacey?" I called out, tryna figure out where she was.

I heard noises coming from her kitchen area. I walked in her kitchen but nobody was there. I heard the noise again then I saw a door attached to the kitchen that was shut. I twisted the door knob and opened it. I heard the noise clearer. It sounded like a plastic bag rattling or something. There was steps that led to the basement. I started to grab the gloc on my hip and pull it out while I walked down the stairs, but instead I just kept my hand on it in case some shit jumped off.

I went down each stair slowly and quietly. I still heard the sounds of a plastic bag moving around. I saw a bright light at the bottom of the stairs; so, I was sure somebody was down there. Once I made it to the bottom I peeked around the corner and saw Lacey with mask and gloves on, holding a garbage bag full of weed, shaking it up and down.

"Aaahhh! Oh shit! Chedda, you almost gave me a fuckin heart attack! Wat you doing here?" Lacey asked. Lacey's screaming almost made me draw my gun and shoot her ass until I realized it was her.

She was so scared that she dropped the bag of weed she was holding.

" I knocked on yo door and tried to call yo phone but you didn't answer" I told her, examining everything that was in front of her.

She had tons of weed spread out on a table with a bowl full of light greyish tan powder and a spray bottle full of liquid next to it.

"Wat da fuck you doing?" I asked, as I approached the table she was standing over.

"Wat da fuck you doing, just walking thru my house?" She snapped back defensively.

I reached my hand to grab hold of the bowl on the table with the powdery substance in it, but she quickly smacked my hand and stood in front of it.

"You need not touch dat without any gloves on?" she said with attitude.

"Wat I need gloves for? Wat da fuck is dat, you putting on the weed?" I drilled. She paused and looked at me silently.

"Chedda, just go upstairs and wait for me please" Lacey replied calmly, but I wasn't going nowhere without answers. It all started to click in my head and I dug in her brain a little deeper to see what I could find.

"I ain't going nowhere until you tell me wat da fuck is all this?" I told her. "I already heard about the clean weed and the dirty weed; so, you might as well tell me wassup?"

I was acting like I knew more than I really did. Lacey took a deep sigh behind the mask.

''You, have to swear that you won't say shit to nobody Chedda, Benji would literally kill me."

"It seems like everybody already know except me. So, wat the fuck is going on?"

"Don't nobody know shit other than me and BB. We just told our main girls who live in the house with us not to fuck around with our Wedding Cake strand anymore; but they don't know wat it is."

 "Well quit beating around the fuckin' bush and tell me or I'mma find out for myself" I told her, and I meant every word.

 "Ok. just chill. . .It's Fentanyl."

"Fentanyl? Wat da fuck is Fentanyl?"

"It's some type of addictive drug that Benji gets from his connect. It's usually sold to heroin addicts but we put just a little bit of it on our weed to keep our clientele coming back to shop with us. Why do you think people are so addicted to our weed?"

I couldn't believe the shit that just came out of Lacey's mouth. She handed me a mask and a pair of gloves so I could examine the drug closely. It was a powder substance that resembled Heroine, except it was a lighter color. This whole time, y'all had me smoking this shit!? "

"Sorry Chedda it's all part of the business. I don't put that much on there, just enough to get a person hooked. Now you gonna keep this between me and you right?"

I aint know what to think or how to feel but it was all starting to make sense to me. Benji must've started off giving the laced weed to girls he wanted to pimp out so that they would get addicted to his product and keep coming back to him. Then he would have them hooked on the drug and eventually hooked on him, giving him the opportunity to convince them into selling pleasures and working for him; luring them in with his lavish lifestyle he provided for them.

"Chedda!" Lacey shouted breaking my train of thought. She was looking at me searching for some assurance that I wouldn't tell the streets her and BB's secret. "You got it. This between me and you" I said, thinking in my head how much of a grimey, clever nigga Benji was.

"Good. Now hold the bag open while I put the rest of this weed in here with our special ingredient," she directed.

I held the bag open; Lacey grabbed the spray bottle full of liquid then shook it up and began spraying the inside of the bag. After she stopped spraying, she began to put the pounds of weed in it, one at a time.

"Alrite now give me the bag," she said , while reaching for it.

She grabbed the garbage bag full of pounds from me, closed it up then began shaking it up and down and all around. You can tell she was making sure the drug she sprayed inside the bag spread thoroughly through-out the marijuana. Her method was to mix the powdery fentanyl substance with a liquid and use a spray bottle to disburse it on the inside of the bag where the weed was going. She told me that she never spray it directly on the weed so that the weed wouldn't get soaked. We continued doing this until we were done with ten pounds worth, then we went back to the venue to prepare for tonight's event.

We got back to the venue around 7:00pm. I followed behind Lacey's Benz in my Hawk and thought about what I just found out about their made-up strand of Wedding Cake marijuana, the whole ride there. When we walked inside all the Diamond Stars were already there and most of them were waiting on me to give them their supply so they could venture off into night clubs and start their days work. I went straight into their changing booth with my backpack full of drugs and started handing out packages to them.

"About time," Big Booty LaLa complained, while brushing her hand up against my dick purposely.

I ignored her advance I had too much on my mind for me to be worried about a piece of pussy. I continued handing out the drug packages to all the Diamond Stars. All together I handed out five pounds of Wedding Cake, eighteen ounces of Coke and eighteen ounces of Molly. I put up the same exact amount so that I could give it to them for tomorrow's event and the rest of the drugs I had left were for Dirty. I started walking upstairs until I heard a soft voice call my name.

"Chedda baby" I turned around and seen Kharisma standing there looking bowlegged with her ass poking out like a pumpkin.

"Wassup Queen?" I answered.

"I was hoping you was gonna stop by today. I was looking for you, I had a present I wanted to give you" She said turning all the way around, doing an about face to make sure I seen all dat ass she was working with.

"My bad, it was a lot going on. Maybe you could skip the club and come up here with me to give me my gift?" I shot in the dark but I think she was with it.

"But then; I'll be missing out on money daddy, is dat wat you want?"

"I'll miss out on wat-eva as long as I get a piece of you, I said to her, licking my Lips and looking at her tempting body. She smiled a blush and then started walking in my direction up the stairs. She made it to my step and I took her hand in mine, leading the way to my private room. I was finally about to fuck another one of BB's top Diamond and I couldn't wait to check her off my list.

I held the bag of drugs in one hand and Kharismas's hand in the other as we walked inside my private room. But I was caught by an unexpected surprise. Stormy was laying in the bed on top of the sheet's ass naked with a bowl of strawberries and chocolate syrup. Stormy locked eyes with me and I was stuck in shock with Kharisma's hand still in mine's, tryna see wat was going to be Stormy's reaction next.

 Stormy took hold of the bowl of strawberries that was sitting on the bed with her and heaved them at me like she was a baseball pitcher. They flew everywhere in my direction.

"Maybe another time" Kharisma said as she let go my hand and walked back downstairs, laughing and snickering.

"See dats wat da fuck I'm talkin' bout Chedda, you neva fuckin satisfied!"

Stormy screamed in anger and hurt. She was up out of the bed, putting back on her clothes.

 "Wat da fuck you talking bout, we wasn't bout to do nothing." I lied.

"Yeah, whatever! You think I'm fuckin stupid?! That hoe does the same shit with BB when he's here!"

"Baby, chill".

"Aint no baby, chill. Here I am going out my way to please you by allowing Taylor into our relationship, but, nooooo, dats still not enough for you."

I walked up on her and attempted to calm her down but she was overheating.

"Get yo fuckin hands off me. I waited here for you all day and when you finally do get here, you choose to walk in with another bitch by yo side. I'm out, done for tonight, I'm not working until Benji gets back!"

She had nothing but a pair of pants and high heels on but she still stormed out of the room half naked with the rest of her clothes in her hand. She had caught a niggah off guard, I didn't know wat to say.

"Are you Benji's bitch or my bitch!? "I yelled.

That must've gotten her attention because she stopped dead in her tracks, turned around, squinted her eyes at me and flicked me off before she turned and continued marching out.

I looked at all the strawberries and broken glass on the floor then just took a seat on the edge of the bed. This day was getting crazier and crazier by the minute. I took off all of my clothes and put on the Fendi robe and slippers that Lacey bought me. I rolled up a blunt of the Wedding Cake weed, not giving a fuck about what was on it at the time. I got up and walked into the money room and watched the video monitors looking at everything that was going on around me.

I fired up the blunt and took in a huge cloud to ease my mind, "Cough! Cough! Cough! Cough!" My lungs begged for forgiveness but my body craved for more. I inhaled again and blew the smoke into the air. I watched Stormy on camera as she walked through the parking lot and drove away in her Durango. I looked to my left at all the neat stacks of money that were on the tables to the side, I felt like a boss. Like I belonged exactly where I was standing.

I looked back at the screens showing all the half-naked women who were preparing their selves to work for me tonight. I now know how Benji felt as the one in position of power. I smoked and smoked as I thought about everything that happened so far and the night was only just beginning to get started. Allot of shit never seemed to surprise me in these streets, but I never expected to find out that Benji and Lacey was powdering their weed with a highly addictive hardcore drug. I was making this my last time smoking this shit; on top of that, I didn't want it to trigger my asthma. I inhaled another cloud easing my mind even more, I thought about the hundred thousand dollar play that I had on the floor for tonight.

Dirty was loving the drugs I was given him, so that meant the streets must've been eating them up. I don't believe no one in the city was putting fentanyl on their weed except for BB and Lacey, so there was no wonder he was known for having the most powerful strand marijuana around. I admit, it was a dirty move, but it was smart. It turned his clients into addicts; all of his clients were Diamond Star addicts. As a matter of fact, any and everybody associated with DSE became a Diamond Star addict and that's exactly what Benji wanted.

The users were addicted to the drugs DSE supplied, the sex addicts were addicted to all the beautiful erotic women that DSE offered and the Diamond Stars themselves were addicted to the money; attention, fame and love that Benji gave them, once they did what he wanted.

Benji Bands was a DSE addict himself and it was clear for me to see he was addicted to POWER. DSE gave him power over all of these things he created for himself and it all started with his bottom bitch Lacey and his special strand of weed to lure in attractive women, who smoked marijuana. Lacey promoted it for him, then motivated the women to be a part of Diamond Star Entertainment, while BB sealed the deal giving the women a lifestyle of attention that they only could Dream of.

They were selling drugs and sex, turning Johns' fantasies into reality, while Benji was the one molding these women visions and turning their fantasies into reality. They were all addicts of different habits and creatures of the same habit; which was to feed their addiction by any means necessary. I took another puff of the smoke while I was deep in thought tryna figure out my next move, so I could benefit off this DSE movement that Benji influenced everyone to create. I now understand why Benji stood in front of these damn video monitors, smoking in silence all damn day. It was therapeutic for the mind. It was peace, it was power...it was addictive.

Chapter: 11
"Business Comes with A Price"

It was fifteen minutes past midnight and the place was in full effect. The money was flowing in rapidly just like last night and the clients were more active than usual. The VIP section was in rotation nonstop. After one room was done being occupied, we had to send the cleaning crew in to disinfect and change the sheets for the next customer in line. It was the first time we had to make a waiting list for VIPs.

Allot of regular clients were looking to spend some time with Stormy but she was a no-show, thanks to me getting caught up earlier.

We missed out on a nice chunk of change because of that. One thing I can say about most of her clients; they were loyal to her. The majority of them turned around and exited as soon as they got the news that she wasn't working tonight.

I read the text that I received from Dirty. I laid on the bed getting my dick sucked by one of the Diamond Stars named Tongue Ring. She was on break and she wouldn't stop crying and complaining about the other Diamonds stealing her shine so I gave her something that would shut her up till it was time for her to go back to work. She twirled her tongue ring around the tip of my dick then spit on it. She went back to sucking all the saliva off my dick. She had a mean head game on her, but it was only money on my mind; so, I interrupted the li'l freak recreation time and sent her back to work.

"Hey li'l momma, it's bout that time" I told her. She took my dick out her mouth.

"You don't wanna buss fa me boss? Just buss in my mouth so I can tase it" She said looking at me with her sexy brown eyes.

"Naw, It's time for you to get back to work, I gotta take care of something" I told her.

"Awww, I was just about to get to the center of the tootsie pop" She complained, then kissed the tip of my dick and got up. "See you later Chedda." She walked her short li'l body out the room.

I got out the bed and got myself together for the meeting I had with Dirty. He just sent me a message, saying that he was on his way and I wanted everything to be on point. I had a special booth that I told Blondie to keep empty just for him. I put a bottle of Moet in there along with a fifth of Grey Goose to quench his thirst. I grabbed the bag of work I had for him along with my Gloc then headed to the money room where Hershey was, so I could watch the camera monitors and wait for him to arrive.

Mean While

Honk! Honk! Honk!

"Damn man, who hell is dat beeping they fuckin horn like that in front of da spot?" Dirty asked the other drug dealers on the porch as he walked up the steps to enter the house.

"Oh, dats for me, I'm bout to serve him now" A young dealer from his block responded.

"Well hurry up and go handle dat; and make sho you let him know to never beep his fuckin' horn in front of this house again. He making the block hot with dat shit. That's yo last sell for the night, it's past twelve. We'll get back to this money tomorrow." Dirty finished instructing the young hustla then went inside the house so he could prepare the money he was about to bring Chedda for the supply of drugs.

The undercover federal agents were parked on the next corner over, watching Dirty's every move. They noticed the rapid increase in drug traffic that picked up on his street within the last seventy-two hours, and they were monitoring his phone calls more than usual aiming to locate the source of their problem. They sent an undercover to pose as an addict to buy some of the product earlier from one of the dealers. Once they tested the drug that they bought, they noticed the quality difference. It was purer which meant it was stronger and that was clearly the reason for the growth of drug traffic that was occurring in front of their eyes. They've been on Dirty's trail for the past two years and still have not seized the opportunity to catch him with a big load. They were only able to catch him with a petty ounce and a few thousand dollars. That wasn't enough to satisfy them. They wanted Dirty's drug operation put to rest for good and if they could catch a bigger fish with him; then that would make the cake taste even sweeter. They had caught a potential incriminating conversation between Dirty and a guy who he addressed as Chedda, during a phone call earlier. They were interested in finding out who Chedda was. Judging from the phone conversation they heard earlier; he could be Dirty's new supplier. They sat in the car awaiting on Dirty to come out so they could follow him to his drug transaction, with plans to initiate a traffic stop on Dirty once he departed from his supplier, in hopes to catch him with a significant amount of drugs in his possession.

Dirty exited the house with a backpack over his shoulder and walked off the crowded porch to get inside his vehicle. He started his car and drove off his million-dollar block to meet up with Chedda, while the undercover federal agents trailed behind him.

* * *

"Ohhh shiiittt! Mmm Chedda yes! " Hershey screamed as she came all over myself face. Her juices even got on the money that her body was sitting on.

I stood up wiping my mouth, while Hershey tried to get herself back together before someone walked in on us. I helped her get off the top of the table I sat her on. It was fifties and hunnit dollar bills stuck to the back of her thighs and inner legs from the sticky nut that came out her cat. I snatched all the bills off of her and set them back on the table next to the money counter machine.

"Damn baby, now I see why they call you Hershey; You taste just like candy" I said while licking the sweet taste of her cream from my lips.

''I want to sit on yo dick so bad Chedda, why you won't give me none?" She whined.

"Just keep staying on my good side and I'mma bless you ma" I said to Hershey grabbing on my dick thru my boxers to tease her.

I knew exactly what I was doing too. Once she showed me that she wanted this dick at Benji's house the other day; I knew exactly how to play her. She was a weak link that Benji kept close to him and now that I discovered I had something she wanted; I planned to keep it in the safe, then use it to attack her weakness when the time was right. Like my uncle Jughead say ''This is Chess, not checkers''.

I looked on the monitors and paid attention to Road Kill and Hitman as they opened the door for a client. Dirty appeared on the screen with a bag in his hands. It looked like he was having trouble entering through Road Kill with his bag until he opened it and showed him that it was all money inside. I saw Blondie approach Dirty to assign him a booth. I texted Blondie immediately alerting her that the client who just arrived was my special guest I was waiting on. I saw her look at her phone than she walked Dirty to the booth I had assigned for him. I grabbed my bag, tied my robe and headed down to the booth where Dirty was.

"You going somewhere already Chedda?" Hershey asked as I started walking towards the door.

"Yeah, baby girl. Just hold it down and keep counting dat money, so we know how much we brought in tonight."

I worked my way through the crowd but it was jam packed and everyone was stopping me to give handshakes and dap. One of them even offered to buy me a plate of food from the food bar and a lot of them knew my name. They all remembered my face from last night and thanked me for the good time they had. I saw Blondie dealing with another client, so I figured she already had Dirty situated. I pulled the curtain to the side and entered the booth.

"Dirty what's good my man?"

"Yo Chedda, this place is poppin' my nigga, is it a birthday party or something?" He asked.

"Naw man, this Diamond Star Entertainment my nigga; where fantasies get turned into reality!" I said, geeked up while I popped the top on the bottle of Grey Goose I had on the table for him.

I poured both of us a drink then sat down across from him in the booth. He took a sip from the glass and eyed the menu that Blondie left him to look at.

"Man, this shit wild. It's naked women walking all around like it's a strip club or something. And look at you in that fancy robe, like you working at the playboy mansion or something" He said with nigga please type of look.

I burst out laughing at Dirty's reaction to the DSE event. I was use to the activities going on around me; but to a nigga who was just experiencing it for the first time it was unbelievable and their reaction was always the funniest.

"Yeah man, this the type of lane I'm into now. All that robbin' shit for the birds it's all about milking the game off these bitches" I said, taking another gulp of the Grey Goose.

"Oh, so you a pimp now?" He asked. The word insulted me inside. I think it was because BB always planted the seed in my head to never call him a pimp.

I asked BB once before, if he was a pimp; and he smacked everything off of the table in anger. I never knew why the word made him so angry but he told me to never call him that ever again.

"I'm nothing like a pimp my nigga and don't eva call me that, I don't get down how pimps get down" I said, staring at him with a still face.

"My bad, my bad, playa. I' m just tryna figure out wats going on here? No disrespect" He apologized; probably because he felt like I had home court advantage if anything was to turn sideways between us in here.

"None taking" I told him. I reached for the bag and handed it to him.

"Take a look at that... . It's twenty-seven ounces of Coke; twenty-four ounces of Molly and five pounds of green. He unzipped the bag and peeked inside it.

"Is it ok for me to check it out on the table?" Dirty asked, referring to the drugs.

"Yeah go head, it's just you and me in here. Dirty poured the drugs onto the table and counted each Ziplock package, one by one. He handed me the black bag that he had sitting next to him.

"It's all yours just empty it out so I can put my work inside it he said, happy about the drugs he just received. I emptied

217

the rubber band stacks of money on the table. I gave Dirty his bag back and he started placing the drugs inside of it. I counted up a hunnit thousand, then placed all of it inside my bag which once held the drugs Dirty just purchased. Now that I had Jughead adding cut on the Coke and Molly; a hundred percent of the proceeds from my transactions all belonged to me. I was just hoping I didn't receive any complaints about the potency from Dirty once he put it on the street.

"So, you really liking the product huh?" I said, tryna lower the uneasy energy in the air.

"Man they can't get enough of it. I really need you to hit me off with some more pounds of that tree. Five pounds ain't gonna be enough my nigga. Everybody around me fell in love with it including my damn self. What the name of that strand anyway?" Dirty asked.

 "It's call Wedding Cake" I told him.

"Wedding Cake?" He repeated with a puzzled look on his face.

"Yeah, they call it Wedding Cake because the shit so good, it make you wanna stay married to it." Dirty burst out laughing, raising his fist to give me some dap.

"Well, I need some more of that Wedding Cake asap!" Dirty said while dapping me up and catching his breath from laughing so hard.

"Don't even trip, I'mma try to get my hands on some more of it soon, just work with me''.

I poured another glass of the Grey Goose and took a gulp. Then Dirty broke the short moment of silence.

"Tell me what is this place?" He asked with a curious stare in his eyes.

''I can show you better than I can tell you" I said to Dirty.

"Wat you mean by that?"

"Grab that menu and find you somebody of yo choice."

Dirty looked at the menu.

"Ooowweee, I wouldn't mind this sexy thang right here" he said, pointing at Stormy's picture. I let out a small laugh.

"Pick another one, she not working today."

"A'ight then, give me her. He pointed at the bad bitch Barbie and I couldn't be mad at him for it.

"Now pick another one," I said grabbing the bottle of Champagne out of the ice bucket.

"Wassup with this one?" Dirty asked pointing at a Diamond Star named Cakes.

I pressed the red button, and five minutes later Blondie walked into the booth right on cue.

"Is there someone you'll like to share your time with?" Blondie asked Dirty, assuming that he was the one who pressed the button to place an order on one of our Diamond Stars.

"Yeah, You!'' Dirty joked and took a sip from his cup.

We both started laughing. Blondie looked at me.

"Blondie, I want you to get Barbie and Cakes and bring them in here for my manz Dirty. He wants the three-way special'' I told her.

"Ok; that'll be thirty-five hundred'' Blondie said, waiting for the payment.

As soon as I heard the amount, I instantly realized how the girls was bringing in so much money in one night. It was fifty of them and they were all charging a fortune for the PLEASURE.

"Blondie I'll take care of the tab" I told her.

Blondie looked at me with her eyes squinting as if she wanted to say something.

"Ok, well give me a few minutes and I'll send your stars right in sir" Blondie said to Dirty, then walked out.

"So you telling me, these two girls bout to come to me and let me have my way with them?" He asked as if he didn't believe it.

"Aye, you owe me one for this."

"Nigga if these bitches show up in here and have a threesome I owe you two!"

We chopped it up for a few minutes and drunk a little champagne, waiting on the girls to come. Hershey walked inside the booth, catching both me and Dirty's attention.

"Excuse me, I didn't mean to interrupt" she said, holding a stack of money in her hands.

"Chedda, we are all booked up in VIP but clients are still requesting VIP rooms, what do you want me to do?"

"How many stars are on break or not occupied right now?" I asked her.

"It's a handful not occupied right now. Why you ask dat?"

I want you to ask the clients would they accept an extra diamond star along with their choice, for the same VIP price instead Of a VIP room because they're all booked. If they agree, then grab whichever Diamonds not occupied and have them aid and assist the client's choice in turning his fantasy into reality. If the client doesn't accept that, then just tell him he'll have to be patient until the ones before him finish up".

"That's clever" Hershey said, before leaving the booth.

I filled both me and Dirty's champagne glasses and made a toast. This nigga was officially my new business partner. Everything about his business made the night much better for me. The girls were supplying the night clubs and DSE events with the product, and Dirty was happy with the load he just received from me to supply his block. Everybody was happy.

"To our new business partnership. May it be prosperous and long lived."

I held the flute glass in the air towards Dirty's and we toasted our glasses, tossing back the Champagne.

"Ooooh la la. . . Who 's the cutie next too you Chedda?" Cakes asked while stepping into the booth with Barbie right behind her.

I looked at Dirty and saw his eyes grow real wide, staring at Cakes and Barbie's naked titties and pussy. They both had devil horns on their heads.

"That's my cue, dawg" I said as I got up, grabbed my bag of money and gave Dirty some dap, preparing to leave.

"Whose champagne is this? Is it yours daddy?" Barbie asked Dirty while grabbing the half-filled Moet bottle from the table.

"Yeah, you want some?" Dirty asked.

Barbie took the open Moet bottle and stuck the neck of it inside her pussy.

"Ummmmm" she moaned, then pulled it out and handed it to Dirty. "No baby, the question is do you want some? Now drink up and taste wat you finna get" Barbie ordered, while Cakes sat on top of his lap.

"Ladies, why don't you turn his fantasies into reality for me I said to them, then looked towards Dirty. " And Dirty... welcome to Diamond Star Entertainment!" I walked out the tent so Dirty could enjoy his stay.

Mean While

"Wat in the hell you think is going on in there?" detective Timothy asked his partner.

They were parked across the street in a small parking lot trying to keep an eye on Dirty's vehicle and the front entrance of the club he went into. They were getting more exhausted and more suspicious about the activities that was going on inside the building as the hours passed by.

"I don't know, but I do know it's well past three o'clock and the night club's curfew end at two. So, whatever is going on in there is officially illegal. Do you wanna call for back up and raid the place? Detective Timothy's partner asked him.

"No, that 'll gives our fish a chance to get away. We can't prove it's his if we just find it in the building with a bunch of people, we have to make sure it's on him. We'll just sit and wait until he comes out".

"But he's been in there forever!" Detective Timothy's partner was growing tired from their days work. They been staked out, watching and following Dirty since seven O'clock in the morning, yesterday.

Detective Timothy stepped out of their Hunter green F-150 truck for a smoke break. He was truly exhausted as well but he didn't want to miss out on his opportunity to finally bring Dirty down and possibly open up a new investigation on the guy Dirty called Chedda.

Detective Timothy lit his cigarette and stared at the busy night club across the street. He watched as heavy traffic left in and out constantly. Something didn't seem right about the

223

crowd. He saw a few females enter but it was mainly all men who went inside the building. At first, he thought he may have been over thinking it when he saw more than a few men in their fifties and sixties going inside the club, but now that his partner pointed out the time; it was clear something was strange about this gathering that was happening. All night clubs were supposed to be closed by two and it was three forty-five in the morning; well past the curfew. Detective Timothy took one last puff from his cigarette than tossed it on the ground. He got back inside the warm heated truck with his partner, who was trying his hardest to stay awake.

"We gotta get this son of a bitch" Timothy said to his partner.

"Yeah, we need to find out wats going on inside that place," he shot back.

They both sat tiredly waiting for Dirty to exit the club. They, waited and waited...

***

It was four-thirty in the morning and I was exhausted from the night. I heard the event still in effect downstairs but you could tell it wasn't as live as it was hours ago and I couldn't wait till it was over. As much money as I seen Lacey and Blondie bringing into the money room; I was more than satisfied. I'm not sure if we made as much as yesterday but it definitely was a good night's worth of work.

Lacey entered my private room as I laid on the bed going through my missed call log. I haven't had a chance to return any body's call today; net even Benji's. Stormy still haven't called me since she left. I knew I was going to have to work overtime to get back in good with her. whatever I had to do, I knew I had to do it fast because we still had one more night for her to shine like a diamond and I needed her back at work. Her fan base was too big to go another night without. When she walked out the door, a lot of money left with her.

"Wats wrong daddy, you tired? The night just got fun" Lacey said, approaching the bed.

"Yeah, I ain't gonna lie, today hit a nigga with some curve balls" I said still looking at my phone.

''I know you ain't still thinking bout earlier at my house?'' Lacey said.

"Naw, baby I'm past that. I'm just thinking bout getting ready for tomorrow."

"Runnin the show isn't as easy as you thought huh?" Lacey asked while rubbing her hand on my back."

''Now, you see wat I have to go through every weekend. What happened to Stormy tonight?" She asked.

"I guess she thought I had something going on with Kharisma, so she left" I replied.

225

"Is dat so? Well doesn't she know that a king sometimes has to satisfy the kingdom's needs?" Lacey hit me with a question and a statement all at once. It was some slick shit dat she probably learned from BB.

She climbed in the bed with me and then pulled my boxer shorts off.

"Don't you worry bout her daddy; I'll handle her tomorrow. You just relax and close your eyes, while I fulfill your fantasies" Lacey said then put my dick in her mouth and worked her magic.

She massaged my balls while she sucked my soul away from me. I dropped my phone and closed my eyes. Lacey's wet warm mouth was feeling like heaven. I don't know where she learned how to suck dick but hands down; I have to give praise to her teacher. I felt my nut rising to the top like it was on a mission to Mars. My toes curled and I shook like I got electrocuted as I unleashed every drop of cum, I had left in me. I think I'm in love with this life and everything that it brings me. Sweet Dreams was all she wrote.

Mean While

"Hey Lonzo, Lonzo wake up dammit!" Detective Timothy screamed at his partner. Lonzo woke up and looked at the time on his watch. It read 9:15AM.

"You fuckin fell asleep! I told you to wake me up when you felt yourself getting tired so I could watch out while you took your break and get some rest" Detective Timothy said, in disgust with his partner.

"Awww shit, my fault Detective, I couldn't control it. One minute I was watching the place and then the next minute I was watching the back of my eye lids."

They looked across the street in the club's parking lot and seen that it was close to empty. There were only three cars in sight and neither of them was Dirty's.

"We missed him again!" Detective Timothy said angrily, while slapping the steering wheel of his truck.

"Hey, Hey Detective, take a look at this. Do you know dat guy?" Detective Timothy reached for the binoculars that sat on his dashboard and put them up to his face so he could look through them. He seen a light brown skin guy carrying a duffle bag and a backpack on his shoulders. The guy was approaching an SUV that triggered something in Detective Timothy's mind.

"Hey give me the camera quick" Detective Timothy said to Lonzo.

Lonzo handed him the camera and Detective Timothy snapped picture after picture, being sure to capture the guy's face and the license plate on the Jeep that he remembered seeing on Dirty's street a few days ago.

227

"Don't you remember that Jeep from our suspects street a couple of days ago?" Timothy asked his partner.

"A couple of days ago?" Lonzo repeated unsure.

"Yeah, remember we saw Mr. Glenfield get inside of it when it arrived in front of his house? I said something about it to you but you told me that it was probably nothing and more than likely just another junkie that he was selling to."

"Oh yeah, yeah I remember now" Lonzo lied, aiming to convince his Detective that he actually does pay attention when they're out man hunting.

"There's something up with that guy. I'm going to run his license plate to see who's the jeep registered to, so we can get an identity on him" Detective Timothy replied as he took more pictures while watching the guy set the two bags inside of the SUV then get inside.

The guy drove away giving Detective Timothy a clear shot at the license plate number on the vehicle. Timothy snapped one last shot.

"Alright; now we can go home and get some rest Lonzo, but I'm blaming this slip up on you. We were supposed to have Glenfield in our custody right now. We're coming back at it bright and early after New Year's" Detective Timothy said as he started the engine and drove away.

***

** I was just pulling into my parking spot in front of my building. I looked to the right of me and seen Stormy and Taylor's rides both parked in the same row, so I knew they were upstairs in the loft. They probably didn't expect me to come home today because they both knew wat I had going on for the weekend with' DSE, but this couldn't wait.

I wanted to fix things with Stormy asap before I let it drag out and get worst. I woke up this morning in the venue with Lacey and we both made sure the count was correct from yesterday. I ended up falling asleep while the event was still going on last night but lucky for me, Lacey and Blondie took control of everything and shut it down by six in the morning. We had a good night with only today's event ahead of us before the New Years and before Benji's return. I bagged up all of the drug money made from the last few days and decided to bring it to my loft. I didn't feel safe having all that money in one place; plus we needed some room on the tables in the money room for us to put more money on it tonight. I got the duffle bags out the back seat and walked inside my building. The African who usually worked the front desk wasn't there but there was a fine lil yellow chick I neva seen before. I got on the elevator and went to my floor. Once I opened the door, I was crowded by a bunch of suit cases blocking my entrance. There were purses and women shoe boxes everywhere, so I stepped and hopped over them to get completely inside. I went to my room and Taylor was in bed watching TV.

"Where's Stormy?" I asked her without hesitation. She turned off the TV and looked me directly in my eyes.

"We have to talk," Tay Tay said.

An hour worth of talking to Taylor and Stormy along with three hours' worth of off and on sex between us, got things back on track. I laid in my bed with Taylor and Stormy's sweaty bodies one on each side of me. We were trying to

229

relax after the wild sex we just had. I rubbed on the top of Stormy's head and kissed it.

"Baby you know it's me and you until the end, right?" I asked her, tryna reassure her that I was da nigga for her.

"Yes, I know dat Chedda, during these past months, I've been through allot with you and it's been enough for me to know that I love you" she said softly."But Chedda, can I ask you a question?"

"Wats dat babygirl?" I asked.

"Why do you have to fuck the other Diamond Stars when you have the top one. Not only do you have me, but you have Taylor as well. Wat, we're not enough for you or something? We don't make you happy?" She asked with water in her eyes.

I looked on my other side and seen Taylor peeking, eaves dropping on our conversation. I couldn't think of shit to say, so I just hit her with wat Lacey hit me with.

"It aint that y'all don't make me happy; you just have to understand that I'mma King sweetheart. . . and sometimes a king has to satisfy his kingdom's needs."

A tear dropped from her eyes while she stared at me stuck, searching her brain for a response to wat just came out my mouth. I saw my window of opportunity and took it. I got off the bed while she was speechless and headed to the living room to grab the bags of money that I brought in with me. I went to the hallway closet where my digital safe was and entered the code. The sixty thousand that I placed in there before; still sat untouched just how I left it.

I placed both duffle bags in front of me and unzipped them. It was $163,500 left in the duffle bag for me and $189,600 in the duffle bag for Benji. Originally, I owed Benji $252,800 for the two bricks of molly, two bricks of cocaine and the twenty pounds of Wedding Cake. But I owed him an additional

$40,000 for the ten extra pounds I talked Lacey into giving me yesterday. That made my tab $292,800 I reached in my duffle bag and counted out $40,000, then put it inside the duffle bag filled with Benji's money. That now made it $229,600 inside Benji's drug money bag, which meant I only owed him $63,200; and that's exactly how much I was expected to get made from the drugs I was going to provide the Diamond stars to distribute at tonight's event. I zipped up the bag of money I had for Benji and placed it neatly on the closet floor behind my safe, so I could give it to him when he returned. I unloaded my bag of money and placed the stacks of dead presidents inside my safe. Altogether, I now had $183,500 in my safe, plus the $60,000 I brought from my safe that was at Jugg head's house. That meant I was now sitting $243,500 strong. It was all my own money and I was feeling like a Boss. My dick was getting hard just staring at it. I started doing a little math in my head because it seemed like I was short a few thousand. . . then I remembered the thirty-five hunnit that I paid for Dirty to have a good time last night. Motor city hospitality SMH. I wasn't gonna pay them hoes shit, but that bitch Blondie was serious about collecting that money for her Diamond Stars. She came and got the money from me as soon as they shut things down this morning. I counted the money in my safe one more time. I took out $23,500 for spending money and left exactly $ 220,000 inside. I shut the door and Taylor stood there appearing out of nowhere, almost making me drop the spending money I had in my hand.

"I miss you. you haven't been home in days and I'm tired of being here without you" Tay Tay said, then wrapped her arms around my body, giving me a hug.

"I know baby, I'm only going to be gone one more night."

"Why can't I come with you?"

"Wat?"

"Why can't I come with you? Stormy goes" Taylor whined.

"Stormy works there, that's why she comes."

"Well maybe I wanna work there too, I told you I'm tired of my job."

I looked Taylor in the face but there is no way I could take her serious.

"You don't want this type of job baby, believe me; this ain't for you'' I said, brushing her off.

"How do you know what type of life is for me, when you barely even talk to me anymore Chedda? Maybe I'm made exactly for that life but you just never pay attention to me for you to know!" I could see Taylor was serious but I wasn't tryna hear it.

The main reason why I started fuckin with Taylor heavy was because Stormy chose DSE over me and now Taylor wanted to be a part of it.

"Listen. . .I told you this life ain't for you. If you want a different job then relax. I told you that I'll find sumthin for you to do. Until then, here."

I peeled her off five thousand dollars.

''Now take dat and chill out. Remember you are Taylor, not Stormy! So don't worry about what she does because she's not you!" I walked off back into the bedroom and woke Stormy up.

"Wake up and get Dressed. You didn't work last night, so I know you not tired, you showing up early today with me; but first I wanna take you somewhere" I said to Stormy while she continued laying down in bed.

SMACK!
"Ouuch!" She cried from the smack I gave her on her booty.

232

"I said wake up, go take a shower and get dress, we're Leaving."

"Damn, ok daddy, I'm getting up...But there's only one problem" she whined.

''And wats dat?''

''Well, I was mad at you so all my clothes are packed up in bags and suitcases''.

''I don't care, u beta dig sumthin out to wear and get dressed, I'm taking you somewhere''.

Stormy got herself together and I did the same. Taylor pouted and walked around the loft like she had an attitude, but she'll be ok, if she was smart, she'll go to the mall before it closed and spend some of that money I gave her to shop her attitude away. It was Sunday so the mall closed early.

I ended up taking Stormy out to a nice restaurant downtown.

We chopped it up and spent some quality time with each other. She opened up to me and told me things that I never even knew about her. You'd be surprised how much you can learn about a female just from taking the time to actually ask them questions and listen to them.

She cried at times, smiled at times and laughed at times throughout the date. Shit, she even cursed me out a bit; I didn't know if she was bipolar, having mixed emotions or coming on her period? One thing fasho; after leaving the restaurant she was wrapped around my finger and we were back on better terms than ever. We showed up at the venue together inside Stormy's Durango. She felt if I rode with her than I would have no choice but to go back home with her when the event was over tonight. I was ok with it too. I had gotten enough pussy and head in the last three days than most niggas had in years and my dick needed a break. I thought about maybe getting a checkup just to be sure I didn't catch anything; but I knew Lacey kept her Diamonds clean. They had to do a mandatory STD, HIV test once a month.

As we walked in, hand in hand, I seen the disgust look on Lacey's face. Hitman was already standing by the door, on guard, but he extended his hand giving me some dap. Ever since I caught him getting head from Barbie, he been playing it real cool with me. It was five o'clock and most of the Diamonds were already there. You could tell we all wanted to get this last day over and prepare for the New Years. I went to the changing booth and set out all the drug packages for the girls. I gave Hershey's, Barbie's and Kharisma's to the Mexican Diamond, Daisy. I told her to make sure they receive them. I went upstairs to my private room to get into my robe; Lacey walked in while I was putting it on.

"No, no, no, wat do you think you are doing?" She asked me, while standing in front of me ass naked with just a pair of heels on.

"Damn ma, it's like dat? I'm just putting on my robe, but since you coming through for the dick, I'll take it back off" I said admiring her perfect body.

"Well, I'll be through later for my dick, but it's nude Sunday, sooooo. . . you don't get to wear anything at all but a pair of slippers today."

"Wat?"

"You heard me. Let dat big dick of yours dangle all night so us Diamonds can get a good look at it on your last day in charge."

Lacey, walked up to me and undressed me out of my robe.

"So, I see you fixed things with horny; oops I mean Stormy."

"Yeah, we good. She back at work ain't she?" I said tryna throw her off a bit.

I caught the horny shot she made at her but I ignored it. She must knew that Stormy was fucking Benji just as well as I did.

"Well, let's see if she knows how to keep her man like she knows how to keep her job; because the way I see it, you'll be mine in no time."

Lacey turned around and made her ass jump in front of me.

"Now smack it daddy" she ordered. I overhanded dat ass like it owed me money.

SMACK!
"Mmmhh; hard and rough just how I like it," she said and then walked out of my private room.

I grabbed my robe and walked my naked body into the money room. It was nude Sunday for the Diamond Stars, not Chedda, I don't know what Lacey was thinking. I put on my robe and stood in front of the monitors watching them as the Diamond Stars all began to arrive. I finally had a piece of mind. This room brought me peace. I scraped up a little Molly left sitting on one of the tables in front of me. I snorted it straight to the dome. This was my last night being in charge and I was going to make it one to remember. I watched Hershey walk in on camera and knew dat her first stop was going to be with me in the money room. I felt my dick beginning to get hard, responding to the Molly I just snorted and the freak I just seen on camera. I gripped it and slow stroked it, preparing it to go down Hershey's throat as soon as she entered the room with me. There was no way in hell I was giving Diamond Star Entertainment up. Somehow, someway, I had to take Benj's place.

Chapter: 12
"Daddy's Home"

"Oh Fuck! Fuck yes! Fuck yes! Mmm, yes daddy! Don't stop, don't stop daddy! Yes! Oh, shit I'm cuming! I'm cuming!"

I dug my dick inside Taylor deeper And deeper as her whole body shook. I let go of her and untied her wrist from the bed post.

"This is going to be the best sex tape ever Chedda!" Stormy said as she played with the digital camcorder she had in her hands.

"Oh my God I think my pussy is sore!" Taylor said.

"Same!" Stormy shouted out loud referring to her pussy being sore from me beating it up as well.

It was December 31st and I was ending my New Year eve just right. For the last couple of days shit been really good in my life. My money was right, business with Dirty was falling in order and my bitches was finally both in line. Even Lacey was texting and calling for this dick every-day. I grabbed a towel out of the hallway closet to prepare myself for a shower. Today was the day BB came home. He had a party for us planned at his mansion and he was supposed to be breaking some big news for us at the party. It was the girl's night off and a day for everyone to just celebrate bringing in the New Year. I had all of his money ready for him and couldn't wait to get more work from him so that I could keep supplying Dirty.

I couldn't believe how quick I made all this money. I was two hundred grand strong and I had my eyes set on a mill ticket before I even considered leaving this lifestyle alone. I hopped in the shower with my two main bitches, got out and got Dressed. I had on a Balmain out top and bottom.

Stormy and Taylor both were Prada down to the floor and we all had on matching Montclair's. I had a fresh haircut showing off my 360 waves and had on the Rolex watch that BB got me. You couldn't tell me my momma and my hoe ass daddy didn't know what they was doing when they made me. Either I was fine, or all this money I had just made an ugly nigga handsome.

"Chedda baby, we have a gift for you" Stormy said, holding a box in her hand. Taylor walked up with another box in her hand and handed it to me.

"Here; open it" She said, handing me the box. I opened the box that Taylor gave me. It was a set of Diamond screw on earrings.

"I went to Hutches Jewelry with Stormy and I thought that you might like them. I noticed you had your ears pierced but never wore any earrings, so I bought you a pair" Taylor said in the sweetest and most innocent voice.

"Now open this one" Stormy said, eagerly. I opened the rectangle shaped box and it was a pair of fresh white Cartier glasses. It had square lenses with white buffalo sticks for the arms.

237

"Do you Like them?" She asked with a smile on her face."Their great, aren't they? Hurry up and put them on" She said not even, giving me a chance to answer her. I took the pair of Buffs out the box and started to put them on. Stormy helped place them on my face.

"I knew they would look good on you. Lately you've been extra sweet, so I wanted to buy you a New Year gift."

I was speechless. I grabbed both the girls, gave them a hug and kissed the top of their foreheads.

"Thanks," was all I could say.

My phone went off as I received a text from Lacey.

Lacey: Benji just touched down. I'm leaving for the airport now. Meet us at his house in about an hour.

"A'ight finish getting y'all selves together so we can go bring in this New Year" I told the girls, then grabbed everything I was taking with me.

I put on the earrings Taylor bought me and sprayed on my YSL cologne. I brushed my waves and put my gloc.23 on my hip. It was now ten o'clock. We had two hours before the New Year and I was ready to party.

"I need your help with something" Stormy said, walking in the room.

"Wat?" I replied.

"I need you to put this on around my neck for me."

She handed me a Cartier necklace. It was the one that I bought her when I first met her.

"Oh, you decided to put this on tonight huh?" I asked, not even knowing she still had this.

''Yea . . .I'm putting it on and never taking it off again" she said, looking at me in my eyes. I almost fell for the shit, but I snapped out of her hypnosis quick.

''Turn around so I can put it on you."

She turned around and I clamped the necklace around her neck.

"Now let's go. Benji just touched down.''

I grabbed the duffle bag full of the three hundred thousand that I owed Benji and we all left out the door.

Mean While

Benji sat in the passenger seat of his all-black G-wagon while Lacey controlled the wheel. Lacey picked him up from the airport and they were just arriving at their gated community. She entered the five-digit security code and the gate opened, allowing her to drive inside. They noticed all of the cars parked alongside the street of their house. Damn near all of the Diamond Stars were already there, waiting on BB to arrive so the party could begin. Lacey parked the Benz truck inside the two-car garage then prepared to help Benji carry all of the shopping bags and Luggage that he had on the back seat.

"Hold up Lacey, lemme talk to you for a minute" Benji said to her, stopping her from exiting the vehicle.

Lacey turned in her seat to look at him while he spoke.

"I just want you to know how much a nigga truly appreciate you. Naw, lemme rephrase dat. I want you to know how much I appreciate you. You everything I could want in a woman and more. I know that I've been putting things on the back burner with us starting a family but all of that is coming to an end. My plans are falling into place and our reality is turning into the picture that my vision has painted. None of this could have been done without you. Thank you. I'm preparing to move me, you and the whole DSE to Vegas shortly and I made up my mind; if I can't find my brother Ka'Ron by the date I set for us to move, then we're leaving without him. He saved my life, but I can't allow him to ruin it as well. I can't continue to let him hold me back. Better yet; hold us back. I want this year to be about starting a new life for me, you and all the Diamond Star family. I want to plant my seed in you so you can have my baby and my bloodline can grow. We can start a family and a new life in Vegas."

Lacey's eyes watered and tears fell from them. She couldn't believe BB was finally telling her everything that she wanted to hear. She waited for the day that BB would give her a spitting image of him inside of her. She thought about every word BB said and then the feeling of guilt came over her. She felt like a piece of shit for betraying Benji with Chedda. If only Benji would've said all of this before he went out of town. She broke down in tears. BB gripped her body, given her a hug. He thought her sobs were tears of joy; but in reality, they were tears of guilty pleasures.

***

** We walked inside the epic party, looking like money, Benji and Lacey had the place decorated with so many people, it felt like we were inside a club. The DJ had the place turnt up from the sounds he mixed and mastered. Blondie welcomed us to the Party and walked us inside as if it was just another day at work for her. I gave her the duffle bag full of money and told her it was for Benji. All of the Diamond Star ladies were dressed to impress. Weed smoke and hooka smoke filled the air, damn near everybody had either a cup or a blunt in their hand. You could tell it was a true celebration.

I strolled through the crowd greeting everybody with Stormy on my right and Taylor on my left. Taylor had this humongous smile on her face. She couldn't wait to finally be amongst the presence of the Diamond Star family and she was soaking it all up. Blondie guided me, Stormy and Taylor down the steps to where the party was jumpin off as well. The basement was huge. When we finally made it to the bottom of the steps, you could hear the change in the music, coming from a different DJ's booth that was set up down stairs for the second group of people. It was like two parties going on at once. I looked towards the back and seen Benji with Lacey on his right. They were sitting down on an red suede couch and were surrounded by their top Diamond Stars. There was also a light skin nigga with Dreads with a bunch of tattoos on his face, sitting next to Benji. Benji and Lacey were dressed like entertainers. Benji had his Dreads in two big French braids going to the back with a pair of Cartier glasses on as well. He had the same white Buffs that Stormy just gave me but his had Diamonds flooded all through them. He wore two thick Cuban ropes around his neck. One had the Diamond Star Logo hanging from the front of it and the other had the letters BB. He was Dressed in a colorful Balenciaga outfit. His hoodie had mink fur going around it. His shoes were

Balenciaga runners. Lacey had on a tan Burberry Dress that was only held up by her soft breast, because there was no shoulder strap or zipper to secure it to her magnificent body. It was skin tight as if it was painted on her. She wore tan stilettos to match and also had on a giant Diamond Star logo Cuban link choker around her neck as well. I worked my way through the crowd to approach BB and noticed a white guy with a mohawk tattooing on one of the Diamond star ladies. There was also a long line Of Diamond Stars along the wall waiting to get tattoos.

"Wassup OG?" I greeted Benji and he stood, rising to give me some dap and a hug.

"My main man Chedda!" he shouted above the music.

He hugged Stormy and then paused when he seen Taylor.

"And who is this fine piece of company that you have with you?" He asked me, making Taylor blush.

"Oh this my girl Tay Tay. Taylor this Benji and the Diamond Star fam" I said introducing her to everyone around.

"Hey," Taylor said, waving her hand in the air at everybody in front of her.

"Yeah, lemme introduce you to a new member of the Diamond Star family, since we all here" Benji said, then turned toward dude with the dreads and face tatts, sitting on the couch.

BB whispered something to him and the nigga stood up. He had a red five-point star under his left eye like BB and looked like he could've been his younger brother or something.

"Kash, this is my young dawg Chedda. Chedda this Kash; Diamond Star's first rap artist" Benji said to me, introducing us to each other.

"Wats poppin Chedda, heard a lot bout you" Kash said while extending his hand to shake mine's. I gave him some play.

I noticed the loyalty tattoo under his eye and instantly remembered seeing him on the news a while ago for shooting a guy in the face and chest inside a studio on the west side. He got sent to prison for it when he was only sixteen years old, and if I'm not mistaking; he fucked with them blood niggas from east seven mile. I didn't tell him I recognized him because I didn't wanna seem like I was a groupie dick suckin' ass nigga. So, I just nodded my head, given him a salute out of respect and turned my attention back to Benji.

"Damn, so now you signing rappers?" I asked BB.

"Yea, it's about that time, I'm breaking the news tonight. It's time to elevate. DSE don't stand for Diamond Star Entertainment anymore. It stands for Diamond Star Empire! This shit is an Empire Chedda, we taking over everything; music, parties, Vegas, drugs, sex, tattoos, whatever! If it equals Benjamin's at the end then DSE and Benji Bands want in!"

BB was geeked and I could tell he had a little bit of molly in his system.

"Stormy, wassup star; you ready to get tatted?" Benji asked her, turning his electrifying energy from me towards her.

"Tatted? " Stormy asked, not knowing what he was talking about.

"Yeah, tatted" He repeated pointing at the direction of the white guy who was across the room tattooing the DSE vixens.

"Any Diamond Star of mine that has the logo tatted on her before New Year, gets them a platinum DSE Cuban choker. Lacey, show it to her" BB said to Lacey and she stood up and moved her hair from off of her neck so Stormy could get a good look at the thick Cuban choker that she was wearing.

The diamonds were shining and dancing like a disco ball. There was also a diamond shaped charm with a red star in the middle of the diamond, representing the company while it hung from the Cuban rope.

"Where's mine?" Stormy asked, admiring the sparkling diamonds.

"You know I got one for you. You are one of my top Diamonds, now go on and get tatted before the clock strike twelve."

Stormy pushed her way through the crowd and cut the line, so she could get her tattoo next.

"Can I touch it?" Taylor asked Lacey, referring to the Diamond choker she wore.

"Let's get you a drink and let the girls talk" BB said, then walked me over to a corner in the basement that had a table full of alcohol beverages on it.

"So did you like running the show?" He asked me.

"Yeah, it was straight."

"It was straight? Maaan knock it off, Lacey already told me you had a blast!"

"A'ight, a'ight. Dat shit was the life!" I admitted.

"Yeah, dats wat I'm talking bout! Now you gotta chance to see how it feels to be Big Benji B!" He shouted at the top of his lungs.

"I see you shining in here my dawg" He said, then pointed to my glasses and earrings, along with the Rolex he gave me.

"Yeah, just a lil sumn" I replied humbly, then poured me a glass full of deuce—eight and sipped on it.

245

"And you walked up in here with two dimes on yo arms, looking like I raised you or something" He said, and laughed at his own joke.

"Yeah them my girls.. but look I brought yo money and gave it to Blondie when I walked in"I told him, changing the topic.

"Now you know today was supposed to be your chill day, we could've taken care of bidness another time."

"Yeah I know, but I just wanted to get dat out the way so we can start the New Year off dealing with new money."

"Oh, I like dat one. New year, new money!" He said raising his glass of liquor in the air toasting it with mine.

I killed the last of the Deuce-eight. BB looked at his watch.

"C'mon it's 11:55pm. We bout to take this party upstairs. I gotta few surprises for y'all."

BB looked at the DJ and nodded his head at him. All of a sudden, the music stopped. The DJ's voice picked up over the microphone.

"Everybody upstairs! We got five minutes before the ball drops!"

The crowded basement moved in unison and worked their way up the stairs to the main floor. As soon as everyone was all gathered together BB signaled for the other DJ to cut the music. Benji walked to the upper floor in his house that was above us all and he stood in front of the banister, talking to us on a cordless mic. Lacey stood beside him looking as beautiful as ever. I felt a hand on my shoulders and turned to see Taylor and Stormy by my side, holding me. Benji Bands started to speak. . .

"I first wanna welcome everybody into my home and thank you for coming to celebrate and bring this New Year in with me and the Diamond Star Family."

Benji started his speech and the crowd whistled and clapped at his introduction letting him know they were happy to be there with him. He continued...

"We only have a few minutes, before midnight and I wanna make this quick. As you know, me and my girl Lacey started Diamond Star Entertainment, nine months ago and I am proud to say that we have come a long way."

Everybody started applauding.

"Now we are expanding the company and planning to transfer it to Las Vegas." The cheers from the ladies were nonstop.

"By August we are set to relocate. I'm moving every last Diamond Star model to Nevada along with the DSE company." The girls were going crazy."

"I also want to announce that I am now adding two new members to the Diamond star family. . . Kash, would you come up here, so I can introduce you?"

The light skin dread head nigga, walked up stairs and stood next to BB.

"We are now starting a record label up under the DSE banner and this is DSE's first official rap artist 55Kash."

Benji announced his name and handed him a DSE Cuban link chain just like the one he had on. Kash put the chain on around his neck and all the females in the DSE family were clapping and whistling for their new member.

"I also want to inform you that we are changing, the name of DSE. Instead of Diamond Star Entertainment we are now Diamond Star Empire!"

Whistles came from the crowd uncontrollably.

"The next official member that I want to introduce really needs no introduction. Chedda, get on up here."

Everybody clapped for me as Stormy and Taylor walked up the stairs with me to Benji.

"This mu'fucka filled in for me while I was gone and not only ran the show; but took over the show, making the most money that we ever made in one night. Now tell me dat ain't DSE material?!"

As everybody clapped for me, Benji reached out and handed me a DSE Cuban link chain just like the one he gave Kash. I put it on then stepped to the side.

"Now Lacey, step to me baby" Benji said through the mic. He dropped to his knee in Front of her and opened a small box, revealing a gigantic icey engagement ring. Every Diamond Star in the house took a big gasp for air, unable to hide their shock. Even I was surprised at what I was witnessing in front of me.

"Lacey. I know you've been through a lot in life on your own and I know that we've also been through a lot in life as a couple. No matter the situation what the situation may have been, we also put forth the effort to overcome for the sake of our love and loyalty towards each other. There's no woman that I would rather spend the rest of my life and money with. I have big plans for us in Vegas. I would like to start a family with you and raise our beautiful children there in a whole different environment. Would you please do me he honors of being my wife?"

The whole house was so silent from Benji's proposal that you could hear a pin drop. Lacey had tears running down her face. She wiped her face and held BB's hand.

"Benji, I would love to be your wife and be Mrs Benji Bands."

BB put the ring on her finger, stood up and locked lips with her. The house went wild, hooting and hollering; whistling and clapping. The DJ got on the mic.

248

"Its almost midnight; ten. . . nine. . . eight.. seven. six. . . five. . . four. . .three. . .two. . . one. . ." everybody yelled..

"HAPPY NEW YEAR!"

Taylor

The 23yr old soft-hearted cutie was always a loner. Born, Taylor Hatcher from a married couple and strict household in Lansing, Michigan, she never had many opportunities to mingle and make friends. She missed out on allot of middle school and high school parties. Once she went off to college and graduated from Michigan State University, she moved from East Lansing to Detroit on her own, loving the new found freedom away from her parents. Instead of Taylor taking her career in computer technology serious, she was more determined to catch up on all the fun she missed out on. She had just lost her virginity in college and went through a major heartbreak during her graduation year. Once she moved to Detroit, she landed a gig at Fairlane mall. She met plenty of new sex partners through the clothing store where she worked. The freak was inside of her and she deemed to bring it out each chance that she got. Her original goals in life to become a successful Facebook tech-representative quickly went out the window when she got a taste of the city life. She had plenty of niggas that only smoked with her and had sex with her, but she never had one who put her under their wing. . . until she met Chedda. Chedda was different than the others. He talked to her and truly got to know her for who she was. He gave her good erotic sex on the regular and even spiced up their love life by adding another female to the equation. This was something no other man has showed her. He paid all the bills and took care of her, not leaving her to want for anything. The only thing Taylor wanted from Chedda was for him to allow her to be a part of the Diamond Star Lifestyle that he and Stormy lived. She never had the opportunity to be a part of anything that placed the spotlight on her and she prayed for the day that her chance to shine would come. Since she moved from Lansing, she been out of touch with her mom and her dad. They were getting older and she had a very small family to keep in touch with. In her eyes, Chedda and Stormy were her new family. She would do anything for Chedda and stick by his side no matter what the situation was; but she wanted her chance to shine in the spot light, just like Stormy. She was very submissive when it came to Chedda, and would always do as he tells her. So even though, she wanted to be a Diamond Star with all her heart, she still would never go against her man Chedda's word. He was her everything.

Stormy

Shakora Evans aka Stormy, was an around the way girl. She came up in the Motor City on both sides of town, living house to house like a run away. She started running the streets and having sex with older men at a young age because the lack of parental supervision. Her mother was a known dancer in the strip clubs of Detroit before she was raped and stabbed to death by an obsessed ex-boyfriend. She passed down to Stormy nothing but her attractive looks and a younger sister for Stormy to look after named of Carmen. Stormy and her sister were on their own, but her charismatic personality helped her create opportunities to put enough food on the table for both of them. Stormy was a bitch that any nigga would want to fuck with at just a glimpse of her sensual lips and fit body. It wasn't so much of her beauty that captured a nigga. It was more about her sex appeal. A nigga's dick would instantly get hard just from her presence.

The only family member Stormy had was her sister Carmen, who was only one year younger than her. Carmen ended up graduating from high school and marrying a man who took care of them both. Stormy lived with them until she had a falling out with Carmen.

Stormy left and gave her heart to a street hustler who stepped on it and crushed it. Stormy made a promise to herself that she would always put herself first in any relationship she committed to in the future; but she soon realized it wasn't easy to do. Even though her hunger craved money and the lavish things that the fast life offered her, she also wanted Love. She was sick and tired of being let down by guys who didn't appreciate her and lacked the control to keep their dick in their pants. She wanted a wholesome man like her sister Carmen had. Stormy loved men with power and money and wanted someone who couldn't only control her mind but who could also control the emotions of her heart. She wanted the top dog and would be dammed if she settled for less. She was so determined to get the head nigga in charge that she wouldn't mind climbing up the ladder from nigga to nigga until she captured her prey. She possessed a bone of loyalty in her body but it had an expiration date on it. She was the type to be down for whatever to her man, but the moment a better one came along, she was gone. Her sister was already saved and now she was on a mission to find someone to save her as well.

* Chedda *

Seven Aaron Thomas was born and the streets of Detroit added another misunderstood renegade to its roster. He had two older sisters that were both by the same mother but different fathers. Seven grew up developing a chip on his shoulders as a toddler. He had a hard time getting along with others and an even harder time keeping friends. His mother moved out of state by the time he was fourteen years old and he had no respect for his father to even attempt to build a cordial relationship with him. He dropped out of school and ran the streets attempting to learn how to hustle. After fuckin up his money time after time, he got fed up and started to use his gun for more than protecting himself. He jumped into the robbing game and couldn't get enough of the thrill he got out of it. He found something that he enjoyed doing and at the end of the day he got paid from it. Chedda begin using his gun on regular occasions, shooting niggas stemming from his short temper.

He soon noticed he had an incredible gravitational force to pulling women. After being burnt by women multiple time he learned to never trust them just like he did not trust the niggas in the streets.

Chedda lived life sleeping at his homeboys and girlfriends houses, not knowing the next place where he would lay his head. His family was useless for him and his heart grew numb towards them.

The lack of love; and possessions that he never had, forced Chedda to put his all into trying to obtain more money for his self. He turned heartless in the process. He only seeked for money and power and didn't believe in anyone having his best interest any more. True love to him was only something that would soon expire. Deep down he yearned for it, but in reality, he didn't trust it.

Chedda went to sleep every night gripping his pistol and whatever freak he had in his choke hold. The streets became a part of his mind, body and soul. He couldn't help but to intoxicate every heart that he touched, with his gully way of showing love. Chedda wanted to get rich, but only in a way that catered to his power hunger desires. He yearned for a female that was pure and innocent with no familiarity to the street lifestyle he lived. But he knew that perfect bitch didn't exist in his world.

Chapter: 13
"New Year, New Money... New Problems"

About a month and some change into the New Year, my bank was sitting higher than ever. It was the first weekend of February and I was grinding hard. Benji been flooding me every weekend with the goods and he still had no idea I was doing my own damn thing on the side. Me and Dirty had had our business transaction setup for every Friday and Dirty never let me down with the paypa. He kinda' complained about the quality of the work when I had Jughead and Dee cut it so I didn't put as much cut on it anymore. He still kept shopping and spending his money with me doe, so that lemme know the quality was still good.

Benji continued giving me two bricks of molly, two bricks of cocaine and twenty pounds of weed every week. I took the two bricks of cocaine and mixed them together, then had Jughead and Dee put a thousand grams of cut on top of it. That gave me an extra brick of cocaine for myself to sell without BB or Dirty even noticing the difference in the quality of work. It was still strong as fuck.

I did the same with the molly, which gave me an extra brick as well. I sold both of the free bricks to Dirty every week, then supplied the DSE models with the drugs they expected. The weed was tight and I could only sell Dirty ten pounds of it every Friday with the two bricks. BB gave me twenty pounds of the Wedding Cake every week; but I still had to make sure I gave ten to the DSE models to sell. I added my thousand-dollar tax to each pound I sold to Dirty; making ten thousand dollars profit off of them. I gave the remaining forty thousand from the weed to BB along with the drug money from the girls that he had coming and everybody was happy. I made a hundred thousand off of Dirty every Friday and it was lovely. So far, I had five hundred thousand put up inside my safe and was halfway to a mill ticket. I never felt better in my life. My crackhead uncle Jugghead was even getting money now. He had his spot jumping. It was now a full-time drug house. All of his friends came in and out the house constantly spending their work or unemployment checks on the drugs Jughead was selling. I make sure I always give him a little something every week to keep his operation going but sometimes he would run out of dope so quick that he would be forced to buy some of the same drugs from Dirty just to keep it going. It was like we were spending, money with each other so we could make more money. My name was ringing on the eastside for having the best work and everybody was trying to get in good with me so I could plug them.

 After Dirty had the time of his life at the DSE event I hosted, he came back and let his whole hood know that I was on top and the nigga to fuck with in these streets. I was getting eager to splurge and spend my money on jewelry, clothes and cars but I had to play it smart so Benji wouldn't catch wind I was making extra money on the side. He boosted up my pay from twelve thousand a week to twenty-five thousand a week and I basically gave that money to Taylor. I finally let her quit her job and made her a full-time house bitch. I brought the bacon home and she made sure all of her duties as my bitch were taking care of. She went and paid the bills with the money, kept the house clean and smelling good, cooked and sucked my dick every morning and night.

 Stormy continued to put dat good pussy and head on me too. She caught me loading my safe one day and ask where did I get so much money. I was mad that I let her see my stash but so far, she has kept her mouth shut. I didn't need BB or anyone else in my bidness. Lacey still on my dick but ever since BB came back and proposed to her, she only let me hit the pussy one time. And it was kinda weird after I made her cum, she started crying and kicked me out of the house. I don't know what's going on with her.I think maybe she was having some type of guilt trip, so I just fell back a little with her.

   **I pulled up at the gas station in Dirty's hood. It was two o'clock in the afternoon and I was headed to his block to make our weekly transaction. I been ripping and running to the money so much I didn't even realize my tank was on E. I told Taylor to fill up the last time I let her use my Jeep but she must have forgotten. I stood there pumping gas in this grimy neighborhood looking for jackers. I had all my weekly supplies inside my ride and I wouldn't looking to take a lost right now. I kept my right hand on my waist and watched the usual traffic that was coming in and out of the gas station. A black Impala pulled up at the pump next to me and a dark skin nigga jumped out the driver's seat. He left his door open with his music blasting loud so everybody could hear it. He just so happens to be listening to BB's new artist 55Kash. It was one of his latest hits that the whole city was listening too. It was called Die-troit. I listened to the sounds and stayed on point while I finished up filling my tank. "This Die-troit this ain't Chi-raq for a couple dollars niggas will get whacked; BLATT!" The Lyrics of the song echoed out of his car speakers. I put the pump back, and began to close up my nozzle. The dark-skinned skinny nigga came back to his car, looking at me like he either knew me. . .or had a problem with me.

"Aye homie, yo name Chedda aint it?" The skinny black nigga asked me above his loud music.

"Yea, why wassup?" I said back. He dipped his head low inside his car through the open driver side door. I gripped on my gloc and pulled it out just in case. I heard the volume of his music turn down than he brought his upper body back outside of it. He looked down and seen me clutching my pipe.

"Naw, naw, homie it ain't no beef or nuttin' like that. I was just turning down the music so I could hear you. Dirty my manz from da block" he said , making who he got his point across.

"My bad, ain't know wat da fuck you was on. But yea, Dirty my dawg, wassup?"

"I was just tryna see if you had some of dat wedding cake weed on you? It ain't none in our hood rite now and I need to smoke. I'm hooked on dat shit nigga."

I burst out Laughing.

"Thats some good shit aint it? But nawl I ain't got shit on me," I lied then continued, "but when I do, I'll hit Dirty up and let him know."

"A'ight fasho my nigga," he said, than started to pump his gas .

 I put my gun up and got inside my ride and pulled off. I texted Dirty letting him know I was on my way and only around the corner. Five minutes later, I was parking across the street in front of the crowded house. Dirty immediately disperse from the crowd and walked down the steps of his porch with a duffle bag in his hand and got inside my Passenger seat as usual.

"Chedda my man, wats da deal?" He said, slapping my hand and giving me some dap.

"Ain't nothing much, wats going on with you?"

"Same shit my nigga, just getting to this paypa. The block been extra hot lately dawg, so next week I'm opening up shop two streets over. It's time for me to switch locations. I caught a narc over here trying to buy some drugs the other day" He said while looking over his shoulder, left and right like he was paranoid or something.

The shit kind of made me nervous. I reached in the back seat and grabbed my bag; careful not to grab the wrong one with all of the DSE models supply inside. He handed me the one he had and I looked inside and zipped it back up happy with what I saw. I tossed it in the seat behind me. Dirty examined the work inside the backpack I gave him and seen one whole brick of molly, one brick of cocaine and ten pounds of the wedding cake.

"Look like it's all there to me" He said, closing it back. "Listen man, next week I'mma give you the new address to pull up at, because this block way too hot right na'. Be smooth nigga, I'm bout to hurry and get inside" he said, stepping out out the ride. He then turned back towards me.. "Oh and Chedda. . . make sho you invite me to whatever the hell that was the next time you have one man. That shit was poppin."

He shut the door and I pulled off and headed towards Daisy's apartments over at Anthos Garden , so I could give the girls their supply for the week. My weekly transaction with Dirty was complete and my weekend was officially starting.

Mean While

"This our time. Alpha unit move in on target and detain suspect."

Detective Timothy spoke through the walkie talkie to the Federal agents that he had on standby. Detective Timothy and his partner Lonzo had been staking out Dirty's drug house since six am this morning. They had been monitoring him and his drug operation daily and this was their time to finally let the sleepless nights pay off. They eventually noticed that the gold jeep was always arriving to meet up with Dirty on his street every Friday. They knew that was the moment Dirty received packages of drugs from his connect, because he always carried a bag with him too and from the vehicle every time it arrived.

Detective Timothy didn't receive much information on the background check ran on the gold jeep as he had hoped. When he ran the plate, he discovered that the jeep belonged to a 23yr old female by the name of Taylor Hatcher and was registered to an address located in Downtown Detroit. Detective Timothy knew the guy driving the vehicle more than likely was the owner's boyfriend because when he ran a background check on the 23yr old female the vehicle was registered to; it showed she had no siblings.

He was determined to get a clear identity on him. His strategic plan was to wait until Dirty had exited the gold jeep with the drugs and then send in the raid team to arrest Dirty with the bag in his possession; then arrest all of the other drug dealers who crowded the porch of the known drug spot. He had another agent in a squad car on standby to follow the gold jeep to initiate a traffic stop after it leaves Dirty's block. He told the agent in the squad car that once he made the traffic stop to wait on the call through the walkie talkie for the confirmation of it being drugs inside the bag that Dirty just received from him and then detain the driver of the jeep for conspiracy to run a drug operation, trafficking and delivering.

As the gold jeep turned off Dirty's street, two all black raid vans bent the corner and jumped out on all of the drug dealers who posted on Dirty's porch. They blocked Dirty off as he tried to run across the street. Dirty dropped the bag of drugs and tried to sprint but than a masked FBI agent ran full speed and tackled Dirty to the ground, detaining him. All of the other drug dealers scattered, jumping off the porch, running inside the house and through the back yards of houses close by. Most got caught while very few got away. Five back-up Federal squad cars swarmed the block and secured the area. Detective Timothy and Lonzo arrived and walked over towards Dirty, he picked the bag off the ground that Dirty dropped.

He opened it and seen a supply of drugs.

"Good work fellas!" Detective Timothy yelled. "Lonzo; radio in agent 21 and see how that traffic stop is going? Tell him the drugs are confirmed and to detain the suspect at the stop."

"I'm on it!" Lonzo replied.

Dirty put his head down face first on the pavement as he felt the feeling of defeat settle in. Detective Timothy walked the drugs to his vehicle so it could be documented into the evidence log report. He felt relieved that he finally got his target Mr. Rodney Glenfield aka Dirty and now he was just waiting on the update of a confirmed arrest of the unknown supplier in the gold jeep; who went by the name of Chedda.

***

** I just left Dirty's house and was driving down eight-mile road on the way to Daisy's, then some bull shit happened. I didn't know what the fuck was going on but as soon as I stopped at a red light, waiting for it to turn green, I notice something odd. A white crown Vic vehicle pulled up behind me close to my bumper. I looked in my rearview mirror to see if I could get a glimpse of the driver's face but before I could make anything out, a flashing blue and white light on the side of the dashboard went off, with the noise of a police siren. I was getting pulled over and I didn't know why.

"Fuck!"

 I pulled to the side of the curb on the right to get out the middle of the street. I put my truck in park but knew better than to cut off the engine. My gun was in my lap, a hundred thousand dollars' worth of cash was in a duffle bag and I also had another duffle bag filled with two bricks of coke and molly along with all ten pounds of weed. There was no way I could get caught with all this money and drugs. The officer got out of his car and started to approach my driver's side window. I covered up my gloc with the end of my shirt and prepared myself for the unexpected.

Tap! Tap! Tap! Tap! The officer knocked on my window and I cracked it; rolling it down just an inch for us to hear each other better. He was dressed in all black with an FBI bulletproof vest on, instantly my heart started pounding I knew something wasn't right.

"I'm going to need you to turn off the vehicle and step out sir" The officer said.

"Ok no problem officer," I replied, as if I was going to follow his orders. I reached for the gear, put it in drive

Skrrrrrrrtt!!I swerved onto eight-mile road driving through traffic, recklessly. In my rearview I could see the FBI officer getting back in his car and attempting to catch up to me on the road. I turned up the music and searched for anything decent to listen to on the radio so I could speed too while running from the police. 102.7 FM was playing a song by Da Baby and I turned it up to the max. I looked in my rearview again as I swerved in and out through traffic, then out of nowhere two more police cars shot from the side streets in front of me, trying to cut me off. Skrrrt! I whipped my Track Hawk to the left, then to the right, almost crashing into one of their vehicles. I regained control of the Track Hawk and sped up the road, making a turn on a residential block. One of the police cars was right on my ass. I bent corner for corner trying to lose him, but he was in a Charger and was driving, that mufucka like a speed racer.

 Finally I got him on a street that had a nice straight away. I pushed the nitro button in my Track Hawk and the air shocks on the truck dropped it lower to the road for better handling. I pushed my foot on the gas full throttle and shot off like a bullet. I sped down the sideway street watching the police car behind me get smaller and smaller as I left him. I made a right turn then jumped on the closest freeway. I turned down the music as my heart pace began to slow back to normal rhythm.

That shit was a close call. I tried to regain my composure, collecting my thoughts. The FBI? Man, I ain't know what was going on but I knew shit wasn't right. I picked up my phone and called Dirty so I could tell him what happened.

Ring. . . Ring... Ring click. The call was answered but he didn't say anything. All I could hear was a Little commotion going on in the background but I couldn't make out what it was.

"Hello Dirty?" I said through the phone. Still there was no response.

"Dirty! "I shouted through the speaker again but it was still the same. Then I heard a voice.

"Chedda, we will find you and get you. You can run but you can't hide" The voice said. I hung up instantly. This shit was getting more wicked by the second.

I merged onto I-75 so I could head to BB's house. There was no way I was going to Daisy's with all the heat in that area, so I figured I'd go head and drop off the top Diamond Star's at BB's, their supply before they got their night started. I didn't know how I was going to get the others their shit, but I'll figure it out once I got settled. My head was spinning out of control.

I focused my attention back on the road and thought about the phone call that just happened. I wish I had a blunt already rolled up so I could smoke. I wouldn't give a fuck if it was the shit Lacey hit with fentanyl or not, I needed something to calm my nerves. All type of thoughts was running through my mind. Did Dirty get locked up? Who was that answering his phone?

He did mention his hood was hot. Was Dirty setting me up the whole time? I didn't know what to think? But one thing fasho, I had to figure out something fast because if the mu'fucka on the phone knew my name was Chedda, then it ain't no telling what else he knew? I checked my rearview and looked over my shoulder feeling paranoid just like how Dirty was acting when he was in the car with me. I was looking in the air to make sho helicopter's wouldn't following me and all type of shit.

Forty-five minutes later I pulled up to the gated community and punched BB's house number into the keypad.

"House of beauty, number one cutie, who's there?" Lacey's voice said through the speaker.

"It's Chedda" I replied. She paused for a brief moment.

"Hey Chedda" she said, and opened the electronic gate, for me to enter.

I pulled up in front of BB's house and parked. I took the bag of drugs out the back seat and walked into the house. Luckily, they left it unlocked this time for me to walk in, instead of leaving me in the cold. As I entered, I was faced with Barbie sitting on the couch and BB sitting in between her legs getting his Dreads twisted. Blondie was sitting at the table drinking wine and watching TV

"Chedda, wass up?" BB asked. Barbie was looking at me and licking her lips in a flirtatious way behind his back.

"Shit man, I was stopping by to hit the girl's off before they got tonight started. Wass good with you?" I asked making small talk.

"Different day, different dollars to make. Ain't shit change. I want you to stop through tomorrow at the event and show DSE yo love and support."

"Ok, I can do that. Wassup, something special going on?"

"Yea, matter fact it is, my artist 55Kash is coming through to have a video shoot while the event is going on; It's going to be live! We shooting a video for his new club banger called Can't U Tell. You can't miss it" BB said, making sure I knew how important it was to him for me to be there.

"Say no more, I'm there" I told him.

"Good. Now talk to me, how err thing going on yo end? I ain't seen Stormy this whole week, she a'iqht?" he asked.

"Oh yeah, shit been good on our end. She getting some rest now so she come in to work tonight" I replied.

Just as I was reaching in the bag to pull out the packages for the girls, Lacey walked down the stairs and entered the room dressed in some green boy shorts and a sports bra.

"Daddy did you see my Chanel earrings anywhere around the house? I can't find them?" Lacey said to Benji, ignoring my presence as if a nigga wasn't standing in front of her.

I just picked up the bag of drugs from her earlier this morning at her house and now she was acting like I was a ghost or a stranger. It even made me mad inside to hear her call this nigga Daddy the same way she was calling me Daddy when he was out of town.

"Yeah, they fell off when we were in the shower yesterday and I picked them up this morning and put them in the top drawer of your night stand" BB told her.

"Oh ok, thanks Daddy" Lacey said, then looked at me and rolled her eyes before switching her round booty back upstairs.

I continued placing the packages of drugs on the table.

"Aye Blondie, you wouldn't mind bringing the rest of the girls they weekly supply for me at the venue tonight, would you? I asked her hoping she ain't ask for an explanation on why I couldn't go to Daisy's and do it myself like I normally do.

"Sure, I got you. Just set them out and I'll bring them with me when I head out."

"Good lookin out my baby, I really gotta run" I told her.

I unpacked the bag, making sure I got all of the drugs out of it.

"I'm gone Benji" I said, then turned and walked towards the door.

"See you tomorrow!" He shouted and I left; jumping back in my truck to drive my ass to the loft so I could wrap my mind around the weird shit that was happening.

I drove home, looking in my rearview every second of the way, praying and hoping that another police car didn't get behind me. It felt like I was on the road forever before I finally made it home.

This time I didn't park my truck in front of the building, I parked it across the street in a group home parking lot. I walked to my building from there and made it inside. I walked in the lobby and the usual African man was at the front desk. I gave him the thumbs up as I walked in and he nodded his head alerting me that everything was good. I got on the elevator and headed to my loft.

Once I made it inside my loft, I put every single dollar that I just made inside my safe. I was up to six hunnid thousand. I asked Taylor to run me a hot bath so I could relax and think of what to do next, then I told her to immediately call the police station and report the Track Hawk stolen. I made sure to stay in the house and end my day early. I wanted to wash this one away and use tomorrow as a fresh start.

Mean While

Detective Timothy was working overtime going back and forth from the Dickerson jail and the Mound Intake Center, interviewing all of the drug dealers that were arrested in the DEA's Federal drug raid earlier that day. After numerous interviews with the suspects, he was exhausted and only received small amounts of information from the drug dealers who Mr .Whitfield aka "Dirty" had working with him. Dirty was caught red handed and already convicted in Detective Timothy's mind, but he wanted to arrest the guy they called Chedda as well. He was highly pissed that his squad agent let him get away without even getting his identity. He didn't have any information about his government identification and his last resort was to interview one of his arch nemesis: Rodney Carlton Whitfield aka Dirty... just as the thought crossed his mind, he received a phone call at his office desk. Ring! Ring!

"yes, yes ok, thank you sir, I owe you one" Timothy replied to the caller on the other end of the line and hung up the phone.

Detective Timothy screamed in joy as he was working on getting a warrant signed for them to search the address that the Jeep Track Hawk was registered to; and a warrant out for the vehicle itself. Since the car was registered to a female named "Taylor Hatcher" and was involved in a high speed Federal chase, then the warrant would have to be put out on her. Even though he knew they had no evidence that she was the one driving, he now would have the right and opportunity to pressure her into telling him who the guy named Chedda was. He celebrated the good news, relieved with how much he had accomplished today. He was ready to take off for the weekend and come back to work on the case

Monday morning. He looked at the picture of the old man who Chedda phone number was linked to. His name was William Dillard and his state Id information hasn't been renewed or updated in twenty years. He knew there was no reason to look for a ghost whose last address was the homeless shelter on Peterboro. He knew that old man wasn't the young guy who he had snapped pictures of weeks ago, getting into the gold jeep in that parking lot.

 He turned off the light's in his office as he stuck a thumb tac through Chedda's picture on his bulletin board above his desk. He walked out his office and shut the door as he saved his worries about Chedda for Monday morning.

***

Chapter: 14
"Me My Bitch & My Gloc"

I woke up the next morning and sent Taylor to the cell phone store to get me a new phone. There was no way I was gonna' continue talking on that phone after the strange police chase and strange phone call yesterday. I told her to get me a little cheap Metro phone and put it in a fake name.

Before I went to sleep last night, I ended up seeing Dirty's face and his whole neighborhood plastered across the TV screen on Fox2 news.

The DEA been watching Dirty for three years. They even put the description of my truck with its license plate number on the news and requested for the public to call in if they spotted the vehicle.

I was getting a bad feeling all over my body. I didn't tell anybody about what was going on because the last thing I needed was for BB to find out I was selling his drugs to an indicted drug dealer. After Taylor came back with my new phone, I transferred all of my contacts into it and broke the old one. I wanted no parts of it. From the looks of things, Dirty was going to be facing some serious drug charges and I was just praying I dodged getting caught up in his bullshit. That was fun while it lasted. I made a good six hunnit bands, but a prison bid wasn't going to be worth it at the end of the road.

I got myself together and prepared myself for my day. I was laying low on driving my Jeep after seeing the shit I saw on the news yesterday. I planned on riding with Stormy to the venue tonight, but for some reason she didn't come in last night or this morning after work. That was kind of different, but maybe she just went home with the other girls to BB's house. Since Stormy wasn't there to take me to the DSE event, I had Taylor drive me to my spot on the east side with Jughead, so I can hop in my charger and drive it until I figured out what to do with my Jeep.

When me and Taylor pulled up to the spot, it was crowded and full of junkies coming in and out just like usual. I gave Taylor a kiss and told her she could pull off and I would be home later.

Jughead greeted me with a hug and a big smile on his face when I walked in the house. There were dope fiends sprawled out across the floor in sleeping bags with crack pipes griped tightly in their palms.

"How ya doing nephew?" Jughead asked.

Knock! Knock! Knock! As soon as we started talking, we were interrupted by knocks at the door from Jugheads normal neighborhood clientele. He served him, made his money and closed the door.

"Sorry nephew, wat you was saying?"

"I Just stopped by to pick up the car Unc."

"The car? Wat happened to ya fancy truck?"

"Dats a long story Unc, Where's the keys?"

Jughead walked inside the kitchen and grabbed the keys to the Charger and handed them to me.

"Here; be careful when you driving it in the snow, it ain't got four-wheel drive like yo jeep. I just got an oil change and tune-up for it the other day; so, it should give you a smooth ride."

272

"Good lookin' Unc" I said and walked out the spot then drove off in my Charger.

It was still hours before the DSE event started, so I decided to swing through to Daisy's at the Anthos Garden apartment's.

I cruised the streets of the east side feeling a lot safer in my charger. I knew the DEA wasn't looking for me in these set of wheels and on top of that, niggas in the streets had gotten used to me driving in my Track Hawk; so I was low-key all around. My head was still spinning from the shit that happened yesterday and what I saw on the news; but my nerve was a lot better.

I arrived at the ghetto apartment complex that reminded me so much of the projects. I knocked on the door, waiting for her to answer. I saw the curtains move as she looked to see who was at the door. The locks quickly clicked and she let me inside.

"Hi Papi, I miss you!" She screamed excitedly as she jumped on me, giving me a hug. She had on nothing but a thong and a bra and she smelled like peaches.

"Damn baby, Daddy missed you too. You walking round here looking all sexy and shit" I told her while looking her up and down enjoying the beautiful Latina in front of me. She blushed.

"I just got out of the shower Papi. You know I have to get ready for tonight. I'm supposed to be in some type of music video for BB's rap artist." I could tell by how she was prancing around her apartment, she was excited about it.

I took off my coat and shoes, making myself comfortable.

So, wat bring you by? I already got my weekly supply fromBlondie yesterday" Daisy asked.

"I just wanted to come by and check on my hot Latin mami of DSE. Damn, is that a problem?" I asked.

She walked from the kitchen area and stepped to me.

"So, you mean to tell me, you not over here to take care of business? You come to check up on me without any business to handle for DSE?"

"Yeah, why you acting like dats so hard to believe?" I said to her.

Daisy placed her hands on my shoulders and leaned in, giving me a kiss on my lips.

"Si Papi, doing shit like this gets my punanni wet. Come with me." Daisy grabbed my hand and led me back to her bedroom.

As soon as I entered her room, I knew what time it was. She pushed me onto her bed and unbuckled my belt, while I laid flat on her mattress, looking up at her ceiling, she pulled down my jeans and started sucking on me; making my dick come alive.

"Oh shit!" I said out loud.

I tried to scoot back on the bed to get out of her throat a little but she stayed swallowing my dick, making me feel like I was about to cum quick. After spittin' and dribbling all over my dick head She finally stopped sucking and then looked me in my eyes. She took my pants and pulled them all the way off from around my ankles, then got on top of me. She slid my dick inside her wet gushy pussy, and started riding me, bouncing up and down on top of my pole.

"Oh fuck!" I let out. Her pussy was so tight but so wet at the same damn time. She was going up and coming down on my dick so hard it felt like I was ripping through her insides and she was just taking it.

''Papi! Papi! Daisy screamed as she rode my dick. I gripped her waist tryna control the freaky Mexican who was putting that Latina pussy on me.

"Choke me Papi! choke me!" she yelled. I put my hands around her neck and she rode my dick even harder. Just when I thought her pussy couldn't get any wetter, my dick felt a rush of water. She was raining on me and she couldn't hold her nut back any longer. She was dreaming on me uncontrollably.

"Oh My God Papi, Si" she said and began screaming some Spanish shit I didn't understand.

I quickly pushed Daisy off of me onto the bed and turned her over doggy style. I slid right back inside the wet Ocean gap between her legs and started deep stroking.

"Oh, Papi! Papi! Papi! dont stop! Papi!" she screamed and started speaking in Spanish again. I pulled her hair and choked her, while I pounded and enjoyed her Spanish Pussy.

By the time me and Daisy finished fucking it was ten o'clock and she was definitely behind schedule for the event she had to attend.

I followed behind her as we drove to the venue where it was hosted tonight. It was located, right across the street from the Motor City Casino and it was already jammed packed. I never seen a DSE event so crowded this early. It usually didn't start jumping until eleven or twelve, but tonight mufuckas was there partying early. Me and Daisy walked in together and I saw the stares that I got from Hitman and Road Kill. Hitman held his hand out to give me some dap and for the first time, Road Kill did too. I dapped them both up and continued inside the packed place.

I made sure I wore my DSE Cuban link for the first time, since it was the first DSE event I attended after Benji gave it to me.

Daisy walked off, trying to hurry up and get changed before anybody noticed she was late, but I saw Blondie on her ass hawking her down through the crowd to give her a piece of her mind. I saw Lacey walking hand in hand with a trick going towards the VIP section. There were camera men filming all over the place. Barbie was on the center stage dancing while niggas was throwing money at her. I worked my way through the crowd and noticed a big gathering towards the left. There was a bunch of niggas dressed in red. I approached the gathering and seen Benji with a bottle of Ace of Spade in his hand, standing next to his artist 55Kash. 55Kash was surrounded by a bunch of niggas with Dreads that had on a lot of red bandannas tied around their wrist and neck; some even had them hanging out their back pockets. On the front of their shirts, there were big letters that read "Free Lloyd" and "RIP Block", another nigga had on a shirt that red "Free Da Squad" with multiple criminal mug shots under it. They were all posted in front of the camera while Kash was recording his new video. It was clear these were members from the notorious eastside gang he was affiliated with, and he was aiming to make them famous as well.

"Chedda, get yo ass over here!" Benji shouted to me above the music as he spotted me.

I walked in closer to give him some play. Kash held out his hand for some play too and I gave him some after I shook hands with BB.

"Now we can really get this video poppin" Benji told the nigga Kash.

"Here nigga, drink some of this so you can knock dat edge off you, it's time to show out. This video going on BET Jamz to showcase how DSE doing it in these streets."

BB gave me the Ace of Spade bottle and I took gulp after gulp, tryna catch a quick buzz. I was going through a lot so I needed it.

"Hold on, hold on; slow down with dat my dawg, its molly in there" BB said as he took the bottle from my hand. I was killing that mufucka, but if I knew it was molly in it, I wouldn't never drunk that much dat fast.

"And action!"

The man on the side of the camera yelled. The next thing I know, everybody around me and Benji were all performing for the camera that was focusing on us. A bunch of Diamond Stars were dancing and shaking their ass and BB was throwing money in the air, show boating. I started to feel the molly entering my system and I joined in by holding my DSE charm in front of the camera; vibing to Kash's new hit.

"Cut!"

The director yelled. Everybody stopped performing and started back talking, giving each other props on how they acted in front of the camera.

"It's over all ready?" I asked BB.

"It's far from over. We just taking a quick break and rotating the girls."

I turned my head and seen Stormy walking in our direction. She was looking fine as hell with nothing on but a thong and some high heels I ain't even gonna front, I was missing her like a mufucka since she ain't come home last night and the way she was looking tonight, made a nigga feel good to call her my girl. I looked her up and down while she got closer and closer to me, I noticed she had on the necklace I bought her a while back. She must've really meant that shit when she said she was never goin' to take it off again. As she walked amongst the crew that was here for Kash's video shoot, she stopped in front of Benji's artist Kash and engaged in conversation with him. I thought it was going to just be a few seconds or so before she made her way over to me, but after ten minutes passed, along with a bunch of flirtatious laughs and touches I began to get pist. I was steaming hot. I ain't know if it was the molly or the fact that this nigga had his paws all over my bitch.

"Ok, everybody in positions... Three; two; one and action!" The director shouted and the cameras began rolling while the show started up again.

BB threw his arm around my shoulder and began acting out the lyrics to the song. I watched Stormy' dance on Kash; I tried not to get on no sucka stroking shit bout it. I started nodding my head to the beat of the song.

Stormy bent over, bussing it wide open and Kash smacked and gripped on her booty for the camera to see. My temperature began to rise by the second. Kash pulled out a credit card than slid it down the crack of Stormy's ass like he was swiping it at a cash register, she shook her ass nonstop with a smile on her face from his gesture, just like on the tip drill video by Nelly. I couldn't take the disrespect any more. I tossed BB's arm from around my shoulder, walked over to Kash in front of all the camera's and dug right off in his shit. He hit the floor instantly. I pushed Stormy to the side and got right on top of him to finish beating his face in. I heard a lot of commotion going on around me, but I was in my zone and didn't pay it no attention. I cocked back and hit Kash in his face with a right, splitting his nose wide open. Before I could get another hit off, I felt a kick in my back and another kick to the side of my head. I went flying to the floor face first.

"Get the fuck off of him!" I heard BB yelling. There was a bunch of screaming going on and the music stopped. I rolled over on my back and seen a brown skinned nigga with extra-long Dreads, holding a gun with a beam on it, pointed at me. His shirt said, "Free Hob" in red letters. Before I knew it, I heard gun shots go off. The nigga with the Dreads turned his head to see who was shooting and that's when I got up and took off running through the crowd. Gunshots was still going off. I stumbled and followed the historic crowd that was rushing towards every exit. Everybody was panicking and stomping on top of each other, tryna find their way out. I finally made it outside and searched for my car in the packed parking lot, my shirt had blood all over the front and shoulder. My mind was racing but I knew I had to check my body to see if I been shot. Police sirens started to erupt throughout the night air and I heard engines began to roar from the partiers attempting to flee the scene. I finally found my charger and I got right inside. I started my car and bullied my way through the traffic. Police swarmed the parking lot as I was vacating the premises. I drove at a normal speed, careful not to make my car stand out from the others on the street. I rode past all the police cars that were going inside the Diamond Star's venue parking lot, I could taste my own blood dripping down my face into my mouth. I touched my left ear and felt the blood that was coming out of it, probably from one of the kicks I took to the head. It was dripping all over my shirt. Everything that just happened was like a quick flash. I couldn't believe Stormy and Kash thought they could be that disrespectful in front of my face. I prolly wouldn't even had tripped if she would've came and spoke with me but I aint seen or heard from her since yesterday. She didn't even acknowledge me, then on top of that, it was getting recorded on camera. I didn't care if it was for a music video or not; it was still disrespectful because Stormy was supposed to be my bitch. I felt all over my body with my left hand to make sure I wasn't shot, while I steered the wheel with my right hand. It was clear that this was just blood coming from the wounds I received from fighting and not from bullets. A flashback of the nigga standing over me with a gun crossed my mind and I quickly made a vow to myself to never go anywhere without my blic. I thought about how BB might've felt about me assaulting his artist right in front of him. He probably was pist about it.

   I turned onto a dead end and parked my car. I don't know if it was the molly in my system, or the effect of everything that just transpired but I had to sit still and clear my mind. I pulled out my phone and called BB's phone but I didn't get any answer. I tried to call Stormy's phone next, but she didn't pick up either. I dialed Blondie s number and waited as I heard the phone ring..

"Hello?" She answered.

"Blondie!" I shouted into the phone.

"Yeah, who is this?" I forgot had switched phone numbers earlier and no one was hipped yet.

"This Chedda. Is err thing alright?"

''No, no, it's not Chedda'' she said sounding like her world was coming to an end.

"Wats going on; you still at the venue?'' I asked her.

"Yes, I'm still here... they're arresting BB."

"Wat? Why is he getting arrested?"

''I don't know, but they have him in handcuffs. The police are all raiding the venue and kicking people out" Blondie said with pain in her voice.

"Wat about Stormy; is she ok?" I asked.

"She's right here with Lacey, talking to the officers who have BB in cuffs."

"Ok, well call me back and keep me updated on what they do with him."

"Ok, Chedda, bye."

I ended the call with Blondie and sat there in silence, taking in everything she just told me. I couldn't believe BB was the one in handcuffs. He didn't even do shit. Why would they arrest him? Then I thought about the police raiding the inside of the building where the event was held. I know BB and Lacey keep allot of money in the money room and I'm sure that would've raised a bunch of red flags if the police were to stumble across it. I looked at the time and seen that it was one o'clock in the morning. Usually, the event last until six in the morning but thanks to me and my hot-headed temper; it was shut down early with BB in handcuffs. I couldn't wait to talk to Stormy about her disrespect that triggered me; but right now it was bigger things for me to worry about and I needed to clear my mind and keep a level head, so I could figure it out.

I started up my car and decided to head home to Taylor for the night. When I arrived, I noticed the black African working the front desk. I was glad because I had to give him my new phone number.

"Yo Michael Blaxton, wat you doing working this late?" I said to him as I walked in the building.

"Do I look like Michael Blaxton to you Muddafucka? No! So don't call me no damn Michael Blaxton. I am from North Africa and he is from south. Fuck you and your jokes Muddafucka; Wat do you want? And wat da fuck happened to you, why is all that blood on your shirt?" He said with his heavy African accent.

"I'M just fuckin with you damn, calm down; and don't worry bout this blood, I'm good, just be lucky it ain't yours. Here, take this phone number and tear up the old one, I gotta new one." I wrote it down and gave it to him. "Now don't forget, call me if you see anything suspicious going on or concerning anything or anybody connected to my loft. "

"I know, I know. I got you, you drug dealing muddafucka. You want me to watch out for five-O for you."

"No; I want you to watch out for everything for me. Even the bitches that come and go out of there."

"You don't trust the bitches you sleep with? That's a damn shame, you Americans."

"Yeah yeah whatever, you African booty scratcher, just do wat I say."

I reached in my pockets and peeled off five hunnid dollars for him and set it on the desk.

"Go buy yo girl something nice for Valentine's Day this weekend" I said, and walked away from the desk.

"Fuck you Chedda. Tell ya girlfriend I got this African mandigo for her on Valentine's Day!" He shouted as I entered the elevator and laughed at his joke inside my head; while the elevator door closed.

I stepped inside my loft, it was pitch black. I saw that Taylor was sleep, so I slid in the bathroom to take off my clothes that were covered in blood and took a long shower. I was in there clearing my head for about forty-five minutes to an hour. I threw my bloody clothes into a garbage bag and tied a knot before I tossed the bag into the trash. I walked inside the bedroom quietly, careful not to wake Taylor. She was sleeping peacefully, looking like she didn't hold a worry in the world.

   I looked at the time on my phone before I slid into bed beside my sleeping beauty. It was five minutes to two and Stormy still hadn't called or even texted me to check-in. I set my phone on my night stand right next to my Gloc .23 sitting in the same place where I left it. I'll never leave home without my gun again. I got under the thousand count blanket with Taylor and she blinked a little then positioned her body up against mines. She wrapped her arm around my body and laid her head on my chest. I stared up at the dark ceiling in my room and thought deeply to myself in silence. Life was moving fast than a mu'fucka and I had to figure out how to get ahold of it, before I spiraled out of control myself.

I didn't even know where to begin. Dirty was locked up and indicted for drugs that I sold him; on top of that, I just dodged gettin' arrested with him. If it wasn't for my Track Hawk and my driving skills, I would probably be on the news with him and all the other niggas from his hood. Was the DEA on to me? Did they know who I was? Did Dirty open his mouth and rat me out? Did he stand strong? Everything crossed my mind. I thought about how BB was going to be towards me, once we crossed paths again? How was he going to feel about me punching his artist in the face and causing all of this drama along with bringing heat to the DSE event? Obviously, the nigga wasn't going to be happy about it, but the real question; was he going to be able to move past it so we could continue running his DSE operations the same we 've been doing the last couple of months? I was making the most money I've ever seen in my life and I didn't want it to stop now. I thought about how weird Lacey's been acting towards me ever since Benji came back from Vegas and proposed to her. As I felt myself drifting off to sleep, Stormy's face popped in my mind. She was looking extra fine at the video shoot tonight, but for the past couple of days, she's been acting weird herself. She hadn't been smoking with me anymore and she never had a drink with me and Taylor' when we poured up some Tequila; and tequila's was her favorite.

I noted her strange actions in the back of my head a few weeks ago, but tonight took the cake. The way she was all up on Kash in front of my face was total disrespect. The fact that I just went through all of that shit at the venue over her and still hadn't received a call or nothing from her; was an ultimate sign that she no longer gave a fuck about the bond or relationship we were supposed to have with each other as a couple. A distant noise awakened me from my thoughts and I quickly opened my eyes and reached to grab my gun off the dresser. I clutched it in my palm, ready to shoot at anything moving; until I realized the noise I heard was just one of my neighbors unlocking their doors, entering their loft. I kept my pistol in my left hand and rested it beside me on my bed. I turned to my right and seen Taylor still asleep with her head resting on my chest and right shoulder. Ever since I started fucking with her, shorty's been proving to me that she was down for a nigga 110%. I gripped her in my arms and gave the top of her forehead a kiss. I gripped my gun in my left hand and thought to myself before dozing off to rest... all I needed in this world was Me, My bitch and my Gloc 23.

**After eight hours of good rest and forty-five minutes of some fiya ass head and wet ass pussy; I was re-energized and ready to tighten up all loose screws. The moment Taylor got done riding my dick I decided me and her needed a getaway for Valentine's Day. Valentine's Day was this Friday and it was already Sunday, so I didn't have time to plan no enormous trip. Taylor was a simple girl anyway. She wasn't hard to please. As long as a nigga was spending some time with her and dicking her down good like she was the last woman on this earth; then she was good. I booked a suite at the Waldorf Astoria Chicago. I booked it for Monday thru Saturday Night. That way we could stay the whole week and that would give me time to clear my head, then we can check out Sunday morning and head back to Detroit early. I even bought us some VIP passes for a concert that Lil Durk was headlining on Valentine's Day. Taylor was a fan of that nigga; so, I planned on surprising her, after all, she's proven time after time to be more loyal to me than Stormy was; so why not reward her for it?

Ring... Ring... Ring.. Blondie's phone continued to ring without an answer. I've been texting and calling her through out the day and I still hadn't received a response. I couldn't get in touch with her, Stormy, nor Lacey via phone or text.

 I didn't know what the hell was going on. I looked on all three of their snap chats and Instagrams and seen that they were posting videos on their story, so I knew that they weren't locked up. They mostly were posting videos of them whining and complaining that BB was locked up.

They kept crying about how they couldn't wait until tomorrow for a judge to give him a bond so they could bail him out. That was all cool or whatever; but' why the fuck was these hoes ignoring my calls?

 "Aye Tay Tay", I hollered from the living room.

"Yes baby" She answered as she stepped from the kitchen area, holding a spatula dressed in nothing but a small t-shirt and no panties.

"Hurry up with breakfast so you can go to executive rentals and get us a car before they close. We' going to Chicago for the week."

Mean while

Benji sat there in silence waiting to see who had the audacity to request a one-on-one interview with him in an interrogation room, as if he was going to talk. He usually wouldn't even had left the bull-pin and even allowed the deps or c-o's to walk him inside an interrogation room, but since he'd been sitting in the Mound prescient, bored out of his mind for hours; he figured he would take advantage of this opportunity to get out of his cell. It was Sunday afternoon and he'd been detained for possession of twenty-eight grams of marijuana. He knew that was bullshit because marijuana was now legal to possess as recreational use in the state of Michigan, as long as it wasn't over two ounces. However; the k-9 dog that they brought through to search the venue, after shots was fired; barked and scratched at the marijuana that was pulled from BB's pocket while he was in cuffs. The K-9 dog was giving off a signal to the arresting officers that the marijuana was a hardcore drug identified as fentanyl, that he was trained to detect. The officers didn't understand why the k-9 was responding to the marijuana so persistent; so they tested it with a quick drug kit and discovered that there was Fentanyl on it. Benji had voiced to the officers that he bought the marijuana from an unknown dealer and wasn't aware that fentanyl was on his weed. After officers revealed the identity of who they had in their handcuffs, there was no way that they were missing out on an opportunity to detain Benji Bands and bring him down to their station. They knew he had a strong defense and no charges would likely stick, because marijuana was now legal

286

for recreational use; but the fact there was fentanyl on it gave them an excuse to keep him until the weekend was over for a magistrate to come in and release him. They also came across one hundred-sixty thousand in cash upon the search of the venue. It was technically an abandoned building and everything they confiscated wasn't in any one 's possession; so, they had no name to legitimately blame. BB fell deep in thought as he waited and waited for his fan to arrive. Even though nobody got shot and the police barely had anything against him; he was still pist at Chedda for causing all of this. He even told Lacey to make sure none of the girls communicate with Chedda until he comes home and had a talk with him first.

Boom!

Detective Timothy slammed the door shut as he entered the interrogation room. He stepped up to the table where his familiar suspect was sitting at and just stared at him with a smirk on his face. In Detective Timothy's head; he knew the arresting officers didn't have much that they could keep their suspect in custody for; but he was still happy that they were able to detain him just so he could have the opportunity to see him face to face again. It was a Sunday afternoon and he was off the clock until tomorrow morning; but as soon as he got the call that Benji Bands was in custody at the Mound police station, he rushed to the station for an interview quicker than a reporter from TMZ.

"Well, well, well, If it ain't my favorite superstar; Mr. Daevion Allen Jones, a.k.a Mister Benji Bands, himself. No matter how much cream you let a rodent get away with, they can't help but to be a greedy pest and try to steal some more. When are you going to change?"

BB sat there, staring the pig eye to eye, with his mug tore up. His nostrils flared up from the stench of him.

"I see yo fat ass wife still buying you that cheap; stanking ass cologne from the dollar store. When is that gonna change so I aint gotta smell that shit?" BB shot back.

"Enough!" Detective Timothy yelled, slamming both of his palms on the table that stood between him and BB.

BB smiled with pleasure, knowing that he was still able to get under the skin of the insecure Detective who's been a pain in his ass for a long time. Detective Timothy reached inside his leather coat pocket and pulled out a ziplock bag, then tossed it on the table in front of Benji. Benji looked at the contents inside the bag. There was a sandwich bag of weed, a sandwich bag of cocaine and a capsule of molly inside it. He even noticed a label taped to the outside of the zip lock which read: Evidence-"Daevion A. Jones".

"That ain't my shit!" Benji said with his mug tore up.

"Now it is," Detective Timothy said with a big smile on his face.

BB sat there in anger, gritting his teeth, grilling detective Timothy, eye to eye through his long Dreads that covered his face. The excitement that Detective Timothy was feeling inside was one of a kind and long overdue. He's waited for the day that he could finally have some type of evidence against Benji to make him sweat and even though he knew that there wasn't enough to send him away to the penitentiary, he still enjoyed the moment like it was. Besides; detective Timothy had already taken one of his arch-nemesis down when he booked Dirty, so he was feeling great about his self these past couple of days.

"It seems as though, my boys found a hundred and sixty thousand dollars' worth of money along with some drugs such as marijuana, cocaine and MDMA all throughout the location of your little get together, mister Music Mogul. Who the hell do you think you are, Puffy?" Detective Timothy asked sarcastically, then continued his rant while BB sat quiet in frustration."Out here dancing in music videos and shit. You see I wasn't even going to interrupt my football Sunday schedule and interview your low life ass about these petty drugs found at your so-called video shoot; until the boys at the station ran a test and notified me that the same drugs you had, were the same drugs that were found on an indicted drug dealer that you may know as Dirty."

''I don't know anybody and I ain't have shit!" BB shouted from the chair he was cuffed too.

"Yeah, yeah tell it to the jury" Detective Timothy mocked.

"As I was saying... these are the same drugs that my other suspect is getting from a guy on the streets who goes by the name of Chedda."

As soon as BB heard the name that came out of Detective Timothy's mouth, he lifted his head up so hard, his front Dreads that were hanging in front of his face, swung to the back of his head, giving Detective Timothy a clear view Into BB's eye's.

"Oh, I see that got your attention" Detective Timothy said, while smirking and pointing his index finger directly in Benji face.

"Now here is what's going to happen here'', detective Timothy paused then finished his ultimatum. "You're going to tell me who the hell this guy Chedda is and where I can find him."

Detective Timothy reached in the folder he was carrying and placed three pictures in front of Benji on the table, next to the drugs. It was three pictures of Chedda that Detective Timothy took when him and his partner followed Dirty and ended up falling asleep.

BB stared at the pictures and couldn't believe what he was seeing. Chedda was standing behind his parked Track Hawk with two black duffle bags in his hand, as if he was placing them inside his trunk. Benji could tell it was outside of where the DSE event was held when he went out of town to Vegas.

"If you don't tell me who this guy is; than not only am I going to make sure you get charged for every gram of dope that was found at your little DSE video shoot'; but I'm going to also have the FBI Bureau investigate you for possibly being the source of how these extreme potent drugs are being disbursed on the east side of Detroit. That's not all either," Detective Timothy said, as he dug inside his folder again.

Benji sat there feeling defeated as his heart dropped to his stomach. Detective Timothy slowly pulled out a menu from the DSE event that was raided. He opened it and placed it in front of Benji next to all of the other evidence he's been antagonizing BB with.

"Now I'm not sure what the hell type of music video requires a menu where you can order sexual favors from the video girls? But if you don't want me and my people to look more into this; then you better be using my card and giving me a call to tell me everything I want to know."

The very moment Detective Timothy finished that statement, he plucked his personal contact card from his fingers and it went spinning in the air like a Frisbee until it dropped on the table in front of Benji. The look detective Timothy seen on Benji's face was priceless. He opened the door and started to leave but paused and turned around when he remembered something.

"Ooopps; I almost forgot something Detective Timothy said as he reached and grabbed the ziplock bag full of drugs off of the table.

"You won't be needing this while you're in here now, would you?" He asked with an uncontrollable smile on his face. "Have fun superstar, I'll be waiting on your call.

Detective Timothy finished his trolling of Benji Bands and exited the interrogation room feeling like he just hit the mega millions jackpot. He was always use to BB making him look stupid in front of his superiors throughout his career and he finally got a last laugh from an encounter with BB. He knew that Benji would never call him and rat anybody out; and he knew that it would take much more evidence than this to convince his department to initiate a full investigation on Benji; but to Detective Timothy, it took him to ecstasy just to prove to Benji Bands himself; that he was on to him and still watching his every move.

Benji sat there handcuffed to the chair in absolute shock and disgust. He couldn't believe everything that he worked so hard to build was now spotted by the authorities and could be destroyed before he had a chance to move it to Vegas and become legit. "FUCK!" He screamed aloud and listened to his own voice bounce off the walls, echoing through out the small interrogation room, detective Timothy left him in. He thought about everything the detective had said to him. Then he looked at the pictures of Chedda that still sat in front of him on the table, he thought about Chedda selling his drugs in the streets behind his back when he told him not to do so. Benji felt like that is what brought the DEA's attention to his operation in the first place. He also thought about the blatant disrespect from Chedda, when he hit his artist Kash at the video shoot, right in front of him. Benji knew if Chedda respected him he wouldv'e spoken to him and allowed Benji to resolve the issue, instead of just taking it upon himself and starting an in-house war. On top of that, Chedda's actions caused DSE to lose allot of money and his freedom, and that was something Benji Bands couldn't allow. All this heat from five-O was because of Chedda's actions. Benji wasn't only working on building an Empire; but he was also working on building something every smart hustla in Detroit wanted for their team.... and that's an escape route out the treacherous city they were raised in.

291

BB glanced at Chedda's pictures again and it made his upper lip cringe. He couldn't wait for the judge to come in tomorrow and give him a hearing so he could bond out on these phony charges; and have his chance to see Chedda face to face.

"Aye Dep! Aye C-O! Come get me out this mufuckin room and bring me back to my cell!" Benji yelled at the top of his lungs until the C-O's came and escorted him back to his cell to wait his court hearing on Monday morning.

Chapter: 15
"Ready for Whateva"

   It was Monday evening; two days after the incident at the video shoot took place. Lacey had given me a call earlier while I was in the middle of packing and preparing for my Valentine's Day trip to Chicago with Taylor. She notified me that BB was home and that he wanted me to come out to there to his house so we could talk. I asked her why he didn't call me himself and why hadn't she or the other girls been accepting my calls? She never gave me an answer, but instead asked me, was I going to show up or not? "I'll be there" is all that I told her; then finished packing and drove the Charger to Jughead's house, while Taylor followed behind me in the rental.

   I parked the old Charger in the driveway and left Jugghead the keys. He had the usual on-going traffic coming in and out the spot. I told him I was going out of town, then I got inside the passenger seat of the 2019 Dodge Challenger we rented. Taylor was ready to get us on the road to Chicago for a week away from Motor city aka Murda city; but there's one more stop we had to make before we headed out to our Valentine's Day getaway...

** BB's house had more cars parked in front of it than usual, when we arrived.

"Park right here," I told Taylor as she pulled behind Stormy's white Durango, that read, Top Star on the license plate.

Taylor turned the engine off and prepared to get out the car while I was in the passenger, making sure I had a bullet in each chamber of my twin gloc.23's. I didn't like how the girls stopped communicating with me after the incident at the event and more than anything, I didn't like how Benji had Lacey call me instead of doing it himself. I didn't know where his head was at on the situation so I brought both guns with me. I switched my standard clips and loaded my thirty round extendos just in case. When we reached the doorstep of Benji's house; I could hear the bass beating from loud rap music being played. I knocked on the door and waited, nobody came. Lacey had just spoke with me through the intercom at the security gate, so I don't know why she wouldn't be waiting for me at the door.

I pressed the doorbell and knocked a little harder. I heard the locks of the door being turned. I hurried up and tucked my gloc a little deeper, just to be sure the extendo clip wasn't budging too hard. The door swung open.

"Damn nigga, you knocking on the door all hard like you the police or something" Hershey said over the loud music. She stood in the doorway in nothing but white panties and a bra, making her slim dark petite figure stand out.

"Yall acting like ya'll can't hear in dat mufucka. Lacey knew I was out here; wat da fuck ya'll doing, having a party or sum'n?" I sounded agitated, tryna match her tone. I don't know what it was, but ever since the little fight with Kash, these hoes been acting like they gotta attitude with me.

"Yeah we having a party nigga, what the fuck you thought? You act like you don't know Daddy just got out."

"Daddy?" I questioned with a screwed-up look.

"Bitch you was just calling me dad –Uuh" I had to stop myself in midsentence because I forgot Taylor was standing behind me.

295

"Excuse me, what was that Chedda?" Hershey said, with her hand on her hip.

"Nothing, just let us in" I replied.

"Mmmhhmmhh, I didn't think so, and next time introduce me to your little friend you brought with you before you step up in our house!" Hershey snapped, looking Taylor up and down, head to toe as she walked in behind me. I could've sworn Hershey and Tay Tay had already met at the New Year's Eve party but I didn't even continue the back and forth, with Hershey.

"Don't mind her" I said to Taylor while grabbing her arm and pulling her along inside the active get together for Benji Band's return home. We stepped further into the house and seen all the Diamond Stars drinking, smoking and dancing to the music; all dressed in lingerie. It was like they were having a lingerie party. Hitman was in the corner fondling Barbie. I saw a handful of hustlas just sitting on couches getting lap dances from some of the girls. If I wasn't mistaken, it looked like they were some of the same guys who were at the video shoot. I entered inside the living room where it smelt like they set a pound of marijuana on fire. It was so cloudy from the smoke in the room that Taylor begun to cough and choke on it behind me.

"If it a'int young Chedda" I heard BB's voice say over the music and chatter, then I looked up and seen him sitting on his sofa in his boxers and a robe, Stormy was laid up on him in some lingerie to his left and Lacey was in her lingerie, sitting up against him to his right. This nigga had a fat ass blunt that was still lit in his right hand and a drink of white liquor in his left hand. It looked like he was hosting a DSE event right here in his house instead of at a venue. I looked at Stormy all hugged up on this nigga and I instantly felt rage creeping up inside of me. This disrespectful ass bitch was the reason why shit went left at the venue and she still hadn't learned from her disrespectful actions.

"Damn bitch, you don't know how to answer yo fuckin phone?! I snapped.

"What?" Stormy replied to my directness looking all dumbfounded.

"You heard what I said, you ain't picked up my call in three days and the first time I see you, you all hugged up under this nigga?"

"Woe, woe, woe, hold up" BB said, cutting me short from dog checking Stormy.

He stood to his feet.

"Aye turn that music off BB instructed to the Latina Diamond Star, who was closest to the remote in control of his sound system.

The music stopped and everybody in the house got quiet.

"Here, take this and go pour me another drink beautiful" Benji said to Stormy as he passed her his glass. She brushed pass me, rolling her eyes at me, as she followed his orders.

BB cleared his throat and stepped towards me, we locked eyes, standing toe to toe. He was only bout an inch taller than me. He placed the blunt to his lips, inhaled, then blew a cloud of smoke in my face. I started to pull out one of my glocs and finally get the revenge on him that I craved for from months ago; but I held my composure and stopped myself from jumping the gun too early. I at least wanted to hear what he had to say. I felt Taylor's hand on the back of my shoulder and it calmed me down a little.

"You ungrateful, disrespectful, hot headed little nigga "BB growled, then continued attempting to chastise me.

You come into my house three days after getting me arrested and don't even greet me when you see me? No, welcome home Benji? No, my bad for fuckin everything up and making you lose money Benji? No concerns what so ever of what da fuck I just had to go through because of yo sucka-stroking ass actions! And on top of that, yo disloyal ass is out here selling my product in the streets behind my fuckin back!"

The words came out of his mouth so loud and aggressive, that the whole house heard them. Out of all the many activities that were going on in this lingerie party, I superseded all of them and was now the center of attention. The music stopped playing... I couldn't believe what he just said. How the fuck did he find out that I was selling? Did he bump into Dirty or something while he was locked up? I didn't know what to say and I felt the tension start to rise; so, I tried to brush it off and leave.

"Man you trippin', I'll holla at you when I get back from Chicago" I spat; then turned to walk away but was stopped when I felt Benji place his hand on my left shoulder and turn me back around to face him.

"Don't you ever turn yo back on me lil nigga, is you tryna die?" He asked with a look in his eyes I ain't neva seen before. I gripped the handle of one of my Glocs, pulled it from my waistline and pointed it right in his face.

"Oh my God, he going shoot Benji!" I heard one of the girls scream over all the gasps and shocked faces that surrounded me. I see Lacey staring at me with tears in her eyes.

"Baby no, don't do it, lets just go" Taylor said on the side of me tryna to snap me out of it, but I was zoned out and ready to kill.

I had made a vow to myself months ago that I was going to get revenge on Benji for having me and Stormy stripped naked, handcuffed in a vacant building. This wasn't how I seen it happening, because it was clear that BB definitely had home court advantage right now, but if it had to go down like this, then I damn sho was ready to pop this bitch off. BB didn't budge nor did he even blink. Everybody in the house was still and caught off guard with shock.

"Don't freeze up now, lil nigga. Let yo nuts hang, you pulled yo gun; now you gotta buss it." BB said arrogantly.

"He ain't bussing shit daddy!''I heard Stormy's voice say, while feeling nothing but cold steel pressed up against the back of my head.

"Drop the gun nigga, or, I'mma kill you and this dingy little bitch next to you,'' Stormy whispered in my ears.

I dropped my gun to the floor, only because I knew I had another one tucked for the action if it went any further than this. You heard everybody in the house let out a sigh of relief, but still looked attentively for what BB was about to do next. He stared me in my eyes through his long Dreads and then put a tuff smirk on his face. He turned, walked back towards his sofa and sat back down next to Lacey, right where he was sitting before. He reached for a liter and lit his blunt that had happened to go out during our standoff. I still felt Stormy holding a gun to the back of my head. Benji took some puffs from his blunt and stared at me while he blew the smoke in my face from where him and Lacey sat.

"What you want me to do with him daddy?" Stormy asked him. The sound of her voice made me want to strangle her dead where she stood. I now wanted this bitch dead just as much as I wanted BB dead.

BB took a big puff and blew out another big cloud of smoke.

"You know you dead right?" Benji said, while pointing his index finger at me, like he was talking to a child. I knew none of his questions were actually meant to be answered from the first time he had me in a compromised position at gun point. He ain't wanna hear the words that would've came out my mouth anyway. I remained silent, careful not to make this shit worse than it gotta be. I just ain't want to make this more uncomfortable for Taylor.

"I give you a chance and try to teach you some game, so you can make you some real money instead of robbing hard working women, who get on the grind for theirs... and this is how you repay me?''

I knew he was insinuating that I robbed Lacey for the thirty grand she paid on Johnny Boys behalf, but I ain't even say shit, I just let him rant.

''I should've killed yo ass last summer. The only thing I got from you was Stormy.''

Benji took another hit of the blunt while Lacey kissed on him and played with his Dreads.

"The only reason I don't have her blow yo brains out on the floor, right here, right now, is because then I'd have to kill this pretty little thang that you brought with you; and she shouldn't suffer any more than she already has for her bad taste in men; plus Hershey just got my twenty-thousand-dollar carpet cleaned today and I don't want yo filthy ass blood on it."

Everybody snickered and laughed at what Benji had said, Hershey's laughed was the loudest.

"Stormy..Hitman; grab this little nigga's gun off my floor and escort him and his pretty bitch up out of here. If he try anything stupid; kill em both."

Stormy pushed the gun up against my head, directing me to turn towards the door, but as soon as I did, Benji stopped me again.

"Aye Chedda" I turned to look back at him, and I saw Hitman approaching me.

"The fuck u gotz too say na?" I hollered back.

300

"If I was you, when you get out of town to Chicago ...I wouldn't come back" he threatened.

"A'ight c'mon, it's time for you to get the fuck up outta here!" Stormy shouted, as she held me at gunpoint and pushed Taylor towards the direction, she wanted me to follow."

Hitman grabbed my shoulder and walked with us.

"C'mon Chedda move it; we gotta party to get back too!" Stormy yelled. I wanted to back hand this no good, sack chasing bitch so bad, but I held back and obeyed her orders. I walked towards the door with Taylor in front of me leading the way. Every Diamond Star was staring at me as I passed their eye sight, along with all the niggas who were attending the gathering as well. I looked up and seen 55Kash posted against the wall with his eyes glued to me. His mug was torn up and he had a look on his face that made me know I was going to have to watch my back from him. He still was salty from the beat down I put on him. I saw the brown skin nigga with the long Dreads, standing right next to him. I couldn't forget his face if I tried. He was the nigga who pulled the gun out on me. I continued walking towards the door, making my exit, and just taking in all the faces I was seeing. They were all watching me as I left. Barbie was still in the same corner where Hitman was before Benji ordered him to escort me out, but this time I noticed Blondie next to her as well. Blondie had tears in her eyes and she blew me a silent kiss so nobody would notice.

I fucked with that white bitch, a hunnit. We approached the door and Hershey came outta no where to open it. Taylor stepped outside on the porch.

"Too bad I ain't gonna be able to get none of dat dick before you die" Hershey said as I brushed past her onto the porch.

As soon as I stepped outside pass the door way, my gun came flying out the house onto the pavement.

"Take yo shit with you" Stormy blurted through her dick suckas.

Hitman and Hershey left the doorway and went back to join the gathering inside. I heard the music start back playing I turned around and faced Stormy face to face. She raised the gun she had in her hand, still pointing at me; but I knew this bitch wasn't goin to shoot. I stared at her in her eyes then looked her up and down, while noticing the necklace I bought her, shining around her neck.

"You no good heartless ass bitch. I knew I should 've just got my dick sucked and left yo ass in the back seat of Dre's ride, where I found yo ass".

"Oh, whatever Chedda, if it wasn't for me, you wouldn't have half the money you have put up in yo safe. You didn't captain save a hoe me, I built a bear work shopped with yo nickel and diming ass. You was out here chasing crackheads down for money that you were never going to see." I

 squinted and looked at this slut ass bitch in disbelief as to what the fuck just came out her mouth.

"What, this pussy cat still got yo tongue? Go ahead and get lost. I'm Benji's girl now. I'm on to bigger and better things. And if you haven't figured it out by now, the reason I haven't been smoking or drinking with you anymore..." Stormy paused, then looked over both her shoulders as if she was checking to see if anyone was near by listening, then finished her point..

"Its because I'm pregnant with BB's baby."

My heart dropped to my stomach as soon as the words entered my ear drums. She rubbed on her bare stomach with one hand to signal that she was pregnant by Benji. I was speechless and filled with rage.

" I'mma make sho you regret crossing me, you low life bitch" I said, then reached out and snatched the chain from around her neck.

She placed her hand on her neck from the instant pain she felt from my the white gold breaking her skin. I picked up my gun, turned and walked away with Taylor, towards our rental car.

"It was cheap anyway nigga! I gotta Diamond Star chain to replace that piece of shit!" Stormy yelled, as I continued to climb inside the passenger seat of the challenger.

"And you crossed me first Chedda! You taking this bitch on a trip for Valentines' Day but couldn't even remember my birthday; you selfish ass community dick piece of shit! fuck you!" She screamed as she turned and went back inside the house and shut the door.

Taylor opened the driver's side door and began to climb into the driver's seat but then stopped.

"Here start up the car" Taylor said as she stuck one leg in and pressed on the break. I pushed the start button on the car. As soon as it started up, Taylor took off running away towards Benji's neighbor house, leaving the driver's door wide open.

I looked to see what she was doing. I saw her bending over grabbing something from their lawn. She started running back towards Stormy's truck that was parked in front of us and I noticed a brick in Taylor's hands. She stood in front of Stormy's truck and heaved it through her windshield.Crack! All you heard was hard glass shattering. Stormy's car alarm went off, echoing thru the brisk winter breeze. Taylor jumped back into the driver's seat, put the car in drive and sped out of the complex.

"That will teach that bitch about calling me dingy!" Taylor said, while driving us away from BB's house, so we can finally get to our much-needed couple's vacation.

** After hours of driving and smoking, we finally arrived at our destination in Chicago. We took a few rests stops during the trip. I also drove a few hours of the ride, but I let Taylor do most of the driving. My head was still spinning from all the bullshit that was being thrown my way. It's starting to seem like, one thing after another and it's beginning to pile up quick.

It was Tuesday, around noon and we were just checking in to our suite at the Waldorf Astoria Chicago. I carried our light luggage into the hotel lobby, while Taylor went to the front desk to retrieve the key to our suite. I looked around and took in how fancy the lounging area was. There was a bar, ball-rooms, luxury furniture in the lobby, and a shoe shining stand, next to a massage booth. Some real upper class type shit.

"C'mon let's go baby" Taylor said, breaking my relaxed train of thought. "I got the keys, here is one for you. We're on the seventh floor, room 762."

Taylor led the way to the elevator andy I followed behind her. We entered inside our suite and Taylor was blown away by how luxurious it was.

"Oh my god it's beautiful Chedda!" She jumped on me and wrapped her legs around my body so she wouldn't fall while hugging me with excitement.

She gave me a wet ass kiss and I felt my dick move a little bit, but I was too exhausted from that long ass drive to break her back in at the moment. I took back my tongue from inside her mouth, then set her down on her feet.

"Lemme hit the shower and get a little rest first, lil momma. That long ride got me a little exhausted" I told her.

"You want me to join you in the shower so we can break it in together?" Taylor asked with a tempting look on her face, but I had too much on my mind to indulge.

"Naw; maybe after I get some rest baby girl."

I reached in my pocket and peeled off about five bands.

"Why don't you check out a few stores in the mall and buy you a little sum-sum'' I said while handing it to her. I kissed her on her forehead than found my way to the shower.

When I woke up it was six o'clock in the evening.

"So wassup Chedda, are you going to take me to the Navy Pier tonight?" Taylor asked me, cutting my thoughts short.

"The Navy what?"

"The Navy Pier, didn't you listen to anything I said? That's what I'm all dressed up for. I want us to spend a little time and enjoy the cool night air together at the Navy pier. I always wanted to go there. Please Chedda; don't do me like that. It's the week of Valentines Day and I never get to spend time with you. I really wanted to go tonight."

She begged like a little girl who dreamed of this her whole life.

"How could I say no to a face cute as yours? Plus, dat ass is looking fat in them Dior pants you got on" I told her, and reached to grab on the softness of her booty.

"Good. Now hurry up and get dressed while I roll up another wood for when we get there" She said eagerly, as she grabbed the weed from the dresser and begun to break it down.

I took the blunt that was already lit from her, hit it a few times and then started getting dress to take my only loyal bitch to whatever the fuck the Navy Pier was.

** Two days in Chicago and I was already burnt out. Taylor had me site seeing all across the whole damn city. We went to every popular restaurant. I took her to Oprah Winfrey's building, The Jordan outlet, a movie theatre, a play for Madea and endless shopping sprees. I was spending way more money than I expected and way too much time doing things I had no interest in. She betta enjoy this trip like it's our last because it just might be. It was Thursday afternoon and Valentine's Day was tomorrow. I had one last surprise for Taylor and that was the Lil Durk concert tickets that's scheduled for tomorrow evening at Douglas Park.

"Do you want me to order blueberry muffins with our brunch, or do you want chocolate chip muffins?" Taylor asked with a menu in her hand.

"It doesn't matter li'l momma, just make sho you tell them to fry my chicken instead of baking it" I replied, fed up with her happy go lucky bullshit.

"Ok, chocolate chip it is!" she said, jolly as an old man with a jar of Viagra's and virgin pussy in front of him.

Mean While

Stormy pulled into the Downtown Detroit Broadway lofts parking lot and found a parking space close to the front. She knew that she'd be having to walk back to her rental car carrying a heavy bag and she didn't want to have to carry it far. She drove a rental because her truck was at the shop getting the windshield replaced, thanks to Taylor. The sun was high in the sky, beaming on the white winter snow and the birds were chirping. Stormy woke up on a mission to start her day off with a fresh start, closing an old chapter in her life. Even though she was living comfortably with Benji along with the money she was pulling in from her regular tricks; she still was always on the hunt for opportunities to make her future more promising. Ever since Chedda exposed his hand that he was going out of town to Chicago, she'd been thinking of a way to get into his safe and take him for everything he's worth, without him knowing. The fact that they had a big fall-out at Benji's gathering, with a brick through her windshield, didn't make the matters any better for him. She looked in the rearview mirror and applied her lip gloss.

"Time to show his ass, I could break him, just like I made him" she said to herself as she exited the all-white impala.

Her six-inch heels clicked amongst the concrete as she took each step. The censored automatic sliding doors opened as she entered inside the lobby towards the elevator. She noticed the usual black African man, working at the desk, but

307

this time she gave him a flirtatious look and a small smile instead of ignoring him like she usually does. He looked her over, amazed at how good her body frame looked in the tan dress she was wearing. She stepped in the elevator and gave him a quick wave before the doors closed; making her body vanish from his eye sight.

The elevator stopped at Chedda's floor and Stormy strutted her seductive body to his loft. She found the key on her key ring that Chedda gave her. She walked inside, closing the door behind her. She went straight to the hallway closet where Chedda kept his safe. She slid the doors open and approached the keypad on the safe. One night when Chedda thought Taylor and her were asleep; Stormy had tip toed behind him and caught him entering the code to his safe. She never thought she would come to stealing from him but she wrote it down and put it up just in case a fallout ever came between them; such as this one. Stormy reached in her Chanel bag and retrieved the piece of paper that held the five-digit code. Seven, six, two, one, two Bepp beep, beep, beep. The light on the electronic safe lit up green and the door was unlocked.

Stormy turned the handle and pulled the safe door wide open. Neat stacks of money were lined up on each rack in front of her eyes. Her heart beat begun to speed up instantly from the adrenaline rush that begun to flow through her body. She searched inside the closet and found two black duffle bags. She started filling up each bag with as much money as she could until the safe was empty without a dollar left inside. She grabbed a handful of rubber band stacks of money and placed it in her Chanel handbag for a specific purpose soon to come, then zipped up both duffle bags. She closed the safe door, locked it and carried the bags of money in each hand while exiting Chedda's loft.

She knew she had a nice amount of her possessions still left inside the apartment, such as clothes, jewelry, shoes and perfumes; but she also knew she'd be able to buy much more of it from Chedda's stash. She entered the elevator and prepared for the last task in her mission for it to be a clean get away.

 The elevator reached the main floor, down to the lobby and the doors slid open at the sound of the bell. She reached down and picked up both bags of money and tried not to look suspicious carrying them out the elevator, but they were too heavy for her little arms and weighing her down with each step she took.

"Hold on, hold on, hold on, stop right there pretty lady" The African man from the front desk blurted out. He came from behind the desk with a phone in his hand, attempting to block her path to the doorway.

Ever since Stormy was staying with Chedda and Taylor, she would pay attention to the small conversations Chedda would have with the African whenever her and Chedda walked inside the building together. At first, she thought it was just small chit chat, but one day she caught Chedda sliding him a few hunnit dollar bills, then she knew it was something more to it. She figured Chedda was paying him to watch the loft while he was gone; so, she was already prepared for this once she seen him working the front desk when she walked in.

"Is there a problem handsome?" Stormy replied, batting her eye lashes, tryna to seduce him.

"I just want to call Chedda to make sure everything on the up and up. I neva seen you come and go so fast, carrying two bags. You Americans are very clever. So lemme just call and see if this is ok."

The African held a piece of paper in his left hand and was holding a phone, dialing the number with his right hand.

"I don't think that would be necessary sexy" Stormy said, while reaching out to grab hold of his hand that possessed the phone.

She looked the African man in his eyes, then stuck her tongue out and — licked her juicy lips from left to right. The African felt his manhood rise at the thought of Stormy using those glossed lips of hers on him. He'd always caught a hard on just by the sight of her when she came and went from the building of the loft.

"Here, why don't you take this and keep this between me and you. It will be our little secret. Stormy said to him while reaching in her Chanel bag that was around her shoulder. She pulled out the stacks of cash that she purposely placed in there before she left the loft; specifically, for him. His eyes became bigger at the sight of the money that was being handed to him.

"Oh my God! Yes ...Yes This can be our little secret. I love you American muddafuckas" The African said, while putting the phone away and taking hold of all the money Stormy was handing him. "Oh God yes. Thank you, Thank you so much you pretty muddafucka. You are a gorgeous woman by the way."

The African was filled with excitement and stuffing his pants pockets with stacks of cash.

"Now make sure you don't say a word to nobody about this. I never was here" Stormy said.

"I see nothing" he replied, covering his eyes with a stack of the money Stormy gave him too add emphasis.

Stormy began to lift the bags back up and walk them to her car but then was offered a helping hand, from the super thankful African.

"Lemme get that for you. I will carry it to your car for you. Go, go and I follow" he said, than took hold of the duffle bags and carried them, following Stormy.

Stormy approached the rental car and opened the trunk for the African to place the bags inside. She got into the driver's seat, shut the door and started the car engine. Just when she was about to pull off. . . Tap, tap, tap.

The African man was at the driver side door knocking on the window. Stormy rolled down the window to see what the bootleg Michael Blaxton look alike had to say.

"What is it cutie?" Stormy asked keeping the fake act that she was attracted to him, alive.

"I don't mean to be a pest and I know you are used to these American men, but in my country, a woman as beautiful as you are considered a Queen. I was just wondering whenever you're not spending time with your American men, would you please allow me the privilege to spend some of my time with you? You are so beautiful I just want to rub your feet and be your servant. Is that Ok?" The African man asked and flashed a wide smile across his face. He had a big gap in between his front teeth and they were as yellow as the sun.

Stormy didn't know if it was her pregnancy fucking with her hormones that made her vulnerable to the ugly African man's advance; or the fact that she liked the thought of her being pampered like a Queen with her own servant? But whatever it was, she chose to give him her phone number. She grabbed a business card from her purse and handed it to him through the crack of the window.

He took it and read it aloud.

"Top Diamond Star Stormy. Where fantasies get turned into reality?"

"Yep, that's me" Stormy said reassuring him, then continued with instructions and a dismissal. "My number is right below it. Call me during the week and never on weekends, ok?"

"Oh yes, yes, thank you my beautiful queen, you have an amazing day my Zamunda Goddess". The African man double tapped the vehicle than walked off, back inside his work place. Stormy rolled back up the window and locked her doors.

 "Creep" She mumbled under her breath.

She searched for her favorite radio station before pulling off, but she felt her stomach bubbling a little bit. Ever since she discovered she was pregnant; she'd still been having a little morning sickness where she would vomit sometimes. She hurried and grabbed her vitamins out of her purse and used the bottled water in the passenger seat to wash it down. She was only six weeks pregnant and nobody knew yet; except for Chedda. Not even the man she proclaimed to be the father of her unborn child knew that there was a bun baking in the oven.

Stormy turned up the "Big Latto" song that played through the car speakers and placed the car in drive. she was impressed with herself on how she came in and handled business just like she'd planned, the moment she seen a brick through the windshield of her Durango.

"Now who's the sack chasing bitch Chedda! I bet you won't t forget my birthday next time!" She screamed as if Chedda could hear her. She pushed the pedal to the floor, speeding out of the Broadway Lofts parking lot with every last dollar that Chedda had to his name. Skrrrrrttt!!!

***

Chapter: 16
"When It Rains It Poors"

It was eleven o'clock at night; and we just now entering our hotel suite.

"You can place all the bags right there on the sofa!" Taylor shouted to the two doormen who helped her with her shopping bags.

We were out all-day shopping, jumping from store to store this afternoon. I heard having a gurl and keeping her happy was hard work, but this shit right here was beginning to feel like slavery.

" Thank you so much for your assistance, sir. Chedda baby, why don't you tip the nice gentlemen for their generosity" she said to me as if she worked and hustled for the money in my pockets.

I reached in my pocket and peeled off something nice for the two of them.

"Appreciate y'all" I said dryly and handed them their tip. I closed the room door behind them and headed to the back room. I been on my feet all day and it was about time for me to smoke a fat ass blunt and just relax. I kicked off my Timbs, took off my pants and shirt then hopped in the bed, so I could roll up comfortably. I looked at the bag of weed and realized I was down to my last seven grams. The bad part about it was that I didn't have no way to get any more of it for the time being. I finished rolling, then I lit the blunt. I scanned thru my phone and looked at all the missed calls while I smoked on this good ass weed. I was surprised to see a call from Daisy and one from Blondie. It was good to know that not all the Diamond Stars had black balled me after the fall out between me and Benji. I see allot of missed calls from my dawg Dre. Ever since I texted him my new number, he had been tryna to hit me up, but honestly, my head has been all over the place and I'm just now finding time to sit down and clear it. I couldn't believe Stormy was pregnant by Benji. I wondered if Lacey knew.

You mind if I smoke with you big daddy?" Just as I formed that thought, it was interrupted by the sound of Taylor's voice; I looked up and was surprised by what I saw. She had changed into a red see through lingerie, with red fish net stockings. She was also holding a fifth of Belvedere in one hand and a silver tray in the other. The silver tray had two glasses, a bowl of strawberries, a bowl of ice and a can of whipped cream.

"Damn ma, you bring me dessert?" I joked. She giggled seductively.

"Ummm, Sumthin like that. The only thing is... you are the dessert" She said, as she climbed into bed with me.

"I Like the sound of that lil momma" I said, throwing my phone to the side and passing her the blunt so we could hurry up and get this party started. I grabbed the tray from her hands, threw some ice cubes in both glasses and filled our glasses.

"Look at you looking all sexy and shit. I told you red was my favorite color. You know what that shit do to me when you wear it." She blushed, then took a sip from her glass.

"Well, maybe I just wanted to do something nice for you to show my appreciation. You know; for all of this."

"Baby gurl, this right here is nothing. Any nigga would be the luckiest man alive to have a solid one like you, and I'll do much more then this to keep you by my side."

She hit the blunt, then necked what was left in her glass.

"I'll be right back" she said.

Taylor ran into the other side of the suite and came back with two of her shopping bags.

"Oh damn; what, you bought me a valentines present?"

"You can call it that" she replied.

She reached in the bag and pulled out a blindfold.

"Come here, lemme put this on you" She said.

"Hold on, hold on, you bout to blindfold me?" I asked.

"Yes, c'mon Chedda, it will be fun, just trust me. Have I done anything for you not to trust me?"

I sat back and looked at how fine shorty was looking in her red lingerie, but if I was thinking with my upper head instead of my lower one, I wouldn't had let her do it.

"Ok lil momma you got that" I said. She covered my eyes with the blindfold.

"Now lay back and just relax."

I felt Taylor get on top of me and rub my shoulders and chest massaging it. It felt like she was using some type of oil or something. She used her hands working them all over my body.

315

It definitely was pulling away all of the tension I had built up. She worked her way to my stomach and ran her hands across my six pack; up and down. The next thing I know, she took hold of my left hand, lifted it in the air and begun tying it to the bed post.

"Wait a minute now my baby, I think you going a little too fa.."

"Shhhhhhhhhh!" She cut me off in mid-sentence, placing her finger over my lips. I stopped talking and she continued tying.

I felt my right wrist being tied to the bed post as well.

"Tay, I swear to God, you betta not.." SLAP!

"Didn't I tell you to stop talking!"

I didn't know what the fuck she hit my stomach with, but that shit sent a chill through my spine. She took the blindfolds off my face and I see her holding a short black whip with a ruffled leather feather or some shit on the end of it. It looked like some Dominatrix type shit. I looked at Taylor in her face to see what the fuck type of shit she was on, but I saw a different look in her eyes.

"Taylor, I…" SLAP!

She used the whip to hit me again.

"Didn't I tell you no talking? Now you are under my command. Now, just lay still and take this like a good boy" She said to me, at the same time running the whip from the top of my chest, all the way down to my stomach.

"These boxers need to come off" She said dropping the whip and going into one of the shopping bags to pull out a pair of scissors.

She placed them right on top of my dick, looked up at me and gave me an evil laugh. I aint know what the fuck was

316

running thru Taylor's mind, I aint neva seen this side of her. She started cutting my boxers right off of my body.

''Good, now they are out of my way'' She said.

I laid there wondering what the fuck type of kinky shit she was on. I ain 't know if this bitch was a psycho with a split personality, or just a good ass role player. She stared at my manhood, then back up into my eyes.

"Time for me to get him at full attention so he doesn't miss the show" she stated; then grabbed an ice cube from the tray she brought in.

She stuck it in her mouth, climbed into the bed and crawled on top of me. The ice cube was at the front of her lips, poking half way out. Taylor planted her lips in the middle of my chest with the cold ice cube touching my bare skin.

"Ohh shit!" I yelled jumping a little from the coldness, but beginning to love the feeling of her warm lips taking the coldness away as she ran the ice cube down my chest, past my stomach to my pelvis.

She grabbed hold of my dick with her hand and started stroking it while she circled the ice cube around the tip of it with her lips.

"Damn dat shit feel good ma" I told her.

My dick grew solid in response to the pleasure Taylor was providing. Her small hand gripped my meat as I felt her stroking and placing the head of it inside her wet warm mouth, I felt the ice touching parts of my dick while she sucked me good with the ice cube now locked in the side of her jaw; making room for my man hood to fill her throat. I felt an incredible sensation as she slurped me down, sending chills through my body and causing goose bumps to rise.

"Damn baby gurl!" I moaned through the deep breaths I was gasping for.

"Slurp! Slurp! Slurp!" is all you heard from her mouth as my nut began to build up.

"Pop!" Taylor's mouth made a poppin' sound as she took my dick out of her mouth.

she continued to slow stroke it with her hand while she looked at me.

"Why you take those soft lips of yours off of me?" I asked, wishing she would've kept on sucking.

"I just wanted big daddy wide awake, so he won't miss out on the action.

"Oh yea.. well he's up now; so wat you gonna do with him?" Taylor kissed the head of my dick than let go of it.

I was now standing at attention. She got off of the bed then grabbed her phone. She played some music on it through the blue tooth speakers that were on the dresser, then started dancing to Chris Brown's song called Under The Influence. She twirled her hips and made her ass jump, making it jiggle to the beat of the music. She stripped off each piece of her lingerie; while seducing me with her dance moves until she was completely naked. The sight of her nipples and clean shaved pussy had pre cum leaking from the tip of my dick. The show she was putting on for me, reminded me of how Ciara was dancing for Future in the Body Party, video. She stood right on the side of me, then slid two fingers inside her pretty pussy.

"Mmmmmhhh" she moaned while sliding them in and out. I got more aroused from the sounds she was making.

"Oh yes... look at how wet I am."

She held up her hand that she was pleasuring herself with and all I seen was juice covering her index and middle finger.

She placed her fingers inside my mouth and I sucked on them getting a good taste of Taylor's honey pot. She pulled her fingers from my mouth.

"Taste good, don't I?" She said with a giggle behind it.

Taylor reached over me, then grabbed a strawberry from the bowl. She spread her pussy lips with her left index and middle finger than stuck the strawberry deep inside of her with her right hand; still holding on to the strawberry by the green leaf, while it was smothered in between her pussy. She pulled it out and held it in the air, and all I saw was wetness covering and dripping from the strawberry.

"Ready for dessert?" she asked, then placed the fruit inside my mouth. I took a huge bite and tasted nothing but sweet syrup on top of the tasty fruit.

Taylor did the same thing over and over with the strawberries, feeding me until she was satisfied. She even sprayed a few of them with the whipped cream after she saturated them with her juices and tasted one for herself.Man this girl was a true freak and I was loving it.

She climbed in the bed and straddled my face while I ate her alive, finally getting the meal I craved for instead of the taste teasers. I flicked my tongue like a lizard while she rode my face, chasing my tongue action.

"Oh God, Chedda! Mmh. That feels so good" she said in a sexual tone.

"Right there daddy...keep that tongue working...oowwee, yea don't stop." Taylor was smothering me, drowning me with the water works from her pussy as I brought her to ecstasy.

"Uh-hmm yes... Yes! Chedda.. Oh, daddy I'm cum—ming! she shouted in a high-pitched voice and I felt her whole-body trembling and shaking on top of me. Her juices sprayed all over my face, up my nostrils and inside of my mouth. I swallowed as much of my baby's sweet juices as I could before she finally lifted her body weight up off of my face so that I could get a breath of fresh air. I laid there with both wrists still tied to the bed post as she continued to have her way with me.

"Now it's my turn to make you cum daddy," she said, as she got on top of my dick reverse cow girl and positioned my dick right into her slit.

I felt her clench her pussy muscles around my girth then she sat on it, allowing me to stand straight up inside of her belly. She leaned forward, grabbing hold of my ankes with her hands than made her ass clap up and down on top of my dick.

"Oh shit!" she screamed as my meat stick ripped through her insides. she wiggled her ass and hips, making sure my dick was positioned right where she wanted it. She continue leaning forward with her knees bent on the bed. All I saw was the back of her, hunched over with her ass tooted, while my dick was still inside of her pussy.

Taylor continued to rise her lower body, up and down, bouncing her ass against my balls and pelvis as she rode my dick.

"Ooowwee, ok then ma" I couldn't help but respond to how Taylor was taking advantage of this dick while she had my hands tied to the bed. Splat! Splat! Splat! Her wet ass pussy was splashing up against me every time she threw dat mufucka back on me. She had my dick in a tight grip while bouncing her ass on top of it, making her pussy cream on me.

"Got damn! Oh shit!" I was breathing hard tryna to control my pace but the way Taylor was riding me; there was no way I could hold my nut back, It was rising up more and more with each bounce Taylor delivered onto my anaconda.

"Ooohh shiiit!" I screamed out. Taylor was showing me no mercy.

My dick felt nothing but her warm soaking wet sticky pussy that was squeezing the life from it as if she was tryna to take my soul from me.

"Oh shit think I'm bout to buss!" I moaned. Taylor didn't talk, but instead just started to ride me even faster and harder.

She was putting the pussy on me in no way that she ever did before. I had no control over her because my hands were tied. I closed my eyes and just allowed my bitch to drive my dick however she wanted.

"Aaaaahhhh shit!" I hollered as I bussed the fattest nut. I felt a load shooting out of me all inside of Taylor.

She slowed down her bounce then leaned back sitting all her weight on top of my dick. She then rocked back and forth, then worked her hips side to side, making sure she soaked up every drop of nut that came out of me.

Tay Tay released my dick from her vice grips and laid her head on my chest while I tried to catch my breath, still laying there with my eyes closed from the riding session she just puton me.

"Now go to sleep daddy. Mommy will untie you shortly "Taylor said then kissed me on my cheek while I dozed off, relieved from the big nut I just bust.

**I woke up feeling like a new man. The kinky sexcapade Taylor shared with me last night was exactly what a nigga needed to get a level head. I rolled over to look at the time and seen that it was ten-thirty a.m. Tay Tay usually wouldv'e been up by now, asking me what I wanted her to order for breakfast from room service; but she was on the side of me knocked out with whipped crème smeared around her lips and all over the sheets. I could tell she was drained from all the dick riding she was doing last night. Luckily she untied me before she passed out. I reached over and grabbed the hotel phone off the night stand and called room service.

"Room service, how may I help you?" said the soft voice on the other end.

"Can you tell me what the brunch special is today?"

"Today the brunch special is grilled turkey with your choice of blueberry or strawberry waffles. A side dish of fried potato tots, a honey glazed croissant and three six-inch deep-fried chicken fingers with your choice of beverage."

"Yea, I'll get two orders of that to room 7621 please."

"O.k. and what type of waffles would you like, strawberry or blueberry?" the lady asked.

Just then, I thought about how good those strawberries tasted last night when Taylor was feeding them too me.

"Lemme get strawberry" I replied.

"Alright then, strawberry it is. And what type of beverages would you like with that order?"

"Two sweet teas, and go light on the ice" I told her.

"No problem. Your order should arrive in twenty to thirty minutes. Have a good day sir."

" You too" I replied back, then hung up the phone.

I sat up in the bed and searched my thoughts in silence. My vacation away from the streets was coming to an end in a day and a wake up. I planned on getting back on the road Sunday morning and it was already Friday; Valentine's Day. Taylor still had no idea that I booked her an appointment for a full body massage and had two back stage passes for the Lil Durk I love India concert tonight; but it was about time I wake her up.

I wanted to give Taylor her Valentine's Day gifts . The Durk concert was the last major thing for me to do with Taylor here in Chicago and I was ready to get it out the way, fast not slow. I pulled out the drawer from the dresser and retrieved the bible from inside where I was hiding the concert tickets. I opened it up and grabbed the envelope. It had the tickets and the brochure with her appointment for the massage. The spa was located inside the hotel. She was scheduled for twelve noon, so there was no better time than now, to wake her freaky ass up. I rubbed the side of her cute yellow face.

"Get up lil momma, brunch is on the way."

She opened her eyes at the sound of my voice. I instantly held the envelope in the air so she could see.

"You got a full body massage scheduled for noon and we got back stage passes for Durk concert that start at six o'clock. Happy Valentine's Day baby gurl. Now wake up and get yo day started."

"Oh my God, you got back stage passes to the Durk concert?!" She screamed while she raised up and snatched the envelope from my hands.

Taylor opened it and pulled the tickets from it. She gave me the biggest hug and wouldn't stop kissing on me.

"I love you; I love you; I love you! Oh my God, I love you so much Chedda!"

She was screaming at the top of her lungs with excitement like kids on Christmas day.

"Miss me with all that talk. I want you to show me how much you love me" I replied.

"Oh, you want me to show you huh, big daddy?" Taylor teased seductively than planted some kisses on my neck.

"Last night you was acting like this pussy was too much for you, and now look at you begging for more?"

"That pussy ain't neva too much for me to handle; you must 've forgot who name you was screaming and hollering all night" I shot back, then gripped on both her ass cheeks as she straddled me like a cow girl.

Taylor placed both her hands on my bare chest and pushed me, so that I was lying flat on the bed. She began planting kisses from my chest, down to my stomach, pass my pelvis.

"I'll give you some more cat once I wake this dog all the way up" she said, looking up at me and grabbing hold of my pole that was half way aroused.

She stroked it back and forth with her hands and tongue kissing the tip of my dick. she sucked on the tip while she stroked it with her hands, letting saliva drip out of her mouth down my manhood. She then let go with her hands and took my whole pole down her throat; back and forth she went. I felt my dick grow harder and harder from the wetness and warmness of her mouth. I laid back, closed my eyes and just relaxed my mind while I enjoyed the bomb ass head my bitch was putting on me. Now this was exactly what a boss like me supposed to wake up too in bed on Valentine's Day.

Mean While

While Chedda was enjoying getting his dick sucked in the Chi on Valentines Day, detective Timothy had something else in mind. He was hard at work. His plans were all forming together to finally get one giant step closer in discovering the identity of whoever this drug dealer was that went by the name of Chedda. He'd been working on getting a search warrant for the address that the vehicle involved in the high-speed chase was registered to, and he finally got it signed Wednesday morning. He spent all Thursday gathering his agents and planning a knock, knock raid into the person of interest, Taylor Hatcher's loft; but he was really hoping to catch the guy who's pictures he had pinned up on the bulletin board in his office. He knew deep down that Taylor Hatcher wasn't the one responsible for the distribution of these high-quality drugs or the high-speed chase; but his plans was to at least detain her and get some answers out of her about Chedda's identity? The search was scheduled for Friday and it was now Friday afternoon. He sat in his office and radioed all of his agents, instructing them to report to the equipment room, so that they could prepare to suite up and handle the task at hand. He wanted to be entering the door of Taylor Hatcher's loft by one O'clock and not a minute later. His wife promised to cook her famous meatloaf for him tonight for Valentine's Day; so, he wanted to be in and out by five. Detective Timothy picked up his office phone and dialed extension number 319.

"Yes, this is Detective Timothy," he said thru the headset of the phone and continued speaking to the clerk on the other end.

" I want you to unlock the equipment room and authorize the ten alpha and omega agents to enter within the next ten minutes."

He paused, listening to the response, then replied.

"Ok, thank you so much, I 'll be on my way down in just a couple of minutes."

He hung up the phone, then leaned back in his office chair. He thought to his self in silence. He'd been feeling really confident and joyful about his work this past week. He brought down Dirty; he made a mockery of Benji Bands and now he was working to bust the guy responsible for supplying Dirty's whole drug operation. He looked at his outdated Movado watch on his wrist. He was excited for what awaited him next, and was eager to get another corner cutting hustla off the streets of Detroit. He stood to his feet, grabbed his leather jacket and walked out of his office to prepare for the raid.

***

**   It was five minutes to one and I was just drying myself off from a steaming hot shower. Taylor's been gone for the past hour, thanks to the massage I scheduled for her. That gave me some time to get a nice piece of mind. I turned on the television to the Chicago news channel and listened to the reports while I put the lil outfit on that I was rockin' for the day.

The ring tune from my I-phone echoed thru the room and the face of it lit up while vibrating on the dresser. I looked on the screen to see who was calling, but I didn't recognize the telephone number.

"Waddup, who this?" I answered.

"Oh, you then did it now, you muddafucka you" I heard a voice say thru the ear piece speaker, but I couldn't figure out who it was.

"What? Man, who the fuck is this playing games on my phone?"

"I'm not playing any games. Listen, they are here. The police are here! They are going up to your loft right now!" The sound of the heavy African accent finally registered in my head and I realized I was on the phone with the black African muthafucka who worked in my building.

"Hold on, Hold on, You say what?" I asked as I grabbed the remote and turned the volume down on the T.V.

"I said, the police are here with the DEA vest on and everything. It's about twenty of them and they came in here with a search warrant for the loft you are living in. Oh my God, I have to go. You did it now, you slick muddafucka. They are on to you. I have to go. You told me to call if I see something suspicious, so I called like you pay me too. If I were you; I would run to Africa and never come back. You fucked up now with these Americans."

The call ended and my fuckin heart dropped to the bottom of my nut sack. My head began to spin uncontrollably and I had to take a seat on the edge of the bed. If it's not one thing, it's another. I thought about all the money that I had inside my safe.

"Fuck!!" I yelled to the top of my lungs, not caring who da fuck heard me.

I heard the card enter the electronic key reader on the door and Taylor walked in with a hotel robe covering her body. She closed the door behind her and looked at me.

"Chedda, was that you just doing all that hollering?" I looked at her, than stood up. "Pack yo shit and get dressed. We goin' back to tha D Now!"

Mean While

"I want you to go through every drawer, flip every mattress and crack open any safe!" Detective Timothy instructed his agents, while he monitored them ram sacking Chedda's and Taylor's loft.

Since nobody answered the door when they knocked; detective Timothy threatened to kick it down and the active supervisor decided it was in the Broadway Loft's building best interest for him to use the master key and let authorities do their job. He didn't want any property damages on his watch. They been in there thirty minutes but hadn't stumbled across anything incriminating other than boxes of bullets.

"Hey Tim, I found something!" One of the agents called out from a hallway.

Detective Timothy walked towards the agent in the loft to a see what his discovery was? he reached the closet door where the agent was standing and looked inside. He noticed a new wave safe, standing inside the closet.

"It's a safe."

"No shit Finstein." detective Timothy replied sarcastically

"Good job. Hey agent Anderson! Get over here and get this safe open."

The agent stopped his search and obeyed Detective Timothy's order without hesitation. While the agent got hard at work, trying to crack Chedda's safe, another agent appeared with a small garbage bag tied with a knot. He handed it to detective Timothy.

"I think you might wanna send this to the lab sir" the agent who held the garbage bag said.

"What is it?"

"Well, when I had untied it to take a peek, it appeared to be a shirt stained with blood spots all over it. So, I tied it back up and brought it to you" he revealed to detective Timothy.

"Good job, good job. Put it with the rest of the evidence and make sure you place that in a bio hazard bag."

Beep! Beep! Beep!

"I got it" agent Anderson hollered with excitement at the sound of the alerts from the safe, signaling that it was unlocked.

Detective Timothy stepped inside the closet where the safe was located and began to open the door. His head dropped to the floor in disappointment when he seen that nothing was inside but empty racks filled with space.

"I did all of that work just for this broke muthafucka not to have a dollar or any drugs for us?!" Anderson screamed, displeased at the results.

Detective Timothy Looked at his watch. It was now a quarter til two and he knew he still had to book things into evidence and schedule items to be shipped to the lab. He also knew that he had to complete the equipment inventory after each agent turned in their raid uniform and that was going to take up a lot of his time. He wasn't happy with the outcome of the raid, but he still was a step closer to getting his target and he could feel it.

"Alright guys, that's enough, lets wrap it up here!" He said loud enough for everyone to hear.

"I want everybody to bag and tie any evidence discovered and carry everything down to the vans. Let's go! Let's go! Let's go! It's Valentines' Day gentlemen and I got a meatloaf waiting in the oven for me at home."

** As soon as my head stopped spinning from the bad news I just got. I packed all of my shit and hopped right on the road and headed back to Detroit. Taylor broke down in tears and was crying most of the ride because she missed out on the Durk concert, but I didn't give a fuck. I was too busy worried about all the fuckin money the Feds probably found. I listened for every Detroit news station and searched social media. I even looked up crime in the D and I haven't found anything on a raid in the Broadway loft building. I couldn't believe my life was falling into shambles right in front of my eyes and it felt like I could do nothing about it. Everything was happening so fast, one minute I'm leaving Dirty's block than the next thing I know, I'm in a high-speed chase. Then I look up and I'm in a club fight with a nigga holding me at gun point. Three days later after that, Benji cut ties with me and threatens my life and tells me I should never come back to Detroit; and now this shit with the damn police running up in my spot. All these problems, and I don't know where to start at to fix them? But one thing for certain, I ain't give a fuck who Benji thought he was; or how much money he was making; there wasn't no nigga on the face of this earth that was running Chedda out of no city!

I pulled into the busy gas station off of 94 and telegraph and parked next to a pump. I 'd been driving on the road for hours with no break at all. Taylor was too busy crying most of the trip back; so when she finally went to sleep, I did my best not to wake her. I was tired of hearing that cry baby ass shit. It was one in the morning and the streets was still crowded with Valentine Day couples. I hopped out the car with both my glocs showing on my hip and went inside to put a fifty on the pump. I walked out and was approached by one of the niggas who was standing by the door.

"Aye homie, you wanna buy some weed?"

I looked up to see who the chubby brown skinned nigga was talking to; studying his body language just in case I had to pull out and put some hot ones in his ass.

"You talking to me?"

"Yea, I got that fire on deck," he said as he got closer to me to make out his facial features better. Just then I thought about how I didn't have a weed connect anymore, since the beef with Benji. . then I thought about the fact I might not have any more fucking money other than what's in my pockets.

"Naw, I'm straight bro, good Looking though" I told him then began walking off.

"Aye hold up, hold up... do I know you from somewhere?" The chubby nigga asked.

I turned around to look at his face a little longer.

"Naw, you don't know me my dawg. You probably just seen me around the neighborhood before.

He paused and just stared at me for a moment, then walked off. I ain't know what that shit was all about, but I was on point with my hand right by my gloc if anything popped.

I pumped my gas and glanced at Taylor through the driver's window. She was rubbing her eyes, with her hands, just coming out of her deep sleep. She looked around as if she didn't know where she was, then opened the car door. She stood up and noticed me pumping gas.

"We back in Detroit already?"

"Surprise" I said sarcastically pumping the gas, looking into the city lights that lit the dark night. She went inside the gas station.

I had a lot on my plate and most definitely was tired as hell from the drive, but I got to admit; it felt good being back home in my grimy ass city. I just needed to find a way to check and see if my safe was hit, without me actually stepping in the building. I've been calling and calling, trying to get ahold of the African nigga who worked at the front desk; but his scary ass was sending my calls straight to— voicemail, Click! Click! The gas pump stopped. I placed the pump back on the lever and got inside the car, but this time I sat in the passenger seat instead of the driver's. I was tired of driving; and since Taylor finally woke her cry baby ass up, it was her turn to drive. I looked towards where I seen the chubby nigga posted up next to a black F-350 truck just to make sure he wasn't up to shit. Everything looked normal. He was over there with some other nigga; I could barely see from where I was parked. They probably was both just tryna sell some weed and make some money. I instantly thought about my nickel and dime days before I ran into Stormy and Benji, then I started to feel sick to my stomach. I had to figure something out fast because i'd be damned to go back to them days. Taylor came back walking towards the car with a juice in her hand. She walked up to the passenger door than paused and stared at me thru the window when she realized I took her seat. She walked around to the driver's side and entered the car.

"I can't believe I slept the whole ride back from Chicago. What time is it?" she asked.

"It's like one in the morning and I'm tired as fuck" I told her.

"So where do you want me to drive, you still want to go to the loft even after what you said happened?"

I sat in silence so I could come up with an answer.

"Yea. I just need you to run in there and see if my safe is still in the closet. If it is; then I want you to facetime me while you in there and I'ma give you the code to bring out the money. Then we are going to spend the night at Jughead's until I figure something out."

She started up the car and drove onto Telegraph Road and back on to the 94 freeway. I knew Taylor didn't do anything wrong out here in these streets; so there's no way they could arrest her if they were still watching the place. I wasn't taking the chance of going inside the building myself by no means necessary. For them to go out of their way to raid where I lay my head, made me wonder how much they really knew? Was Dirty snitching? I couldn't see nothing clear in my mind at the moment. If you already got your drug bust, why the fuck was I still so important?

We cruised down 94, I was still deep in thought about all the bull-shit going on in my life. Skrrrtt! I jumped at the sound of screeching tires, then looked to my right and seen a black F-350 truck on the side of me, with a nigga hangin' out its driver's side back window, aiming a draco at me. It was the same truck from the gas station I stopped at back on the west side.

"speed up!" I yelled to Taylor. She slammed on the gas instantly at the sound of my voice while gunshots were firing.

She sped down 94 and exited at the Connor exit.

Skrrtt!Boc! Boc! Boc! Glass windows shattered from flying bullets, as Taylor made an illegal left turn onto Seven Mile rd; tryna to escape the ambush.

Blatt! Blatt! Blatt! They were still shooting but I was already on top of it raising both my glocs up from the passenger window shooting back. Boc! Boc! Boc! BOC! Boc!

Taylor sped across a set of train tracks, getting a wider distance between us and the masked gun man hangin out the back window of the truck. I raised up out of the passenger seat and stretched both my arms thru the shattered glass window, then let both my glocs blow at the windshield of their vehicle.

Boc! Boc! Boc! Boc! Boc! Skrrrttt! SMACK!

I seen the windshield glass shatter than the driver lost control of the high-powered F-350. Their truck swerved and flipped, crashing us onto the front lawn of Anthos Garden apartment complex.

"Oh my God! Chedda! Help!" Taylor screamed in my ear as we were shaking off the hard hit, we just endured.

I looked through the windshield and seen the F -350 tipped on it's side from the collision. I reached for both my guns and climbed out of the car as fast as I could; but o-boy was already on me.

Blatt! Blatt! "Oh shit!" I yelled from feeling a bullet penetrate my shoulder and chest. BOC! BOC! BOC! I shot back.

I saw him lift the Draco, aiming to shoot again and I just came out like Tony Montana, letting both my guns bust. BOC! BOC! BOC! BOC ! BOC! BOC!

I seen him drop to the ground but I felt another bullet enter my body when he was shooting back.

"Oh my God, don't let me die Chedda. Come back!" I heard Taylor scream but at this point, I was locked into kill mode; her voice didn't even matter.

I walked up, limping to the gunman who was on the ground. I couldn't believe my eyes when I pulled the mask from his lifeless head. It was the face of a nigga named Tez. He was responsible for shooting up my car at the club a while back. I saw that his eyes were stuck open and his body was breathless; but I still pointed the barrel of my gun to his head.

BOC! BOC! The sound of my gloc went off and his blood splattered on my Gucci loafers. I was proud for my gloc to add it's first body on it.

"R.I.P. bitch nigga" I spat.

I began to walk away back towards the wrecked vehicle so I could check on Taylor but was alarmed by a door of the F-350 swinging open, and a mufucka climbing out of the wrecked vehicle.

"Cough! Cough! Cough!" The chubby fat nigga was coughing up blood as he waddled his way out of the tipped over truck.

He stumbled and stood to his feet; I noticed it was the same fat nigga who approached me to buy some weed at the G-station. Our eyes locked, then his fat ass tried to take off running through the Anthos Garden apartment complex. BOC! BOC! I let my gloc go some more as I chased behind him. BOC! BOC! BOC!

"Ugh" I heard him grunt, signaling that I'd hit him a few times in the back, but he kept running.

I don't know if he was faster than yo average fat boy or was it the fact I was limping from a car crash with bullets inside of me; but I couldn't keep up with his ass for nothing. I started losing breath and breathing heavy, so I just stopped in my tracks and took one last try at killing this fat son of a bitch. BOC! BOC! BOC! BOC! BOC! BOC!

I don't know if I hit him or not, but if I did, he still kept on running.

I turned back around and tried to follow the trail back to where Taylor was but I was out of breath and getting lite headed. I took another step and felt my legs getting weak. I looked down and seen that my whole shirt and pants leg was Drenched in blood, my head started spinning. I dropped my guns to the ground and everything went black.

**I opened my eyes and woke up from the winter sun shining bright in my eyes through the blinds of a picture glass window. I heard the   sounds of something beeping than turned to the right of me. I was speechless, tryna to take in everything that was in front of my eyes.

"Oh, hi there, you're finally awake" a brown skin older lady said to me. She was dressed in a flowery set of nurse scrubs. I tried to sit up and move, but then felt aches in my body.

"AAHH shit" I grunted.

"Oh no, no, no; you have to relax yourself Mr. Thomas, you been injured pretty badly. You've been shot three times. Once in your shoulder, once in your chest and once in your right thigh. The one in your chest could've been fatal if your girlfriend did' nt get you to the hospital in time. You owe her big time. I'll be back, don't move, i'm going to tell them your awake. The Lady walked out of the room and I finally started to realize where I was at. There was tubes running thru my body and I.V's in my arms. I was hemmed up in a hospital bed. I tried to lift my right arm and realized it was handcuffed to the rail on the bed.

"What the fuck!!!" I screamed out in agony, sickened by what I just woke up too.

"Here he is right here" The older lady said as she entered back inside the room with two muthafuckas dressed in police uniforms and one Italian looking muthafucka dressed in regular clothing with a badge hanging around his neck.

The Italian muthafucka approached me first, popping his big red gum out loud like a female.

 "Well before I introduce myself to you. . let me first start by saying, you are under arrest. You have the right to remain silent, anything you do say can and will be used against you in the court of law.

I gave the spaghetti eating greaseball a glare that let him know I wanted to shoot his fuckin face off.

"Now that's out the way, let's get down to business. I'm Sgt. Clark and I work for Detroit Homicide's unit. Now before I have one of my detectives waste their time, coming down here to the hospital to interrogate you, I decided I'm going to pick your brain myself. Especially since I had to be present to serve as a witness of your arrest. Now my question to you is... are you going to tell me about the shooting you were involved in last night, which left one dead and another in critical condition? Or are you going to be one of those stupid guys who stick to the so-called G-code by making me do my job?"

As soon as the stinking pig stopped talking, I coughed up a loogie filled with flym and blood then spat it right in his face.

"Pheww! Ugggh! You dirty piece of shit"... he paused and looked at the nurse who was present watching the whole thing before he did something or said something she might report.

"You two get in here, I'm done with this prick. Read him his charges so I can enter his name into booking back at the station. He wiped his face with the tissue the nurse handed him then looked at me once more.

"We got enough evidence to hang your ass until a next lifetime anyway. Good luck tryn not to drop the soap."

He stepped to the side while the other two officers read me my rights again along with some charges. I was under arrest for a second-degree murder, one assault with intent to murder and two felony firearm charges.

Taylor came in my room right after the police walked out but the nurse only let her talk to me for five minutes because it wasn't visiting hours. She was looking a mess from the shootout and car wreck that occurred last night. She had a patch over the top of her shoulder from a bullet that grazed her. I told her to go to the loft and clean herself up, then make it back before visiting hours. I also gave her the combination to my safe so she can check on my money. Even after all this bull shit; my money was still the number one thing on my mind.

Mean While

Detective Timothy and his favorite partner to hate was side by side, at a staking the scene out again. Even though it was a Saturday, Detective Timothy called his poor excuse of a side kick, Lonzo and setup a small surveillance on the entrance of the building that his person of interest, Taylor Hatcher; was living in. After the search of her loft yesterday, he felt like he had just missed them or either was on Chedda's heels so close that he must've smelled him coming. He knew all it took was a little over time and his hard work would pay off.

"Well I been seeing a whole lot of fine girls walk in and out of this place but I ain't seen the one that's on this state I.D. photo. You sho we at the right place?" Lonzo asked sarcastically.

"Oh just shut up and pass me another donut; she'll be here and hopefully she has the drug dealer with her" Detective Timothy spat back.

"Fool, you know you ate the last donut hours ago. We been here since 10 AM and its half past two. Let's go get something to eat.

"No, No, then we might miss her. I can't afford that. I already have the boys at the station ready to aide and assist me if I spot her and if I miss her coming in, then that means we'll have to be out here on a Sunday morning. My wife's not having that shit. Further more, I'm not missing the Lions game for nothing or no one tomorrow."

"Well how about I walk to the gas station down the street and buy us both something while you stay and watch?" Lonzo offered, but Timothy refused.

"Dammit Lonzo, just relax. It's not a stake out if you're doing it alone. I'm telling you she'll be here. The African at the desk said she was a home body and that her boyfriend comes in late at night."

Just when he finished his sentence, an all-black beat-up challenger parked two rows in front of them.

"Damn that car is fucked up, with bullet holes in it. What type of people live in this building?" Lonzo questioned aloud. The roughed-up girl exited the wrecked challenger and Detective Timothy's eyes were glued to her. The girl shut the damaged car door and begun to strut inside the building

"It's her!" Timothy said while tapping Lonzo.

"Thats her in that beat up as car? This gurl on the picture looks better than her. That's not her" Lonzo grunted.

''C'mon lets go" Detective timothy said, ignoring Lonzo 's comments. He hopped out the truck and walked into the Broadway building with Lonzo tailing behind him.

Just when detective Timothy and Lonzo were entering the building, the elevator doors were closing with Taylor inside of it. Detective Timothy approached the desk and spoke with the African man who was present when he came in earlier.

"Was that her'' he asked him with no hesitation.

"Yes, that is the girl" he assured him.

Timothy pulled out his cell phone and dialed to the station where he had his trust worthy weekend crew on standby.

*Meanwhile continued..

-Taylor

Ding! the elevator sounded as it opened, allowing Taylor to exit on her floor. she was feeling overwhelmed from all that she'd been through last night and she couldn't wait to take her a nice hot shower to help wash her worries away. She entered inside her loft and was met with another terrible surprise. The furniture was flipped and their belongings were tossed everywhere. Chedda told her the police showed up looking for him but he never told her they came and destroyed the place. No wonder he was so anxious to get back and check on his money she thought to herself.

"Just great!" Taylor said aloud as she closed the door to her loft and walked through the mess in front of her. She made it to the hallway closet where Chedda instructed her to go and she pulled out the piece of paper with the safe combination on it. She slid the hallway closet door open where the safe was located and heartbreak sank in as she wasn't prepared for what she seen next. The safe was standing there with its door wide open, emptier than the inside of the Tinman. She dropped to her knees and burst out crying from the breath-taking scene in front of her. She once seen how much money Chedda had in there when he left the door of it open one day and she knew how distraught he was going to be when she delivers him the news. Knock! Knock! Knock!

She jumped from the sounds of someone knocking on her door. Knock! Knock! Knock!

"C'mon Ms. Hatcher, we know you're in there. Just open up so we can talk" she heard a voice say through the door.

Taylor stood to her feet, closed the closet door and tried to wipe the tears from her face. Her mind was racing and she did'nt know what to do. She looked around the loft clueless. She took in the sight of how messy the police left the loft, then she thought about the fact that they already had taking the money, so what else could they possibly want?

"Well, it can't get much worst than this" She said to herself, then looked through the peep hole at the two rugged detectives standing outside her door step. They look like criminals they themselves, she thought; then opened the door to face her destiny.

***

** Hours later in the St. John's hospital, and I was losing my shit. It was nine o'clock' PM and visiting hrs. for patients were about to end in the next thirty minutes. Taylor was supposed to had been here at seven o'clock sharp and she was nowhere in sight. I wanted to snatch all of the tubes out of my fuckin body and walk right out of the hospital, wounded or not, but that wasn't possible because they got me handcuffed to the hospital bed with a bitch ass Detroit Police officer sitting outside my room on guard duty.

"Nurse! " I pushed the button alerting the nurse who was assigned to my room and she came walking in.

" What is it now Mr. Thomas?" She asked me as if she really was concerned.

"Did she answer?" I asked her referring to Taylor. The police had my phone and all my other personal shit that was on me in an evidence locker; so I was forced to use the hospital phone; trying to reach Taylor .

"No, I 'm sorry it's only been ringing once and going straight to voicemail. I've called three times, but I left her a message for you. would you like me to call anyone else?"

" Naw, Im good, Just try to get me a glass of Remy if you can."

"Now you know I can't do that Mr. Thomas'', she said as she walked out of the room leaving me stressed and pist.

Mean while

"Unfortunately Ms. Hatcher, you are free to go, but I will be in touch with you as soon as we catch Chedda and charge him for fleeing and looting and possibly much more serious Federal charges. I'm not buying your whole stolen car story, but being that you were smart enough to put it on records and backdate the theft; I have no choice but to let you go" Detective Timothy told her as he walked her out of the interrogation room.

He had tried every tactic in the book to break the young sweet innocent college graduate and she still would not change her story. She never gave him any info on who Chedda was or what he does, nor anything about his where abouts. she was more solid than half the so-called thugs he'd interviewed throughout his career. Detective Timothy wasn't discouraged at all though, because he still had one more major piece of evidence that he was hoping would answer every question in the book that he had about Chedda's identity. He was just waiting on the lab to do the testing on the bloody clothes to identify whose blood it was through DNA testing. He talked Taylor into allowing their health care staff to draw blood from her so that they could compare the DNA and see if it was her blood, if there was no match, then he planned to do a search through their database and see if they'd come back with any matching results. Detective Timothy looked at the time on his watch and knew he'd have a mouthful to hear from his wife when he finally got home.

Taylor ran out the police station in a hurry. she grabbed her phone and turned the power back on. "Got dammit!" Taylor screamed as she read the time across the screen of her phone. It was Nine forty-five pm and visiting hours for Chedda were over until tomorrow. She dialed up an uber fast to come get her from her location because she didn't have a car. Detective Timothy and his partner Lonzo arrested her at the loft and had her escorted to the police station in a squad car. She'd been in there for hours, just for them to tell her she can go and she was passed pist about it. The only thing on her mind was visiting Chedda to make sure he was ok; and now it would have to be prolonged a whole nother day.

***

Chapter: 17
"Everything That Comes With The Game"

It was exactly one month after the shootout and they had me hemmed up in the Wayne County Jail. I had been cleared for release from the hospital two weeks after the shooting, but my body was still aching from the bullets I caught during the shoot out. One thing fasho, I was still breathing while one of their momma's was planning their funeral. Too bad for her son thinking he could've out gun a nigga of my caliber. May he rest in PISS! One of the bullets hit close to my lung and aggravated my asthma, but I'm ok. The homicide charge that I was facing on top of my other charges made my bond an amount that only a millionaire would pay. Even if my money would've still been in the safe when Taylor checked, I would've had to go to a bail Bondsman to help me out with this one. I was stuck in here fighting for my life and it wasn't nothing I could do about it. I had no money to my name. The only mufucka that reached out and came through for me was my dawg Dre and my uncle Jughead. Taylor pulled up on him to let him know what happened and he ended up giving her ten grand for me. Dre gave her five bands, but to be honest, that was only enough for me to retain a lawyer. Taylor was Left out there dry. She didn't want to stay in the loft anymore after she had gotten interrogated, so I moved her in with Jughead until she found a cheaper apartment to stay. She had to pawn all the jewelry I bought her and even started back working a nine to five job. Things were tight. I only had three hundred dollars on my commissary and I had to budget like it was my last. Taylor went behind my back and reached out to Benji and Lacey for some dough, hoping they would help out, due to my situation; but Taylor said Benji only laughed, ignored her cry for help then offered her a job with diamond star. I felt an amount of anger I couldn't even explain built up towards that nigga BB; and I couldn't wait for the day to release it on him. I was feeling overwhelmed but this wasn't no time for me to fold under pressure.

Mean While

Detective Timothy drove around searching for a parking spot downtown on St. Antoine Street. It was the middle of the week during business hours and downtown Detroit's curbs was filled as usual with parked cars from workers and tourist of the motor city. He was so excited to finally had gotten the test results back from the lab this week, that he could barely sleep at night. The test results provided him with all the information he was looking for. After doing a lien search on the blood in the DNA database, he discovered the DNA belonged to a 23yr old male by the name of Sevyn Aaron Thomas.

Once he ran the name, he discovered a photo and recent mugshot pictures of Sevyn Thomas with a list of serious charges he was being held for in the Wayne County detention Center. Detective Timothy also believed that the mug shot he'd pulled up of Sevyn, clearly matched the images of the guy he suspected to be going by the name Chedda, from the photos he'd taking of him in the parking lot. He even went as far as doing an extensive search on Chedda with a little help from his friend that use to work for the CIA. They discovered Chedda has a 2010 Dodge Charger in his name registered to an address located on Detroit's east side. Detective Timothy was pleased with the information and couldn't wait to go check out the residence, but right now he was going to speak with the man whom the streets called Chedda; face to face. His case against Dirty's drug operation was getting stronger and stronger but Timothy wasn't satisfied. He not only wanted the man who was supplying Dirty, but he also wanted the man who was supplying Dirty's drug supplier. Deep in his heart, he suspected that man was an old fling that happen to get away by the name of, Benji Bands. He felt like this may be his one and only chance to finally nail BB to the cross and he was aiming to take full advantage of the situation. He knew BB had to have something to do with the distribution of these drugs because they were found at his so called, video shoot; on the night he was arrested. Detective Timothy planned to pay Chedda a little visit and see if Chedda was willing to trade a favor for a favor. His freedom against all those charges he was facing, in exchange for Benji Bands?

***

**   The steel gated doors squeaked loudly as the deputy pulled them back and everybody on the rock turned towards him.

"Inmate Thomas! Is inmate Thomas on the rock?!" the deputy yelled.

"Yea that's me, wassup?"

"C'mon out here, you got a professional visit!"

I grabbed my inhaler, got up from where I was sitting and walked down the rock to see who the fuck was here to see me. My visiting day wasn't until Friday and my lawyer didn't plan on seeing me until next week, so I didn't know who the fuck this could be. The Deputy escorted me to the visiting area for lawyers, then handcuffed me to the table.

 "Just sit here, your visitor will be here shortly" He said, then walked off.

Ten minutes later a dark brown skin guy with a goatee and a fade, looking like Denzel Washington on training day entered.

I looked him over and seen a badge dangling around his neck that brandished FBI.

"Waddup, who da fuck is you?" I cut right into him as soon as I smelled pork. He let out a laugh and sat across from me opening a folder. He pulled out three pictures and set them in front of me, lining them up horizontally. I took a closer look and realized it was me outside of my Track hawk, loading a black duffle bag inside. My heart dropped just a little bit, but I didn't let him see me sweat.

"Damn I knew I had fans, but I ain't know I had an obsessed stalker" I spat, then continued, "I know you ain't here to talk to me about publishing my picture, so wat da fuck you want?" He smiled than begun clapping his hands, applauding me sarcastically.

"Bravo! Bravo!" He shouted, adding to his sarcasm.

"That was a good introduction from a piece of shit who's two court dates away from a life sentence. You'd think a muthafucka fighting for his life would start using his fuckin' head and be a little nicer to the ones who can help him.''

"I don't need yo help" I spat back.

"You don't even know what help I'm offering for you to tell me what you don't need" He said.

"I don't care what you offering. You're a pig and I don't buy pork" I snapped sharply. He looked me in my eyes with a serious mug for a minute, then burst into laughter.

"It's nice to finally meet you Chedda, I'm detective Timothy. Your girl Taylor probably told you about me, from the little chat me and her had about a month ago" he paused. . . "Now maybe we started off wrong with each other. I'm only here to ask you a few questions and see how it is that you can help me, help you. Now my department wanted me to come down here and question you about a DEA traffic stop that turned into a high-speed chase; but honestly, I couldn't care less about you running from the police that day."

"So what the fuck you down here in my face for, if you don't give a fuck?"

"Well, I'm down here in your face because of Benji Bands."

As soon as he said his name my eyes and facial expression beamed, hate, but I sat in silence.

''You know it's funny… When I showed him your pictures and said your name, he had the same exact look on his face, as you do now."

"Yea; well, I don't know who da fuck Benji Bands is."

"Sure you do. He's the guy you've been getting the drugs from to supply Dirty."

My heart beat begun beating faster and faster as this mufucka kept dropping bombs on me left and right.

"Wats the matter young Chedda; cat got ya tongue?"

I looked at him and didn't budge or blink. I honestly didn't know how this mu'fucka had the drop on me like this. I mean, Taylor told me about a detective interviewing her and asking her a bunch of questions about who I was and things like that; but she never said shit about him having pictures of me or accusing me to be selling drugs for Benji.

"Oh C'mon don't sit there like you had no clue I was on your ass because you had to have some type of idea I was coming. That's why you were so quick to move your stash of drugs and money out of your safe in your girlfriend's place. Let me tell you, that was the smartest thing you could 've done because we just missed hitting the jackpot on your ass."

"What da fuck is you talking about, moving a stash of drugs and money out of a safe?" I asked.

I couldn't help but bite the bait he was tossing because Taylor told me the police found the money, but this muthafucka acting like he found nothing!

"Don't play stupid with me, that safe is too expensive for it to be hers and definitely too expensive for someone to buy and keep empty. You moved your stash because you knew I was coming."

I studied his face to see if he was just tryna get a reaction out of me but I didn't sense any bullshit in his demeanor. I could tell he didn't find shit in my safe and he was pist about it. Now the question is; who da fuck got my money?

"Listen here, let's stop beating around the bush and get straight to it" he said interrupting my thoughts. "You can go down with the federal indictment of your homeboy Dirty's drug operation, as well as fight all these extreme charges that you have with the state, or... you can tell me all of what you know about Benji Bands distributing drugs to dealers such as Dirty and I'll makes all of your charges disappear. Now what is it going to be?"

I sat there and stared this man in his eyes, and braced myself for my signature move. I hacked up a big loogie filled with flym. . . SPLAT! I spit and it landed right on his face.

Mean While

Stormy blew a kiss at her African patron as they both parted ways. They were leaving Stormy's new house, both pleased from their little erotic session that just took place. Stormy satisfied with his payment and Ahkbar satisfied with his climax. Ahkbar walked down Stormy's driveway and got inside his silver accord that was parked in front of her house. He waved and beeped the horn as he drove away. Stormy finished locking her front door and setting her alarm system. Ever since she stole Chedda's money, her life has been just like she dreamed it to be when she was a little girl. She moved out of Benji's and Lacey's house and bought her own house on the outskirts of the east side. She even went and upgraded her ride to the same exact G-wagon Benz Truck that Benji had, except that hers was especially painted a hot pink color so she could stand out as the top Diamond Star when she arrived. She had her own; and wasn't depending on a nigga for shit, but to spend his money on her if he wanted her attention.

She opened the door to her Benz Truck and climbed into the driver's seat. She shut the door, pulled out the stack of money the African just paid her and began to count it out Loud.

"one-hunnit, two-hunnit, three hunnit, four hunnit, five-hunnit, six-hunnit, seven-hunnit, eight-hunnit, nine-hunnit a thousand! As long as his stank breath ass keep paying this good, he might just become one of my regulars. She said too herself referring to the list of companions she had paying to be pleased by her weekly. She set the money inside her Birkin bag and started up the motor in her truck. She had no worries at all. She heard about Chedda's legal problems and she felt even more confident that she didn't have to look over her shoulders for retaliation if he ever found out. She looked in the mirror feeling an ounce of guilt when she saw her reflection. Not from stealing Chedda's money, but for still selling her body to men even while she was pregnant. She pulled out her favorite lip gloss and ran it across her lips. I'll stop when I'm six months and showing, she thought to herself. Then she turned up the sound system and drove away to the surprise gathering; Lacey was throwing for Benji and the Diamond Stars.

Inside the DSE surprise party

"Wheeeww!" Kharisma screamed. She was sitting beside Benji while they both threw money on the stage as Lacey worked the pole. The music was bangin'. The different color disco lights were shining and had everybody's diamonds flashing and dancing with the lights. The punch was spiked with the finest and purest Molly in the city of Detroit. Lacey's Diamond Star party was jumping and off the chain. Acrobatic strippers were hanging from ropes and swinging from pole to pole, pleasing the crowd with their every move. The place was flooded with pink and baby blue colored balloons and party favors along with no other than, the whole Diamond Star family. You had Road Kill, Hitman, Benji's artist Kash and his entourage, an unknown exotic looking chick, as well as Hershey, Blondie, Daisy, and all the rest of the Diamond Stars. The place was packed and everyone were showing each other love.

"Alright, Alright, Alright," Lacey shouted into the microphone as the DJ stopped the music. "Everybody give it up for Diamond Star ENT!"

The Diamond Star crowd went crazy, hooting and hollering, surrounded with whistles and applauding to Lacey's shout out to the company.

Stormy walked into the crowded location looking like the dime piece she was. She was just in time for her to hear

Lacey tell them what this gathering was all about. As Stormy walked through the pink and blue balloons, approaching the front of the stage, Her and Lacey locked eyes. A few Diamond Stars noticed Stormy presence and smacked their lips while rolling their eyes in disgust. Ever since Stormy hit the lick on Chedda's money, she'd been acting even more stuck up with the big head and she was gaining a new enemy within DSE everyday.

Lacey continued her rap on the mic, as the roar and applauds from the crowd faded away. She strutted across the stage in a baby blue g-string with a matching bra. Her body was sprinkled with glitter from her Victoria Secret lotion, and she wore a Diamond star Cuban link choker around her neck with a pair of white Bottega Veneta stilettos that had baby blue trim to top it off.

"Now I know all of you are wondering why Me and Benji chose to put together this only the family gathering.. Sooooooo lemme explain to y'all what's going on before I call Benji to the stage to speak. First off, I want to let all of you know that you all have this weekend off!"

Whistles and gurly cheers of happiness aroused from the crowd.

" Ok, Ok quiet down, y'all all seemed a little too happy about us missing out on all that good money we've been making."

"I know dats right!" Hershey yelled from the back.

Lacey continued..

"I called yall here today because Benji and I have two major announcements to make. So, I thought, why not do something special for the ladies at the same time us sharing our surprise with them?"

They all applauded again and Lacey paused, giving them time to get it out their system.

"Now, Benji's going to come to the stage and give you all the first announcement, but we got a lot of turning up and partying to do tonight before I give yall the final surprise for the DSE family. So, it may be a minute before I share the last DSE announcement with yall. You gotta stay to had what it is" she teased, than walked off the stage, handing the microphone to Benji as she left everybody in curiosity about what the surprise announcements could be?

As Benji began to talk on the mic to the Diamond Stars, Lacey walked over to the unknown exotic looking chick who was in the building.

"Waddup doe ladies, how's everyone doing tonight?" Benji asked the crowd on the microphone, posing like he was an instructor in an auditorium full of his students. They all laughed at his gesture.

"That's good, that's good. I'mma take that as everyone's having a good time. We've got the best erb in the city circulating in the atmosphere" he said, while pointing at Hitman and Road Kill passing a lit blunt of his so call wedding cake strand back and forth.

"We got the sweetest and tastiest molly juice in our cups" He gloated as he held his cup of spiked fruit punch in the air. "We also got the sexiest women that's alive under one roof right here, right now!"

The cheers and screams from the Diamond Stars were through the roof and full of excitement after that statement. Even Stormy stuck up ass had to clap her hands and smile. Barbie bent over and clapped her ass a little bit to show how pleased she was with Benji's praise.

"Now I know this year started off a little rocky and we had a little speed bumps from me getting locked up or what not. . . but we've clipped all Loose ends and banded the rotten apple from Diamond Star Empire; now we're back making extreme progress just like I promised yall on New Year's Eve."

The girls just stood there attentively, listening to Benji's every word as he spoke.

"We are still prepared to move the company; which means each and every last one of you, out to Las Vegas, Nevada this summer in August. I need everybody to stay on their A-game and stay focused on the goal. We' re going platinum with this, fuck gold. No matter fact, we going diamond with this shit!" All the gurls begun cheering and whistling again at Benji's prosperous rant.

"Alright, now calm down so I can give yall the first big announcement of the night.

Everybody in the place got quiet as Lacey walked the fine unknown exotic looking chick up the stairs and onto the stage. She looked as if she came from a Native American or Arab descent, with long black hair that hung down to the bottom of her heart shaped booty. She was blessed with a bangin' body that was shaped like an hour glass. she wore skin tight purple velour pants with a velvet color halter top and matching stilettos. Her belly ring was an added attraction that glistened off her coconut brown sugar skin tone. Her stomach was flat as an ironing board.

"Now I always told yall that DSE is always recruiting and expanding. Not only do I want us to expand in different cities and states but I also want us to expand ethnically for the many desires of our clientele. Being that one of our top stars that goes by the name of Miss Stormy along with our two other most loved Diamonds by the name of Blondie and Hershey, have moved out of the mansion, leaving three rooms vacant, It's was time to add some more flavor to our roster. I want all of yall to give a big warm welcoming into the Diamond Star family for our first set of Triplett's; Miss Coco and her two twin sisters, Ginger and Spice."

The DJ was on cue with the music, playing MeganTheeStallion's song "Savage", while Ginger and Spice swung from ropes onto the Stage and danced alongside their sister Coco, as she worked the pole, bouncing her perfect ass to the beat of the Savage baseline. Lacey and Benji pulled out a wad of money and begun making dollar bills rain over top of all three women, while they showed the whole Diamond star community what they all were working with. Ass and Pussy was clapping everywhere across the stage, and everyone's money was flying out of their hands to motivate the new Diamond Star members to keep on going. Lacey grabbed hold of Benji's hand and walked him down the stairs off stage while the music continued to play, keeping the party alive. Lacey led the way through the packed gathering with Benji still in her grasp and spotted Stormy ahead of her. They both stared at each other for a second time tonight. Lacey approached her, reached and took hold of Stormy in her free hand, then walked them both down a back hallway that led to a private V.I.P. section.

Once they entered inside VIP, Lacey escorted them both over to the burgundy sofa that accompanied the secluded room. There was a stripper pole, a table setup with alcohol, fruit punch that was spiked with molly and small finger foods as well. There was a lazy boy chair alongside the sofa and a big flat screen TV, that was playing a celebrity exposed porno flick on it. Lacey poured a cup of fruit punch for Stormy and a glass of patron for BB.

"Here drink up you two" She said while handing them their cups.

"Why you being so nice to me?" Stormy asked, as she accepted the drink from Lacey.

"What you mean, why I'm being nice you? You my gurl.

"Oh, really, am I? Because any other day you act like I didn't exist. . . like I'm an enemy of yours or something."

Stormy took a sip from her cup making sure she didn't taste any alcoholic beverages in the punch, then continued to drink it while Lacey talked.

"I didn't look at you like you're my enemy sexy." Lacey sat beside Stormy.

She reached out and ran her fingers under Stormy's chin, lifting her head so she was looking her directly in her eyes.

"I just look at you Like you are my mini me," she said, then leaned forward from the sofa she was sittin' on and tongue kissed Stormy.

Stormy didn't know what to do. She took Lacey's tongue in her mouth and felt Lacey caressing her breast while she kissed her. Stormy felt her pussy start to tingle at Lacey's advances and she pulled back, breaking the kiss. The sexual arousal that was coming over her from Lacey's touch was the same feeling she remembered having the first day they met. Stormy looked at the cup she was drinking, confused at why her pussy was getting so wet just from a kiss? She didn't know if it was because she was pregnant or if there was something in her drink?

"What's in this punch? This isn't the same shit they're drinking out there that BB was calling Molly Juice on stage, is it?"

"Why? You don't like it?" Stormy remembered that she was keeping her pregnancy a secret and changed the tune of her attitude quick. She set the cup down on the table next to her, before she answered.

"Oh naw, it's fine with me" She lied, but what I don't like is the fact that you called me your mini me." Stormy stood to her feet and pulled down her skirt. She wasn't wearing any panties.

362

She took off her top and was standing in between Benji and Lacey butt booty naked. She straddled Lacey cowgirl style and begun riding her, moaning in her ear as if Lacey had a dick that Stormy was sitting on top of. She moaned and licked on Lacey's neck, getting Lacey a little wet from her tongue action. Stormy looked back and seen BB sitting across on the other sofa with his pants down, stroking his dick while he enjoyed the show. Stormy twisted her head back around facing Lacey and spoke in her ear.

"You know I'm far from your mini me. . .I'm your competition" Stormy whispered; then got up off of Lacey's lap and walked over towards Benji.

She stood in front of him and took off the rest of her clothes while he eyed her voluptuous curves with his meat in his hand. She dropped to her knees, looked at Lacey, then took Benji's erected dick in her mouth.

"Oh shit!" Benji let out at the feeling of Stormy's wet mouth. Stormy was going to work, putting her best dick sucking skills to use, right in front of Lacey's face.

"Damn ma, oh dat shit feel good" Benji said in pleasure. Stormy spit on the top of his dick head, then deep throated his whole pole, making sure not to gag.

Lacey watched and played with her pussy then she got up and walked towards the sextivities."

"If your my competition; then lemme show you how it's done" She said as she dropped to her knees and began sucking on Benji's dick as well. She took one hand and massaged his balls while she and Stormy sucked and licked all over his manhood.

"Oh fuck! "Benji hollered out, enjoying his two bottom bitches. Drool was everywhere. It was so much he felt the spit from their mouth running down the crease of his ass. Its like they were literally lip—boxing over who can get the most licks and sucks on Benji's tootsie pop. It was a whole dick suckin competition on the same dick at the same time, and Benji was reaping the benefits of their competitive spirits'.

 Lacey stood to her feet. She pulled down her G-string and stepped out of it. Benji sat there on the couch looking and wondering what was to come next?

"Stormy, I want you to sit on his dick and ride, reverse cowgirl, while I ride his face and he eats my pussy. The first one to cum loses Let's make this a real competition."

Stormy took BB's dick out her mouth at the sound of Lacey's challenge. She didn't know who had the upper hand in the challenge because Benji's dick game was just as good as his pussy eating skills; but she wasn't about to back down from this bitch no longer. She had the fame like her, she now had the money like her and little did anyone know; she even had Benji's seed in her stomach. She was now confident enough to take Lacey's thrown.

"Dats a bet" Stormy said standing to her feet.

''The loser has to eat the other ones pussy. . . on camera!" Lacey shot back, staring at Stormy's bubble lips seductively.

"Get ready to take yo tongue to the water works then bitch" Stormy snapped. Stormy was high off molly and ready for action. The porno flick played on the big screen, while the music from the party echoed throughout the vip section where the threesome was taking place.

"Baby eat my pussy like you neva ate it before'' Lacey demanded to BB.

She stepped on the couch, then placed her left leg over his right shoulder and her right leg over his left shoulder. BB leaned his neck all the way back and used his arm strength to prop and position Lacey over his face so that his tongue and lips was right on her clitoris.

He began licking away at Lacey's clit and she cooed in pleasure.

"Oh yes! Eat this pussy daddy. . . eat it!"

Stormy stood in front of Benji, turned around so that her ass was facing him. She reached back for his dick, then positioned it right inside her pussy as she sat down right on his lap; causing his dick to enter all the way inside her wet pregnant pussy.

"Ohhh shit!" BB mumbled while he was eating Lacey's pussy from how sticky slippery Stormy's pussy already was. Stormy leaned forward a little bit but not too much. She was just getting a good grip with her footing. She began riding Benji's dick , up and down. She made her ass cheeks and pussy muscles grip his dick every time she rose up but loosened them up every time she came down on top of him, working her hips in a circular motion. Stormy s pregnant juices were splashing all over Benji's dick,and balls. He couldn't believe the feeling.

"How you Like dat daddy?" stormy asked while she bounced up and down on his pole.

Benji ate Lacey's cat even more intense because of the dramatic wetness from Stormy's pussy. He hadn't fucked her in a minute, but he didn't recall her pussy ever feeling like this. Even Lacey's pussy was dripping all over his face, wetter than usual and she was beginning to drown him as the proof.

"Oh my God, daddy yes! oooohhh yes! Please daddy! Please! Lacey begged as Benji's tongue flickered on top of her clit in every which direction. She moved her hips to the rhythm of his tongue, catching his every beat.

Stormy begun bouncing up and down uncontrollably craving to catch her nut that she felt rising to the surface.

"Benji! Benji! I feel you in my stomach daddy!" Stormy yelled. BB motioned his hips and pumped his strokes as much as he could from his sitting position so he could go deeper and deeper inside of Stormy's pussy as she came up and down on top of him. He felt his nut cumming and he thought about how he was going to pull out; but Little did he know there was no need for that because Stormy was already pregnant.

"Oh my God, I'm cumming daddy! I'm cumming!" Stormy shouted. She wanted to feel the ecstasy from the pleasure Benji's beef stick was bringing her so bad that she didn't no longer care about losing to Lacey. She just wanted Benji's dick filling her insides up and that's exactly what she was getting.

"Ahhhhh Ahhh Ahhhhhh Yes! Oh my God, I love you Benji! She screamed as her super wet pussy came creaming all over Benji. Stormy's body shook in pleasure.

"Oh shit. . .Daddy, lemme get down" Lacey said as she moved Stormy out the way so she could get some of BB.

Lacey looked at stormy while stormy laid still on the couch breathing heavily. Lacey wore a smirk and let out a laugh.

"Lemme show you how it's done. . . Mini -Me!" Lacey yelled, then grabbed BB's dick and straddled him.

"Ummmm, she moaned as she took his dick inside of her and began to ride him, looking at him face to face.

"Ummm Yes!" she cooed.

"Yes! Oh, shit, yes! She screamed as her and Benji sped up the pace of things. Benji gripped on both her ass cheeks and began to control Lacey's pace and rhythm.

"Damn this pussy good as hell" Benji grunted out loud.

"Give me daddy-dick baby" Lacey shouted back.

Benji started lifting her ass up and pulling her right back down on his dick while Lacey followed his guidance. He held her down and stopped Lacey from bouncing on him. She sat all of her weight on his dick, feeling every inch of him inside of her then started grinding her hips.

"Get up" Benji ordered.

" What?"

"I said get up, so I can beat this mufucka down."

"Ohh I like it when you talk like that.''

Lacey was just about to get up until Benji took hold of her and turned her over onto the couch without letting his dick slide an inch out of her vagina.

"Woe daddy" Lacey said, surprised at how quick and aggressive Benji was being.

He was on top of her with his knees on the edge of the couch. He placed his arms under each leg and pushed them all the way back to her shoulders then held them there. She looked like she was folded together and there was nothing but bare ass and pussy exposed for Benji to take advantage of. Benji got a good grip on the sofa with his knees and began getting into rhythm as he deep stroked Lacey's warm wet pussy from the angle he desired.

"Oh my God   ! Oh God, Oh God yes! Yes Daddy! Lacey screamed

Benji dug deeper each stroke, with his sweaty body hoovering over Lacey. His dreads swung back and forth tickling Lacey's body while he pounded her out.

"Damn this pussy soo good. Who's pussy is this?" Benji talked to her while he beat the pussy down.

He sped up his strokes and added more back into it.

SMACK! SMACK! SMACK! SMACK! SMACK! SMACK! It sounded like somebody was whipping up a pot of mac and cheese. Her pussy was that creamy.

"who's pussy is this?!"

"Yours Daddy! "

"Who's?

"Daddy this yo pussy!"

"Wass my name bitch?!

"Benji, this Benji's pussy!" Lacey finally was able to cry out between her deep breaths from the pressure Benji was applying to her.

"Oh shit . ..damn you wet as— hell . . .I'm bout to nut" Benji managed to get out in between his hard deep strokes.

"Me too daddy. . . Me too"

Benji dug deeper into Lacey's guts and pounded her out while they both came in unison.

 "uuggh!"

"Oh Yessssssssss!"

Benji unfolded Lacey and pulled his dick out of her, standing to his feet. He looked at Stormy and Lacey tryna catch their breath, destroyed by his dick game. He approached Stormy and he placed his moist dick on top of her lips. It was soaked with all of Lacey's juices on top of it.

"Suck Lacey' s cream off of me and clean me up with those lips of yours so i can go back to the party."

Stormy opened her mouth obeying his every command. He stuck his dick down her throat and she sucked everything but the skin off of Benji's dick. Benji looked to the left and seen Lacey' s pretty pussy still out and exposed and he just couldn't help his self. He stretched his body across Stormy's, laying on her a little bit, while at the same time making sure his dick stayed in here mouth while she sucked away. Benji put his head in between Lacey's legs and began licking at her slit.

*** About an hour and a half after BB, Lacey and Stormy's rendezvous; the party was still jumping. The place was cloudy with the heavy stench of Wedding Cake smoke that was being blown into the air, and molly juice kept on getting poured. The place had more people that joined the festivities, thanks to Benji making a few calls. He even had a special guest of his who flew out from Vegas in the building. It was his deceased father's old friend "Dude;" also known as Benji's plug. The Dj was on point with his music selection and kept the crowd turned up the whole night. It was now getting close to twelve midnight and lacey was ready to make her special announcement.

It was such a secret that even Benji had no idea what it was.

She worked her way through the crowd with her sweated out edges. She took the stage, grabbed the microphone and signaled for the DJ to stop the music. Everybody looked around, wondering what happened to the music.

"Uhmmm Mmh—mmm, Lacey cleared her throat.. Ok yall, I want all of you to give me just a few seconds of yall time, then we can go back to enjoying ourselves."

Everybody turned towards the stage, watching Lacey as she spoke.

"Now anybody who've been with me, Benji and Diamond Star Ent knows — how far me and Benji has come as a couple.

"Mmmm-mhmm, sho'll do!" A diamond star in the crowd shouted.

"So, tonight I wanted to surprise Benji and all of my Diamond Star Family with an announcement that means so much to me and I hope it will be special to yall as well. I held this in all night; well actually I held this in since I found out in January."

Lacey scanned the crowded place and found Benji posted up next to Dude and Hitman.

"Baby, I waited so Long to tell you this because I wanted to be sure the test and the doctors were right. I honestly was so excited that I didn't know how to tell you" Lacey paused for a minute, took a deep breath and wiped her eyes before she spoke.

"We're going to be bringing in a new member to the Diamond Star Family. I'm two and a half months pregnant!" Lacey revealed with excitement.

Cheers and screams from all of Lacey's day one Diamond Stars surrounded the place. Everybody started clapping and Lacey started crying. BB Left where he was standing and walked up on stage to dry his Lady's tears, he wore a smile on his face that none of the DSE models ever seen him wear in their whole career working for him.

As the applauds were going, Stormy vomited on Baby Cakes attire at the sound of the news Lacey just dropped. She was sick to her stomach and couldn't believe what she was hearing. All this time she was keeping her pregnancy by Benji a secret and tryna figure out a way to tell him, but here was Lacey taking her shine again. She grabbed her bag and stormed out of the building without anyone noticing.

***

** "All rise!" The bailiff shouted then an old white man in a gown walked in.

It was the beginning of May and I was in a court room facing sentencing. Everything up till this day happened so fast and I didn't know how to keep up with the pace of my Life anymore. Being broke, robbin' niggas, selling drugs, fuckin' bitches, gettin' money, shootin' niggas, all the way back to being broke again. Now I was facing my freedom being taken away from me. The good thing is My lawyer was able to talk the prosecutor into dropping the Murder charge.

We had video thanks to the spot-shot surveillance that was installed in the street lights of the Anthos Garden apartment buildings and the green light gas station where I first stopped st.

It showed that the two pussies followed me from the gas station and started shooting, first. They were seen on camera chasing the car as Taylor was trying to speed away. Thank God for that because the footage saved my ass! But it also nailed me to the cross at the same time. See they accepted the murder as a Justifiable-Homicide because the nigga was on camera shooting at me and I shot back to defend myself. But the other nigga who I shot, got hit in his back five times from my bullets; which showed he was trying to retreat and I was the aggressor. He survived, so they offered me a plea deal for" Attempted Murder" and Felony-Firearm. They gave me eight 8 to 15yrs, for the Attempt Murder, plus another ?yrs for the Felony-Firearm charge. I started to take that shit to trial and tell the prosecutor to suck my dick; but they had threatened to charge me for over-kill and enhance my charges because I was on camera shooting the nigga in the head twice after he was already dead. So, I just took the ten years instead of having to fight a life sentence against a racist ass judicial system.

371

Taylor sat in the courtroom next to my uncle Jughead and my nigga Dre. We all had on mask due to some outbreak going on. The judge was even behind a plexi-glass window. Whatever the virus was,they were taking it serious just like they did the corona virus. The judge talked and talked, asking me did I agree to a bunch of bullshit and blah blah blah.

I just was lost in the daze thinking about my life and staring at Taylor. Tears were filling up her eyes and I felt like I was helpless to heal her pain. I thought about everything she was telling me during our last phone call. She said Benji, Stormy and Lacey have just been having the time of their life and making so much money. She said she saw all of them on TV, in BB's rap artist music video and now Lacey was even advertising that she was pregnant by Benji. I couldn't believe how big BB's Diamond Star legacy was beginning to grow and it was hard to accept that I was no longer a part of it. I thought about all the shit I did for him, Stormy and Lacey. I couldn't believe they'd just leave me to rot like trash. It really fucked with me that Stormy was pregnant with BB's baby. Anger built inside of me even more as I heard the judge issue out my time.

"one hundred-and twenty-months total in the MDOC before eligibility for parole."

I looked at Taylor and blew her a kiss then thought about it all, before I walked out the court room. Shoot-outs, money, bitches, betrayal, graveyard and prison. Whoever is there, is now gone. Life goes on and I gotta accept it.. Time waits on no man.

Too Be continued....

Sneak Peek

Paid N Plea$ures
pt.2
''The Takeover''

Chapter:1 "Pandemic!"

"Breaking news! The whole United States is under a mask mandate. The public is instructed to stand at least six feet apart from each other. We want everybody to wash and sanitize their hands frequently and most importantly, practice social distancing! This is Monica Chambers, reporting live from Detroit's Fox 2 News."

Mean While

It was now the end of May and business was booming ten times harder than usual for the Diamond Star Empire. Being that almost the whole damn world was experiencing a pandemic, almost every place of business for entertainment was shut down. There were only certain vital places for the community that were still aiding to the public but there were certainly no places for social lounging open. . . Except for the private events that DSE was still throwing every weekend. The Pandemic didn't do nothing but make Benji and his Diamond Stars even richer than they were before. Benji had so much money coming in; that it was hard for him to keep count. Being that partiers were limited on the places they could go turn up; BB's venues were packed and overcrowded. It got to the point where he even capitalized and started charging his customers for parking amongst the set locations. The virus of the Pandemic was certainly a disease to be taken seriously. Benji ordered everyone to wear mask inside the building. He only allowed for them to remove it while his clients were in tents or VIP sections, exchanging cash for sexual pleasures. With all the extra business coming in and the un timely exit of Chedda; Benji inserted his rap artist 55Kash into the operation to help him with the flow of things. He didn't have him doing as much as Chedda but he was definitely in the mix helping him distribute the drugs to the girls so they would always have enough to supply the demand.

"Alright bet" Benji said through the phone as he was wrapping up a call with his business partner and connect; Dude.

Dude had flown out to Detroit from Vegas not long ago to discuss a number of things with BB face to face. He flew back to Vegas after getting things handled, and just as Dude expected; all the airlines were shut down for traveling because of the crisis. Dude had some strong politician connects in the game; so, he knew ahead of time that a pandemic was about to hit the world. He warned Benji months before and Benji was glad that he took heed in his deceased father's friend warning. Not only did Benji Load up on all the drugs that he needed to continue flooding his DSE events, he also took care of all the significant business in Nevada for him to transfer and relocate his company when the pandemic ended.

The only problem that still dangled over BB' s head was his lost brother Ka'Ron. He still hadn't seen or heard anything from him.

His worries were that his brother was somewhere dead in a vacant house from over dosing or somewhere in somebody's dope house, smoking the rest of his life away. Even Dude helped Benji search the streets of Detroit for his brother when he was visiting, but they both came up empty handed. BB started to accept the fact that his big brother was forever gone and if he continued to search for him; the price could amount to him losing his self as well.

"I'll get right on dat" Benji responded through the phone again; ending the call with Dude, then went back to focusing his attention on the native beauty that was giving him his morning blow job.

Spice pulled Benji's dick out of her mouth then began to circle her tongue ring along the shaft and head of his penis.

"You got to spit on it baby" He told the dry mouth freak. She followed his instructions without hesitation.

Benji reached over and gripped her apple shaped booty as she pleasured him with her mouth.

"Here, get on top of this big boy and lemme see what yo dick riding skills like."

She came from under the covers exposing her fully naked body. Her breast were nice perky D-cups and they were staring Benji directly in his eyes as she positioned her body on top of him, ready to test drive the horse beneath her.

It was Friday morning and Benji was taking full advantage of Lacey's absence. She had gotten up early and left the house just as she usually does on Friday. As soon as Benji noticed she was gone he went into one of the triplet's room so he could enjoy the fresh pussy he flew into the states all for himself without Lacey intervening.

"Uh-mmmm" She moaned, while easing his manhood inside of her. Benji felt how tight Spice's pussy was and helped her fit his dick into her pussy.

"Damn baby, this shit feel like virgin pussy!"

"I keep it tight just for you to buss down Papi."

"Is dat right? Well show Papi how fast you can bounce on this dick and make me cum."

She eased down all of her body weight on top of him and fought to take all his dick inside of her stomach.

"Don't be scared lil momma, I ain't gonna hurt you" BB said, as he placed his hands around her waist and guided her slowly up and down onto his pole.

"Ahh shit, just like dat."

"Oh yes! Oooooooh yes!" Spice moaned.

She followed Benji's guidance and worked his dick in between her sugar walls. Benji felt nothing, but tight, wetness gripping his erection. He couldn't believe how tight her pussy was. Spice sped up her pace as she became more accustom to Benji being inside of her. She wasn't use to a man Benji's size penetrating her

pussy. She never had sex with a man outside of her race and they were nowhere near what she was experiencing.

" Oh my God Benji Bands yes! I love America!" She shouted in pleasure while riding Benji more energetically.

"Damn; Ma. . . Damn ok, da--mn. Oh shit! Yea like dat."

"You like dat papi?"

"Hell yea, keep riding just like dat."

Benji gripped on her hips tighter as he felt his self about to explode.

"Shit I'm about to nut ma!" As soon as the words escaped Benji's lips she lifted up off him. She grabbed BB's dick and started sucking it and stroking it at the same time. She put his dick as far as she could down her throat and then pulled it back out.

"Ooh shit that feel good" BB uttered. She continued stroking and sucking the tip of BB's dick, making his nut rise to the top.

As soon as Benji let his nut go, Spice took his dick out of her mouth and held her tongue out catching most of Benji's fluid on the tip of her tongue while the rest covered her lips. While still holding Benji's dick in her hand, stroking it. Benji then felt her moist tongue running up against the inside of his ass hole..SMACK! Benji gripped the fine foreign freak by her long jet black her and tossed her off of him.

"Ouch!" Spice cried out as she plowed onto the floor from the blow delivered to her.

"Wat da fuck wrong with you bitch?!" Benji looked at the confused recruit on the floor with a look that would've put Freddy Kruger to bed.

"I...I was just"

"You was just nothing! Don't ever stick yo tongue, yo fingers or nothing else near my there!"

"I'm sorry. . .I'm sorry, she cried, "thats just how we do in my country, where I'm from" She tried to explain while holding her face from where BB slapped her.

"Well don't do that shit with me!" BB snapped then got his naked body out of her bed and marched out of her room.

** Benji puffed on his high-quality marijuana and contemplated the upcoming moves for Diamond Star. He sat on the couch in his white room and stared at the music videos on his flat screen. He looked at his I-pad and continued to scroll through the Instagrams of his potential recruits.

"You want me to pour you a glass of Don Daddy?" Coco asked Benji, breaking his train of thought.

''Yea baby, do dat for me, and leave out the ice" He replied.

It was twelve-thirty in the afternoon and he knew he had a lot on his hands this weekend. The business was picking up and he needed more women at bay for him to keep up with the growth of his clientele. He thought about if he would've kept Chedda around, would he have more help?

Then, he thought about how fucked up Chedda's situation turned out. . .

"Man fuck dat lil nigga, he lucky I ain't kill him" He said out loud to himself.

He looked at his phone to see if stormy had text him back. Ever since she heard the news that Lacey was pregnant, she hasn't been to work at any of the Diamond Star events. Benji was upset about it but business was coming at him too fast for him to have time to give a fuck. Stormy had left a voice message on BB's voicemail the next day after Lacey's pregnancy announcement crying and he hadn't heard from her since. No one has, she had clientele asking about her every week and BB was getting annoyed each time he had to watch money walk out the door. She had some of the most loyal clients.

"Here you go daddy." Coco handed Benji a glass of Don Julio. "No ice, just how you like it."

BB grabbed the glass, took a sip and anticipated looking at Coco's booty jiggle while she walked away. But she had one more thing to say before she walked out.

"Daddy?"

"Wassup, sweetheart?"

"I had over heard and I want to apologize for my sister's actions. She didn't know any better. She's just a freak like dat. Dat's how she gets down. She wasn'n attempting to try you or anything" Coco explained to BB, trying to help her sister out. BB just looked at her and took a sip from his glass, while he eyed her walking away.

BB didn't see a response from Stormy on his phone, so he googled the Wayne County Jail' s phone number just like his connect, Dude instructed him to do. This was the last place he could think of to call in search for his brother. If he cant find him there, then Dude told Benji to start preparing for his move to Vegas without his older brother by his side. It was time to elevate his life and move on from his past.

*Meanwhile continued...

-Lacey

"Ok mam please sign right here by the patient's name you are here to visit" The receptionist said to Lacey.

"Thanks, remember to only remove your mask for eating or drinking purposes and please respect the six feet social distancing rule while you are here visiting. Have a good visit." The receptionist buzzed Lacey into the visiting room to attend her weekly check up on her Daddy, Johnny Boy.

Lacey surprised Johnny Boy with the news of her pregnancy and chatted with him for hours until visitation was over. Johnny Boy was extremely happy that Lacey chose to have a baby with BB, rather than any other guy. Johnny Boy knew for sure that BB would provide for her and her baby, no matter what. He was positive Lacey was in good hands.

   After the visit she walked back to her car satisfied at how clean and healthy Johnny Boy was looking. He was almost starting to look like his old self again before he started using drugs. She was happy for him. She got inside the new silver i-8 BMW that Benji bought her for her Birthday, that recently passed, and instantly rolled down the windows. It was a nice spring day and the sun was still shining. She looked at her phone and seen that it was the usual time that she left from her weekly visit with Johnny Boy, 3:35pm. She knew she still had allot to get in done for the event tonight and she didn't want to be behind.

   She dialed Stormy's number, hoping for an answer, but her voice mail came on. Lacey hung up the call at the sound of Stormy's voicemail. she was done leaving her messages and not getting a response. She didn't know why? Where? Or what happened to Stormy? But it surely was bothering her; especially since she knew Stormy was forwarding her call to voicemail and leaving her on read.

Lacey Looked in her passenger seat and seen the package she had put together. It instantly caught her attention and she remembered that she still had one more errand to run before she linked back up with Benji and the girls for the weekend. She searched through her notes on her phone and found the address she stored under Taylor's name. Lacey had shown up late and missed Chedda's sentencing, in court but she ended up spotting Taylor leaving the courthouse. She saw her crying and knew that the news they received couldn't have been good. Lacey decided to follow Taylor without her knowing. She followed Taylor that day until she parked at a complex and walked into a condol.Lacey took the address down just so she could re visit it today. She wasn't sure if Taylor lived there but to her, it was worth a shot. Deep down Lacey didn't have any hard feelings against Chedda and Taylor. There was just no way she could go against Benji. Benji's been there her whole life and it was hard for anything else to trump that.

 She grabbed the package from the passenger and wrote Taylor's name on it with a black sharpy. If Taylor didn't live there, she obviously knew someone that did, so Lacey was confident that the package would find her. She typed the address in the navigation app, put her car in drive and went to complete her last task before she gave her weekend to Diamond Star Empire.

*Meanwhile continued...

-Stormy

"Oh, Gotdamn.."

Stormy's legs shook while her juices squirted all over Ahkbar's face. He couldn't get enough of Stormy's wet pregnant pussy and she was making sure she squeezed every last dollar out him for his new uncontrollable addiction. She pulled his head from between her legs and bossed him around her new play den she bought with Chedda's money.

"Now go get a nice tall glass of ice water" She told the African.

"Yes, my dear."

Stormy grabbed some wet wipes off her dresser and wiped between her legs. Her sheets were a mess, but she'll make her African servant change them later, she thought. She laid in bed and counted the money that Ahkbar had handed her earlier. She was satisfied with his payment. What was better than getting paid just to boss a nigga around and get pampered?

Bing! She turned her attention to the sound of her phone receiving a text message. She read it and seen that it was from Benji.

Benji: Come to work this weekend, we need to talk.

That was all that Benji messaged, and she was pist about it.

"Tisss whatever" She muttered to herself then threw her phone to the side.

" Here you go my beautiful brown queen" Ahkbar appeared, handing her a glass of ice water. He started to get in the bed with her but she stopped him.

"Uh-uh," what you think you doing?" She asked.

"My queen I just wanted to lay up and cuddle with your body."

"oh no, grab that baby oil and rub my feet first, then I'll think about letting you cuddle with all this. Do you got some more money to afford cuddling?"

"I still have most of the money you gave me for not calling Chedda that day." He replied.

"Good, cause I'mma need some more if you want to cuddle" Stomy said, milking the obsessed man for all that she could.

''Whatever you want my queen, I'll be honored to give it to you." He bowed, then dripped some oil into his hands and began to rub her feet

 Stormy Laid back, relaxed and drank her ice water. She thought about Benji and began to rub her stomach where his seed was growing. Tears started to form in her eyes at the thought of Lacey having his baby. She was still upset that Lacey beat her to the punch. She planned on surprising Benji with the news of her being pregnant ,but as always Lacey stole her shine. She thought about both the men that had been consistent in her life recently, Chedda and Benji. She had developed love for Chedda but she was deeply in love with Benji and she knew he was the man she wanted to be with. He was rich, powerful and knew how to control her mind whenever he wanted to.

***

** I laid there on my bunk deep in my thoughts. I been at an in-take prison for almost three weeks and I was getting sick and tired of it. They called this place Quarantine. They had me waking up early every morning, going to get my blood drawn, teeth checked and shit like that. They even had me watching movies about how niggas be leaving candy bars on niggas pillow in prison for sexual favors. It was like a whole health care check up, along with all the do's and don'ts while you're in prison. They even had me take a HIV test. I was scared shitless to read the results. All the Diamond Stars I was out there fucking raw; I just knew I had something. But I'm proud to say my dick still clean. I dropped to my knees and thanked God when I read the negative results. Everybody who was about to do prison time had to come here first and go through the process. Well, my process was done and I was ready to go on to whatever prison they were going to send me to, so I can get this show on the road.

They only allow us out of our cell for an hour worth of yard every three days at this place; so I've just been reading books to pass my time. I had Taylor order me a few books about "Ice Berg Slim", and some self-help books for me to feed the brain. Shit like The Millionaire Prisoner, The Sevenism of Pimping, 48 Laws of Power, The prosperity Bible and The Art of War. If I was going to sit still, I wasn't about to be sitting still doing nothing, letting myself rot. I was going to learn all that I can Learn, so that I can come home and surpass Benji. Even though I hate that nigga and want to kill him myself, I had to give it to him; he had a lot of game about making money. I paid attention to him closely while I was under his wing and I saw that he used women to do a lot of his footwork. Women was the reason a lot of lucrative doors were open for Benji to walk through. That's one thing I know for sure. That's why I bought that pimp book by Ice Berg. Even though I grew to hate the word, I still had to learn the story behind it. I thought about life so much in this cell, my fuckin brain started to hurt. I was bored out my mind and taking myself through an emotional roller coaster. My dawg Dre and my girl Taylor been keeping in touch, writing me e-mails on some shit called J-pay. They can send me pictures and all thru J-pay, and from the looks of things, Dre been coming up in the world. He always sending money to Taylor for me on cash app and he sent me a picture of some Icey ass watch he just bought. It looked like an "A-P". I noted that in the back of my head. Jughead wrote me a letter while I was in the county asking if I could introduce him to the connect I had, so he could continue his business? He complained about how everyone else's shit was trash and he wasn't able to make as much money. I ignored him and I haven't heard from him since, I thought about Stormy and Lacey as well. I even thought about Johnny Boy's ass. I was moving so fast when I was in the streets that I almost forgot about him.

I couldn't believe his crackhead ass had a daughter as fine as Lacey and she was getting real money in these streets. Who would believe that one instant of me about to kill his ass was the same moment that changed my life? I would've never touched that much money if it wasn't for his daughter Lacey saving his ass. Then, how in the hell was it possible that the Lil bitch Stormy; who Dre introduced me too, was buying weed from Lacey's man; BB? When I thought about it with a sober mind; I realized this was a story that belonged in a book. It was mind blowing. I also wondered what the fuck happened to Johnny Boy?

I rewind the conversation I had with that bitch ass detective. Where the fuck did my money go if the police wasn't the one who seized it? That shit didn't even add up. I bet them crooked ass pigs took my shit and split it amongst themselves without reporting it. They had to.

"Hey Thomas!" I Looked up attentively at the CO standing in front of the bars of my cell. "Congratulations, you made the emergency ride out list. We're finally transferring a bunch of you level four inmates out of here. Get up, get ya stuff packed in this green duffle bag and I'll be back to pick it up in a minute. Consider yourself lucky to leave this shit hole early because of your asthma. Health care has you and a few others on an emergency transfer, thanks to the outbreak in the facility. You'll probably be getting picked up in the next few hours. So, get up and get ya stuff packed, I got twenty-two more guys to do."

The C.O. whistled a tune and shook his keys as he walked away from my cell. This the first piece of good news I've gotten since I been here. I got out bed and started stuffing the duffle bag with my belongings. I was anxious and ready to go to the next chapter in my journey.

Mean While

"Oh Chedda that feels amazing, Taylor purred as Chedda traced his tongue around her clit. He slid two fingers inside of Taylor's juicy pussy while he used his tongue to flicker up and down on her Love button.

"Yes, just like that baby" she moaned and worked her hips to the rhythm of his fingers sliding in and out of her.'

"Yes!" Taylor screamed as Chedda sped up the pace. She looked down and seen her juices spilling all over Chedda's face as he continued to eat his meal. She wrapped her legs around his neck. "Oh yes I'm cumming Chedda! I'm Cumming! I'm Cumming!"

Ding -Dong! Ding-Dong! Ding-Dong! Knock! Knock! Knock! Taylor was awakened out of her Dream by her doorbell and knocks at her front door. She opened her eyes and looked straight at her phone to see if she missed any calls from Chedda. It was 4:15 in the afternoon and she realized she had fallen asleep while day dreaming about Chedda. She got up and noticed the wet puddle on her bed that came from between her legs. She put on some pants and walked to answer the door but when she Looked through the peep hole, she didn't see anyone.

She unlocked the door and cracked it a bit just to see if anyone was there but only noticed a manilla envelope on her stoop, with her name big ass the moon, written on it. Taylor looked from left to right attempting to see who dropped it off but seen no one. She grabbed the package and locked the door back. She tore open the envelope and was shocked by want she saw inside.

"What the Fuck" She uttered out loud in disbelief.

There were ten neatly rubber banded stacks of money in her hands. No notes or anything suggesting whom it came from. Just money, nothing else.

*Meanwhile continued..

-Detective Timothy

Detective timothy sat in his chair, wrapping up his files and case-before he left the office for the weekend. He was getting closer and closer to having to appear in court for a testimony on the arrest and investigation of Rodney Whitfield's drug operation; aka Dirty. He was getting aggravated that he didn't have enough evidence to tie Benji Bands into the indictment.

He was extremely upset that Chedda literally spat in his face and refused to help bring down Benji; but he still wasn't ready to give up just yet. He been paying attention to the streets more closely since the pandemic arrived and he's been noticing some things about the drugs he recovered from Dirty and Benji's video shoot. He noticed that, they were nowhere to be found in the streets. He had undercovers shopping in the most known drug neighborhoods in Detroit and he couldn't find anyone with the same type of quality. But three days ago, He got a call from the local Detroit Police department, stating after test results; They noticed that they had recovered the same type of drugs with the same percentage of potency that he asked them to look out for. He asked where did they get it? They told him, from a crowd of females that they were dispersing from overcrowded areas Downtown. They informed him that it looked Like some type of party or club scene going on in a vacant establishment which was not supposed to be happening because of the social distancing mandate. The first thing that popped in detective Timothy's head was the so called, music video shoot that Benji was arrested at. Being that an outbreak was going on and everybody was attempting to throw parties because of clubs being closed; he wasn't sure.

Detective Timothy decided to put some over time in over the weekend and called up his partner Lonzo. His plan was to ride around the downtown Detroit area searching for large crowds so he could investigate the activities amongst them. He opened up the file for Chedda.. He thought about getting a search warrant for the address his Dodge Charger was Linked to just to see what he could recover, then remembered he just got sentenced to ten years in the department of corrections anyway. As much as he wanted to get him back for spitting in his face; he knew that he had bigger fish to fry and wanted BB even more. With Dirty or Taylor not snitching Chedda out, he would've had to go through a lot just to prove to a jury, that Chedda was the one supplying Dirty. He had no physical evidence against him, just a picture of him outside his Track hawk, with a duffle bag a distorted recorded phone conversation between Dirty and Chedda. He knew a good lawyer would eat that up. He looked at Chedda's picture one last time, than closed up his folder.

"Maybe next time kiddo. . . maybe next time. Cause there will always be a next time" He said out loud. He got up from his desk and walked out his office to start his weekend preparing to place his focus back on Benji Bands.

***

Paid N Plea$ures

Part 2: The Takeover

Scheduled for release very soon

www.ingramcontent.com/pod-product-compliance
Lightning Source LLC
Chambersburg PA
CBHW060343260626
47160CB00006B/2193